6.21, 0

ORSON SCOTT CARD

HART'S HOPE

A TOM DOHERTY ASSOCIATES BOOK

This is a work of fiction. All the characters and events portrayed in this book are fictitious, and any resemblance to real people or events is purely coincidental.

HART'S HOPE

Copyright © 1983 by Orson Scott Card

Cover art by Dennis Nolan

A Tor Book
Published by Tom Doherty Associates, Inc.
175 Fifth Avenue
New York, N.Y. 10010

Tor ® is a registered trademark of Tom Doherty Associates, Inc.

ISBN: 0-812-52135-8

First Tor edition: February 1988

Printed in the United States of America

0 9 8 7 6 5 4

To Mark Park,
Who knows the Little King
From the heart out.

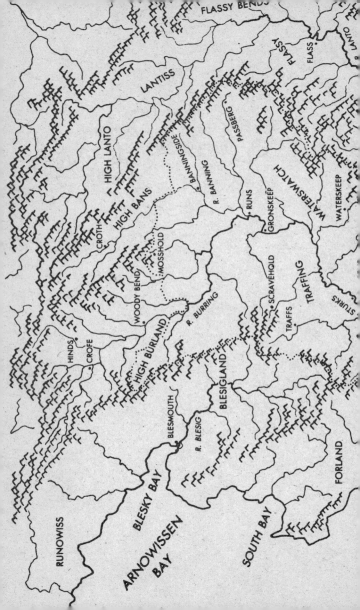

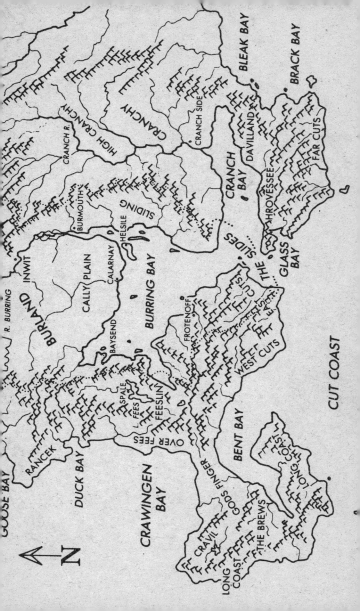

Proem

O Palicrovol, with death and vengeance in your eyes, I write to you because over the centuries there are tales you have forgotten, and tales you never knew. I will tell you all the tales, and because my tales are true, you will withhold your blade-filled hand, and no longer seek the death of the boy Orem, called Scanthips, called Banningside, called the Little King.

THE EXILED REBEL AND THE FLOWER PRINCESS

This is not the earliest of the tales, but it is the first that I must tell, because if you remember this, you will hear me to the end.

He came to her in the garden, where her women were draping her with flowers, which they must do every day of the spring. "What is the name of the girl?" he asked.

Her women looked to her for permission to answer. She nodded at sharp-tongued Cold-in-the-Western-Waters, who would know the proper words to say.

"Our lady will know the name of this man who walks boldly in the holy garden, and risks knowing all the secrets that only eunuchs know."

The man looked slightly surprised. "But I was told I might walk anywhere in the city."

Again the women looked to her, and this time she chose Bent-Back-from-Birth, whose voice was high and strange.

"You may walk where a man may walk, but you must pay what a man must pay."

To her surprise, the man did not look afraid. By his fearlessness he was a fool. By his clumsy accent he was a foreigner. By his presence in the holy garden, he was new to Isle-Where-Winter-Is-But-One-Day-in-the-Mountains. But above all, by his face he was strong and beautiful and good, and so she nodded to Born-among-Falling-Lilac-Petals.

1

"You are in the presence of the eldest child of King Over-the-Sea-on-a-Swan's-Back," said Mesmisfedilain in her most velvet voice.

At once the stranger dropped to his knees and bowed his head, but he did not bend his back. This was remarkable. She nodded to Truth-without-Torture.

"If you are a king in your own land, Man, why do you kneel? And if you are not a king, why does your unbent back pray for your death?"

"I am Palicrovol," said the man. "I am one battle away from death or a throne. My enemy is Nasilee, who rules by right of blood in Burland."

Truth-without-Torture took the challenge of his words. "If he rules by right of blood, how do you dare oppose him? Answer truthfully, for your life is in your tongue."

"Because I am a good man," answered Palicrovol, "and Nasilee is one of those who rule by right of blood, but earn the hate of all good men. Still, I would not have rebelled if the gods had not chosen me."

"If the gods have chosen you, then why are you an exile here in Isle-Where-Winter-Is-But-One-Day-in-the-Mountains?"

Palicrovol leapt suddenly to his feet. For a moment the girl was afraid that he meant to harm her, and even more afraid that perhaps he meant to flee. But instead he flung out his arms and half-chanted the tale of the battle. In her language the words were clumsy, but she soon realized that the awkwardness was because he was translating from poetry. You know the poem. He told her that he stood on a hilltop late in the evening before the battle, the campfires of the largest armies ever brought to war in Burland spread out before him, and he saw that whether he won or lost, too many men would die. There would not be army enough left to defend the borders against the raiders from the inland mountains, or the coasts against the raiders from the sea. So he told his great general Zymas to break the army into pieces and send them into hiding before morning. Let all men think that Palicrovol is a coward, and then Palicrovol will come and win his battle when the cost is little and the prize is greater. In those days, Palicrovol was wise.

And she smiled at him, for he was a fit king.

"May I live then?" he asked her.

She nodded.

"With my lifelong accoutrements intact?"

The women giggled, but *she* did not laugh. She only nodded, gravely, once again.

"Then may I risk my life again, and tell you that you are only a child, and yet I have never seen such perfect beauty in all my life."

She nodded to Born-among-Falling-Lilac-Petals.

"Of course she is beautiful, Almost-King-of-Burland. She is the Flower Princess."

"No," he said. "I do not speak of her perfect face or the flowers that look harsh beside her perfect skin or the way her hair looks deep as a new-plowed field in the sunlight. I say she has the perfect beauty of a woman who will never tell a lie in all her life."

He could not have known, unless a god told him, that she had taken that most terrible of all vows when she was given to the sea at the age of five. She was bound to the truth, and though she had said not a word to him, though not even the Sea Mothers knew of her vow, he had looked at her and seen it.

"She is not a woman," said Born-among-Falling-Lilac-Petals. "She is only eleven years old."

"I will marry you," said Palicrovol. "When you are twenty years old, if I am King of Burland I will send for you and you will come to me, for I am the only king in all the world who can bear the beauty of a wife who will not lie."

She stood then, letting the flowers fall where they would, ignoring the gasps of her women. She reached out and touched his wrist, where he opened his hand to her. "Palicrovol, I will marry you then whether you are King or not."

Palicrovol answered, "My lady, if I am not King by then, I will be dead."

"I do not believe that you will ever die," she said.

Then her women wept, for she had now betrothed herself, and it could not be undone however her father might grieve or rage at her choice.

But Palicrovol cared nothing for their keening. "My lady," he said, "I do not even known your name."

She nodded to Bent-Back-from-Birth. She could not say her own name, for in those days her name was not true.

Bent-Back-from-Birth found her voice despite her weeping, and said the name of the Flower Princess. "Here-Is-the-Woman-with-the-Joy-of-All-Women-in-Her-Face. The-Pain-of-All-Women-in-Her-Heart.''

Palicrovol repeated the name softly, looking at her lips. ''Enziquelvinisensee Evelvenin,'' he said. She listened joyfully, for with his love she was sure that someday those words would be true, though she feared the path that would lead her to her name. ''I will send for you,'' he said, ''and you will be worth more to me than the Antler Crown.''

He went away, and the Flower Princess waited for him. In all her life she has never regretted her betrothal, nor grudged the terrible price she paid for him, nor lied to Palicrovol, even when you wished her to lie, even when you commanded her, so cruelly, not to speak.

Palicrovol Becomes a King in His Heart

This is the story of how God taught an unambitious man to seek a throne.

THE DREAM OF ZYMAS

Zymas was the King's right arm, the King's right eye, and—so the irreverent said—the King's right cobble, too. Zymas was born to a stablehand, but first his strength, then his skill, and at last his wisdom brought him such fame that now he was general of all the King's armies, and the terror of Zymas spread throughout all of Burland.

Zymas had only five hundred soldiers, both horse and foot, but this was a day when a village had five families and a town had fifty, so that five hundred soldiers were quite enough to subdue whoever needed subduing. And if some group of barons or counts combined their petty forces so that they outnumbered Zymas, they were still foredoomed. If there were ten such barons, they could be sure that one had joined the rebellion as the King's agent, two had joined as Zymas's men, and the rest would hang before the month was out.

Zymas had known days of glory on the frontier, where wild tribes from the inner mountains destroyed themselves against the pikes of Zymas's army. And there were days of glory on the littoral, when the raiders from the east beached their craft and died by the hundreds before they could get beyond the tideline. Oh, Zymas was a mighty warrior! But now, with the King's outward enemies all broken and paying tribute, Zymas led his men from mountain to coastline, not to defend Burland from attack, but to protect the tax collectors, to punish the disobedient, to terrorize the weak and defenseless.

There were those who said that Zymas had no heart, that he killed for pleasure. There were those who said that Zymas had no mind of his own, that he never so much as questioned any order that the King gave him. But those who said such things were wrong.

Zymas camped for the night with his half a thousand men on the banks of Burring, high on the river, where the locals still called the stream Banning. The village was too small to have a name—four families, recorded in the books as "seventh village near Banningside." It was recorded that this village had not paid their assessment of thirty bushels. This was causing resentment and was a bad example to the other villages. Zymas was here to punish them. Tomorrow he would come with fifty footsoldiers, surround the village, and then call for their surrender. If they surrendered, they would be hanged. If they did not surrender, they would be spitted and hung over fires or seated on sharpened stakes or some such thing, the normal these days, men and women and children, the normal. Zymas contemplated tomorrow and felt his heart drain away as it always did, so that he would not be ashamed.

When at last his heart was empty, he lay on the cold ground and slept. But tonight his still rest was broken by a dream. It surprised him to be dreaming, surprised him even within the dream, for dreaming was something he had given up long ago. It was a most holy dream, for in it he saw an ancient stag walking painfully through a wood. What was the pain? A rat hung by its teeth from the hart's belly, and at every step the stag shuddered with the pain. Zymas reached out his hand to take the rat, but a voice stopped him.

"If you take away the rat, what will close the great wound in the hart's belly?"

Zymas looked closer, and now he saw that the rat's teeth were holding together the lips of a long and vicious wound that threatened to split the stag from breast to groin. Yet he knew the rat was poisoning the wound.

Then a fierce eagle stooped, and landed brutally on the hart's back. Zymas saw at once what he must do. He took the eagle in his hands, turned it upside down, and thrust its feet under the hart. The talons reached and seized, spanning the wound, binding the edges together far more firmly than the rat's teeth. Then, still upside down, the eagle devoured the rat, every bit. The stag was saved because Zymas had set the eagle in its place.

"Palicrovol," said the voice, and Zymas knew it meant the eagle.

"Nasilee," said the eagle, and Zymas knew it meant the rat.

Nasilee was the name of the King. Palicrovol was the name of the Count of Traffing. Zymas awoke then, and lay awake the rest of the night.

Before dawn he took his fifty men and went to the village, and in moments the people had surrendered. The patriarch of the little village tried to explain why the taxes had gone unpaid, but Zymas had heard the excuses a thousand times. He did not hear the old man. He did not hear the moans of the women, the crying of the children. He only saw that each one stood before him with the face of a great old stag, and he knew that his dream had not come to him by chance.

"Men," he said, and all heard his voice, though he did not shout.

"Zymas," they answered. They called him by his un-adorned name because he had made it nobler than any title they might have given him.

"Nasilee gnaws at the belly of Burland like a rat, and we, we are his teeth."

Puzzled, they did not know how to respond.

"Does the true King hang these helpless ones?"

Unsure what kind of test Zymas was posing, one of the men said, "Yes?"

"Perhaps he does," Zymas said, "but if he is the true King, then I will follow a false King who is good, and I will make him true, and the people will no longer have to fear the coming of the army of Zymas."

It seemed impossible to the soldiers that Zymas could speak such treason, but not so impossible as the idea of Zymas telling a lie or making a jest. So Zymas was going to rebel against the King. Was there any man there who would choose the King over Zymas?

Zymas let them choose freely, but all five hundred marched with him away from the bewildered villagers, toward Traffing. He did not tell them whom he meant to put in the King's place. The dream had said Palicrovol, but Zymas meant to see the man for himself before he helped him to revolt. Dreams come when your eyes are closed, but Zymas only acted with his eyes open.

THE GUARD AND THE GODSMAN

In the land of Traffing, in the dead of winter, a figure in a white robe walked like a ghost upon the snow. The guard at the fortress of the Count trembled in fear until he saw it was a man, with his face reddened by the cold, and his hands thrust deep into a bedroll for warmth. Ghosts have nothing to fear from the cold, the guard knew, and so he hailed the man— hailed rudely, because the guard had been afraid.

"What do you want! It's near dark, and we do no work on the Feast of Hinds."

"I come from God," said the man. "I have a message for the Count."

The guard grew angry. He had heard all about God, whose priests were so arrogant they denied even the Sweet Sisters, even the Hart, though the people had known their power far longer than this newfashioned deity. "Would you have him blaspheme against the Hart's own lady?"

"Old things are done away," said the Godsman.

"*You're* done away if you don't go away!" cried the guard.

The Godsman only smiled. "Of course you do not know me," he said. And then, suddenly, before the guard's very eyes, the Godsman reached out his hands beseechingly and the bar of the gate broke in two and the gate fell open before him.

"You won't hurt him?" asked the guard.

"Don't cower so," said the Godsman. "I come for the good of all Burland."

From the King, then? The guard hated the King enough to spit in the snow, despite his fear of this man who broke gates without touching them. "The good of Burland is never the good of Traffing."

"Tonight it is," said the Godsman.

Suddenly the sunset erupted, hot streams down the slope of the sky, and the guard became a Godsman himself from that moment.

THE PROPHECY

"Were you invited?" asked Palicrovol.

The Godsman looked about him at the nearly naked men sitting on ice-covered rocks around a fire. "I am invited to the feasts of all the gods." Palicrovol was young and beautiful, even with the treebark mantle on his shoulders; the Godsman loved the sight of him, even though the Count was angry. Anger would pass. The Count's beauty would not.

"My guard is impressed with you," the Count said.

"Such men are easily impressed," said the Godsman.

"I've seen magic before," said the Count, for beside him sat Sleeve, the pink-eyed wizard who served only the master that he chose.

"Then I will give you what no other can: I will give you truth."

Palicrovol smiled and looked at Sleeve, but Sleeve was not smiling, and Palicrovol began to wonder if he ought to take this Godsman seriously. "What sort of truth?"

"Words can only tell two kinds of truth. Words can name you, and words can say what you will do before you do it."

"And which will you do?"

"To name a man is to say what he will do before he does it. So I will name you, Palicrovol. You are King of Burland."

Suddenly Count Palicrovol grew afraid. "I am Count of Traffing."

"The people hate King Nasilee. They have given him their life's blood, and he has given them only poverty and terror. They long for someone to set them free from this burden."

"Then go to a man with armies." If Nasilee heard that Palicrovol had even listened to this Godsman, it would be the end of the house of Traffing.

"General Zymas will come to you and follow you to the day he dies."

"Which will be very soon, if he dares to rebel against the King."

"On the contrary," said the Godsman. "Three hundred years from now you and Zymas and Sleeve will all be alive, with a man's life yet ahead of you."

Sleeve laughed. "Since when does your magic-hating god give gifts to a poor wizard?"

"For every day that you're glad of the gift, there will be five days when you hate it."

Palicrovol leaned forward. "I should have you killed."

"What would be the point? I'm only a poor old man, and when God lets go of my body, I will know even less than you do."

Sleeve shook his head. "There is no poetry in this man's prophecy."

"True," said Palicrovol. "But there's a tale in it."

"This is not a prophecy," said the Godsman. "This is your name. Zymas will come to you, and in the name of God you will conquer. You will enter the city of Hart's Hope and the King's daughter will ride the hart for you. You will build a new temple of God and you will name the city Inwit, and no other god will be worshipped there. And this above all: You will not be safe upon the throne until King Nasilee and his daughter Asineth are dead."

These words spoken, the Godsman shuddered, his jaw went slack, and the light departed from his eyes. He began to look about him in tired surprise. This had no doubt happened to him before, but plainly he was not yet used to finding himself in strange places—particularly in the midst of a very serious Feast of Hinds.

"What bright servants this god chooses for himself," said Sleeve.

Palicrovol did not laugh. The fire that had left the old man's eyes had left a spark in Palicrovol. "Here before you all," he said, "I will tell you what I have not dared to say before. I hate King Nasilee and all his acts, and for the sake of all Burland I long to see him driven from the throne."

At these treasonous words, especially spoken at the Feast of Hinds, his own men grew still and watched him warily.

"It is good that we love you," said Sleeve. "We will all keep silence and tell no one that you spoke against King Nasilee. And we will pray to the Hart that you will not be seduced by the flattery of a strange and jealous god."

Sleeve's words counseled against rebellion, but Palicrovol had learned that Sleeve's words rarely gave Sleeve's meaning. Sleeve might mean that it was already too late for Palicrovol to change his mind, for now he would live in constant fear of betrayal by someone who had heard his words. And as to the Godsman's prophecy of victory, was Sleeve doubting? Or testing? Palicrovol looked at the unnaturally white face of the wizard, his transparent skin, his hair as fine and pale as spiderweb. How can I read your strange face? Palicrovol wondered. Even as he wondered, he knew that Sleeve did not mean his face to be read. Sleeve probed others, but was not himself probed; Sleeve comprehended, but remained incomprehensible. "You came to me for no reason I could understand," said Palicrovol. "Until now. You came to me because of now."

Sleeve pursed his lips contemptuously. "I follow the entrails of animals. I use the power of their blood and in return they teach me where to go. Whatever plans God has for you, they're no concern of mine." But his denial was a confirmation, for never had Sleeve bothered to explain himself before.

A trumpet sounded outside the palisade. Count Palicrovol leapt to his feet. The treebark mantle slipped from his shoulders as he stood. "The King," whispered some of the men, for such was the terror of King Nasilee's Eyes and Ears that they thought he had already heard of this treason and come to punish Palicrovol. They felt no easier when they saw an army of five hundred men gathered outside the fortress.

"Who are you, who bring an army to my gate!" cried Palicrovol from the battlement.

"I am Zymas, once general of the King's army. And who are you, who stand naked at the battlement!"

Palicrovol felt the winter cold for the first time in the Feast of Hinds: the prophecy was already being fulfilled. In that moment he made his decision. "I am Palicrovol, King of Burland!"

But the army did not raise a cheer, and Palicrovol felt the giddiness of despair: he had spoken treason in front of the King's right hand, all because he had believed the mad prophet of a foolish God.

"Palicrovol!" called Zymas.

"Can these gates keep you out if you want to come in?" asked Palicrovol.

Zymas answered, "Can these soldiers keep you in if you want to come out?"

"If these soldiers are my enemies, then I will not come

out. I will stay here and make them pay in blood for every step they take inside my walls.''

''And if we are your friends?''

''Why did you come to me?'' cried Palicrovol from the battlement. ''Why do you taunt me?''

''I dreamed of you, Count Traffing. Why did I dream of you?''

Palicrovol turned to Sleeve, who smiled. ''It is the Feast of Hinds,'' said Sleeve.

''It is the Feast of Hinds!'' called Palicrovol.

''The tripes were heavy, and the womb was all but five days full,'' said Sleeve.

''The tripes were heavy, and the womb was all but five days full!'' called Palicrovol. As he echoed Sleeve's words, Palicrovol was relieved. When the hind that gave herself at the Feast of Hinds was utterly full, the enterprise of the master of the feast could not go wrong. *Someone's* enterprise, anyway, and it was usually polite to read all good omens for the host.

''I know nothing of augury,'' said Zymas. ''Who is the wizard who is teaching you what to say?''

Sleeve spoke for himself then. ''I am Sleeve,'' he said. ''The Sweet Sisters showed me a heavy hind. God spoke to Palicrovol through an old fool. And the Hart has come to you in a dream. If all the great gods are with Palicrovol, what will withstand him?''

Zymas had not said there was a hart in his dream. ''What need has he of me?''

''What need have you of him? It is enough that you are both committed to treason now. If you work together, you can bring down this King. If you oppose each other, Nasilee will find his work much easier.''

Zymas thought of still another argument. Sleeve, the greatest of the living wizards, is with this Count Traffing. ''Palicrovol, if you would be King, I will help you wed the King's daughter and have the throne. Will you be a just and good king?''

''I will be the same sort of king as I have been Count,'' said Palicrovol. ''My people prosper more than the people of any other lord. I am a just judge, as far as any man can be.''

''If that is true, I will follow you, and my men will follow you,'' said Zymas.

So the Godsman's prophecy was perfect, though it had predicted an event as unlikely as Burring flowing backward. Zymas had come to him, and come even before Palicrovol himself had taken one single act toward rebellion. God was now his god. "And I," cried Palicrovol, "I will follow God."

And I, whispered white-skinned Sleeve, pink-eyed Sleeve, I could shake the earth and unmake this fortress, and with my left hand I could cause a forest to rise in the place of Zymas's five hundred men. Why should I link myself to these unmagicked men, particularly if they fear that ridiculous god named God? They have no need of me, nor I of them. But Sleeve felt the hind's blood hardening on his arms and hands, and he was content that Palicrovol should be king, even if he did it in the name of this angry young God.

And that is how Palicrovol began his quest for the throne of Burland.

2

The Girl Who Rode the Hart

Three times in her life, Asineth learned what it meant to be the King's daughter. Each lesson was the beginning of wisdom.

ASINETH'S LESSON OF GOOD AND EVIL

When Asineth was only three, the ladies who cared for her walked her in the palace garden, in the safe part, where the gravel walks are neatly edged and the plants all grow in animal shapes. One of her favorite games was to sit very still, dribbling sand or gravel from her fingers, until the watching women grew bored with her, and got involved in their own conversations. Then she would quietly get up and walk away and hide from them. At first she always hid nearby, so she could watch the first moments of panic on their faces when they realized she was gone. "Oh, you little monster," they would say. "Oh, is that a way for a princess to run off and leave her ladies?"

But this time little Asineth hid farther away, because she was getting older, and the world was getting larger, and she was drawn to that part of the garden where moss hangs untrimmed and the animals are not rooted to the ground. There she saw a great grey beast drifting slowly through the underbrush, and she felt a strange attraction to it, and she followed. She would lose sight of the beast from time to time, and wander searching for it, and always she caught a glimpse of it, or thought she did, and moved after it, farther and farther into the untamed garden.

She did not hear the ladies searching for her; she was not nearby when, frightened, they reported to the Butler that she was missing; only when the sky was getting red and the soldiers found her bathing her feet at the edge of a large pool of water, only then did she remember her game of hide and seek. The soldiers took her away from the pool and carried her through the woods to the safe garden where she had been playing. There she saw the three women who had not watched her well enough, naked and staked out upon the ground, their backs and thighs and buttocks bloody from flogging. She was afraid. "Will they beat me, too?" she asked.

"Not you," said the soldier who carried her. "Never you. King Nasilee is your father. What man would dare to take a whip to you?"

So it was that Asineth learned that the daughter of the King can do no wrong.

Asineth's Lesson of Love and Power

King Nasilee's favorite mistress was Berry, and Asineth loved Berry with all her heart. Berry was lithe and beautiful. When she was naked she was slender and quick of body, like a racing hound, and all her muscles moved gracefully under her skin. When she was clothed she was ethereal, as distant from the world as a sunburst, and as beautiful. Asineth would come to her every day, and talk to her, and Berry, beautiful as she was, took time to listen to the little girl, to hear all her tales of the palace, all her dreams and wishes.

"I wish I were like you," Asineth told her.

"And how would you like to be like me?" Berry asked.

"You are so beautiful."

"But in a few years my beauty will fade, and the King your father will set me aside with a pension, like a house-keeper or a soldier."

"You are so wise."

"Wisdom is nothing, without power. Someday you will be Queen. Your husband will rule Burland because he is your husband, and then you will have power, and then it will not matter if you are wise."

"What is power?" asked Asineth.

Berry laughed, which told the six-year-old girl that she had asked a good question, a hard one. Adults always laughed when Asineth asked a hard question. After they laughed, Asineth always studied the question and the answer, to see what made it such an important question.

"Power," said Berry, "is to tell a man, You are a slave,

and he is a slave. Or to tell a woman, You are a countess, and she is a countess.''

"So power is naming people?" asked Asineth.

"And something more. Power is to tell the future, little Asineth. If the astronomer says, Tomorrow the moon will come and cover the sun, and it happens as he said, then he has the power of the sun and the moon. If your father says, Tomorrow you will die, it will also happen, and so your father has the power of death. Your father can tell the futures of all men in Burland. You will prosper, you will fail, you will fight in war, you will take your cargo downriver, you will pay taxes, you will have no children, you will be a widow, you will eat pomegranates every day of your life—he can predict anything to do with men, and it will come to pass. He can even tell the astronomer, Tomorrow you will die, and all the astronomer's power over the sun and the moon will not save him.''

Berry brushed her hair a hundred times as she spoke, and her hair glistened like gold. "I have power, too," said Berry.

"Whose future do you tell?" asked little Asineth.

"Your father's."

"What do you say will happen to him?"

"I say that tonight he will see a perfect body, and he will embrace it; he will see perfect lips, and he will kiss them. I predict that the seed of the King will be spilled in me tonight. I tell the future—and it will come to pass.''

"So you have power over my father?" asked Asineth.

"I love your father. I know him as he does not even know himself. He could not live without me." Berry stood naked before the glass and drew the borders of herself, and told Asineth how her father loved each nation of her flesh, told her which he came to as a gentle ambassador, which he dealt with sternly, and which he conquered with the sword.

Then her voice softened, and her face became childlike and peaceful, even as her words became colder. "A woman is a field, Asineth, or so a man thinks, a field that he will plow and plant, and from which he means to reap far more than his little seed. But the earth moves faster than a man can move, and the only reason he does not know it is because I carry him with me as I turn. He only plows what furrows he finds; he makes nothing. It is the farmer who is plowed, and not the field, and he will not forget me.'' Asineth listened to all of

Berry's words and watched the motion of her body and practiced talking and moving like her. She prayed to the Sweet Sisters that she would be like Berry when she grew; she knew that there was never a woman more perfect in all the world.

She loved Berry even on the day she spoke of her to the King. Nasilee let her sit beside him in the Chamber of Questions, and though she was young, he would sometimes publicly consult her. She would give her answer in a loud voice, and Nasilee would either praise her wisdom or point out her error, so all men could hear and benefit, and so that she could learn statecraft. This day the King asked his daughter, "Who is wiser than I am, Asineth?"

In the innocence of childhood she had not learned that there are some questions whose answer you must pretend not to know. "Berry," she answered at once.

"Ah," said her father. "And how is she so wise?"

"Because she has power, and if you have power you don't have to be wise."

"I have more power than she has," said the King. "Am I not wiser, then?"

"You have power over all men, Father, but Berry has power over *you*. You can never get a farmer to plow the same field twice in a year, but she can get you to plow twice in a day, even when you have no seed left to sow."

"Ah," said Nasilee again. Then he told the soldiers to bring Berry to him. Asineth saw that her father was angry. Why should he be angry? Didn't he love Berry as much as Asineth did? Wasn't he glad that she was wise? Hadn't he poisoned Asineth's own mother because she was angry at him for taking Berry into his bed?

Berry came with manacles on her wrists and hands. She looked at Asineth with a terrible hatred and cried out, "How can you believe the words of a child! I don't know why she is lying, or who told her to say these things, but you surely won't believe the tales of my enemies!"

Nasilee only raised his eyebrows and said, "Asineth never lies."

Berry looked in fear at Asineth and cried, "I was never your rival!"

But Asineth did not understand her words. She had learned

her first lesson so well that she was incapable of imagining that she had done something wrong.

Berry pleaded with her lover. Asineth saw how she used her beautiful body, how she strained against the manacles, how her robe parted artfully to show the swell of her breasts. Father will love Berry again and forgive her, Asnieth was sure of it. But Berry's lover had become her King, and when all her pleading was done, he sent for a farmer and a team of oxen and a plow.

Out in the garden they did it, plowed Berry from groin to heart with a team of oxen pulling, and her screams rang in the palace garden until winter, so that Asineth could not go outside until winter changed it into another world.

It was a cruel thing her father did, but Asineth knew that he, too, heard Berry's screams in the night. Berry dwelt in every room of the palace, even though she was dead, and one day, when Asineth was nine, she found her father slumped in a chair in the library, a book open before him, his cheeks stained with half-dried tears. Without asking, Asineth knew who it was he thought of. It comforted Asineth to know that even though Berry had not so much power as she had thought, she had this much: she could make herself unforgotten, and force her lover to live forever with regret. Yet Berry's death itself was still a half-learned lesson, with the meaning yet ungiven, and so Asineth asked her father a question.

"Didn't you love her?" asked Asineth.

To her surprise, he answered, "If I did not love her, I never have loved anything."

"Why did you kill her, then?"

"Because I am the King," said Nasilee. "If I hadn't killed her, I would have lost the fear of my people, and if they do not fear me, I am not King."

Asineth knew then that of the two powers Berry taught her, the stronger power was naming. It was because Nasilee was named King that he had to kill what he loved most. "You did not love Berry most of all," said Asineth.

Nasilee opened his eyes, letting their light shine narrowly out upon his young daughter. "Did I not?"

"More than her, you loved the name of King."

Her father's eyes closed again. "Go away, child."

"I don't want to go, Father," she said. I loved Berry more than I loved you, she did not say.

"I don't want to see you when I think of *her*," said her father.

"Why not?" asked Asineth.

"Because you made me kill her."

"I?"

"If you hadn't told me of her treasonous words, I wouldn't have had to kill her."

"If you had merely laughed at the words of a child, she could have lived."

"A King must be King!"

"A weak King must be what other Kings have been; a strong King is himself, and from then on the meaning of the name of King is changed." The words could have been Berry's, for Berry understood these things, and Asineth only still guessed at all that she meant.

"What does it matter?" said the King wearily. "You said the words, the King heard them and had to act, Berry had to die, and now I mourn her and wish that you had died in birthing, and taken your mother with you, by the Hart I wish it, by the Sisters I swear it, now leave me, little girl."

She left him. Until that time, she had been the one person in all Burland who did not fear King Nasilee. Now there was no one left who did not fear him, for he was King, and could break anyone with a word.

ASINETH'S LESSON OF JUSTICE AND MERCY

It was the day of Palicrovol.

The terrible rebel had roused all the people of Burland against the King. With that traitor Zymas he had defeated army after army, not in open battle but by cutting off their supplies, separating, wooing soldiers, troops, whole armies to desert and serve Palicrovol. Now, at last, after fifteen years of a war that had never come to battle, Palicrovol's army was outside the walls of Hart's Hope. Hart's Hope, the great city on the Burring, the capital; and Nasilee looked out and saw no help.

For the last ten years tax payments had fallen steadily, ceasing first in the outlying counties, and finally diminishing to almost nothing. The commerce of Hart's Hope itself had failed, for Palicrovol had built a highway in the west and forced all the river traffic to travel overland, though it raised prices; Hart's Hope was starving, and the people fled. Now Nasilee waited inside the impregnable walls, watched as Palicrovol, a Godsman, gathered his white banners, each with a hundred men around it, until the land outside foamed white as the crests of the sea.

Asineth also waited. She watched her father consult his wizards—the few that remained. She watched him wander the half-empty halls of the palace, haunted by the knowledge of his own death. Everyone knew that the walls of Hart's Hope could not be breached. They were miles long, rods high, yards thick; even the few soldiers Nasilee had left could hold it against Palicrovol's army, even with Zymas the traitor in command.

But Asineth was afraid. She was old enough now—twelve years old, with her womanhood newly on her—to know that her father was a wicked man, that the people were right to hate him. Asineth knew that Palicrovol was beloved of the people, for even the servants in the palace, loyal as they were, talked wistfully—and quietly—of the freedom and prosperity that Palicrovol brought wherever he conquered. Asineth feared that her father's soldiers would betray him and open the gate for Palicrovol. And so she prayed to the Sweet Sisters. She brought the blood of the moon with her to the altar of women in the secret place, and said, "Make the hearts of these men loyal to my father, so we are preserved from our enemy."

The morning after the night when she burned blood for the Sweet Sisters, the gates of the city swung open, and the soldiers of the outer wall raised the white banner of Palicrovol's God. Word was that Zymas had come to them alone in the night, unarmed, and with his stirring words had won their hearts.

Asineth took four strong guards with her to the Sisters' shrine, where no man had ever been brought before, and commanded them to break the altar in pieces. They broke in with four blows of a sledgehammer. Inside, the solid rock of the altar was hollow. Like a little pot it held ancient water that had been there since the world first gleamed upon the point of the Hart's Horn. The water spilled upon the floor, and Asineth trod in the water and muddied it with her shoe. "I hate you," she said to the Sweet Sisters.

Now Palicrovol's army held even the city of Hart's Hope itself. Word was that Palicrovol had changed the city's name. Now he would call it Inwit, and he was causing half his soldiers to work on building a great temple to his God. He forbade anyone to offer blood at the shrine of the Hart.

This gave Asineth hope. Even though the Hart was a strange god to her, as to all women, she was sure that the Hart would listen to her. Weren't they allies now? Wasn't Palicrovol an enemy to both of them? She prayed to the Hart, then, to be a shield around the Castle walls. There was no chance of treachery now—only a few guards remained, and King Nasilee himself held the only keys that would open the rooms where the gate could be lifted or the postern door unblocked. But Palicrovol had Sleeve, the greatest wizard in the world, and what no man could do, Sleeve might do. So Asineth prayed to the Hart to protect them.

And in the night, at the very moment she was pleading with the Hart to preserve her father and herself, she heard a great cracking noise like a thousand trees breaking in a storm and knew at once what it meant. The huge gate of the castle had been broken by Sleeve's magic, and there was no more thwarting Palicrovol now.

Asineth ran searching for her father through the labyrinth of the Palace. She looked in every hiding place; she did not know her father as well as she thought. He was not in a hiding place. So she did not find him until the soldiers did, in the Chamber of Questions.

"Father!" she cried.

"Fool!" he shouted. "Run."

But the soldiers knew her at once, and caught her, and held her until Palicrovol came.

I hate you, Hart, said Asineth silently.

They came into the Chamber of Questions within the hour: Palicrovol, tall and strong, with the light of God in his face, or at least the light of triumph. Zymas, the traitor, with arms and legs like the limbs of an ox, and the look of battle black in his eyes. Sleeve, gaunt and ghostlike with his white skin and white hair and pink eyes, drifting like a fog over the floor.

"He should die as so many thousands of his people died," cried Zymas. "Sit him naked on a stake, and let the people spit on him as he screams in agony."

"He should be burned," said Sleeve, "so that the power of his blood is returned into the world."

"He is King," said Palicrovol. "He will die like a King." Palicrovol drew his sword. "Give him your sword, Zymas."

"Palicrovol," said Zymas, "you should not take this risk yourself."

"Palicrovol," said Sleeve, "you should not dirty your hands with his blood."

"When the singers say that I vanquished Nasilee," said Palicrovol, "it will be true."

So Asineth watched as her father raised the sword they gave him. He did not attempt to fight—that would have been undignified. Instead he stood with the point of the sword upraised. Palicrovol beat twice upon the sword, trying to force it back, but Nasilee did not flinch. Then Palicrovol thrust his sword under the King's arms, beneath the breast-bone, upward into the heart. Asineth watched her father's blood rush gladly down Palicrovol's blade and wash over his hands, and she heard the soldiers cheer.

Then she stepped forward. "I am the daughter of the King," she said in a voice that was all the more powerful because it was so feeble and childish.

They all fell silent and listened to her.

"The King my father is dead. I am Queen as of this moment, by all the laws of Burland. And the King will be the man I marry."

"The King," said Zymas, "is the man that the armies obey."

"The King," said Sleeve, "is the man clearly favored by the gods."

"The King," said Palicrovol, "is the man who marries you. And I will marry you."

With all the contempt she could manage, Asineth said to him, "I scorn you, Count Traffing."

Palicrovol nodded, as if he honored her verdict upon his honor. "As you wish," he said. "But I never asked for your consent." He turned to one of the servants cowering under the gaze of the soldiers. "Has this girl her womanhood?"

The servant stammered, as Asineth answered for her. "Why don't you ask *me*? I do not lie."

At those words Palicrovol's face brightened, as if in recognition. "I knew another woman once who would not lie. Tell me, then, Queen Asineth. Have you your womanhood?"

"Three times," said Asineth. "I am old enough to marry."

"Then marry you shall."

"Never to you."

"Now. And to me. I will not have it said that I do not rule in Burland by right."

They dressed her in a wedding gown that had been made for a child bride eight generations before her. It had never been worn, for the child had died of a plague before her wedding. Now, as they carried Asineth in a prison cart through the streets of Inwit, with ten thousand people jeering at her, cursing her though she had never done them harm, she prayed.

She prayed to the only god left, Palicrovol's God, whose temple was rising in the southeast corner of the city. God, she said to him, your triumph is complete, and I also scorn the Sisters and the Hart. Be merciful to me, God. Let me die unmarried to this man.

But there was no miracle. No unwatched knife lay near her hand; she stood at no precipice; there was no water larger than the contents of an urn. She could not slit her throat or leap to her death or drown. God had no mercy on her.

The image of the Hart had been torn from its place at the Shrine and now stood shabbily in front of Faces Hall. A thousand generations of wizards had stood upon the back of the Hart to pray for Burland and offer the blood of power. Now only Palicrovol stood there, waiting for her, dressed in the short tunic of the bridegroom. There would be no Dance of Descent, no rites; it was plain to anyone with eyes that Palicrovol intended to consummate this marriage in full view of ten thousand witnesses, so that no one afterward could say that he had not been the duly wedded husband of the daughter of the King.

Asineth had known all her life that as daughter of the King, her body was the Kingdom, and whatever man had her, had Burland. What she had not realized was that as daughter of the King, above all laws and customs, she had no protection now. There was no law that said a girl of twelve could not be publicly ravished by a husband she did not want—if she was the daughter of the King. There was no custom that said the people should turn their eyes away in shame at such cruelty to a child—not if the child was daughter of the King.

They forced a ring upon the thumb of her left hand—it was Palicrovol's only gentle gesture to her at that time, to name her Beauty at her wedding day. She saw also that he had his ring upon the thumb of the right hand, signifying strength. "Now everyone will know how strong you are," she said, "to conquer a dangerous enemy like me."

He did not answer her. He only watched.

They tied padded boards to her hands, making them so heavy and unwieldy that she could hardly lift them. They put a gag on her mouth, with barbs in it so if she so much as touched it with her tongue or tried to clamp her teeth upon it, it cut her painfully. Then they lifted her to the back of the Hart, and before all the citizens and soldiers of Inwit her husband said the words of the vow, then cut her dress from her. Asineth felt the breeze on her naked skin as if it were the darts of ten thousand eyes. *I am the daughter of the King, and you have made me naked and defenseless among the swine. You gave my father the dignity of a King's death, but me you will degrade as the worst of whores is not degraded.* Asineth had never known such terrible shame in her life, and she longed to die.

But her maidenhead was Burland, and Burland would be his. Zymas the traitor took Palicrovol's clothing from him; his wizard, Sleeve, anointed him for the marriage bed. And as he was anointed, Palicrovol looked upon the girl he meant to defraud of all she had, saw in her anguish how terrible a thing it was that he must do to this child, and yet for the kingdom's sake he did not flinch from what he must do.

Because she was the daughter of the King, she looked back at him. *These gawking churls will see a princess broken, but they will not see her bow.* She bit savagely into the barbs of her gag, hoping to drown in her own blood, but the barbs were too slender to draw the heavy stream she needed, and she could not keep her throat from swallowing.

Then she saw the pity in his face, and she realized for the first time that he was no monster of power, but a man; and if a man, then an animal; and if an animal, then a prisoner of his body. Palicrovol was not as strong as a god, for the gods had no mercy, and the gods were weak or malicious anyway. Palicrovol had the power to ensure that she would be alive when he broke into her secret chamber and left his slime. But did she not have the power Berry had taught her: to make this man remember her? She began to move her girlish body as she had seen Berry move. She saw Palicrovol's surprise, and then

Palicrovol's eyes filled with—desire. Her movement was so
subtle that it could not be seen by anyone but Palicrovol; but
once he saw it, he could see nothing else. Asineth was not
surprised at his fascination—she had learned from Berry, and
Berry was perfection.

Palicrovol trembled as he took her, and Asineth ignored the
pain and tried to use him as Berry had said a woman must use
a man if she is to be remembered. When he was done at last,
he stood, her blood glistening upon his triumphant horn, and
she watched them set the Antler Crown upon his head, and
put the Mantle of the Stag upon his shoulders. His eyes were
distant, and his knees were weak, and she knew that she had
shaken him. She thought he was trembling with the memory
of her body, as men had trembled for Berry.

"The Hart has ridden the Hind," he said. He cast away the
Mantle, and instead donned the white robe of a Godsman.
And he was King. The people cheered and cheered.

The rite was finished, and the few participants withdrew
from the crowd into Faces Hall. "Kill her now," said Zymas.
"You have what you need from her. If you let her live, she
will only be a danger to you."

"Kill her now," said Sleeve. "Women can take vengeances
that men cannot understand."

Kill me now if you dare, Asineth challenged him, her
tongue flicking painfully against the barbs. All gods have
forsaken me, I have done what little I could do, and I long
not to live. Kill me now, but I will haunt the inner chamber
of your heart.

"I will not kill her," said Palicrovol.

And Asineth believed, for that moment, that she was Berry's true disciple, that he had found her body too beautiful,
too desirable to be slain. Of course the others, who had not
known her flesh, did not understand his need.

"Mercy to her is injustice to Burland," said Zymas. "If
she lives, you promise us all a future of war and suffering."

Palicrovol's eyes flashed with anger, and he said nothing
for a long moment. Asineth waited for him to speak of his
love for her. Instead he looked at her and tears came from his
eyes and then he said, "I can kill a King, I can ravish a child,
all for the sake of God and Burland, but in God's name,
Zymas, wasn't it to stop the killing of children that you first
came to me?"

Sleeve touched the King's shoulder. "She is Nasilee's daughter. Imagine how much mercy she would have if she ever had the Flower Princess in her power."

At the mention of the Flower Princess, King Palicrovol bowed his head. "I remember the Flower Princess, Sleeve. I have not forgotten. This girl is so much Nasilee's daughter that even as I took her, she tried to seduce me. That is the sort of animal that was bred in Nasilee's palace."

Asineth went cold, for he sounded horrified at the memory. She had tried to be Berry, but this man only pitied her, and the others looked at her with contempt. Her shame before had been the shame of a King's daughter degraded; now her shame was of a woman despised, and she hated herself for having tried to make him love her, and hated Berry for being so much more beautiful than she, and hated Palicrovol and Zymas and Sleeve for knowing her pitiable attempt at womanhood, and hated most of all this unknown Flower Princess who never would be raped upon the Hart. She cried out against the gag, and Palicrovol ordered them to free her tongue.

"If I am an animal, kill me!" she cried. With no crowd to watch her now, with all dignity gone, she was willing to beg. "Kill me now! Like my father!"

Palicrovol only shook his head. "It is not her fault that she is what she is. If she had been born in any other house, to any other father, she would not be what she is. If she had been born across the southern water, she might have been the Flower Princess."

"But never Enziquelvinisensee Evelvenin," said Sleeve.

"No," said Palicrovol. "But we ask the gods for only one miracle in a lifetime."

"You have broken and humiliated her," Zymas said. "Nasilee's daughter will not forget."

"I have broken and humiliated her," Palicrovol echoed, "and killed her father before her eyes, and taken away her kingdom, and to harm her any more would make me despise myself more than I can bear. If I do not temper my victory with one act of mercy, even one that is dangerous to myself, then how will I look in the crystal and say to God that a better man than Nasilee now wears Nasilee's crown?"

There was a moment of silence, and then Sleeve stepped forward and took Asineth by one of the clumsy boards that encased her hands. "If you insist that this broken creature live, then put her in my care. I alone am strong enough to guard her in her exile, and hide her from the eyes of all your enemies who would love to find her and use her to destroy you."

"I need you by me," protested the new King.

"Then kill this woman."

Palicrovol hesitated no longer. "Take the little Queen, then, Sleeve, and be kind to her."

"I will be as kind to her as you will let me be to one whose only desire is to die," said Sleeve. "By my blood I wish that you had truly been merciful."

Sleeve enclosed her in the folds of his own robe, so that no one could see the naked body of the little Queen. Little Queen, thought Asineth. I will remember the name he called me, she told herself. He will know someday who is little, and who is great. Are you the strongest of all men, so strong that you can be merciful to me, a weak woman? Here is the undoing of your strength: I am not a weak woman. I am not a Little Queen. And your mercy will be your undoing. You will regret leaving me alive, and someday you will remember possessing me, and yearn to possess me again.

What was the third lesson that Asineth learned? She told me herself, many times, when she dwelt in your palace and you hopelessly wandered the forests of Burland.

Asineth learned that justice could be cruel, and crueler yet necessity, but mercy was the cruelest thing of all. That would be useful to her. She would remember that. That is why she left *you* alive for three centuries when she had the power to kill you whenever she wished. As the Godsmen say, no act of mercy goes unrewarded. Ah, Palicrovol, will you not learn that mercy is as good as the person to whom the mercy is given? You spared Asineth, who should have died; now you will not spare Orem Scanthips, called Banningside, whose good heart should be born a hundred thousand times upon the earth. Are you like Asineth? Will you learn all your lessons backward?

3

The Descent of Beauty

This is how Beauty came into the world, struggling to find her true image among many faces.

THE PRIESTESS OF BRACK

The wizard fisher came in a smallish craft and without greeting built his hut on an unused place at the bottom end of the bay. The other fishermen of Brack eyed him carefully. His ship was too slow for a pirate, which was just as well—a pirate would starve on what he could steal from their fishing boats. His ship was rigged for just one man, and from the look of him he was not a sailor. So it was not jealousy that made them fear him. It was the way he kept himself covered in all weathers, as if he feared the sun; it was the stark white hair of his head, the gleam of pink in his eye like a crazed treehopper; it was his secret way. He knew more than they did, knew more than the wind as it teased the sea, knew more than the air-breathing octopus that spread himself on the water, knew more than the priestess of the Sweet Sisters who tended her burning stones at the point of the bay.

"What is he?" the fishermen asked their wives. "Who is he?" the wives asked the priestess. She touched the hot obsidian; the flesh of her finger sizzled; and she looked deep into her pain and said, "He rules by the power of blood. He finds shelter from storms in the open ocean. He finds shoals that make no whitecaps on the sea. He can dip into salt and bring up fair water. And the fish follow him dreaming, dreaming."

A wizard then, but not to be dreaded. So they took to watching him respectfully, and in a matter of weeks they learned that he meant to be kind. For if they followed him out to sea in the early hours before dawn, he would sail in his clumsy fashion for an hour or so, then stop and cast in his

net. If the fishermen cast in their nets at that time, they found
nothing. But if they waited until his net was full, if they
watched as he laboriously brought it aboard, then he would
sail back home, and they could then dip their nets into the sea
and catch well, every day that they followed him, boats full
to the brim with fish on some days, and never a day that the
fish escaped entire.

So the coming of the pink-eyed wizard brought good to
Brack. Not that they ever became *friendly* with the man. It's
never good to mingle with folk who draw their power from
the living blood. Besides, even if they had lost all their fear
of the wizard fisherman, there was his daughter.

It seemed at first that she hardly knew she was a woman.
She never left his side, and when he drew in his heavy nets,
there she was beside him, pulling on her side, and pulling
well—when the fishermen still thought she was a lad, they
praised the boy among themselves for his hard work, if not
for his skill. They knew soon enough that she was a woman,
though. If the wizard dressed too much under the hot sun of
the southern sea, his daughter dressed too little, wearing
dungarees like a man, and casting away her shirt when the
day was blazing, until back and breast alike were burnt dark:
She seemed at first to care nothing for their gaze; as time
passed, however, they began to think she was something of a
wanton, shedding her clothing deliberately, so they would see
her. They saw how her breasts grew fuller and more sluggishly pendulous as she worked. They saw how her belly
swelled. She could not be more than a year or two into
womanhood, and yet she was full of a child.

Whose child? When at last the fisherman's daughter had
her confinement, it was not hard to guess. The wizard fisherman had come in the end of autumn, only weeks after the
coronation of the King, and the babe was being born now,
well into the new autumn. Ten months. The child must have
been conceived since the little ship first came into the bay of
Brack, and the father of the child could only be the child's
grandfather as well. It was a terrible thing, but the ways of
those who buy their power from the living blood are not to be
questioned.

The priestess of the Sweet Sisters knew better, however.
She, too, could count the months, but when she poured tears,
sweat, and seawater drops on the hot pumice, they beaded up

and stayed, skittering for a moment, then drifting across the rough stone like a fleet of sailboats in a bay, runing for her the message of the Sweet Sisters to this watcher by the sea. It was no incestuous child that would be born, but a daughter whose blood was filled with awesome power: a ten-month child ruled by the moon from her birth.

What should I do? asked the priestess, terrified.

But the water evaporated at last, leaving thin trails of salt upon the stone. It was not for her to do anything, only to watch, only to know.

Some of the wives saw the fear in her face as the priestess looked across the water to the wizard fisherman and the hut where the babe already crawled in the sand.

"Should we drive them away?" asked one.

"Wizards come and go as they like," said the priestess. "The Sweet Sisters do not ban, they quicken what they find in the world."

"Should we leave, then?" asked another.

"Do your men come home with empty boats or full?" asked the priestess in return. "Does the wizard do you good or ill?"

"Then why," asked another woman, "why are you afraid?"

And the priestess caressed the quartz crystal at her throat and professed not to know.

At last the priestess could bear no more. She got onto her feeble raft and poled her way across the placid water of the bay until she beached before the wizard's hut. The fisherman's daughter was playing with her child in the cool afternoon of early spring. She looked up curiously at the priestess who picked her way along the kelpy sand. The babe, too, looked up. The priestess avoided the baby's eyes—a ten-month child is not to be caught in the gaze of a stranger—and so stared instead at the mother. She was younger than the priestess had thought, watching her from a distance. She might have been the babe's sister. Her eyes were hot and challenging, cold and curious, and for the first time it occurred to the priestess that the mother might be more dangerous than the child.

But it was the wizard she had come to see, not the women, and so the priestess of the Sweet Sisters went to the door of the hut, pushed aside the flap, and went inside.

"Close the flap!" barked the wizard. "I could go blind

from the sunlight, coming sudden like that." When the flap was back in place, the pink-eyed fisherman stopped squinting. "You," he said. "Took your sweet time about coming."

"I need a good day on the sea," said the priestess. "I rarely travel."

"You witches, who use the dead blood, you don't ever seem to have much life in you at all."

"Out of death comes new life," she answered. "And out of living blood comes old death."

"May be true. I don't much care, actually. You women never teach us your rite, and you may be sure it's a fool who teaches a woman *ours*."

She looked around the hut and saw that it was better equipped with books than with the tools of fishing. "Where do you mend your nets?" she asked.

"They never break," he answered. "Child's play."

"The child must die," said the priestess.

"Must she?"

"A ten-month child is too powerful to stay in the world. You must know that."

"I've never studied the lore of births and bindings," confessed the wizard. "There's not much use a man can make of it anyway. I'll look it up, though, now that you've mentioned it."

"I've come to do it for you."

"No," said the wizard.

"You cannot use the blood. It would consume you."

"I do not intend to use or not use the blood. I don't intend the child to die."

"My tears stayed forever on the pumice."

"It's not in my right to decide. The father of the child extends his protection over the girl and over her little one. Both will live."

"A wizard who draws the fish up from the sea, and you let the father of the child keep you from acting for the safety of the world?"

"The child's mother loves her."

The priestess saw that he did not mean to listen to her, and so she said no more and left. As she came from the hut she looked to where the childmother and the ancient child had been playing. They were gone. And then the girl's voice came from behind her, and the priestess knew that she had heard all that was said indoors.

"Can a woman use the living blood?" asked the girl.

The priestess considered the question, and shuddered. "No," she said, and walked quickly away. And all the way across the bay she cursed herself for coming to see them: for the girl had asked the question that no decent-hearted woman would ask, and the priestess feared the girl was wise enough to know that her answer was a lie. There were living bloods that a woman could use, but no woman who was not a viper ever would. Let her not use them, she prayed all night, washing her hair again and again in the tidewater that lapped against her skirts. Forgive me for having raised the possibility in her mind, and undo my day's work.

THE CAREFUL WIZARD

Warned by the witch, Sleeve watched the babe more carefully. He had had little to do with children in his life, and so he had not kept track of how quickly the infant was learning things, how bright her mind seemed to be, until now. And now he began to find the passages in his books and pore over them, trying to learn what it was that the witch so feared. The hints were vague and obscure, and Sleeve grew more and more frustrated with his books. They spoke so little of women's magic, for only men wrote and read these works. The ten-month child—they dreaded her, it was plain, and called for the child to die at birth, its blood poured out upon mouldering vegetation. But why the child was so dangerous they did not bother to explain, not in so many words.

All the while the child grew. In spite of his fears, Sleeve found himself liking the little one; even more surprising, he liked Asineth as well. She was not just enduring captivity, but thriving in it. Her habit of fishing with him bare-breasted was annoying, since it was obviously meant to discredit him with the local fishermen, but now that she had the child, she seemed alert and alive and the hate left her face for hours, for days at a time. Asineth was no more friendly with Sleeve, but she babbled on with the child.

"What will you name her?" asked Sleeve.

"Let the father name her," she answered coldly.

"He never will."

"Then let her go unnamed," she said. That was the only sign that she had not forgotten her woes. No matter how much her love for her daughter cheered her, she would not name the child.

"Is it fair to punish the child because you hate her father?" asked Sleeve. Then he heard his own words, realized that it was a question Nasilee's daughter might well have asked him, and left the conversation alone after that.

The visit from the witch undid him, really, though no doubt the woman thought her mission a failure. Sleeve had been growing contented there on the edge of the sea. Even though Asineth almost never spoke to him and the fishermen shunned him, still this life was the least solitary he had ever been. The fleet of little ships that put out to sea with him in the morning—they were a comfort to him. Though his fragile skin could not bear the sunlight, so that he remained forever clothed against the eyes of the other fishermen, still there was friendship in this: that his arms knew what their arms knew, that he lived as they did with the smell of fish and salt spray and sunlight hard on the wood of the boat. For the first time in his life, he felt at one with other men, and if they could not match his wit, they were still brothers of the flesh. Asineth and the child had been a comfort, too; he had almost come to understand the home-feeling that he had always despised because it turned other men weak.

Well, it turned him weak, too. Weak—or careless, anyway. Not that he was not alert to some things. He read all day until his eyes ached, trying to discover the menace of a ten-month child. Then he slept, letting his mind study again in dreams. Then he went out before dawn, leaving mother and child asleep, and the kettle of fish simmering on the fire. He would sail alone now, let down and haul up the nets alone. All the while he fancied he was studying out the problem. In fact he was only thinking about it now and then. Most of the time he was thinking a fisherman's thoughts. Sometimes he even wondered if he would not have been better off to be born a fisherman than to have lived as he had, following the blood of the Hart.

What he never noticed was that Asineth spent all morning every day inside the hut, reading whatever he had read, studying also to learn women's magic from the books that were written to men. What he never guessed was that she knew enough of the Sweet Sisters' lore that things that meant nothing to him meant much to her. Every book began with a page of warnings to guard these secrets, especially against the prying eyes of women—but Sleeve was careless of women, since only men had ever tried to steal knowledge from him. It did not occur to him that Asineth could understand what was written there.

On a day late in summer, when the child was nearing her first yearday, Sleeve finally understood a passage that had long eluded him. It was while he was on the boat, feeling the rhythm of wind and current with his feet, his buttocks, and his arms; suddenly he trembled with discovery and nearly capsized himself as the jib went flying. Only one person had anything to fear from a ten-month child, and that was the child's mother. Sleeve turned about at once and tacked back into the harbor, right among the fleet of fishermen who scrambled to maneuver their boats out of the way. They asked him for no explanation, and he did not offer any. True, the infant had done no harm till now, but now that Sleeve knew the truth he would not delay in taking precautions. It would not do to report to Palicrovol that Asineth had died because Sleeve had to finish his day's fishing before getting back to save her life.

Sleeve did not know that Asineth matched his reading day by day, and that she, too, discovered what he knew. She understood even more, however, much more, and when Sleeve got back to the hut, Asineth and the child were gone.

He tried to follow her afoot, but she lost him in the rocky hills behind the shore. He bled himself copiously to buy power enough to search magically for her, but his searching eye could not see her. He knew then that he had moved too late. The infant already understood some of her powers.

It was only when he realized that four of his books were missing that he first suspected that it was not the infant, not the daughter of Asineth and Palicrovol who was thwarting his search. It was Asineth herself, for the babe could not yet read. He cursed himself for having let her study what it was his duty to protect. But beyond that, there was nothing he could do. And so he waited, and built up his strength against the return of his adversary. He was not sure just how strong women's magic might be, and he wanted to be sure of the victory in case the contest proved to be a difficult one. He was almost pleased at the prospect—he had not had a difficult battle in decades, for there was no wizard that he knew of in the world who was a match for him.

On the tenth night of his waiting, a woman called him from outside the hut. It was a voice that he did not recognize at once, but when he saw her face, even by the light of the cookfire he knew her.

"Berry," he said. "I thought that you were dead."

She smiled and raised her eyebrows. "And I had no idea that you knew me."

So this woman who wore Berry's flesh was not Berry at all. "Asineth," he whispered. It was a bad sign, if she had the power of changing shapes to such a degree that it fooled even him.

"Asineth?" she asked. "I do not know her."

"Who are you, then?"

"I am Beauty," she answered. "I am the most powerful of all the gods." With a single perfect, graceful motion she was naked. "Am I not perfect, Sleeve?"

"You are," he freely admitted. To see Berry's body again, so perfectly recreated—Asineth could not have known that he had been Berry's lover long before Nasilee had her, but the sight of Berry there on the beach unnerved him as no other ploy could have. Still, Sleeve was not one to be completely distracted by his own memories of love. "You are perfect—but you are not a god."

"Am I not? I came from battle to you, Sleeve," she said. "I had learned so much, and I had to try it out. First I challenged the brute Hart, for I thought he would be easiest to rule. I was wrong, for my first battle was the worst of all, and he nearly won, and as it was I still fear him a little. But no matter—he is in chains at the root of the world, and you will have no help from him."

She was mad, of course. To challenge the Hart and win—absurd.

"The Sweet Sisters next, for I had a quarrel with them. I was surprised at how easily they bowed—they have no weapons for the kind of war I wage. They have been born into the most amusing bodies, and in flesh they will stay, bound up as long as I want them there."

"And God?" asked Sleeve, amused.

"He's slippery. I'll have to keep him where I can watch him over the years. But *you*, Sleeve. You I do not fear at all."

His love of theatricality would have made him say some heroic epigram in answer, but he had learned at an early age that theatricality is no substitute for sure victory. So he bit down upon her heart with the teeth of his left hand, to fell her at once with a single magical blow. Even if she endured it she would be too shaken to fight him after that.

But she did not so much as flinch, and as he squeezed with his cruel inward hand, he was surprised to find that he felt the agony in his own chest. He stopped, but her pain went on, and in a moment of anguish he realized that her words were not brag. There was no help for him from the Hart, and that presence of gods that he had always felt underlying all his power—it was gone.

"What have you done!" he cried.

"Took you by surprise, didn't I," she said. "Oh, never mind, Sleeve. If the gods could not resist me, how could you?"

The pain in his heart eased, and he found himself lying on the sand, looking up at her through blurred eyes.

"Can't you see me well?" she asked. And suddenly his eyes were clear of tears. It was that which frightened him most of all. A magic that could break the power of gods was terrible indeed, but a magic so delicate it could take the tears out of a man's eyes—that was a thing he had never heard of before in all his reading, in all his life.

"Look at me," she said again. "Berry was the most beautiful woman I know, but I am Beauty, and I thought of some improvements. Here, is this better? And this?"

He lay in the sand and told her yes, yes, it was better.

"Well, now," she said at last, dressing herself as she spoke, "well, now, Sleeve. I suppose you'll want to come with me."

"Where are you going?" he asked.

"Why, to Palicrovol," she said. "Am I not his wife? Did he not marry me with many, many witnesses?"

"I told him he should have killed you."

"I remember that," she said. "But he didn't, and here I am. Do you think he'll find me beautiful?"

It was impossible that she could mean to live with him as his wife.

"Oh, I don't mean to," she said. "*Live* with him? Absurd. But I heard that he was bringing the Flower Princess to him from the southern islands. She is of age, I hear. And apparently he thinks that he can marry her. While I still live, he thinks that he can marry her. When he sees me, will he still think that she is beautiful?"

Sleeve took a bit of satisfaction in telling her, despite his fear, "Asineth, improve on Berry all you like, but no woman of flesh has ever been so beautiful as Enziquelvinisensee Evelvenin."

Suddenly his tongue was thick in his mouth, and he felt snakes slithering inside his clothing, a forked tongue tickling at his throat. "Never call me Asineth again," she whispered.

"Aye, Beauty," he answered.

"You will come with me to Palicrovol. I will keep you as a pet."

"As you wish," he said.

She giggled, and the snakes were gone. "Get up," she said.

He got up, and in the process discovered that she was not content with changing her own shape. She had changed his, too.

"Tell the truth," she said. "Don't you like yourself better like this? Weren't you tired of standing out, a pale giant among other men?"

He did not answer her, just stared at his hands and nodded. This is what defeat feels like, he told himself, but he knew it was not true. This was only the beginning of defeat. He knew that Asineth had plans. And he pitied Palicrovol, for there was no hope for him now. It was plain that all the warnings about the power of a ten-month child were feeble compared to the danger of its mother, and now it was too late to think of how he might thwart her. Asineth's power was so beyond his that she could swat away his strongest effort with a laugh. It would be something besides the power of the living blood that would undo her now, if anything ever did. He had never been so afraid in all his life.

Only when he had packed his books and hoisted them on his back, only when she led him away from Brack on the end of a golden chain, only then did he invent a role for himself that might just keep him alive. He wrapped the long chain around his legs to hobble him and toddled after her like a child, singing loudly,

> I have captured Beauty,
> I have her on a string,
> I keep her in the cupboard,
> And poke her with my thing.

She looked back at him in annoyance and pulled on the golden chain. Immediately he fell forward against the rocks, gashing his shoulder. Ignoring the pain, he sat upright and poked the wound with his finger, then licked off the blood. "The wine is strong, but the vintage is wrong," he declared solemnly.

Looking down at him, she smiled in spite of herself. She had given him a ridiculous shape; now he was living the part she had assigned him. It pleased her. "What is the name of the wine?" she asked, playing along.

"Splenetic Red, from the fields of Urubugala."

"Urubugala," she said, and she laughed aloud. "Urubugala. That is the language of Elukra, isn't it? What does it mean?"

"Little cock," answered Sleeve.

"My little cock," she said. "My Urubugala." It was a good name for the creature he had become. And the name did not displease Sleeve. If it kept him alive, he was happy with it. Sleeve was not one of these weak, proud men who can be controlled by the threat of humiliation. There were times when he even enjoyed the freedom that he won through his fool's part.

> Beauty's daughter
> By the water—
> Did you wish
> She were a fish?

At that Beauty glowered, but Sleeve immediately raised his tunic and strutted toward her, showing off his grotesque genitals. "If you like to be a mother, I'll gladly sire another!"

"You are not always funny," said Beauty. "I don't like you when you aren't funny."

Sleeve sidled up to her and whispered, "Where is the baby?"

Immediately he felt an excruciating pain in his head, as if his eyes were being forced out by the pressure of something growing behind them. After a few moments it stopped. He refused to be so easily vanquished. "The baby is dead! It lives in my head!"

"Shut up, Sleeve."

Sleve drew himself up to the full height she had left him. "My name, Madame Beauty, is Urubugala." He whispered again. "You are a very quick learner. Was all this in those books you read?"

Asineth was only fourteen years old—she was susceptible to flattery. She smiled and said, "The books were nothing. They knew nothing. All I learned was how to get the power. Once I paid the price for it, the power was its own teacher. So far, I need only to think of a thing, and I can do it. And the most delicious thing of all is that Palicrovol himself gave the power to me. Gave me the power, but only a woman can ever have it."

"A man can have it," said Urubugala.

He saw the fear leap into her face. She was not secure yet with her power. "How can a man have it, when a man cannot create a child out of his body?"

Again he answered her in rhyme:

> If we fasten our balls to the walls,
> And then if we feed on our seed,
> The power will come in an hour
> To pee like the sea and to fart like a flower.

"You are disgusting," she said. "No man can have a power that is the match of mine. And no other woman, either, for no woman has enough hate in her to do what I have done." She said it proudly, and Sleeve again hid his fear of her behind mockery.

"I am your minstrel and you are my monstrel. Where is your teeny one, tinny one, tiny one?"

"Oh, we had an argument." Beauty carelessly tossed her head and smiled. "I won," she said. Sleeve fancied he could still see the blood on her tongue.

4

The King's Bride

How the Flower Princess lost her body, her husband, and her freedom all in an hour on her wedding day.

THE ROYAL PROGRESS

She came to the mouth of Burring with her father's fleet of tall ships. Palicrovol had a thousand singers meet her at the port. So perfect was their singing that the deafest sailor on the farthest ship heard all the words.

She was rowed up the river on the only galley that her father ever built, but the oarsmen were free, not slaves, and all of them wore robes of flowers. Every day of the voyage, a hundred women sat below deck, winding fresh flowers into new robes, so that every day the robes were new. And when she reached the great city Inwit, a thousand bags of flowers were released upstream, and all of Burring, from shore to shore, was a pond of petals for the coming of the Flower Princess.

Palicrovol himself met her at King's Gate, with the white-robed priests of God surrounding him, and white-robed virgins from the nunnery led the Flower Princess from her father's ship. Palicrovol knelt before her, and the carriage that met her began the Dance of Descent.

The Dance ended in the palace, in the Chamber of Answers, a room not opened for a century because it was too perfect to be used. Ivory and alabaster, amber and jade, marble and obsidian were the walls and floor and ceiling of the Chamber of Answers, and there the Flower Princess chose to wear her ring on the middle finger of the left hand, but high on the finger, to promise fecundity and faithfulness; and lo, of all miracles, Palicrovol also wore his ring on the middle finger of his right hand, high on the finger, to promise worship and unwavering loyalty. The watching hundreds cheered.

And then an imperious woman walked out onto the floor, leading a grotesque black dwarf on a golden chain, and Enziquelvinisensee Evelvenin turned to face the woman, and the wedding was broken at that moment.

THE USER USED

"I see," said the strange woman.

The dwarf piped up in a strange little song.

> Ugly Bugly, Mercy Me,
> You are not as fair as she.

Palicrovol spoke from behind the Flower Princess. "Who are you? How did you get into the palace?"

"Who am I, Urubugala?" asked the strange woman.

"This lady is Beauty, the greatest of all the gods," said the dwarf. "First she chained the Hart at the root of the world. Then she captured the Sweet Sisters and trapped them into such comical bodies. Then she bent God and imprisoned him. And at last she came home to poor Sleeve, and undid him, undid him, undid him."

"Sleeve," said Palicrovol. "Came home to Sleeve."

"Do you know me, Palicrovol?" asked the strange woman.

"Asineth," he whispered.

"If you call me by that name, you do not know me yet," she said. Then she turned to the Flower Princess. "So you are what he loves best in all the world. I can see that you are beautiful."

Again the dwarf chanted in his strange voice.

> Beauty is fair, Beauty is fair,
> But Beauty chose the wrong body to wear.

"I can see that you are beautiful," said the stranger, "and so it is only fitting that Beauty should have that face and form."

Enziquelvinisensee saw the woman change before her eyes, into a face that she knew and did not know. Knew because it was her own face. Did not know because it was not mirrored, as the Flower Princess had always seen it, but exactly as others had seen it. "This is what others have seen in me," she whispered.

"Do you worship?" asked Beauty. "Am I not perfect, Flower Princess?"

But Enziquelvinisensee Evelvinin had taken a vow to tell only the truth, and she had none of her women beside her to lie for her, and so she destroyed herself by saying, "No, Lady. For you have filled my eyes with hate and triumph, and I have never felt such things in all my life."

Beauty's perfect nostrils flared a bit with rage, and then she smiled and said, "That is because you have lacked the proper teachers. So let me teach you, Flower Princess, as I was taught."

The Flower Princess did not feel a change, but she saw the watching people look at her and gasp and turn away. She was afraid of what had been done to her, and spun on her toes to face her husband, gracious Palicrovol, who loved her. But Palicrovol, too, was revolted at what he saw, and stepped back from her. It was only a moment, and then he came to her again, and held her close to him, but in that moment Enziquelvinisensee Evelvinin knew the truth: Palicrovol thought of her beauty as part of herself, just as everyone else did; he did not know her without her face. Yet she was comforted that he still embraced her; and that he spoke with courage against Beauty.

"Did you think I could be so easily deceived, Asineth?" he asked. "You may startle me, but my heart belongs to another heart, not to a face."

Beauty only smiled again. Suddenly the Flower Princess felt Palicrovol take her brutally by the waist and throw her from him onto the floor. She looked up at him in horror, and saw the anguish of his face as he cried out to her, "It wasn't I!" Then, though he tried to speak, he fell mute, but the Flower Princess had heard enough to understand. It was Beauty, it was Asineth who had used his arms to hurl her away.

"Lie on the floor, Weasel," said Beauty. "Lie on the floor, and see what your husband does when he finds a virgin body to despoil. *Your* body, Weasel. Too bad you won't be wearing it when your fine new husband takes his pleasure."

At first Palicrovol moved jerkily, as Beauty learned to control his body. It cost her more power than anything else she did, to battle the King for control of his flesh and win—it was the rarest of the powerful acts she did. But she was clever, and soon learned to overmaster him. Then his body moved smoothly, and others forgot that Palicrovol did not act of his own free will. But the Flower Princess, now named Weasel, she knew truth as no other knew it, for her lips had never spoken a lie, and she remembered easily that Palicrovol acted with another will. Beauty had power, but not wisdom yet. At that time she was still a child, and thought vengeance would come at the price of a cheap and easy show.

So Palicrovol's hands cut the clothing from Beauty's body, which was the body of the Flower Princess. And Palicrovol, act for act, ravished her as he had ravished Asineth two years before. Only this time he did not disdain her attempt at seductiveness. Now when the body of the Flower Princess moved so subtly for him, he cried out with the pleasure of it. Now when his arms lifted his body from her, he moaned in protest. Let it not be over, cried his flesh. Let it not finish. And as long as he looked at her naked before him, as long as he remembered the pleasure that her body and her power had given him, his body again and again convulsed in pleasure; even after his seed was spent, even after the pleasure had turned to agony, he writhed against the impossibility of having her, the memory of having her, the longing to have her forever.

"Kill her!" he cried, but his guards had long since fled.

"Help me," he whispered to Urubugala, but the dwarf only said a little rhyme:

> In the morning
> Heed no warning.
> In the night,
> No respite.

"Weasel," said Queen Beauty, "you know how I was served. Tell me—is my vengeance just?"

"You were wronged," said the Flower Princess.

"Is my vengeance just?"

"You are just to take vengeance."

"But is my vengeance just?" Beauty smiled like the blessing of a saint.

"Only if you avenge yourself on those who harmed you,

and only if your vengeance is equal to the wrong done you.''

''Come now, I heard I could count on Weasel Sootmouth to tell the truth. I ask you a fourth time—am I just?''

''No,'' said the Flower Princess.

''Good,'' said Beauty. ''I was unjustly treated, and unless my vengeance is monstrously unjust I won't be satisfied.''

''I'm the one who wronged you,'' Palicrovol said. ''Take your vengeance on me.''

''But don't you see, Palicrovol, that it is part of my vengeance on you, that you know your woman and your friends suffer unjustly for your sake?''

Palicrovol bowed his head in helplessness.

''Look at me, Palicrovol,'' said Beauty.

Against his will he looked up and convulsed again in passion for her.

''Here is my vengeance. I will not kill you, Palicrovol. I despise you even more than you despised me when I was weak. You may keep your army—as many as you want. Fill the world with your armies and bring them against me—I will vanquish them with a thought. You may keep your Antler Crown—I need no crown to rule here. You may govern all of Burland outside this city—I can overrule you any time I please. You will send me tribute, but not so much that it will harm the people—I do not have my father's greed. I will not undo your laws or your works. This city will still be called Inwit. The new temple you are building to your God may continue to rise. All the worship they give your God will please me, for I also rule God. I will leave you everything except for this: you will never enter this city again while I am alive, and you will never be alone again while I am alive, and you will never know a moment of peace again while I am alive. And Palicrovol—I will live forever.''

Urubugala somersaulted and sprawled on the floor between them. ''There are limits on the life of a daughter and a wife!'' he cried.

''I know that,'' Beauty said. ''But when my power wanes, I will simply have another child. Next time, I think, a twelve-month child. Find some wizards, Palicrovol. Have them study *that* in their books.''

She laughed then, and compelled Palicrovol to gaze upon

her, throwing him into paroxysms of rapture until he sprawled on the floor, exhausted and retching.

As she laughed, a powerful-looking man strode boldly into the hall, carrying a sword and wearing heavy armor, though the helmet was cast away.

"Zymas, run!" cried Palicrovol.

"Oh, stay, Zymas," said Beauty. "Today would not have been complete without you."

Zymas did not pause to listen to either of them, just kept moving relentlessly toward Beauty, his sword rising above his head. He was nearly upon her, and they all knew a moment's hope that perhaps Zymas's direct action was the antidote to this sudden sickness that had come upon the world. But no. Suddenly his hair turned steel grey, his face went old and wrinkled, the sword dropped from gnarled, arthritic fingers, and he staggered feebly under the weight of the armor.

"Zymas, so bold, so brave, is dead," said Beauty. "In his place is the Captain of my palace guard. Craven, I call him. Craven, we all call him. Because he was such a coward that he was afraid of a woman."

Beauty looked around at those she had hated so long, and smiled. There was real beauty in her smile, and the Flower Princess knew that when the face had been her own, it had never worn such an expression of ecstasy. "Craven, Urubugala, and Weasel. My strength, my wit, and my fair face. I will keep you with me always, Captain, Fool, and Lady of Ladies. You will be the jewels of my crown. And outside Inwit, where he must forever dwell, will be Palicrovol, King of Burland, always remembering me, always longing for me. If he ever begins to feel sorry for himself, he can always remember *you*, and imagine what I do to *you*, and that will cheer him up immeasurably." She walked to the writhing Palicrovol and touched him gently on the flank. He cried out, he reached for her, and then he fell back witless. "Carry him out," said Beauty. And the guests who had watched the scene in helpless horror obeyed her, carried him out of the palace, out of the castle, out of Inwit through West Gate.

Outside the city waited a few of his bravest men, who dressed his naked body and carried him away. A nun was there, and she prophesied that the man who killed Beauty would enter through that same gate. Because of that, Beauty had the gate sealed up, never to be used again.

Within a remarkably short time, the city of Inwit was back to normal and better than normal. All the laws of Palicrovol remained in force, and all the freedoms he had granted remained intact. Beauty ruled gently enough in her city that the people did not mind the change of rulers. And her court became a dazzling place, which the kings of other nations loved to visit. They soon enough learned not to visit Palicrovol's court themselves, for they found that if they gave Palicrovol the honor due him as King of Burland, they would develop the most uncomfortable infections. So they had to send ambassadors, who soon learned to revile Palicrovol whenever they spoke to him, in order to avoid the plagues that otherwise came upon them.

Beauty ruled in Inwit, and the exile of Palicrovol had begun. Yet as the years passed, she knew that her vengeance was empty and incomplete. For with all her abuse, she did not change you, and she did not change your three captive friends. Our flesh she could alter, our lives she could fill with misery and shame, but we were still ourselves, and short of killing us she could not make us other than what we were. We remained always beyond her reach, even though she had us always within her grasp.

5

The Captive King

This is how a man may be a slave, though he is free to go all places in the world but one.

THE TORMENTS OF BEAUTY

Shall I catalogue the suffering of your exile for you, Palicrovol?

The foreign ambassadors reviled you, or their bladders would burn when they urinated.

Your own soldiers spat when you came near, or they would be infested with lice.

No matter how the cooks labored, all food served to you was covered with mold, all drinks were filmed with slime.

You fenced yourself with wizards, to give you a few moments' respite now and then; Beauty tore away their feeble barriers whenever she chose, and whatever wizard helped you was incapable of coupling from that moment.

You called also upon the priests, even though God had lost all power and was silent in the world; the priests that comforted and honored you all developed huge goiters and tumescences on the head and neck.

For a week she would make you strain at stool, to no avail; then for another week she would give you dysentery, and open your bowels in public places, so that you were forced to diaper yourself out of courtesy to those who kept you company.

You awoke itching unbearably in the middle of the night. You froze in summer, could not bear clothing in winter because of the heat she forced on you. For days terrible dreams would waken you; then for weeks you would doze off even as you sat in judgment, or led meetings of your generals.

One of her worst tricks was to trade vision with you. She would look out of your eyes and see whatever was going on around you, and at the same time you would see whatever she saw within the palace. She did not do it in order to spy on you—she had her Sight, and could sense the whole Kingdom of Burland at will. She did it so that you would be forced to see Weasel being beaten for some offense or other; Craven feebly carrying some burden, or leaning on a serving boy; Urubugala cavorting before a laughing audience of baronets and scions of wealthy merchant families. Your friends, suffering for your sake, and you helpless to save them. So you fashioned golden cups and covered your eyes with them, so that no light could enter at all. That was how you came to be known by one of your names: the Man with the Golden Eyes. They also called you the Horned Man, the Man Who Cannot Be Alone, and the Husband of Far Beauty. And your people were not fooled: You might be Beauty's toy, but you were a good King, and they prospered and lived mostly free, and paid your slight taxes willingly enough, and submitted to your judgment with trust.

Yet, ironically, her plagues did you good as well as harm. You knew if a man stayed to serve you that he was not with you for pleasure or honor, or even because he pitied you or hated Queen Beauty. Those who stayed with you in those hard times, who lived closely with you, and were privy to your inmost thoughts—you knew that they served you either because they knew your heart and loved you or because they loved good government and endured you and the life they had to live with you for the sake of the people of Burland. You had a gift few kings are ever given—you could trust everyone near you.

That good was matched with evil. With bitter injustice, your very justice made it all the harder for you to raise and keep an army—for whose heart stirred to oust Beauty from Inwit, when things went so well for Burland as it was? Only adventurers came to your army, and the Godsmen who hated her for silencing God, and the ne'er-do-wells who had no hope of any other trade. To fill your fifties and your regiments you had to conscript soldiers, which gave you an unwilling, weakish army, on the whole. It was enough to keep the enemies of Burland at bay, but rarely enough for you to hope to overcome the Queen herself.

And thus it was for days, for weeks, for years, for decades, for centuries. Your loyal followers would come to you and serve you, grow old, and die, but still you lived on, and Urubugala lived on, and Craven lived on, and Weasel lived on, for Beauty, broken as a child, could never grow straight however many years she lived: she would live forever exacting painstaking vengeance for a brief and unwilling cruelty so many years before.

Three times you brought your army to the gates of Inwit. Three times Queen Beauty let you hope for deliverance. And then she sent terror into the hearts of your soldiers, faced them with whatever they feared most in all the world, and all but the most resolute handful of them fled from your army, and you retreated from the city that you had won from her father so many years before, forced to begin again, ashamed again before the other nations of the world.

THE HART'S HOUR

After three centuries and more of exile, on a day when you wore the golden cups over your eyes, there came a vision to you. At first you thought it came from Beauty, but in only a moment you knew that it did not. You saw the Hart, the great shaggy stag, the one that Zymas had seen. The eagle clung to his belly, holding closed the wound there. And the Hart stopped, and turned his heavy head to face you, and you saw that he wore an iron collar around his neck, and his hooves were also banded and chained, and he bade you follow him, and set him free.

I cannot, you said.

Come, he told you, though you heard no words.

It will do no good, you said. Beauty will see me, and thwart all my works.

Come, he said. For this hour, she sees not, and sees not that she sees not.

So you took the golden cups from your eyes, and walked forth from your camp into the forest, and armed with your bow you followed the tracks of a deer into the wood, and went where the deer chose to lead you.

It was all the power that the gods could muster, exercised for you that day in the woods not far from the town of Banningside. Did you not wonder why they led you where they led you, why you did what you did? Will you now kill what came from that hour? It was your salvation, Palicrovol. It was your only son.

6

The Farmer's Wife

Now the life of Orem Scanthips, the Little King, began this way: with a man following a hart through the wood; with a woman bathing at a stream.

She Was a Poet of All Things That Grew of Themselves

Molly the farmer's wife had her six sons and didn't long for more. Six sons, three daughters: too many sons to divide the farm among them, too many daughters to marry them off with any sort of dowry. It was not a son she longed to make when she went that spring morning to her hidden place on the banks of the Banning. She went with a twist of magic in her fingers, so none could follow; but she was followed. Or rather, she was found.

It was a dark place, a still place, where the river ran narrow and deep and so swiftly that a twig was lost in an instant, so quietly that all songs were heard, all footfalls noted. The trees reached out over the water and met in a dense roof so that the sun did not dance upon the stream. It was cold here, even in the summer. A cave made of leaves and water, all the cold and terrible things of a woman: it was Molly's truest home, the place where she dared to call herself by her most secret name.

Bloom, she whispered, naming herself.

Hush, spoke the river in reply. Hush, for the end of your life is coming, following the traces of a deer.

The Pandering Hart

A great grey hart stood across the stream from her. Molly knew him well, knew that in the hart and hind were magics beyond the reach of the silly farm women of Waterswatch. Beyond even her own reach, and she was the best of them.

50

The blood of the Hart, they say, stains all the world. So she watched as the hart condescended to drink from the stream; watched as water fell silver from his mouth back to the river; watched as behind the great beast a hunter came, arrow nocked, bow down but ready to be drawn in an instant.

Do not dare to harm the horned head, she cried silently.

And, as if obedient to her utterance, the hunter stood and watched the deer drink, letting the nock slip from the string, letting the bow grow slack. No death today for the hundred-pointed head.

Molly studied the hunter as the hunter studied the hart. He was a strong-looking man. Not tall, and as dark as men of the west always were. He wore the deep green of the King—a soldier, then. But not like most soldiers, for Molly had never seen a slogger who had the wit to recognize the beauty of a deer; nor did she know any man at all who could fix his attention on one thing for such a long time. The man's eyes gleamed in the darkness of her green and silent cave. He was so still, and yet even slack his arms had power in them. Even silent, his lips commanded attention. And she knew, or thought she knew, or dreamed it even as it happened: she knew that this was no common soldier of the King. It was Palicrovol himself, yes, Palicrovol the Exile, the Husband of Far Beauty. No wonder, she thought, no wonder he stares with such longing at the hart. He wishes some god could be freed to bring him ease. Well, Queen Beauty, if you watch today, see how I bring him ease, thought Molly, thought fecund Daughter Bloom, for I will have this man, will have the life of him in me.

I am a chaste woman, a part of her cried out. And his children are born monsters.

But a part of her answered, with peace only the Sweet Sisters could bring, My children are not born monsters, and a woman is not truly chaste if she refuses what man the Hart brings. Her womb, which had been so often full, cried out to be filled again. But this time, this time with a King's son, this time with the Hart's child.

"Man," she whispered. Such was the stillness of the place that he heard and yet was not afraid.

"Woman," he said, and his face showed cold amusement.

"Are you strong as this river?"

"Are you," he answered, "as deep?"

In answer she lay upon the grassy, leafy bank and smiled. Come to me, if there's as much man as king in you.

As if he heard her taunt, he crossed the river, naked now except for his knife—for he would not be unarmed. He fought the current bravely, but still he came ashore far downstream from her, and she watched as he came dripping and exhausted from the water. River Banning was called unfordable and far from safe to swim. Yet the King had crossed it for her. Molly's legs trembled.

He stood over her, leaves and grass and dirt clinging to his shins. He had no beauty to him, and yet there was a quivering deep in her belly as she looked at him.

"Woman, what do they call you?" There was neither lust nor affection in his gaze. He would not pretend that she was young and beautiful, for she was neither. Her belly sagged within her skirts, her thighs were heavy and her dugs hung as loose as the udder of an aging cow. What the Hart brings together is what would not have come together without him. Beauty or not, it was plain that he desired what she desired, and as much.

"I am Bloom," she said, giving her secret woman's name to him, though he was a man. The Hart had led him.

"Has the forest given you to me?"

"I have a husband," she said. "I will not be yours."

To her surprise, he looked angry and stepped back, as if her wifehood would be a bar to him.

"Man," she said, "I will not be yours. But will you not be mine?"

"Yes," he said, "Yes I will. Yes."

He took her as the hart mounts the hind, and she cried out in the pain and pleasure of the giving and the taking. He put the seed of a son in her, and then kissed her at the small of her back, behind her womb. "What comes of this only God will say," he said to her. But she only hummed and lay naked on the bank, not even turning to watch him as he plunged again into the flood and swam away. God had not brought him, didn't he know it? No, it was not God but the Hart that would say what came of this; the blood of the Hart, the blood that flowed from her belly even though she had not been a virgin, as though he had secretly pierced her with his knife. What you have made in me, O Palicrovol, she said to her memory of his flesh, what you have made in me I will make stronger than you. I will make him large and strong. Nine children I have born alive, and always my husband's own. But this one is not my husband's. This one is mine. I will name him Orem, for silver water flowed from his father's body on the morning he was made.

7

The Birth of Palicrovol's Son

These are the signs that came when Orem Banningside, called
Scanthips, called the Little King, was born.

THE SIGNS OF THE MOTHER

As she lay on her childbed, her eyes swimming with the pain
that never eased no matter how often she went through it,
Molly saw the midwife lift the baby up, and in the sunlight of
early morning that streamed through the spring window of her
east-facing house, he gleamed silver to her; covered with the
blood and mucus of birth, he gleamed silver as the water from
the hart's mouth.

She held him, she sang to him, she talked to him long
before the infant could possibly understand. Silently she told
him in every way she could, You are the son of the King, my
son, you are born to be great. The words were never spoken,
but the child still understood. He learned to walk when he
was only eight months into the world, because it did not
occur to him that he could not; he spoke boldly from the first
word, expecting to be understood no matter what he tried to
say. A bright one, all the neighbors said to Molly.

But for two reasons she was not pleased at what they said.
For one, she knew that there were other things said as well,
for the child did not look like her blond giant of a husband.
For another, there were her own doubts and fears. Quickly
she learned that when her seventh son was with her, all her
subtle powers were gone. Her cooking spells were meaningless when he was in the house, no matter how many dead
mice she bled into the hearth. Her loom magics made no
pattern in the homespun cloth if he looked on at her labors.
The household goms were free here, where once they had
been held in the tightest rein of all High Waterswatch.

But the worst was when she made the signs that hid her

path from mortal eyes as she wandered off into the wood. He could always follow her, could always see her despite the blood she pricked from her own finger. What have the Sweet Sisters given me? she asked herself in fear. But it was neither God nor the Sisters, she knew, for the Hart had also found her in her secret place, and Orem was the child of the Hart. These were the signs of the mother, and instead of love for her son, she soon felt fear, for he had made her weak, and she had once been strong in her small and vegetal way.

THE SIGNS OF THE FATHER

When Molly was in her childbed, Avonap her husband waited impatiently in the other room. Nine other times, six times sonned and three times daughtered, he had waited this way. Nine other times he had felt the same impatience. The fields are waiting, woman, he wanted to cry, the soil has called. Did she not know what a farmer's work was?

With the soil as with a woman, it was his work to plow, to plant the seed, to tend, to reap. But the corn did not require that he sit and wait in the next room for the grain to ripen in the husk. No, the ripening, the fruiting, that was the business of God who gave life, or the Sweet Sisters, after the woman's reckoning, which he dared not despise. His business was out with the uncut soil, the unripe corn, the unbound sheaves, not waiting, waiting for—what this time? A daughter to dower? A son to raise to disappointment? Five times he had had to tell a boy of his loins that the fields would never be his, and ever since he had felt their hatred at his back, scythe in hand, or harrow. Not that he feared them; just that there was a weakness hidden in Avonap's heart. He loved his children, and wanted to be loved by them. Not unheard of in a man, but not something to boast of. He spoke of it to no one, but still when he felt the heat of their anger like breath on his sweating back, Yes, he would think, Yes, they hate me, yes I am undone.

So when the midwife came from the room and said, "A son," she was braced for the dark glowering on his face. However, she knew that there was worse to come. For Avonap was one of the blond giant farmers of High Waterswatch that had earned the land the sobriquet "Straw Man's Land," and the baby that was brought forth to him did not have the white-down-covered head of all of Molly's other babes. The baby was red and dark, longer and thinner than the others had been, and worst was the shock of blackish hair on the top of the head. The infant bawled piteously, but the sight of him kept Avonap from pity.

"Changeling," he murmured, and the midwife made the circle upon the cloth of the baby's swaddle.

Changeling? Oh, no, it was no child of goms or wandering Sebastit. It was something worse, he feared. He saw the child and dreamed of the towers of the west, where men grew lean and dark-haired, and women were white of skin and ebon of hair. He dreamed of such a westerner coming somehow to the east. In the army, no doubt. Dreamed of a west-facing tower, and Molly perched at the top, combing her long blond hair to tumble down and cover the face of the soldier leering up at her below. He dreamed of the volcano he had seen erupting in his youth, on his one journey to Scravehold. And he hated the child. Leave him to his mother, thought he. Whatever he is, and whoever his sire, he's none of mine, none of me, and for once I'm glad to be sharing none of my land with him.

But the years will bend all things, even the blond and mountainous men who farm the hilly riverside land of High Waterswatch.

First, it soon became clear to him that Orem would be his Molly's final child, and he remembered the saying

> Last of ten and all alive
> Richest bee of all the hive,
> Cheater of the beggar's grave,
> Thief of all his father's love.

Second, there was the matter of the child's hair. He was a woman-raised child, of course, and so there was some foolishness of combing and washing more than a boy should be combed and washed. But sometimes when Avonap saw the brooding child at supper, glowering over his plate, he saw in the firelight a tough of red gold in the boy's dark hair, and saw in the wan and whitish face what had been kept from all his other sons and daughters—the grace of young Molly, the greatest prize that he had won in all his life. And of a sudden one day he yearned for the boy.

Third, and most of all, he saw soon enough that despite Molly's total rule over the boy, she shunned him. Wouldn't let him play beside the loom, wouldn't let him help her at the stove. Too often Avonap saw him playing strange games in the lee of the house in summer, being neither inside his mother's walled factory nor outside in his father's field, where the men forged wheat and tawny barley in the fires of the sun.

So it was that one day, by chance the fourth yearday of young Orem's life, Avonap let fall his hoe when he saw the boy, let it fall and walked to where he played.

"What are you doing?" asked the father.

"I'm making armies in the dirt," said the son.

"What armies?"

And the boy touched with the point of his stick where the army of Palicrovol stood, a series of circles concealed behind weeds or perched at the tops of inch-high mounds. "And here," said the son, "is the city of Inwit, Palicrovol's capital, which he shall recapture today."

"But those are only circles in the dirt," said Avonap. "Why aren't you inside with your mother?"

"She sends me out when she has work to do. She works better when there are no boys around."

What did Avonap see in the boy's face? Molly's face, yes, that for sure, and perhaps he felt the old yearning for his young wife; but more than that, for Avonap had a soft heart. He saw a child who had no welcome in either world. Not in the still, enclosed, soft world of women, not in the tooled and bristling, windy world of men. Avonap was touched with pity for the boy. A boy should be strong and hale and blond; this strange child was plainly not. Yet a boy should also have a ready smile. When this boy was an infant he had had such a smile, and now it was gone. That much surely could be set to rights.

"Will you come with me, then, since you're not too busy here?"

And the rejoicing in the son's eyes was enough for the father. From that time on his weakness and his darkness were no barrier between them. No thought of cuckolding, no murmurs of changeling children. Avonap did with Orem what he had not done since his oldest boy was little. Said some, "Young Orem is the fruit of the basalak, growing whole from the bark of the fathertree," for that was how it seemed, that

Orem grew whole from his father's shoulder, or sprang from the ground beside his father, tied at the stem, tied at the hand. Root and branch he became his father's son.

These were the signs of the father.

THE SIGN OF THE SON

And what of the other tales the common folk tell? How Queen Beauty wept all night the night that he was born? How Enziquelvinisensee Evelvenin woke up and saw her face beautiful in the mirror for that single night? How Palicrovol himself was overcome with power on the night of Orem's birth, and stood at the door of his tent naked and large with potential, all to be fulfilled in the birth of his bastard son? How stars fell, and wolves mated with sheep, and fish walked, and the Sweet Sisters appeared to the nuns of the Great Temple of Inwit?

Such tales were all made up so the Tale would have more magic. Not Orem nor Molly nor Avonap—no one suspected what had been wrought in the world. There were these signs only: The signs of the mother, who loved and then feared the boy; the signs of the father, who hated and then loved the boy; and the sign of the boy.

This was the sign of the boy: He followed his mother often to her river cave, where the trees were so tall they arched to both sides of the deep and fast-rushing Banning, so only green light could touch the water, and all was rich with the power the women called Sisterhood and the men called God. And there, he watched her bathe in the edges of the tugging current, saw her dip her loose and sagging breasts and belly into the flood, and as these touched the water, he saw a great stag, a hundred-horned head, appear among the leaves, watching, watching. For just a moment he saw; then he glanced away and when he looked again the hart was gone. He did not wonder then what it meant; only feared for a moment that his naked and vulnerable mam might be in some danger from the deer. He did not know the Hart had already pierced her once, as deep as a woman could be pierced. And that was the sign of the son.

8

The House of God

Here is the tale of the only true miracle of Orem's childhood, and how he came to be a clerk.

THE SEVENTH SON OF AVONAP

Because Avonap loved his seventh son, he tried to get him away from the farm as soon as he could. It was no good for a lateborn son to stay long on the farm, for the older he got, the more he ate, and the more he ate, the more the elder sons saw their inheritance being wasted, perhaps being threatened by a child their father loved more. Such lateborn sons had a way of dying in strange accidents. Avonap had no reason to think that Orem would be safe.

He tried Orem as a soldier, with the one-eyed man in the village who had once been a sergeant in Palicrovol's army, but Orem was too slight of build, too small of stature to wield the weapons. And so there was nothing to do but give the boy to God.

Orem took the news well. He could see that his father grieved that he must go, which comforted him. He could also see that his mother was relieved that he'd be gone, and this hurt him enough that he did not want to stay.

So it was that at the age of six Orem was carried on donkeyback to the town of Banningside and delivered into the hands of the clerics in the House of God.

"You will learn to read and write," said Avonap, though he had no notion of what reading and writing were.

"I don't want to learn to read and write," whispered the child.

"You will learn to count money," said Avonap, though never in his life had he held a coin in his hand.

"You will learn to serve God," said Halfpriest Dobbick, taking the boy into the door of the house. And at that Avonap

touched his forehead and bent his knees a bit, for God was
treated with respect in all the lands of King Palicrovol.

Orem wept when the great wooden door closed, but not for
long. Children are resilient. No matter how they are battered,
they have a way of thriving.

FRIENDS AND ENEMIES

The House of God was dark and dead, filled with the white
figures of dour-faced men and frightened boys. There was
never a great booming of laughter echoing through the corridors and cells of the House of God, as there had been in the
tavern of the village or through the great colonnades of the
wood. The children sneaked their laughter as subtly as they
sneaked the oblatory wine. Yet Orem soon found himself at
home there. Home is anywhere that you know all your friends
and all your enemies.

His enemies were the older boys, the stronger boys, who
were used to wielding power in the darkened rooms at night.
Orem had somehow grown up with a belief that unfairness
was to be, not endured, but corrected. So when he saw
injustice being done, he corrected it. Not by telling the
halfpriests—he knew adults never take seriously the wars and
struggles of children. Instead, he taught the younger boys to
organize in the darkness. It took only two times that Orem
out-generaled the bullies in the dark before the younger boys
began to find themselves safe and more free than they had
ever been before. The older boys did not forget. Orem had
undone them when they thought that they were strong, and
with the directness of children they plotted Orem's death.

Orem's friends were not the younger children, however.
Once they had their safety, they stayed as far from Orem as
they could. They were content to let the hatred of the older
boys fall upon him, and stay clear of it themselves. Orem
bore their treachery calmly. He did not expect them to be any
better than they were. He was his father's son.

His friends, such as they were, were the priests and
halfpriests, who recognized his quick and clever mind and
loved him for it. The other boys were long baffled by the
matter of letters and numbers. But to Orem they were magic,
mysterious things that somehow meant sounds and values,

that had names but did not say their names, that stood in rows that meant different things at different times. Arrange the letters vertically and they are numbers, his teacher taught him. Horizontally and they are words. Orem memorized all the runes within a day, was reading words within a week, and within a month discovered that the cleverest scribes order their numbers to make words and their words to make numbers, too, so that in this book the whole astronomy of the universe is mathematically portrayed in the story of Azasa and the absigent, while in this book all the countings of the King's treasury for a decade are figured into acronyms and ciphers that tell of the sins of the courtiers whose specific damnation is told out in the sums. While the other boys struggled to comprehend the plain sense of things, Orem learned the subtlest lessons, and without trying, so that to his own surprise he was doing his exercises with an elegance beyond the reach of many of his teachers.

"Don't you see what you have done?" asked Halfpriest Dobbick. "Here, where you do the sum of the suns of winter, you also spell out 'warm snow.' "

"I'm sorry," said Orem, thinking he had been caught in a secret vice. But he soon saw that Halfpriest Dobbick was pleased with him, and several times Orem noticed that when priests came in to observe the class as they studied, they would look over his shoulder the whole time, never particularly observing anyone else at all.

Once Orem discovered that the teachers were his friends, he turned to them gratefully, and escaped the dangerous solitude of the playyard by spending the free hours indoors, reading and talking with his teachers. Only one of Orem's teachers understood what was happening. Halfpriest Dobbick. "You don't know yet the cost of your power," said Dobbick.

"Power?" asked Orem, for he did not think he had any.

"You acted bravely and wisely when you first came. You must act bravely and wisely among the other children now, if you are ever to do well with them."

"They aren't my friends," said Orem.

"Will they love you better if you ally yourself with us, the teachers, the oppressors, the foes of every child here?"

"What do I care who they love or why? I'm happier here in the dark with the books than there in the light with them. If you don't want to teach me, leave me alone with the library."

But Halfpriest Dobbick would not be dissuaded, and he saw to it that Orem was forced to play outside, forced to take part in the games. When the other boys pitched stones and batted them with sticks. Orem learned to be adroit at dodging the stones thrown straight at his head. When the other boys swam in the waterhole, Orem learned to be long of breath and wriggly as a watersnake, so they could not hold him under water longer than his breath. When the other boys slept, Orem learned to move stealthily and surely in the darkness, and he slept every night in some different corner of the House of God, far from his bed, so they could not murder him in his sleep. He hated Halfpriest Dobbick for compelling him to live and play among the other boys, but against his will he became sure of hand and foot and eye, strong-gripped and quick-witted, and his body was hard and could endure much. No one in the House of God could run as fast or as long as Orem; no one could live on less sleep; and no one could read and write as Orem could. He thought that he was miserable, but he would look back on this as the happiest of times.

FIRE AND WATER

The boys who hated Orem most were Cressam and Morram and Hob. They had not ruled before Orem came, but because of their ruthless torture of the younger boys they had been valuable enforcers for the smarter boys who did rule. Now they had no role at all within the House of God: they were fools at their schoolwork and none of the boys' games rewarded cruelty and ruthlessness. So they plotted Orem's death, partly for lack of anything else to do, and when they had settled on a plan, they practiced until they were sure they could bring it off quickly and unnoticed.

It was the day the offerings of hay came in. Orem stood with the other boys watching the stack grow higher and broader as the farmers brought their gifts to the House of God. Orem hoped to see his father, though he knew the chance was small that his own family would draw the lot to bring the village tithe.

Suddenly Orem found himself gripped by many hands and thrust under the hay. He writhed and twisted, but he was not in water, and they had practiced well. Orem did turn enough to see that Cressam held a torch. Then the hay fell down to cover him. He saw the whole plan at once. Cressam would stumble. The torch would fall. They would count the boys when the fire was out and only then discover Orem wasn't there. If any of the other boys saw it, they would not dare to tell; if Cressam and Morram and Hob had murdered once, they would not fear to do it twice.

So he did not try to leap forward out of the hay, where the flames would first erupt. Instead he plunged backward, burrowed deep into the stack. Behind him he heard the sudden roar, the shout of Fire. He could not see the flame, but he could hear it, and the heat and smoke came quickly. He did not have to think. His arms knew to burrow deeper into the hay, his feet knew to kick down hay behind him so the smoke would not be funneled in to where he meant to hide.

It was black as a sow's womb inside the hay, and because his eyes could not see, his mind did: remembered vividly the haystack fires that he had seen before. It never took more than a few seconds for the fire to reach all the way around, and only a minute or two for the flames to die down. Within the haystack there was always an unburnt core, a place where the flames could not reach. That was his hope.

But he also remembered raking through such a fire once, and he found the corpse of a mouse in the unburnt portion. There was no mark upon it, not a hair was singed, but he was still dead, eyes staring wide. Fire or not, the heat or the smoke had killed to the center of the stack, and Orem wondered what form his death would take and how much it would hurt.

Then came the only miracle of his childhood. The haystack had been built upon firm, dry ground, but now his hand reached forward for support and found none. He slid and splashed into a pool of water that could not have been there. He had presence of mind enough to take one sharp, deep breath as he went under; then he let himself drift downward, downward in the water, not moving, trying only to remember up and down, and to estimate how long till the fire was out.

Suddenly there was ground under his feet and he stood. When his head broke the surface of the water it was not into a nest of hay. It was ash that floated on the surface of the water, ash that covered his face. He breathed and it was hot and smoky in his lungs, but it was air. Then the pain of the heat and smoke in his lungs hit him, and he fell back into the water. Surely he would die, he thought, but he had scarcely splashed when strong hands took him, lifted him out, pressed his lungs. Large male lips closed over his mouth to breathe life into him, but Orem pushed the priest away. "I'm all right," he said.

The priests looked at him in awe, and Prester Enzinn said what they all thought. "We drained this marsh a century ago, and just for you the water came up again and made a spring under the stack. God must love you, Orem. You are not meant to die."

From then on the priests and the other boys knew that Orem was protected, and they raised no hand against him.

In his learning he excelled. His hand was so fine they took him from the scribal class and set him to making manuscripts at the age of twelve. They let him do a new transcription of the prophecies of Prester Cork, and when he finished it they commended him for discovering seven new and hidden meanings in the rhymes and the diagonals. But whenever their praise tempted Orem to be proud, to speak boldly with the other boys, or to presume a friendship with a priest, he felt himself slip helplessly forward into a pool of water, felt his lungs wrench at him in a desperate plea for air, and he could not speak.

So the years passed in the House of God in Banningside, until the day his true father found him.

9

The Man with Golden Eyes

This is how you almost met your son, though you did not know you had a son, and how you set him on the course of life that led him to do the things you wish to kill him for.

THE END OF EDUCATION

Orem sat in tutorial, Halfpriest Dobbick across from him, studying his copy of the Waking of the Wines. He had, on a whim, written the words *bud, bloom, blossom,* and *blood* in the castings of the ages of the coops, and other such figures throughout the book. Dobbick frowned now and then, and Orem feared he had laid too many meanings into the book. He wanted to speak, to apologize, to explain. But silence, he knew, was the best policy.

So he looked out the window at the street below. There was deaf Yizzer where he always sat, at the gate of the House of God, shouting in a voice that could be heard in every corner of the building, "Oh sir kind sir you have the gift of God in your face oh sir you are beneficent God smiles at you for giving and God will name your inmost names with a blessing your inmost hidden names," on and on in an eternal monologue that was singularly effective in drawing coins from passing strangers. The novices were convinced that Yizzer was no more deaf than they were, but no amount of teasing him from the playyard could interrupt his shouting or trick him into anger or laughter; if he was only pretending to be deaf, he was good at it.

If I were hungry enough, would I become a beggar, too?

Dobbick set down the book. "You have excelled yourself."

Orem did not know how tense he had been until he felt himself relax. "Is it good enough, then?"

"Oh, yes. I will certify it as your masterwork."

Orem was shocked. "My masterwork. But I'm only fifteen years old."

Dobbick sat back in silence, forcing Orem to wait patiently for him to speak. At last: "Your education is finished, Orem."

"It can't be finished. I'm not half through the library, and my work is still raw—"

"Your work is the best we've seen in Banningside since God was first taught in this land. Who do you think wrote the manuscript you copied of the Waking of the Wines?"

"I don't know. They're never signed."

"Prester Abrekem."

"Himself."

"The prophet who first taught Palicrovol the ways of God. And you improved on his work. Not slightly—markedly. What more will we teach you in Banningside? The books you have not read contain nothing that you need—you have taken our most difficult books and swallowed them whole."

Orem had known he was doing well, but he had not conceived, not yet, that his education was through. "I am not a man."

"You *are* a man," said Dobbick. "You're the tallest creature in the House of God, will we still call you a boy?"

"I am not wise."

"We never said that we could teach you wisdom. Only that we would teach you what the wise men wrote."

"I cannot take the vows."

Ah. There was the thing he had been so afraid to say, that he thought he would not have to say for years yet.

"Why not?" asked Dobbick quietly. "The life is not bad here. You have been happy with us."

Orem looked out the window.

"Is it the wide world? Is that what draws you? But you need not stay within the House. You could be a mendicant—"

"Not I—"

"Or even an outrider, our purchaser—or we could send you to the Great Temple in Inwit, they'd be glad of you there, and we'd be glad of you upon your return."

"You don't understand."

"Do you think I don't?" Dobbick said. "You worry because you think you don't believe enough to be a priest. It's a disease of the age of fifteen. When the flesh is stirring, the spirit seems unreal.''

"If my flesh stirs I don't know it," said Orem. "My problem is not unbelief. My problem is too much belief."

Dobbick's eyes narrowed. "You were a child when you came here. Haven't you broken yourself of foolish superstitions?''

"There is magic in the world. The women who love the Sweet Sisters don't deny God. Why must Godsmen deny the Sisters and the Hart?''

"The world is more complicated than you think."

"No, Halfpriest Dobbick. The world is more complicated than *you* think. I will not live in one-third of the universe when I might wander through it all."

"So you'll leave the benison and orison and psalm in order to do obeisance to a household gom?''

Orem laughed. He could not help laughing when Dobbick went into rhyme, and Dobbick knew it.

"Come, Orem. There's no choice that must be made today. As long as you're not bored with it, there's plenty of copywork to be done. When a man is certified a master cleric, he usually takes the vows or leaves, but we can make you a brother unsworn—it's an honorable role, and it recognizes that you are our equal in education, if not in holiness. But I'll no longer pretend that I'm your teacher. I don't read your manuscripts to correct them—I read them to learn what bright new things you have made them mean."

Orem spoke the blunt truth then, though he knew it would hurt Dobbick. "How can you look at my work and find truth, when I am only playing games? If my jokes and riddles and puzzles look like truth to you, what can I think but that all your other truths are nothing but jokes and riddles and puzzles?''

Dobbick again fell silent, until he finally said, "Or perhaps you are too young to know jokes and riddles are the only truth we have, and so are precious to us."

Ashamed at having hurt his teacher, Orem again walked to the window and looked outside. There was a stir, a hurry about the people passing back and forth, and it wasn't even a market day. And then trumpets in the distance, getting closer. Was the army coming early, then? And would King Palicrovol ride in at their head? It was the only thing that really interested Orem much these days; the mere mention of King

Palicrovol's name awakened something in the boy. What sort
of man is King, Orem wondered, what sort of man is it who
speaks and armies obey, who calls out and a thousand priests
pray for him?

"You seem drawn to the window."

"It's the banners caught my eye. You can close the
window."

"Which means you want it open. Do you think I don't
know your way?"

You don't.

"You are not different from other boys. You dream of
Palicrovol and his wicked and hopeless quest for a city he
stole in the first place."

"He's a Godsman, isn't he?" Orem retorted.

"In name only. He keeps a few priests for show. It's with
wizards that he guards himself against the Queen, more fool
he."

Outside the window, the gate of the town's stockade was
opening—yes, the King was coming, for outside the gate
were soldiers ahorse and soldiers afoot, shining with steel
breastplates and helmets. It was a dazzling sight, but soldiers
held little glamour for Orem. It was the magic that drew his
dreams. Not the magic of the Sweet Sisters, but the magic of
the hundred-pointed head, the Antler Crown. It was King
Palicrovol, whose wizards battled daily with the Queen. And
as he thought of the King again, Palicrovol rode through the
gate of Banningside, on a high saddle on a tall grey horse,
and on his head the gilded Antler Crown of Burland. He
looked every inch a king. He turned his head not at all, just
stared straight ahead as the crowd cheered and threw roses at
him.

He came closer, and Orem winced as the sun shone brightly, reflected off King Palicrovol's eyes. Where his eyes should
have been there were two gold balls, shining in sunlight, so
that the King could not possibly see anything. "The Queen
looks through Palicrovol's eyes today," said Orem. "Why
does she do it, when she has the Searching Eye?"

Dobbick was surprisingly angry when he answered. "If
you had ever learned anything of God, you'd know that her
Searching Eye can't penetrate a temple or a House of God, or
the seventh circle of the seven circles. So why do you think
King Palicrovol doesn't surround himself with priests to keep

her sight out? Because he's black, too, at heart. Because he's the kind of man who'd rape a child on the steps of Faces Hall in order to steal the crown that was her only gift to give. God has no part of him, Orem. And God will have no part of you, if you draw yourself to magic the way you—''

But now it was Dobbick who stopped the conversation and turned to look out the window. For the crowd had fallen silent outside, and when Orem looked where the halfpriest was staring, he saw that King Palicrovol had stopped, had taken the Antler Crown from his head and now held it before him.

The King turned his blind eyes from one side to the other, as if he could see to search. "No!" cried a strange, moaning voice, and it took Orem a moment to realize that it was the King who spoke so mournfully. "Oh, Inwit, not here, not through my eyes!" And then the King looked up, and the golden balls seemed to fix on Orem's face, and the King pointed at Orem's heart and cried, "Mine! Mine! Mine!"

Soldiers leapt out of line, and suddenly Orem felt himself being jerked back into the House of God. It was Dobbick, and his voice was thick with fear. "O God, O God, O seven times seven the dark days that come from incaution. O God, Orem, he wants you, he wants to have you—''

Orem was confused, but made no resistance as Dobbick dragged him out of the room. Compliance had so long been Orem's way that he had no strategy to escape the halfpriest's grip as he pulled him up and down stairs, through doors usually locked, and finally into a trap door leading to a hidden path.

"The House of God is old," said Dobbick, "from the dark days before God had His victory over all the strangers and all the powers. This path comes out near the river, well outside the stockade. Go home. Go to your father's farm and bid good-bye to your family, and then get away. Far away, to the sea, to the mountains, wherever the King can't find you."

"But what does it mean!"

"It means the King has some use for you in his battle. And you can trust this—it will be to your cost. A man like Palicrovol hasn't lived his three black centuries by paying his costs himself. In the games of power, there are only two players, and all the rest are pawns. Oh, Orem—" and the halfpriest hugged the boy at the secret postern gate, "Orem, if you had only stepped within the seven circles, just a step, you would have nothing to fear from him. God knows I hate to let you go.''

''What's happening to me?'' Orem asked, frightened as much by Dobbick's sudden expression of love and regret as by what had happened with the King.

''I don't know. Whatever it is, you don't want it.''

But in that instant Orem realized that he did want it. In that instant he knew that the safety of the House of God was itself what he most hated. In the House of God he would never make a name for himself, or find a place, or earn a poem. Here at the postern gate he was at the verge of all three, he could feel it in the fear of his belly and the clarity of his vision.

''You're fifteen, you're only a child,'' said Dobbick. But Orem knew it was the age when soldiers went into the army, the age when a man could take a wife. Only in the House of God was fifteen young. ''Ah, yes,'' said Dobbick, drawing the seven circles on Orem's face with a tender finger, ''I was not wrong, you're no tool of Palicrovol's war, Orem. You're God's tool.''

It made Orem angry. ''I'm not a tool.''

''Oh, we're all a tool, every one. You don't want to be a servant of God, do you? Well, serve yourself, Orem, and I think you'll end up serving God anyway.''

And then it was God-be-with-you and gone, the gate closing behind him. Orem tramped down a short run of what looked like sewer but wasn't, and then clambered out of the end of the pipe, where it was fouled and tangled with silt and shrubbery. He heard the halfpriest call to him down the pipe: ''Orem! Anywhere but Inwit!''

Anywhere but Inwit? Oh, no, Orem answered silently. *Only* Inwit for me. Whatever the King's pointing finger might have meant, it did mean this: Orem had a poem in him, and he meant to earn it out. And if Inwit was where God's man thought he must not go, then Orem knew that it was Inwit that called him. First home, as Dobbick had said, to bid good-bye, or his father would grieve. Then Inwit, where the world's water all flowed.

I am fast as a deer, Orem said to himself as he ran the country roads. He ran untired forever, it seemed, and then walked until the air came back to him, and then he ran again. His legs did not hurt him; the pain in his side came and

almost killed him and then went away, abashed. And sooner
than he would have thought possible, he was home. All those
years that he yearned to come back here, and it was only this
far all the time.

"Why not stay here?" asked his aging father. "I'll be
glad of you."

But it was an empty offer, for Avonap would not live
forever. His brothers scowled, and his mother Molly only
stared into the fire. Orem laughed. "With you I'd stay forever, Father, but would you stay with me?"

"What will you do, then? I can teach you the way to
Scravehold. I went there once, with *my* father."

"That's not the fire I yearn to see."

Orem's eldest brother laughed at that. "What does such an
ashen one as you know of fire?"

"More than the straw," retorted Orem, for he was not
afraid of his brother, who knew nothing of astronomy and
numbers and could not write his name.

"Inwit," said Orem's mother.

Orem looked at her in surprise, and for the first time his
enthusiasm was paused. What his mother wanted for him
could not be good. Or was it possible his mother might
actually share a dream with him?

"It is Inwit," said Molly, "where the tenth child and
seventh son must go."

"Hush, Molly," said the anguished father.

"Inwit," said Molly. "Inwit."

So it was that Orem did not leave flying as he had come
home. He walked, and his step was slow and his thoughts
deep. What did it mean, that his mother also wished a poem
for him?

He stood at the river's edge, in his mother's own secret
place, waiting for some vessel to come to bear him out, to
carry him away and down. As he waited he wrote in the mud
of the shore, wondering what his mother would make of the
strange signs when she came here again to bathe. He wrote:

> Orem at Banningside
> Free and flying
> Palicrovol
> Seeing, sighing

And the numbers added downward to say:

> See me be great

He did not notice what Dobbick would have seen, that the numbers added upward to say:

> My son dying

He did not know yet that a man could be playing riddles and accidently tell himself the truth.

Near sunset came the raft of a grocer, keeping timidly to the edge of Banning at this treacherous place where the current was far too fast. The grocer was on the far side, struggling and looking afraid. Orem hailed him.

"Do you want a hand to trade for a river trip?"

"Only if you can swim!" came the answering cry.

So Orem hitched his shirt and tied it around his chest, held his burlap bag in his teeth, and swam his backstroke across the surface of the water. He measured well, and his flying hand struck the edge of the raft. He tossed his bag over his head and climbed aboard. The grocer glanced at him, grimaced, and said, "Your voice is a liar. I thought you were a man."

But Orem only laughed and took the little oar while the grocer kept to the pole, and together they fended the raft through the cave of leaves until the river broadened and slowed and it was safe again. Then Orem laid down the oar, unfastened his shirt, and let it fall to cover him again. He turned to face the grocer and said, "Well, if I didn't do a man's work, say so and I'll leave you here."

The grocer glowered at him, but he did not say to leave. My adventure has begun, thought Orem. I am my own man now, and I can make my name mean whatever I like.

10

The Grocer's Song

How Orem Scanthips found his way downriver to Inwit, where he would earn his name and his poem, but no place.

HIS FATHER'S WATER

"How far are you going?" Orem asked cheerfully. The grocer only eyed him skeptically for a moment, then turned to study the current, using the long pole to keep the raft to the center of the river. Orem knew from the talk of travelers in Banningside that the currents of Banning were dangerous enough, but where the river was slower the dangers were worse, for there were pirates whenever Palicrovol's army was far away, and foragers whenever it was close, and both used about the same strategy for about the same purpose, with the difference that Palicrovol's men didn't kill half so often.

"The King's in Banningside," Orem offered. If the grocer heard, he gave no sign; indeed, he was so silent and surly-looking that Orem wondered that such an unfriendly man would have taken him aboard at all.

Night came quickly from behind the eastern trees, and when the last of the light was going, the grocer slowly poled the raft nearer the shore, though not closer than a hundred yards from the bank. Then he took the three heavy anchor stones in their strong cloth bags and dropped them overboard at the rear of the raft. The current quickly drew them from the stones until the taut lines held them.

Orem watched silently as the grocer crawled into the tent and pulled out a large clay pan. In it the grocer built a fire of sticks and coal. On it he placed a brass bowl, where he made a carrot and onion soup with river water. Orem was not sure whether he would be invited to share, and felt uneasy about asking. After all, if his host chose silence, it was not his place to insist on speech.

So he opened his bag and took out two sausages.

The grocer eyed them briefly. Orem held out one of them, thin and white and stiff within its casing. The grocer took his knife and reached it out. Orem thrust the sausage onto the point. The grocer grunted—a sound, at least!—and Orem watched him slice the meat so thin that it seemed he would cut the one sausage forever. When the grocer made no effort to reach for the second sausage, Orem put it back in his bag. There would be meat in the soup, then, and Orem had done his part to make the meal. He would stay aboard this ship as long as he wanted now, for it is the custom of the high river country that whoever makes a meal of shared food may not refuse each other's company.

They ate together in silence, spearing the lumps of carrot and meat with their knives and taking turns drinking the broth from the brass bowl. The meal over, the grocer rinsed the bowl in the river, then dipped his hand to bring water to his mouth.

Orem held out his flask. "From my father's spring."

The grocer looked at him sternly and, at last, spoke: "Then you saves it, boy."

"Is there no water where we're going?"

"When you gets to the Little Temple, you must pour in the water from your home and take out God's water."

"To drink?"

"To pour into your father's spring. What, is God forgotten on your father's farm?"

Dobbick had often wanted to tell him the rites of the Great and Little temples of Inwit, but Orem had never said the simple vow. Still, it wouldn't do to have the man think his family unbelievers. "We pray the five prayers and the two songs."

"You saves the water. For your life."

They sat in silence as the wind came up, brightening the coals in the clay firedish. So we are going to Inwit, Orem thought. It was, after all, the likely place for the grocer to be headed; indeed, most downriver traffic was going there, for all waters led to the Queen's city. "I'm going to Inwit, too," said Orem.

"Good thing," said the grocer.

"Why?"

"Because that's the way the river runs."

"What's it like there? At Inwit?"

"That depends, doesn't it?" the grocer answered.

"On what?"

"Oh which gate you goes through."

Orem was puzzled. He knew gates—Banningside had a stockade, and there were the walls of the House of God. "But don't all the gates lead to the same city?"

The grocer shrugged, then chuckled. "They does and they doesn't. Now, I wonder which gate you'll go through."

"The one that's closest, I expect."

The grocer laughed aloud. "I expect not, boy. No, indeed. There's gates and *gates*, don't you see. The South Gate, now, that's the Queen's own gate, and only the parades and the army and ambassadors uses that gate. And then there's God's Gate, but if you goes through there, you gets only a pilgrim's pass, and if they catches you out of Between Temples, they brands your nose with an *O* and throws you out, and you never gets in again."

"I'm not a pilgrim. Which gate do *you* use?"

"I'm a grocer. Swine Gate, up Butcher's Road. I get a grocer's pass, but it's all I want. It lets me go to the Great Market and the Little Market, to Bloody Town and the Taverns. Aye, the Taverns, and that's worth the whole trip alone."

"There's taverns in Banningside," Orem said.

"But they doesn't have Whore Street, does they?" The grocer grinned. "No, there's no place else in the world has Whore Street. For two coppers there's ladies'll do you leaning up against the wall, they ups their skirts and in three minutes you fills them to the eyes. And if you've got five coppers there's ladies'll take you into the rooms and you gets fifteen minutes, time to do twice if you're lively, which I am." The grocer winked. "You're a virgin, aren't you, boy?"

Orem looked away. His mother and father never talked that way, and his brothers were swine. Yet this grocer seemed well-meaning enough, though Orem found himself thinking that the trip had been more pleasant before the grocer started talking. "I won't be for long," said Orem, "once I'm at Inwit."

The grocer laughed aloud, and darted a hand under Orem's long skirt to tweak his thigh perilously near his crotch. "That's the balls, boy! That's the balls!'' It was a pinch that Orem remembered too well, and it was with a bit of loathing that he heard the grocer regale him with tales of his sexual exploits on Whore Street. Apparently Orem had passed some kind of test, and the grocer regarded him as a friend of sorts, one who would be interested in all he had to say. Orem was relieved when at last the grocer yawned and suddenly stood up, stripped off all his clothing, bundled it into a pillow, and pushed it ahead of him as he crawled into the tent.

Orem caught a glimpse of the inside of the tent as the grocer crawled through, and there wasn't room for him. The grocer took no further notice of him, so Orem curled up on the deck, nestled against the leeward side of the grocer's load. It was chilly, especially where Orem's shirt was still damp from the swim a few hours before, but it could have been worse.

THE CORTHY PRICE

In the morning, the silence reigned again. This time, however, Orem did nothing to interrupt it. He helped in the work of the raft, bringing the grocer water to drink as he manned the pole, and from time to time dipping the oar into the water to help when the work became hard in swift currents or shallow sandy water. Orem shared his own small bread for nooning, which the grocer wordlessly took. But this time when night fell, the grocer beckoned for Orem to cast the anchor stones with him, and the talk began at once when the meal was done. The grocer got merrier and merrier, though he touched no beer, and he told Orem more and more about Inwit.

"There's Asses Gate, but you're no merchant. And Back Gate is only for them as lives in High Farms, which you doesn't and never could, those families being older than the Queen's own tribe, and near as magical, they says. No, boy, for you there's only Piss Gate and the Hole. For Piss Gate you gets a three-days' pauper's pass, and if you doesn't find work in those three days, you have to leave again, or they cuts off your ears. Second time they catches you on an old pass, or without one, and you gets a choice. They sells you as a slave or cuts off your balls, and there isn't as many free eunuchs as there is horny slaves, I can tell you!''

Three days. In three days he'd find plenty of work.

"What's the hole?"

The grocer suddenly got quiet. "It's the Hole, boy, not just any hole. That's closed, and there isn't passes. Not from the Guard. But there's ways through the Hole, and ways to get around in the city from there, but I don't know them. No, I'm a Godsman, I am, and the ways through the Hole are all magical, them as isn't criminal. No, you takes your chances with Piss Gate and a three days' pass, and when you doesn't find work, you goes home. No good comes from the Hole. It's magical black and God hates it."

Magical. There it is, thought Orem. They say Queen Beauty is a witch, and magic flies in Inwit, even though the priests do their best to put it down and the laws are all against it. Maybe I'll see magic, thought Orem, though he knew that God wouldn't truck with wizards, and there were seven foreign devils to take your soul if a man should do the purchased spells. The clean spells of the Sweet Sisters, the magics the women did on the farms, they were different, of course. But the magics of the Hole would not be that sort, Orem was sure. And he found himself drawn to the idea of passing through the Hole, to find the city that he wanted to see.

"I don't like the look of your face," the grocer said. "You're not thinking witchy thoughts, are you?"

Orem shook his head, at once ashamed of having so betrayed Halfpriest Dobbick in his heart. "I'm on my way to find a place for myself, and make a name. And earn my poem, if I can."

The grocer relaxed. "There's poems to be had in Inwit. I met a man there whose poem was as long as his arm—I mean it true, he had it needled right into his skin, and a fine poem it was." Suddenly the grocer was shy. "I have a poem, given me by three singers in High Bans. It's no Inwit poem, but it's mine."

Suddenly the mood of the night became solemn. Orem knelt on the hard logs of the raft, and reached out his open hands. "Will you tell me your poem?"

"I'm not much for singing," said the grocer. But he put his left hand in Orem's hands, and his right hand on Orem's head. He sang:

Glasin Grocer, wanders widely,
Rides the river, drifting down,
Turns to north, town of Corth,
Feeds the frightened Holy Hound.

"You," said Orem, in awe.

Glasin Grocer nodded shyly. "Here on my shoulder," he said, baring himself so Orem could see the scars. "I was lucky. It was the Hound's first day, and he took little enough before he went back to the Kennel."

"Weren't you afraid?"

"Peed my winders," Glasin said, chuckling. Orem laughed a little, too. But he thought of how it must be, the huge black Hound coming out of the wood without a sound, and fixing you with the eyes that froze you to your place. And then to kneel and pray as the Hound came and set his teeth in you, and took as much flesh as he wanted, and you hadn't the power to run or the breath to scream.

"I'm a Godsman," Glasin Grocer said. "I didn't scream, and the pain was taken from me, it was. They carried me to the city and the singers gave me my song. Best crop ever, that year."

"I heard about that year. They said the Hound took an angel."

Glasin laughed and slapped his thigh. "An angel! I never!"

Whenever Glasin laughed, his breath took the odor of his rotting teeth in foul gusts to Orem's nose, and Orem would have turned away but for the failure of respect. And Glasin was worth it now—only one bite from the Holy Hound, and a good crop, too. "You were the Corthy Price," Orem said, shaking his head.

Glasin punched Orem in the shoulder. "An angel. They doesn't."

"Oh, they do," said Orem, and Glasin sang his song again. He sang it many times on the way down the river, the two weeks as Banning turned into Burring, and they passed the great castles of Runs, Gronskeep, Holy Bend, Sturks, and Pry. The souther they got the more the river was crowded with other rafts and other barges and boats, and the fouler the river got from sewer streams of the towns along the way. But the odors and noises and arguments with other boatmen were no damper to the excitement of knowing that Inwit was hourly nearer. The only thing that marred Orem's days was Glasin himself. There were many times, in fact, that Orem wished devoutly that he and Glasin had not become friends, and he missed the old silence dreadfully. Glasin had a small enough life, after all, to be contained all in only a few nights' talk, and Orem had to force himself not to say, But your whole song is because by chance the Holy Hound found you, and you were clean. Being clean is just a list of the things you've never done. An empty sort of life, and Orem thought, I will have a poem so long and fine that I will never have to sing it myself, but others will sing it to me because they know the words by heart.

One morning Glasin began to talk even as he first poled the raft back out into the current. "I bet you thinks I can't hold my tongue," he said, "but you sees how I keep my counsel. Did I tell that today would be Inwit day, and landfall at Farmer's Port? If I'd said a thing, why, you never would have slept a wink, and today you needs your rest, I said to me, today you needs your sleep. But you looks there, and sees Ainn Woods, and that low hill ahead, that's Ainn Point, and Ainn Creek is just beyond." It wasn't on Glasin's raft alone that the excitement was high. "Clake Bay!" cried a woman on a nearby boat. "Boat Island!" a man shouted.

And then they fully rounded the bend and there, on the lefthand side of the river, there was Inwit, a high stone wall bright with banners, and below it the docks of Farmer's Port, and rising high behind it the great walls of King's Town—no, *Queen's* Town then—and the gaunt Old Castle highest of all. Glasin named all the places until he nearly missed his turning, and only made one of the last slips of Farmer's Port.

11

Piss Gate

How the Little King entered the city first through Piss Gate, with a pauper's pass, no one guessing who he was.

AMONG THIEVES

The nearest portman tied their line to a post at the slip, and Orem was all for jumping ashore. But Glasin glared at him and ordered him to stay. They waited, and soon several men in gaudy southern trousers came to eye them and their raft.

"A weaky ship," said one.

Glasin turned away from that man, and faced another. "All oak," he said defiantly.

"Bound with spit and catgut?" the man retorted.

"Good only for lumber," said a third. "And three days' drying to boot. A cart in trade."

"Cart and twenty coppers," said another.

Glasin snorted and turned his back.

"Cart and donkey," said the man who had called it a weaky ship.

Glasin turned around with a frown. "That and four silvers gives you raft and tent."

"Silvers! And what do I want with a tent?"

Glasin shrugged.

Another man nodded. The third turned away, shaking his head. The first man, who had the eye of a hawk, staring open always even when the other was closed, he raised his hands. "God sends thieves downriver disguised in grocers' shirts," he said. "Two silvers, a donkey and cart, but by God you keep the tent."

Glasin glanced at the other bidder, but he was through. The sale was set then.

Or almost set. Hawkeye looked at Orem. "Boy for sale?" he asked.

For sale? Orem was appalled—how could anyone take him for a slave? He had no rings in his face, had he? He had no branding! But there was the man asking, and the grocer not saying no, but standing, thinking.

"I'm a freeman," Orem said hotly, but Hawkeye made no sign of having heard, just kept watching Glasin. The grocer at last shook his head. "I'm a God's man, and this boy is free."

The buyer said nothing more, just tossed two gleaming coins to Glasin, who caught them deftly so they didn't slip down between the logs to get lost in the river. The buyer waved, and four men came up, one leading a sad-looking donkey and cart while the others quickly unloaded the raft and put all that would fit into the cart, piling the rest on the dock. When all was done, the portman nodded, drove a red nail into the post, and walked away.

Orem mounted the dock and stood near the pile of the grocer's goods. Not that the grocer had asked him to; indeed, Glasin might have forgotten Orem was there, for all the notice he paid to him. Orem simply did not know where to go or what to do. The wide space fronting the river was crowded with carts and men and some women, shouting and cursing; other rafts were being unloaded at other slips, and Orem had only been ashore a few moments when Hawkeye's men had the empty raft free of the slip and were poling it out into the river.

"They takes it to Boat Island," said the grocer. "They trims it into boards and builds sea ships with it. From Boat Island on out to the sea, the big ships comes and goes. Half my profits is from the raft—the donkey alone would bring me twice that lumber in the north, and the cart is worth all my cargo when I'm buying at the country markets. Now, boy, what is our business?"

Orem didn't understand.

"If you stays and watches my things, if you doesn't let anything get taken whatever they offers you, I give you five coppers when I get back."

"Where are you going?"

"To the market, to get a stall. If I go now, while all the other morning grocers is loading their carts, I get a better place, see. But can I trust you?"

Orem only looked at him angrily. Asking a man if he could

be trusted was like asking an unwed girl if she was virgin. The question mattered, but the asking of it was gross insult.

"All right then," said the grocer. "I'll be back. You talks to no man."

Orem nodded, and immediately the grocer was off, trotting heavily among the crowd.

Around him Orem watched the other grocers as they quarreled and traded and disparaged each other's goods. Here and there were portmen standing guard as Orem stood; he suspected that *they* were being paid a good deal more than a few coppers. It didn't matter. He had learned the abstract values of coins at the House of God, but never in his life had he been forced to learn just how much living could be done on how much money. And even if he *had* learned, at Inwit all values were changed. Six coppers would keep a good-sized family for a month at Banningside. It was different here.

There were other differences. Orem was not so naive he didn't know what was happening when a golden-trousered man gave a small heavy bag to a man standing guard. The guard turned his back as two wagons were drawn to the absent grocer's pile and the goods were loaded on. Orem listened for the cry of thief to arise, waited to see the crowd giving alarm; but there was no sound. Neither did Orem make a sound, for he was afraid to raise the cry of thief in a place where a crime could be committed in the open. He guessed that the bribe was only half the transaction. There was a hint of violence in the rough-looking men who did the loading; he wondered if the man who resisted might end up swimming for his life.

Soon enough a red-trousered man with golden bracelets stood at his side.

"I have a bag of coppers here," the man said softly, "which I'll pay to a boy with a wandering eye who stands and watches the river. Twenty coppers have I, my boy."

Orem did not know what to say. It was a fine offer indeed, and gave him some notion of how ungenerous Glasin had been in his payment. It occurred to him that Glasin trusted him rather much—or else was convinced that Orem was a fool who had no notion of money.

The man drew conclusions from Orem's silence. "I'll go to fifty coppers, then. Fifty coppers, but I tell you, boy, the fishes of the river can be hungry, and we try to keep them fed on stubborn flesh.''

There it was—the bribe and the threat, and he only a boy of fifteen. The rough-looking loaders, there they were waiting at the empty wagons. What chance would Orem have if they threw him into the river? They'd have the grocer's goods whether he wanted them to or not; so why not have the coppers in the bargain?

But there was no poem in a hundred coppers, none at all, and no name or place in that, either.

''What, are you deaf? Well, do you know what *this* means?'' And there was a dagger in the man's hands. For a moment Orem was tempted to try a trick the sergeant had taught him long ago; but no, it was too long ago, when he was little, and Orem did not know if he had the strength or quickness to do it against such a man as this. Who could say what a man with trousers might do? But there was an idea in the man's words about deafness.

''Oh you are generous sir!'' Orem bellowed. ''Oh you are kind and wise!'' He hadn't the lungs of old Yizzer at the gate of the House of God, but his voice was strong enough from his years of canting at the prayers. ''Oh your face is a kind one sir, and God knows your inmost hidden name. God and I know your inmost names and we shall name them!'' And with that Orem reached out his hand and drew his palm lightly across the dagger's point. It drew his blood and hurt with a sharp sting, but Orem knew from the magics observed on his father's farm what such a thing would mean. He held up his hand and let the blood trickle down his arm into his sleeve. ''I will name your names!''

It was enough, oh, yes, see the man run, hear the hissing of his trousers as his legs brush against each other. Orem did not know, however, whether he had done right; it was a terrible thing to pretend to have magic. A terrible thing to spill blood without purpose, to pay a price without petition; but it was all that he had thought of at the moment, and there, the man was leaving, he was glaring back at Orem sure enough, but he and his rough servants were fleeing. It was enlightening to Orem. Yes, he said to himself again and again, Yes, this is a deep and high place, but they are still afraid of magics here, in Queen Beauty's own city they cannot tell a deaf wizard from a desperate wandering boy.

More than the would-be thief had been frightened, too; the other grocers eyed him suspiciously. Only the nearest portman seemed to understand—he winked and drew a circle on his trousers. But was the circle to congratulate him or to fend his pretended power? Orem guessed the first; and also realized that the portmen must charge high fees indeed, for no thief bothered to approach the ones of *them* that stood on guard. A hundred coppers wouldn't tempt them, and with hundreds of the green-bloused men around, Orem guessed that even the most desperate men wouldn't dare to drop one in the river, punctured or not. Life in Inwit was more openly criminal, but there were protections, and a good one was the protection of being in a company of loyal men. Orem wondered vaguely how he would look in the portmen's green.

It was near noon when Glasin returned, smiling broadly. "Got a place in the Great Market," he said, "and I don't have to give the pick to anybody." Orem could smell beer on his breath. The grocer had trusted him indeed, to have paused before coming back to his goods on the wharf. "And now I have too much to fit in one load of the cart. You waits another hour for three more coppers." The grocer looked at him with an eyebrow raised.

By now Orem had come to understand how much the grocer was gaining by his services. Glasin had not had to pay a portman, nor had he had to give pick of stall in the Great Market to some other grocer for watching his goods on the wharf. And it occurred to Orem that Glasin had considered claiming that he was a slave and selling him. Glasin might have been the Corthy Price, but he was too shrewd by half. What if he only left behind on the dock the things he didn't need to sell? What if Orem waited all day for him to come back, and he never came?

"First my five coppers," said Orem.

It was a calculated risk; an honest man might have dismissed him on the spot, for sheer rage. But Glasin only laughed. "Six coppers, then, for waiting again."

So he did mean to cheat him. "First the five I earned."

It was only now that Glasin's eyes went narrow. "What, so I can return and find you gone with my five coppers and my goods as well? I pay you only when your work is done."

Orem could not bear the accusation of thief when he had taken risk already to save Glasin's goods. "A man offered me fifty coppers and would have killed me! I frightened him off for you, and all for five coppers!''

Glasin plainly didn't believe him. ''What sort of man could *you* frighten off? You won't cheat me by such a silly lie as that!''

By habit Orem turned to the nearby guards and grocers for confirmation of his tale. ''I did, you saw me!'' he called out. But no one gave a sign of hearing.

''Why should anyone witness for *you*?'' Glasin asked. ''What could you possibly pay them?''

''I could pay them my five coppers,'' Orem said.

''Off with you, then! I have no use for you! Trying to cheat me! After I let such a useless boy as you ride my boat for free! Here's the five coppers, which you didn't earn. Now away, before I call the guards and name you a thief! Off! You gets away!''

And now, to Orem's surprise, the other grocers began to take notice. ''Is the boy cheating you?'' one called. ''Into the river with him,'' cried another. ''Get rid of a boy like that!''

What could he do, then, but leave? He was furious at the unfairness of it, but it was plain enough that just as portmen found safety with each other's company, so the grocers were a band together, and they'd stand up for another grocer however much the right might be with a wandering boy like Orem. It was a weakish, undependable company, for they had said and done nothing when a thief took the goods of one of their number—but it was a company, all the same. Where was Orem's company? Who would protect *him*? It was the House of God again, and his enemies able to throw him into the fire because he had no friends.

He fled from the grocer then, holding his few coppers in his hand. But fear or not, he had to know for sure; so he stayed and watched, and sure enough, Glasin was able to put all his load of goods into the single cart, saving only the rotted stuff. To protect rotten foodstuff Orem would have waited all day, and had no payment at all. There was no honor in Inwit, none at all, and it made him more afraid than even the thief's dagger pointed at his belly. A dagger has only a single point, but a traitor cuts from anywhere, that's what they said, and only now did Orem understand that it was true.

OREM SEES THE FORBIDDEN GATE

Where now? In all his talk on the downriver trip, Glasin had said much about ways into the city. Now Orem felt little desire to follow Glasin's advice—but in this place what other guide did he have? Glasin would have had little to gain by lying to him in his tales of the city. Orem had no choice but to trust his hints. What had Glasin said? Piss Gate, of course, and three days to find work before they thrust him out. Well, nowhere to go but there, for the ways into the Hole were dangerous, Glasin had said; and what would those dangers be, if the open dock was full of such traps?

"Don't buy anything outside the gate," the grocer had said. "And don't buy anything from anyone who offers to sell. They'll spot you as a farmer from the first second, and they'll up their price by tens." It was all the wisdom Orem had right now; it was his only armor as he found himself on Butcher Street, where four great lines of carts and animals and men waited to get past the guards at Swine Gate.

The guards wore skirts of plated metal, and breastplates of brass; plainly they were not the soldiers who defended the city, for Palicrovol's men wore steel mail shirts and carried swords that would bite such brass as a candle bit through paper. And though the walls of the city were high, the huge wooden gates stout, Orem wondered why it was that King Palicrovol, with an army that they said was the strongest ever known in all the world, had never been able to mine or breach the walls, or even, they said, slay a single one of Queen Beauty's soldiers. Surely the Queen had some terrible army hidden away, and these antiquely costumed guards were all for show.

All for show, except that they were as good a bar to Orem's entry into the city as any men in steel mail with steel swords might have been. He watched, and they did not let the huge press of cursing grocers and butchers hurry them; every pass was checked thoroughly, and more than one man was made to stand aside while others went ahead of him. And over all were the archers perched on the tops of the gate towers, alert always to what was happening below them.

There would be no way for Orem to slip in unnoticed even if he had wanted to.

"No use looking, farmer," said a voice behind him.

Orem turned and saw a weasely looking man near four inches shorter than he, smiling at him. Smiles like that, Orem thought, are worn by dogs who have cornered their squirrel.

"I'm not a farmer," Orem said.

"Then you'll not get through Swine Gate, will you?"

"I'm looking for Piss Gate."

The man nodded. "They all are, boy, they all are. Well, when you're done with Piss Gate, you find old Braisy here, and he'll get you through. He'll get you into Inwit for the very small fee of five coppers and a favor, he will." And then Braisy was gone, and because he was so short, Orem quickly lost him in the sea of heads moving in every direction on Butcher Street.

Unfriendly as the city might be, Orem had to find his way. He asked questions, and among the surly replies was information enough to get him to Shit Street, which led between the reeking stockyards and north into Beggarstown. "You'll find the towers of Piss Gate easy enough, if you just look up and keep the wall on your right," said a man with a bloody butcher's apron. But Shit Street quickly became narrow and kept turning away from the main path of traffic. There were fewer and fewer signs the farther he went; who could read, after all, in such a place as this? For Beggarstown was made up of people who had not found work on their pauper's passes and could not stay inside the city walls; it was a poor place, with seedy wooden shops gradually making way for boarded-up buildings that were lived in despite their sag and filth, and even these began to look fine as hovels sprouted up in every space the rickety old structures left between them. The shacks grew out into the road; the people squatting in the shadows of the east side of the street looked hungry; Orem began to be afraid of thieves, for in this place even five pennies might be worth taking another man's life.

Soon he was lost. Only the wall remained constant, high and grey, looming over the filthy town that was already three times as large as all of Banningside. Orem dared not ask directions of any of the people along the way. He kept as far as possible from the buildings. And the farther he walked, the fewer people he saw, until there was no one about when he spotted the twin high towers of a gate.

The streets were utterly empty near the gate. The buildings were boarded up or, even more haunting. left to hang open, roofless and shutterless, as if they were half-completed. Not a person was in sight; there was not even the banging of an open door to break the silence. He knew that this could not be Piss Gate, where paupers passed into the city of Inwit. But that did not deter him, for he knew then what this gate must be, and he wanted all the more to see it.

He stood at the foot of the gate towers, looking up. The street had widened to a plaza and then disappeared. Where the vast wooden gates should have stood open, houses rose steeply to lean against the towers, covering the space where only at the top was there any of the lumber of the gate visible. There was an odd shifting of the view: at one moment it seemed the gate was holding up the buildings; at the next it seemed the buildings were holding up the walls, keeping them from falling outward to crush Orem where he stood and looked.

"Ho, boy!"

Orem was startled, for he had thought he was alone.

"Ho, what are you doing here?"

There, in the shade of one of the boarded-up buildings, two guards. Their bronze looked less polished than the breast-plates of the guards at Swine Gate. But it served to make them more menacing, not less. Without thinking, Orem decided that this was certainly the time to seem to be what in fact he was—a farmer's boy lost in the slums of the city.

"I'm looking for Piss Gate," Orem said. "I'm here for the first time. Have they closed the gate, then?"

The guards glanced at each other, then smiled. There was derision in their mirth, and Orem felt uncomfortable.

"Not Piss Gate, that's sure, you can tell Piss Gate by the stink of thieves and farmers who come down the river hoping to ger rich in the city." The guards approached him, and now Orem saw that there were more than a dozen of them; they had been concealed in shadows or, he suspected, inside the shells of the buildings that were not totally boarded up.

"I'm not hoping to get rich," Orem said, trying to sound frightened and succeeding better than he had expected.

"Where you from, boy?"

"A farm. My father's farm. Upriver, near Banningside."

Now the guards were more alert, and Orem noticed that hands were on hilts and fingers had closed around ax-hafts. "An illegal person is near Banningside," said a guard.

"Illegal person?" The King, of course. And for a terrible moment Orem feared they would suppose him a spy. Spies, he knew, were skinned alive and forced to eat their own hearts. Should he pretend that he didn't know Palicrovol had been in the area? No, they'd never believe it. It was impossible not to know when that vast army came foraging in a countryside. "All I know is the sergeants were out pressing soldiers. I didn't want to go in the army."

The guard who seemed to be in command looked him up and down pointedly, then laughed. "If you were in danger of pressing then the rebels must be more desperate than anyone thought."

At the laughter, Orem tried a smile, hoping to join in the camaraderie. His mirth offended them. The commander did not take him by the shirt; he took him painfully by the skin at his waist, a crushing grip that brought an unwilling cry from Orem. "Do you know how close you are to death?"

"No, sir."

A guard had opened Orem's bag. In it was only his flask, still full of his father's spring water, and the last bit of bread that now was like rock. His coppers were in a better place.

"A rich one, that's plain," said the guard as he tossed the bag back to Orem.

Orem dared to ask a question. "Why is this gate closed?" he asked.

"You're better off if you never learn the answer to that question."

A guard with white hair who looked like he had committed all sins and was still unsatisfied spoke softly. "He's a country fool. It's broad daylight."

"I say question him," said another.

The white-haired guard spoke even more softly. "I say eat shit. The spies all know their way into the city, and it isn't the Hole in midafternoon."

The commander pushed Orem from him, hurting his side again even as he released him. "Get away from here, boy, and don't come back. If you want Piss Gate, follow the north wall and stay close to the wall always."

"Or go home," said the white-haired guard. "There's nothing in Inwit for you. Don't you know this city devours children and flays strong men alive?"

Orem smiled uncomprehendingly and backed away from them. "Thank you, sirs. Good day to you. I'll never come here again."

"Your name, boy!" called the commander. "And don't lie!"

"Orem ap Avonap!"

The white-haired guard laughed aloud. "What a name! Only a farmer would think of that!"

The other guards nudged each other and laughed also. But they watched him out of sight all the same, and he suspected that one was following him much of his way north.

It made Orem angry that they laughed at him, but what made him angriest was that he had earned their laughter. A fool, that's what he had been, and it had not been a pose, no, not half.

The Beggars' Way of Death in Life

The farther north he got, the less dead the place appeared; a child played in the street, and then a beggar sprawled in sleep, and at last litter began appearing at the sides of the road and the sewer down the middle of the street began to be fetid with decomposing filth. Beggarstown was alive again, now that he was away from the Hole, and the faces that had seemed frightening to him before were a welcome sight now. Orem began to see, not their strangeness, not their darkness and filth, but their weakness and grief. They wore elegant clothes, most of them, but so tattered and soiled that the color that had once been bright was now a dull brown or grey. There was a dullness in the eyes, too, as if something in Beggarstown took the mind out of the head, as if the people could go through their days without ever quite awakening.

Orem began to pity them, and almost lost his fear, until a man with just such an empty face walked up to a man near Orem and calmly stabbed him deep in the eye with a dagger. His victim fell without a sound, blood pouring up and out of his face onto the road. Orem felt more anguish than fear, for if a man with such a dead face could kill, when the dead could reach out and drag the living into their graves, then what chance had he to hold onto his life here?

On the dock a thief had been left alone by the witnesses of his crime, but here there was another code. While the murderer was stripping his victim, five or six men calmly gathered around and began throwing stones at the thief. The thief dodged desultorily and finally gave up trying to get the dying man's shirt. As he stumbled away from his victim, the men caught him, kicked him, threw him to the ground, beat him silently, wordlessly. The thief at first tried to cover himself, but at last lay open to the blows. He was not unconscious, Orem saw; nor were the men who kicked him driven by hate. They simply kicked and stamped on him, until a man leapt into the air and landed with both feet on the murderer's neck and head. The neck broke; the mouth went slack as the jaw crumbled; yet the eyes looked no deader than before. The men who had killed the murderer left him to lie on the street by his victim. The rats were already gathering, and no one moved to cover the bodies. Orem felt that he had seen all there was of the whole wheel of life in this place. There was no birth here; only death, only the rats gnawing.

The knife stood upright from the victim's eye. On impulse Orem strode to the body and reached down to take the knife; at that same moment a long thin hand also reached to the corpse. For a moment Orem thought someone was challenging him for possession of the weapon, but no; it was an old woman, and she was holding a cup, catching the last of the flowing blood. A witch, then, who could make use even of unearned blood. Orem wondered what sort of filthy magic could be made of found death even as he backed off and let her take what she wanted.

She finished. She looked up and smiled at him. She bent and kissed the knife. For a moment Orem thought not to take it after all; who knew what the kiss might mean? But then he thought better of it. Even a boy trained as a priest could make use of a dagger if need were, and in this place he had no intention of passively submitting to what the walking corpses might decide for him. So he stepped forward again and drew the knife upward, drawing one last bubble from the man's eye. He cleaned the knife, for lack of a better place, on the man's clothing; then he put the knife in his bag.

The woman spoke, her voice hissing like the last breath of

a butchered sow. "There are three things in nature that know no moderation, in goodness or in foulness." She cocked her head and waited.

Orem shuddered. He knew the litany, and knew as well that it could not be left incomplete. If she chose to stop and wait, he had to go on for her. "When they are governed by goodness," he said softly, "they are most excellent in virtue."

"The tongue," said the woman. "And a priestly man."

"But when they are corrupted, there is no bottom to stay their hellward plunge." Is that enough, or must I name the third name?

"And a woman." She smiled and nodded wisely at him, as if they had shared something lovely; then she took her cup of cooling blood and carried it away.

Orem felt the knife in his bag like a small fire, burning his skin though it could not touch him directly. What had she meant by making him chant the Ambivalence? Was she warning him to curb his own evil desires? But I have no truly unspeakable desires, he thought, and besides, I'm not a priestly man anymore. Why should I worry about the warnings of a woman already so corrupt as to use found blood? Yet still he shuddered. Still the knife burned his back. Still the knife froze his back until he had walked far enough and thought enough of other things and inwardly sung songs enough that the litany of the three boundless friends and enemies of God fled his mind and he forgot even the knife he carried.

How Orem Came to Be Called Scanthips

Piss Gate at last. From a distance it looked like Swine Gate and the Hole; close up it had a character all its own. This place did not belong to the permanent residents. It was not silent and despairing. The line was long and jostled rudely, and only the presence of many guards kept quarrels from erupting into fights. As for the guards, they were grim and busy, and six of them were ahorse, patrolling up and down the line. There were no dead looks among the people in the line. They might be angry or stupid or frightened or awestruck or jocular, but they were not dead. Orem recognized himself in many places along the line, at once ashamed at the plain naivete of the others his age and relieved that it was indeed possible to stay hopeful here. People from the farms; people with dreams of finding some treasure in the city; Orem took his place in the line and felt smaller—but safer than he had in the streets of Beggarstown.

No sooner was he in line than the queue was a hundred people long behind him. The guards had let the grocers in three or four abreast, but here the guards were in no such rush. The huge gates did not stand open. Only a narrow door in the gate served for the paupers to pass. Yet the people themselves had the same sense of urgency that the grocers and butchers had. The belief was strong that if you could just get through the line ahead of someone, then you would get the job that *that* man might have had. Within that gate was the answer to everything, if you could just get through and ask your questions first. A job; a workingman's pass; the right to stay within the city; this was the gate of heaven and the angels in their bronze breastplates held the chains of salvation. Orem could not help seeing the world as the priests saw it; he also could not help being amused at the thought of these foul-faced soldiers being angels. Are these the silver bridge and the golden gate and the chains of steel? Try that for doctrine, Halfpriest Dobbick.

"First time?"

It was the man ahead of him, who bore three thin scars on his cheek, two of them old and white, the other just a little pink. He did not look friendly, but at least he had spoken.

"Yes," Orem said.

"Well, take a word. Accept no jobs from the men just inside the gate."

"I want a job."

The man's mouth twisted. "They promise to take you for a year, but in three days they turn you over to the Guard without your permanent pass. How's that? And they don't pay you, either. They just get three days' work out of you for free and turn you out. The real jobs are farther in."

"Where?"

"If I knew, would I be in this line again?"

And at last, with the sun hot and red through the door in the gate, they were at the questioning guards. The man who had spoken to Orem sullenly answered the questions: Name, business, citizenship. Rainer Carpenter, woodworker looking for a job, citizen of Cresting. The guard took Rainer by the chin and turned his face, so he could see the scarred cheek. It was the pink one that made the guard's eyes go small and angry.

"Still red, Rainer, dammit, are you blind?"

"Got no mirror," Rainer answered. "Woman told me it was white."

"Like I thought, only a blind woman would have *you*. Get out and come back when the time's done."

And now Orem was at the front of the line, only vaguely aware that Rainer Carpenter was still standing nearby.

"Name?"

"Orem."

The guard waited, then said impatiently, "Your whole name!"

Orem remembered the laughter at the Hole over his patronymic. Rainer had used his trade as a surname, as Glasin had. Well, Orem had no trade. Why had they laughed? Perhaps they didn't admit their fathers' names here. "Don't have more. Just Orem."

The guard was amused. "From a village so small, eh?" He looked at Orem's body and his smirk grew. Orem cursed his thinness and lack of height. "We'll just put you down as Orem Scanthips, eh? Scanthips!" He said it loudly, and the other guards laughed. "Business?"

"Looking for work."

"What kind of work?"

"Any kind, I guess."

"Any kind? No one hires a man who can't do anything. What, do you think there's farms in there needing another ass to bear dead burdens?"

Wouldn't they let him in without a trade? What did he know? *I can say all the open prayers by heart. I can name the letters capital, the letters corporal, the letters spiritual, the numbers real, the numbers whole, the numbers variable.* "I can read and write."

The guard made a face of mock surprise. "A scholar, eh?" But the amusement was over. The guard reached out and took away Orem's bag and opened it. A flask of water, a lump of bread, and a dagger with a little blood still clinging to it. Not the safe little dinner knife Orem wore at his waist—that was for slicing cheese. This was obviously a killing knife, long and sharp pointed. The guard held it up. "Read and write. Oh, I've heard *that* before. And what is this, your pen?"

Orem didn't know what to say. The dagger had seemed desirable as he walked through Beggarstown; now it might be what blocked him from the city, or worse than that.

But then Rainer Carpenter spoke from nearby. "It's mine," he said.

"Yours!" said the guard.

"Last time in here I was robbed and I damn well wasn't going to do it again. I didn't think you'd look at the boy's bag. He didn't know it was in there."

The guard looked back and forth between Orem and Rainer. The look of bewilderment on Orem's face was sincere enough, and nothing could be read in Rainer's eyes. Finally the guard shrugged. "Rainer, you're a fool. You know we'd have you whipped with a glass pipe for that, if you once got it inside."

"Glass pipe or a crackhead's leaden rod, tell me the difference," said Rainer. And the guard wrote again on Orem's pass. "Citizenship?"

"Banningside, in High Waterswatch."

The guard looked at him suspiciously again. Again Orem was forced to claim that he ran from the pressmen of Palicrovol's army. Again his body was laughed at, and he wanted to strike out at the guards and break their brittle, mocking smiles. But at least he would get inside, at least he held the pass in his hand; and all thanks to Rainer Carpenter, a man he didn't know. Just when Orem had concluded there was no kindness in this place, a stranger lied to let him into the city. Orem dared not turn and thank him—that would undo it all. But part of his name and poem would be repayment of such debts. Rainer would find it was not unprofitable to help Orem ap Avonap.

He was guided into the gate by the careless, efficient hands of the guards. And they were not through with him once he had passed inside. There was a guard with a short razor, and before Orem could be sure what was happening, two guards had seized him. They held his head still while the cutter sliced his cheek. The cut was thin and not deep, but still the blood dripped quickly from the stinging wound and stained his shirt.

A mouth spoke at his ear. "Mind you, we know from experience when this wound is healed enough that you ought to be back outside. Any guard who sees this scar will check your pass, and if you're overstayed he'll have your ear. Understand? Get caught twice, and it's your balls. You have three days. Sundown, clear? And once you're out, the scar has to be plain white before we let you in again. And stay off Stone Road. Go on.'' With a push at his back, Orem stumbled forward into Inwit.

12

The Sweet Sisters

This is the tale of how Orem, called Scanthips, called Banningside, went to Whore Street and left unsatisfied.

THE WHORE AND THE VIRGIN

When you come into Inwit on Piss Road, on the left is the miserable shantytown of the Swamps, and on the right are the gaudy taverns, and ahead in the distance looms the Old Castle. It is not a hard choice for newcomers to make. Orem turned right, into the Taverns, and wandered along the street in the gathering darkness, wondering how much food and lodging his five coppers would buy.

In the Taverns, all roads lead to Whore Street, and by not knowing where he was going, Orem soon ended up there. He did not know it was Whore Street at first. It looked, to him, like the richest town he had ever seen, for here the buildings were high and clean, and there were trees in the middle of the road, many trees and bushes, so it was like walking in an open wood. The houses were simple and graceful and well-proportioned, and more than one of them was made to look very much like a House of God.

The nature of the place was revealed when a half-drunk, giggling bunch of masked boys stopped two women and handed them each a coin. It took only a few minutes for all the boys to be satisfied, whooping as they leaned the women against trees and slobbered drunken kisses on them and lifted their skirts high while they discussed which was better. The intercourse was like little boys urinating, giggling as they compared each other's equipment and loudly counted to see how quickly each was through. Orem was not ignorant—he had lived on a farm. But he had never seen it done by a man and a woman before, and he could not take his eyes off the scene. Only when it was over did he look at the whores' faces. He saw them just as the boys were leaving, just as the women's smiles were fading and they sighed and rearranged their clothing and pooled their money. They picked up an interrupted conversation in midstream; the interlude with the boys had meant nothing to them. As Orem told me of this night, he was still awed that a man could dip in the Sisters' fountain and the woman would not rue it.

An hour later, Orem leaned against a tree, watching one of the more elegant orgies, where the men and women held forth on philosophical topics for an hour or so among the trees before the coupling began. He did not know the woman had come near him until she touched his arm.

"Unless you have more money than you look to have," she said, "you might as well go home. The deeper you go into Whore Street, the more expensive it gets."

She was all breast and teeth—at least to Orem she was, for all he could see when he looked at her face was the way both rows of teeth were visible when she smiled, and when he didn't look at her face all he could see was the way her breasts hung provocatively within her blouse.

Perhaps she was one of those few whores who haven't lost their taste for beauty or for love. Not that Orem was beautiful. But he had a kind of gangling grace, like a colt first running, and he could look at once childlike and dangerous. (Perhaps only I saw the danger in his face; Beauty would have prospered better if she had seen it sooner.) Whatever her reason, she accepted an offer he did not make. He was so trusting that when she asked, he told her he had but five coppers. She had a conscience—she only charged him four.

His new-engaged whore brought him past the fierce guard at the door of a nearby house, announced in loud tones to all who cared to hear that she had found a virgin stalk to reap, and pushed him toward the stair. She walked behind him, and twice reached under his tunic and pulled his wrapping cloth down below his buttocks. Each time he jumped in surprise; each time she giggled.

At the head of the stairs he made as if to walk down the wide carpeted hall, but she pulled back on his shirt.

"That costs a silver, no bargaining, that's what the house charges and I got no choice." Off they went up another flight. This time the carpet ended at the turn of the stairs, the moment the steps weren't visible from the carpeted hall. "It's like a hundred houses in one," she said, "depending on what you pay." The next flight creaked. And the fourth flight of stairs wobbled underfoot. "It's the cheap rooms, forgive the fleas, but four coppers ain't exactly money."

They walked carefully down a dark corridor, lit only by a torch at each end. Orem glanced into the rooms that were open. Just glanced, until what he saw made him stop and stare.

They sat side by side. Two women, just sitting, still as trees. They were dressed like any other whores, and had bodies perhaps more lovely than other whores. But their faces: which was more terrible? The one with a single eye, and a mouth that opened only on the side, and a nose skewed around so the nostril pointed more up than down? Or the one with no face at all?—neither brows nor eyes nor nose nor lips, just a circumference of hair and a blank of flesh interrupted only by a thin slit that could not be called a mouth, for there were no lips and it hung open in a limp *O* that dripped a steady stream of saliva down on her open bosom.

"Twins of the flesh, they were," said Orem's whore in a whisper, and she drew him away. Though he could not bear to look at the women, he hung back; she pulled harder and he drew away from the door. "Twins of the flesh. Born of a noble house, it's said, and they got the finest physicians and the finest wizards, not to mention priests, who blessed them till they damn near sprouted wings. Then they cut them apart. Twins of the flesh, joined at the face, except that the one was looking away from the other just a little, so she had an eye and half a mouth and half a nose, but the other nothing at all but a tiny hole that was letting air in from the other's mouth. They widened the hole. The blessings worked, for they lived. And the spells worked, for they grew flesh over their bloody wounds. But what was there for them? And which is worse cursed, do you think? The one who cannot see? Or the one who knows mirrors? We call them the Sweet Sisters. Kind of a joke, you know."

Orem had never known a woman in his life who would joke about the Sweet Sisters.

His whore opened a small door and ducked to go in. Orem also ducked, but still banged his head. "Low roof," she said.

His whore pulled her blouse from her shoulders; her breasts pulled up and then jogged back down when she lowered her

arms. Orem saw, but all he could think of was the slack face
with the hole that drooled. The whore undressed him, but all
he could think of was the face with the single eye and the
canted nose and the half-mouth. His whore stroked him and
kissed him but it did no good; he lay trembling and unable
and cold on the thin rug on the floor. Whatever he may or
may not have wanted as he came up the stairs, the whore had
nothing of him, because he had seen the twins of the flesh
who had once been joined at the face and could think of
nothing else.

"Fifteen," his whore said contemptuously. "Might as well
be five. What did you plan to stick there, your knee? God knows
it's skinny enough to fit. You got the balls of a mouse and
the cod of a flea, that's what you got, so don't go telling me
it's my fault, I'm still pretty enough, I didn't hear you telling
me I was ugly down there on the street, did I?" She dressed
quickly, then stooped and took four coppers from where they
lay on the floor. "You pay for my time—it's not my fault
you didn't use it. You're damn lucky I don't take the other
one, for the insult." She spat on his loin wrap where it lay
pathetic and empty on the floor, then stepped on it. "That
and piss is all you'll ever find in *your* wrap in the morning.
Find your own way out, dingle. When you turn ten come
back and we'll see what we can do." And she was gone.

JOINED AT THE FACE

Ashamed, Orem tried to wipe her spittle from the wrap by
dabbing with his shirt. Was this how his poem would begin?

He dressed and ducked back into the cluttered, shadowy
hall. At once he saw the wall of light from the door where the
monsters called the Sweet Sisters waited for him to pass. He
was at once drawn to them and terrified. He stepped carefully, he trembled at the knee, he stumbled, he lurched against a
wall. He was all the noisier for his efforts at silence.

"Who is there?" said a thin, high, wavering voice.

He kept his silence, kneeling on the floor of the dark hall.
Don't come out and see me. Stay where you are, go to sleep,
die. Let me pass.

"Answer. You know it makes my sister angry when you
don't answer."

The last thing Orem wanted was to make a sister angry. In the name of God, Orem said silently, don't be angry at me. "I fell," he said.

"The voice of a child, yes? The voice of a clumsy child, yes? The voice of a boy who was charged four coppers and given nothing. But think, but think, she took nothing from you either. For the price of just four coppers, you're still a lake undrained by any stream." And then a slight laugh that angered him. His whore had been too loud; they knew his failure.

"Come in," said the voice.

No.

"Must I come get you?" He got to his feet and walked weakly forward, turned at their door. The single eye of the one face was looking at him, but if he looked away, the only place for his gaze was the other, the blank flesh, the steady trickle of drool. He forced himself to look about the room. There was a single chair besides the ones they sat in, old and frail and ready to break. There was a small loom, with a cloth half-finished in it, a ragged cloth which was also rotting, and the loom was so strung and clotted with webs and dust that it was plain it had not been used in years. And then the rug on the floor, just like the rug where he had lain helplessly with his whore: only this rug glowed in the light, and Orem realized it was woven with gold thread.

"Sit down."

He did not try the chair, but sat on the floor.

"Four coppers. Was the sight of sagging teats worth the price?" Was that a smile on her deformed face? "She's an old gom of a rutter—you must be fresh in the city not to have known." The one-eyed woman looked at her placid sister. "How old do you think he is?"

To Orem's horror the lipless mouth tried to answer. A moan, a modulated moan like a song of pain, and the one-eyed sister nodded. "Yes, fifteen, but scrawny of body. My sister says your will is stone—you may crumble under the hammer, but long after the hammer has rusted away, you will remain. Isn't that pretty? What's your name?"

"Orem." He still had not learned to lie.

"Orem. Do you want your four coppers back?"

It had not occurred to him that it was possible. "Yes."

"Then you must entertain us."

"How?"

"Tell us a tale of two sisters, who were both twins of the flesh, joined at the face, and who by magic and prayers and surgery were separated, the one with a single eye, and the other with no face at all except a mouthhole that drools constantly and leaves a trail of spittle between her breasts down to her belly."

"I—I don't—I can't tell you that tale—"

"Oh, we won't *believe* it, mind you. Such a thing could not be. Tell us what these pathetic women are doing in a whorehouse."

"They—sit. In a room upstairs."

"And what do these women do while they sit?"

"They—listen."

"And what do you think they hear?"

"The sounds of—of—"

"Love?"

Orem nodded. The one-eyed sister shook her head.

"Not love," Orem said.

"What then?"

"The sound of—of birds."

"Yes, birds. And above the birds, what?"

What was above the birds? What was this tale supposed to mean? "The sound of wind across the roof of the house."

The blank one moaned, and the other hooted with laughter. "Yes, he knows, he knows, he has many many ears inside his head, yes, and what else do they hear?"

He understood now. It was a game, like the riddles and puzzles of the manuscripts. "The sound of the sun rising and falling. The sound of the stars as they pass overhead. The sound of God closing his eyes upon the world. The sound of the Hart as it shakes its head and tosses the planets."

The one eye opened wide; the hole of the mouth emphatically stopped drooling for a moment, so that the mucous spittle broke in midstring, and the top of the thread was drawn up into her mouth like the body of a dangling spider.

"The mouth opens and it speaks," said the one-eyed sister.

"Nnnnnnng," said the other.

"We are bound about with magic," said the one-eyed woman, "yet he speaks with our tongues. Beauty has silenced us, yet our own gifts come from the boy's mouth. Ah, Hart, you have more wit than we."

"What does it mean?" Orem asked.

"Nothing to you, forget, forget, tell no one what you have seen, for it is no favor, you are *just an ordinary boy*."

His stomach clenched with fear at the force of her words.

"We are whores, too, did you know that? We left our father's house and came here because we knew that without faces we had only our bodies. Do you know what it costs to take us? A thousand of gold or a hundred acres of farmland. For a single night. And we are busy twenty nights a year. Oh, we are rich, we twins of the flesh, we sisters of beauty. We are blessed. And not all who come to us are men. There are women who come and spend the night exploring us, trying to discover what makes us so beautiful. They cannot guess. But *you* know, don't you?"

"No. I don't."

"That's right. You cannot know if you think that you know. We hear another thing, we listen to another thing, not just the stars. Not just the heartbeat of the great thousand-horned Hart who holds the worlds on the points of his horns. Not just the great eruption of the sun that ejaculates its gusts of light to inseminate the world. We hear this also:"

And she stopped.

And after a long, long silence, in which Orem heard nothing but his own heavy breathing, she said, "Did you hear it, too?"

"No."

"That is why they pay so much to have us."

The one with the eye opened a small chest beside her. It was filled with jewels that glistened in the torchlight like a thousand tiny fires.

And the one whose face was as featureless as fog, she stood and made a single motion with her hand. Abruptly she was naked, and her face glowed like the sun itself; there was no hair on her body, and her skin was deep as amber, and she was so beautiful that Orem could not keep his eyes from flowing with tears so he could no longer see.

"It is as I thought," said the one who could speak. "His eyes cannot be closed except by his own weeping and his own trust."

The blank-faced woman was sitting again, as suddenly as she had stood; how could she have clothed herself so quickly?

"Hunnnnnnng," she moaned. "Ngiiiiiunh."

"Four coppers, says my sister, and a kiss."

It was not for the coppers that he kissed them, but for fear of them. He kissed their mouths, such as they were, and the coppers fell into his hand, and he fled the room.

As he ran along Whore Street he could hear for the first time in his life the song that his mother had loved best: the steady hissing of the sap up the trees, the song of capillarity, ah, it was beautiful, and he wept until the spittle of the fog-faced woman's mouth had dried upon his lips.

A cot at the Spade and Grave cost only a copper for two nights, not as expensive as he had feared. He lay for some time with both hands pressed between his legs, because of the great ache at the base of his belly. He could hear the sap flowing also in himself. Why have I come to Inwit? he cried to himself. But he knew that the question itself was a lie. He had not come at all. He was shoved.

That is why Orem was a virgin when Beauty needed him.

13

Thieves

How Orem learned what life was worth in Beauty's city.

THE SONG IN THE CISTERN

Orem awoke on the top bunk of the backmost bed in the Spade and Grave. The ceiling was inches from his face, but after the cramped cells of the House of God he had no fear of such small places. He slid carefully to the edge of the splintery board and clambered down the seven tiers of beds. The reek of vomit was strong. Each of his steps bowed the board of some other sleeper; some moaned; one cursed and slapped out at him.

As he passed the innmaster the fellow tossed him a chit. Orem looked at it. "I don't want to carry this all day."

The innmaster shrugged. "As you like. But I warn you, I'll cheat you if you let me."

Orem put the chit in his bag. "Thanks. Will every thief in Inwit be so thoughtful as to warn me?"

The innmaster regarded him calmly. "I'm a Godsman. I only cheat them as want to be cheated."

Nothing in Orem's life had prepared him for the daytime streets of Inwit. The flow of the crowds led him to the Great Market, and for some time he was swept back and forth in the eddies of the buying and selling. In all his life before he had never seen so many people as were in the marketplace that day, rags and velvets, uniforms and livery, all bumping together in the battle to get much for little. Orem gawked, and so marked himself as an easy target for thieves.

A boy brushed up against him and a small hand reached under his shirt, and as fast as Orem could realize what was happening his coppers were out of his wrap. Without a thought Orem swung out and caught the child a blow on the chin. The boy fell soundlessly, and as silently scrambled to his feet—

but Orem had learned to be quick in the House of God. He had the boy by an ankle before he was fairly afoot. The child kicked viciously at Orem's face. Was the battle worth an eye? Orem's few coins were his life and hope here, and so he struggled on despite the blows.

No one seemed to notice the cruel battle going on in the street, except to leave a space for them to roll in the sand. At last Orem got the thief in a coward's hold, legs bent painfully and Orem's hand firmly tucked into the boy's crotch, ready to inflict that irresistible pain.

"I want the coppers, little bastard," Orem said.

"Coppers!"

"Or in Sister's name I'll have your balls off."

"God's name, I haven't got your money!" The boy's wail was loud and pitiful. Now that the fighting was done, people began to take notice.

"Leave be," said a voice in the crowd. "It's a coward who takes down a little child."

The little swine was winning sympathy. Orem leaned down and whispered in the boy's ear. "I'm a farmer, boy, and I've made bulls into steers with my bare hands before." It was enough. The boy's eyes went wide and he spat four coppers into the dust.

Orem released the boy and quickly grabbed up the coins. From the corner of his eye he saw the thief moving in a way that he feared might be an attack—what, a kick? Yes. Orem dodged out of the way just in time, then leaped to his feet to prepare for the next onslaught.

There wasn't one. The child looked at him with eyes all innocent and laughed.

"Don't you know all pissers keep them in the same place? And half of them have soil in their wraps, it's filthy work to put them in my mouth."

"If you don't like it," Orem said, holding his coppers tightly, "find another line of work."

"*You* hire me as soon as *you* find work."

It stung Orem that the boy assumed that he would fail. "I will hire you," Orem said disdainfully. "I'll have a job in days, and take you on."

"Oh, yes, and the Queen wears a codpiece." The boy whirled around and flipped up his shirt to show his buttocks to Orem for a moment. Then he was gone in the crowd.

Orem wandered north, where the Great Market empties into Queen's Road. He marveled at the great houses, he gaped at the spider-wheeled carriages, he stared at ladies as naked as they could decently be above the waist and gentlemen as naked as fashion required below it. And he stood at the base of the hundred-stepped pyramid that led upward to Faces Hall, where Palicrovol had stood and ravished the little daughter of Nasilee, spilt her inmost blood and so became her husband and so became the King and then cast her away. The start of all the woes of the world, there at Faces Hall.

"Damn your liver to be eaten by the eagles!" A guard had him by the shoulder, shaking him. "Didn't they tell you at the gate to stay off Queen's Road? The Stone Road? Are you deaf? Have you the brain of a pudding?" More kicks and blows as the guard took him down an alley, bashing him against one wall and then another, until Orem gratefully fell on his face in the dust of a back street. "And don't come back on Queen's Road or I'll have you hung by your ears till they tear!" Orem lay in the street listening to the footsteps as the guard left. He hurt everywhere, yet he was not so much angry as glad that it had stopped. Even glad that it hadn't been worse. He winced and gingerly got to his feet.

"Gentle, an't they?"

Orem turned painfully to meet the face that went with the voice. It was the child who had robbed him, smiling cocky as you please, hands on hips, legs spread, like God astride the world.

"You look pretty poor, you know." The boy smiled at him maliciously. "Had me by the balls and you were rich and fine."

"You were taking all I had," Orem said dully. He winced at the pain of breathing in.

"And you took all *I* had."

"But it was mine."

"Not while *I* had it."

It was an argument that would get nowhere, Orem could see. "Where am I?"

"What's it worth to you to know?"

"Nothing." Orem looked around. All he could see were the backs of common buildings on one hand and on the other the high garden walls of the great houses, with their cruel spear-topped iron ridges. Except for the alley to Stone Road,

there was only one way to go, so Orem set out along the dirt
street. The thief padded behind him.

"Get away from me," Orem said.

"I followed you all this way."

"You'll never get my coppers."

"You said you'd hire me."

"*If* I get a job." But suddenly the boy was not so neatly
catalogued as a clever thief. "You believed me?"

"You look too stupid to lie."

"Then what makes you think I'll get a job?"

"Because you wouldn't let me go when I kicked your
face." The boy giggled. "You're a bad fighter, you know. A
girl could beat you."

Orem felt himself flush with anger, but he said nothing.
The road was widening, and now there were some sleazy
shops fronting on the street. In the middle of the road was a
short round wall like a well housing, made of crumbly bricks.
Orem made to go around it, but heard a sound. Like singing,
coming from the well. He stopped.

"It's the cistern," said the boy. "All the time singing.
Means nothing. Cistern's empty."

"Why? Drought?"

"They're for a siege. There's never a siege of Inwit.
Besides, you'd drown the voices."

Orem stepped to the cistern rim and leaned over to listen.
Along with the sound he was greeted by a smell so fetid that
he reeled backward and gasped and choked.

"Since it's empty," said the boy, "everybody dumps their
slops in. And shits quite direct." As if to demonstrate, the boy
jumped up and sat perilously on the wall, his backside leaning
far over the edge. Unceremoniously he defecated, then waited
with his head cocked. "Hear the splash? It must be half a
mile down."

"What about the voices?"

"Probably a choir of rats. They live fine on manure. Aren't
you a farmer? Don't you know about the magical properties
of manure?" While he talked, the boy wiped himself with his
left hand, then spat on it and rubbed it in the dirt till it was
dry. "Here," he said, gesturing at Orem's bag. "Let us have
a little water."

Orem shook his head.

"Oh, won't share even water, is that it?"

"It's from my father's spring. For the fountain at Little Temple."

"What are you, a pilgrim? You have a priest's face. Like a hungry rat."

"I studied with priests."

"That's it, then." The boy nodded wisely. "I knew you could read. I can read a little. Taught myself."

"The voices from the cistern. How long have they been going on?"

The boy shrugged. "All *my* life."

Orem recited the Seventh Warning of Prester Zenzil: "Do not learn the songs of voices singing out of empty cisterns and exhausted wells."

The boy looked at him quizzically. "You can't learn them. They got no words. An't no one understands them, anyway."

Orem pulled his wrap halfway down and hoisted himself to the lip of the cistern to empty himself. The voices came more clearly, an echo of wails and high singing that suddenly filled him with fear. Why should I be afraid? he wondered. Then he looked at the young thief and thought he saw murder in his eyes. Yes, murder, and what better time than now, with Orem helplessly over a pit that went deep into the earth where no one would find the corpse even if anyone bothered to look for a scrawny young man with a pauper's pass. The boy could just run up and push him and he'd be dead. And there—yes, the boy was poised, wasn't he? And leaning in! "Stay back, or by God—" And then his bowels opened and emptied and he sprang from the cistern wall and backed away from the thief.

"Just a fancy," the boy said, smiling. "Didn't mean nothing. Meant just to put a scare in you."

Orem did as the boy had done, wiped himself and then his hand in the dirt. Then he pulled up his wrap. He was trembling. Not just because the child had thought to kill him, but because the voice in the cistern had seemed to warn him so. Was this, perhaps, a touch of true magic? For the first time in his life had a spell touched him?

"I'm sorry," said the boy, watching Orem's face. "It was a joke."

Orem said nothing, just walked from the cistern and out into the road. Only a few steps and he knew where he was, Piss Road, with Piss Gate at the western end of it.

"Don't leave me," said the boy.

Orem faced him angrily. "Don't you know when you're not wanted?"

"My name is Flea Buzz."

"I don't want your name."

"I'm telling you anyway. It was the name my mother gave me. She's from Brack, it's ever so far to the east, she was stolen by sea pirates and eventually ended up here as a pisser. She got a pass. They give names like Flea Buzz there, because it was the first thing she saw and first thing she heard after I was born. Her husband is dead at the bottom of the sea. He has pearls instead of eyes."

"What makes you think I care?"

"You're listening, aren't you? Anyway, it's all lies. My father, he's alive enough. He calls me Pin Prick, and worse things when he's angry. He's got no pass, so he has to hide in the Swamp when the guards come. I get no pass until my mother marries another pass man. So I steal. I do all right. I'll steal for you, if you like."

"I don't want you to steal for me."

"The truth is my father's dead. My mother killed him when he went at her with a club. We buried him in the garden. He'll be flowers all over if the dogs don't open him up. Only last night."

"It's a lie."

"Only partly. Let me come with you."

"Why? What do I have that you want? If you think I'll give you a copper to leave me alone you're going to weep at the tale I have to tell."

"My mother's gone, pass and all."

"What's that to me?"

"Her lover took her away after they killed my dad."

Lover. It was a strange word. What part had love in Inwit? Yet the boy looked afraid, his eyes looked weak and he was ready to spring, ready to run at a word. Was this true, then? Had he no parents?

"I've got nothing," Orem said. "Little enough for me, nothing for you."

"I know the city. I'll be useful."

"I'll find my own way."

"If the guard catches me I can be your brother, and then I won't lose an ear for having no pass."

It hadn't occurred to Orem. That they'd take an ear from a child.

"They wouldn't."

"God's name they would."

What did he need with a boy along? Make it look like he was trying to feed a family, like he wasn't free, get in his way, keep him from a job most likely. Go away. "Come on then."

Flea Buzz grinned, and suddenly all the pathos was gone. Was he a fraud, after all? Orem cursed himself for a fool. Yet he did not send him away, even so.

"What's your name," asked the boy.

"They call me Scanthips."

"By God, a name that's worse than mine."

"I'll call you Flea. That's not a bad name."

"And I'll call you Scant."

"You'll call me Sir."

"Like hell. Come on, them as I've heard was hired was hired on Shop Street." And they plunged into the crowd on Piss Road.

Flea was a companion such as Orem had never had before. He was so jaunty that even the coldness of the shopkeepers was cause for laughter. Flea would bow and elaborately compliment the shopkeepers that they met—those that didn't drive them out immediately. And when they had been sent away, Flea would parody and mock. "Oh, I love you like a son, but if I had a son I'd have to send him away without work, lads, you must understand, times is so hard that if it goes on like this another twenty years I'll waste away and die myself, die myself!"

Orem laughed often because of Flea, and covered far more ground because Flea knew his way through Inwit, but by late afternoon it was clear there'd be no work for him on Shop Street. He needed to rest, and Flea led him into the huge cemetery. The trees were a haven to Orem, like a touch of home, even if there was no underbrush and the trees were cropped and tame. A touch of home, only there were no birds. Orem noticed it and said so.

"The dead take them and ride," Flea said. "They go everywhere on birds' backs. It's why you never kill a bird. There might be a spirit there who can't get home, and he'll haunt you forever."

"The dead are gathered up in the nets of God," Orem said.

Flea looked at him blankly. "I thought you weren't a priest."

"I'm not anything if I don't find work," Orem said. "A man *is* what he does to earn his bread. A carpenter, a farmer, a halfpriest, or a beggar."

"Or a thief?" asked Flea. There was an edge of anger to his voice.

"Why not, if it's how you live?"

"I steal, Scant, but that's not what I *am*."

"What are you, then?"

"A man *is* the greatest, boldest thing he dares to do. *I* play the snakes."

Orem shrugged. "I don't know what that means."

Flea grinned. "Then you'll have to see, won't you, Scant."

AT THE SNAKEPIT

Orem guessed they were near the Swamp when the smell of the town became a reek, and what huts there were stood on stilts. "Got to stick tight to me," Flea said. "There's sinking sands here, and clay sucks you down, if you step in the wrong place. Stick tight."

Orem stayed right behind him, imitating as best he could the intricate path that Flea followed among the great-rooted trees and the cattail stands. After what felt like a mile through the meaningless maze, Flea abruptly stopped. Orem jostled him.

"Stand back," said Flea. "You never know what the snake's going to do."

Flea picked up a stick with a short fork at the end—it looked as if it had been cut that way. He dug with it, scraping dirt away from a board hidden in the ground. Then he pried under the edge of the board. A high whining sound came from the hole. Orem flinched involuntarily. Not a child in Burland didn't know that the whine of a keener meant death if you didn't get away. They lived only in places like this, where the country couldn't decide whether it was lake or land. It was as good a reason to stay away from swamps as any.

Flea laughed, but not at Orem. "Three days, and he didn't suffocate. Now that's luck, that's luck!"

Orem watched with fascination as Flea inched the board open, always with the stick. When a keener moved, it moved like a bird, quick and invisible until it stopped again. And there it was, a flash of green skittering over the ground, straight toward the nearest standing water. It got no farther than a few feet away, though, and then it lay wriggling, neck neatly pinned under Flea's stick.

"Can I trust you with my life?" Flea asked.

"Today."

"Then hold this stick and don't let up the pressure."

"No."

"Once this keener hits water and drinks, it'll follow us out of the swamp, you know that."

"Tale to frighten children."

"Tell it to the dead children in Swamptown."

Orem walked over and took the stick. At the faint change in pressure the keener let out a high wail, but Orem held firm. Flea laughed nervously. "That's right, that's right, hold her tight, they say she's just like a woman, lots of music and death when she bites." Orem knew that Flea was just talking to hear the sound of his own voice. The snake began flapping its whole body from the stick down, slapping out with the tail. Flea showed no sign of paying attention to *that*—he reached out his hand and pinched the keener tightly right behind where the stick had it, then pulled slowly backward until the head was drawn tight up against the stick. The keener made a choking sound, but Flea was humming. Now he dared reach right up behind the jaw; he took a tight, tight grip. "Not yet," he whispered. The snake wailed. Flea drew his left hand down the snake's writhing body until he had hold of the tip of the tail as well. "Now let go."

Orem waited another second, afraid.

"Let go, you want to strangle it?"

He let go. Immediately the snake writhed violently in terrible shudders and spasms; Flea held on. The snake whined, the snake cried out, for all the world as if its child had died. Flea giggled in relief. "Tricky, that. Tricky, tricky. If you don't hold the tail it flips you in the eye, you know, and you drop it and it gets you. Now come on. The pit's a ways on."

Orem had hoped that catching the snake would be bravery enough for one day. He would gladly have left Flea then, but he didn't know the way out of the Swamp.

The snake pit was not deep—there could be no deep pits in the Swamp, for the water would seep into any cavity. They had only been there a few moments when other boys began arriving, each holding a keener by the neck.

"Flea!" called several, and "Buzzer!" Flea thrust his keener's head toward them playfully. A few of them eyed Orem.

"Scant," said Flea, by way of introduction. "He's a pisser, but he'll do."

One by one the boys came to the edge of the pit and cast in the snakes. Each keener immediately rushed to the water and drank. Then they began trying to slither out, toward the boys. Each snake that came close to the edge was flipped back with a forked stick. The sound of a funeral filled the clearing as the keeners wailed and whined.

"You, Scant," said a boy. "You got no stick, you do the rats."

Rats? Flea was quick to fill in what Orem didn't know. "Off to your right, there, in the castle."

The "castle" was a fence of stones, roofed with wood. Inside were whimpering and scurrying rats. Orem was not delighted at the prospect of reaching in to take one out. Again Flea advised him. "Take the bag and hold it ready and open a stone in the wall." Orem did it clumsily once, and the first rat got away; the second two went into the bag, and then he was able to kick the rock back into place well enough to keep the others in. The rats fought each other and struggled in the bag, lunging every direction and making it hard to hold.

"Got two?"

Orem nodded at the boy who spoke, the only one who looked to be about Orem's own age.

"I suppose you don't want to grab just one."

Orem shrugged. Not good to label himself a coward. "Whichever way you want it."

"One then. And heave it right in the middle." The older boy didn't bother watching him—he had to keep flipping keeners back into the water in the middle of the pit.

Orem held the mouth of the bag with one hand and used the other to squeeze the bag between the rats. The one in the dead end of the bag he sealed off by holding the bag between his knees at that point. Then he carefully worked the bag smaller until the rat at the open end was tightly trapped and squealing so it could not move. Carefully Orem manipulated the rat until its back was to the mouth of the bag. I may get piss on my fingers but it's better than teeth.

Carefully he opened the mouth against the resistance of the fingers of his other hand and probed the body of the rat until he found a back leg. Then he released the mouth of the bag and pulled on the rat all at once, and with a single motion flicked it out into the snakes.

If he had hoped for a murmur of admiration he was disappointed. The rat landed near the middle of the pit, but immediately the boys were watching the performance of their snakes. The keeners went dead silent and the rat hung between the mouths of a dozen snakes, all of which had a hold. The rat hardly had time to squeal, it had so much poison in it: blood spurted from its mouth, vomiting forth from the deepest part of its bowel, and then it was just fur and mange and meat. The snakes struggled and pulled, and the rat fell apart. Some snakes came away with nothing, some with patches of fur, and finally there were two snakes left attached to the rat, both swallowing furiously until they met fang to fang, jaws distended by the rat they held.

The two boys whose snakes were thus joined hooted congratulations to each other. They had won the first part of the contest. It was the end of their snakes' part in the proceedings, however, for now the other snakes began howling and snapping at them. Keeners are not easily poisoned by their own venom, but with a dozen bites they began to sicken, and with a hundred bites they died. Now the other snakes began biting and trying to eat everything. Some of them died with the body of another keener halfway into their bellies; some died with nothing; and at the end of it, when all was still, the boys came nearer to take a tally. Which of the snakes had swallowed how much of the others?

Orem tried to decipher what the game meant. Those whose snakes were off alone, neither eaten nor eating, apparently were out of things—they grumbled and wandered off. The rest of the boys estimated how deeply a snake had been swallowed before it died, and the boys paired off according to the pairing of the keeners, always with one boy triumphant, the other grim-faced. For the first time it occurred to Orem that none of these boys had money. What was the wager, then? What was the forfeit for those who lost?

"Yours most eaten," said the oldest boy to a younger one.

"Chew yourself," said the loser. "It was a short snake."

"I said," said the older one.

"I said chew yourself. Yours is most eaten."

Orem looked at the snakes and thought the younger boy might well be right. He also thought that unless the forfeit was something dire, it wouldn't be worth arguing the point, for the older boy had an air of cheerfulness that was frightening.

"I say not."

The younger boy looked frightened, but still defiant. "I didn't come here to get cheated by a chewer like you," he said loudly. The other boys began backing away.

"Not I," said the older boy. "I think not I. I say not I. You say it too. Not I."

"Not *I*!"

Now a touch to the chest, a step back, a shove, a step. Orem had seen the look on the older boy's face before—it was the faces of Cressam and Morram and Hob when they thrust him into the haystack to burn him alive.

"Hop, it's nothing," said Flea. Who was Hop? Was Flea trying to placate the older boy or reassure the younger one that losing to him wouldn't be too bad? Orem couldn't tell, for neither boy gave a sign of hearing. The argument was no longer about the snakes. It was about who would do the other one's will.

And then it ended. The younger boy pushed back, just once, and the older one had him by the hands and flipped him pitward in one motion. At first Orem was only sickened at the thought of landing on the corpses of the snakes. Then he discovered that the keeners were not dead. They were only sluggish, only quiet. When the boy landed on the snakes in the water, some of them came alive, quickly enough that the boy came up with five or six snakes dangling from him. Orem could not help himself—he screamed with the boy's own terror. Bad enough the fangs puncturing the skin like sewing needles, but the one snake hung from his eye as if it had grown from there. The boy doubled over and seemed to vomit all the blood of his body. Then he dropped and lay still as the rat had lain, with the snakes fruitlessly trying to open their mouths wide enough to swallow him whole.

For some reason all Orem could think of was the Hound taking Glasin Grocer's shoulder in its maw and tearing away at the flesh. Yet this was no such worthy sacrifice. The boy was acrawl with snakes that fondled him with their bodies and tickled him with their darting tongues, yet Orem could not turn away.

"Seen enough?" Flea asked softly.

Orem could not speak.

"We go now," said Flea, "or we don't get out of the Swamp alive, it's that short. Coming?"

"In High Waterswatch," Orem said, "we wrestled and spun tops. That's how we played."

"There's no name for a man in *that*," said Flea. "But I remember you were quick enough to grab my balls for the sake of four coppers."

Orem followed Flea out of the Swamp, hearing the wails of the keeners behind him all the way. Only when they reached the shanties did Orem realize he was still holding the bag with the rat. Impulsively he swung it hard against the wall of a house.

"Name of God!" cried Flea. "What are you doing?"

"Is the rat so precious to you?" Orem asked.

"Not the rat, Scant, the house. If you break a hole in their wall, you might as well have killed them come winter, if they can't find a patch."

The house was sacred, but a boy could die for nothing in the Swamp. Orem handed Flea the bag. Flea turned it upside down and let the rat out. The animal was not dead, but the blow against the wall had left it dazed. It lurched drunkenly forward. Flea aimed a kick at it and sent it flying thirty yards, wriggling in the air as it flew.

"What was the forfeit?" Orem asked. "For the boys who lost."

Flea shrugged. "Just a little game of plug-the-hole. Hop shouldn't have argued. He has a sister to pay it for him."

"Do *you* have a sister?" asked Orem.

"No," Flea said. "But I don't lose." He grinned. "I'm a good judge of keeners."

"Why do you do it?" Orem asked. "Why do you play so close to dying?"

Flea shrugged. "It's who I am."

THE SECRET OF THE FOUNTAIN

Orem insisted he could find his own way home from Wood
Road, and they parted, planning to meet in the morning to
continue Orem's search for work. Orem had one errand to run
before returning to the inn. He found his way through the
darkening, emptying streets to the Little Temple, and a halfpriest
showed him the fountain where strangers always came.

The fountain wasn't much. No one asked him to pay or
even wanted a gift; he went to the fountain and poured out his
flask of spring water. He wasn't sure what prayer it was they
said here, so he murmured a prayer for his father, then dipped
the flask again to take up the sacred water that Glasin had told
him was so valuable.

Before he left, he looked into the water to see how the
fountain was filled, to find the place where the water of
spring came in. He looked for a little while before he realized
there was no such place. It was just a pool, not a fountain at
all. He poured out the water untasted. The fountain was filled
by all the visitors to Inwit, who left the water of their home
behind and took away nothing of Inwit at all, but just the
half-evaporated gifts of the other fools. A fraud, of course, a
cheat. Orem almost spat into the water, but stopped when he
remembered that the next visitor did not deserve any harm
from him. He could have shared his water with Flea, if he
had known. That's what made him angriest, that he had been
ungenerous with his water.

Back at the Spade and Grave the innmaster demanded
another copper.

"But I paid last night for two nights."

"I know it. The other copper's for tomorrow."

"But that's one night. It should be a half-copper."

"Stay and use it twice." And that was all. The pass was
for three days, the rooms for two and two, take it or leave it.
At least they let Orem have a bowl of soup. They had
consciences, too.

14

Servants

I never knew what seeing was except coming out of the fog.
So said Orem, the Little King; so he said to me when he
thought he was not wise.

THE QUEEN'S WATER

It hardly seemed morning when Orem came out of the inn,
the fog was so thick. Buildings across the street were invisible until he was in the middle of the road. Other walkers in
the early morning loomed suddenly, nearly colliding with
him. He had to walk slowly and watch carefully. There were
curses here and there; now and then the sound of an argument
about whether someone was blind or just a fool. Orem was
afraid of getting lost, and wasting his last full day in the city,
but Flea found him.

"What's fog?" Flea said. "If we let fog keep us indoors
here, there'd be damn little work done in Inwit. For me it's a
golden day. I've had three coppers already without even a
knife to cut a purse."

It made Orem uneasy to know he was companioned with a
thief, but he had no other guide, and on a day like this he
needed Flea more than ever. They had tried the north side
yesterday. Today they went east, hoping to find work for
Orem in a counting house, somewhere that his literacy might
make him valuable.

But it was not readers and writers and counters that they
wanted in the eastern part of the city. It was boys, for the
cruel sports of Gaming, for the beds of the pederasts—boys
who could disappear and no one would care to look for them.
Twice Orem talked them into a place where they should not
have been; twice Flea had to get them out, and not by talking.
They left a gamer nursing a well-kicked crotch. They were in
more danger in the Great Exchange, for when they refused

the lucrative offer of a pimp of a banker, he raised a cry of thief. The fog saved them, that and Flea's ability to find his way through places that adults would not think to look. They found themselves in late afternoon, exhausted from running, near the end of the aqueduct.

The great waterbearing arches ended their progress before fully crossing the street. At the foot of the arch was a small pool of water overseen by guards and surrounded by queues of people waiting to dip and fill a flask, a jar, a watering bag.

"Thirsty?" asked Flea.

"Would it be safe for us to wait so long here? Are you sure they won't follow us further?"

Flea grinned. "Let's see if we can make the line shorter." He walked between queues to a place fairly near the pool, and then with a broad gesture he loudly said, "The kindness of the Queen."

Someone close by hushed them softly, but the others pretended not to hear. "Water," said Flea, "from the great Water House in the Castle. A spring that runs strong all year, without digging, just flows, and out of her kindness the Queen lets fully half the water flow down into the city. And after water has been piped down into the rich houses on either side of Queen's Road, and after the Temple has its water and the Guilds have their water and the water falls in the Park, then there's a bit that dribbles out here and fills a pool for the people of Inwit."

The speech did its work. They were alone at their spot at the pool, for those ahead of them and behind had moved away, separated themselves from the loud discussion of the Queen. Yet nothing treasonous had been said; the guards could only glower as Orem dipped his flask into the water and brought it up brimming. He did not drink, however. Rather he handed the water to Flea, deliberately letting a little spill on the boy's hands as he reached to take it. Flea looked at him in surprise, and then gravely sloshed the water back at him. It was only fitting to do the sharing of water, even if Flea was a thief, and Orem once nearly a Godsman.

A Servant's Servant

They rested north of the pool, by the mouth of a wide alley
that ran between two great houses. Liveried servants made a
heavy traffic in and out of the alley. Orem watched them, all
so busy, all so important, yet time enough for a smile or a
nod at each other, regardless of livery. Oh, there were some
who passed cold as you please, Orem saw, but even that was
so pointed that it was a sign of a quarrel—there were no
strangers among the servants.

"Forget it," said Flea.

"Forget what?"

"You'll never get hired by one of the great houses. You'll
never get past the gateman."

"Then let's not go to the front gate."

Flea refused to go. "If we go back there they'll think for
sure we're thieves."

"We got away once," said Orem.

"We damn near didn't," answered Flea.

"You play with the snakes, and you're afraid of the servants?"

So Flea went in with him, but this time hung back, forcing
Orem to lead the way. The street quickly narrowed, and though
the fog still lingered, it only greyed the buildings on left
and right. At first there were still gates, for a few of the
lesser great houses fronted into the alley rather than the
street. Then the gates ceased, and suddenly the street widened
to a plaza between the high-walled houses. Within the plaza
a little maze of streets, and along the streets little wooden
miniatures of the great stone buildings. Were there stone
colonnades in the great housefronts? Then there were intricately
lathed wooden posts here. Were the great houses pierced with
many large windows, all barred? Then these small homes
were festooned with small windows, and wooden bars echoed
the bronze and iron of the masters. The servants imitated
their masters as best they could, though their small homes
stood among the kitchens of their lords.

Orem had no notion where to go, now that he was here. He
had expected someone to challenge them, but no one did. In
fact there were others without livery, dressed as simply as he.
It gave him hope. There might indeed be work here.

"It's like a little city," Flea whispered.

"Come on," Orem answered. He strode boldly toward the back gate of a great house, where the kitchen fires burned hot and smoky, sending more fog to thicken and yellow the light.

"Ho, boys!" An old man watched them from the portico of a wooden house.

"Ho, old man!" Orem answered.

"You want work?" the old man asked.

"Nothing less," said Orem.

"Ah, yes, wanting work, all the world wanting work except those who presently have employment. And except for me. I'm handsomely pensioned and I sit on a porch all day and hollo to boys in hopelessly rustic clothing. Do you know that within the house, those who buttle and those who kitch and those who bake and those who wait, they know you're coming?"

"They know? How?"

"The odor of a farmboy and a Swamptown lad can be smelt from rods off. The uncouth clop of your sandals on our stony walks can be heard even farther off, and the rough accents of your speech betray you more than anything. You were seen as you walked from the public fountain. You were noted as you squatted by the portals of our humble alley. And now you are being examined by an old man who has nothing better to do than turn away the pathetic strangers who think there's work for them here."

Orem had been turned away too many times now; he had lost his fear of the rejectors. "There's work here. Why shouldn't I do it?"

The old man cackled. "Oh, you *should*, you *should*—but you can't. Any man can learn to be a noble or a beggar, but you must be *born* a true servant."

"I was born to be a cleric or a soldier," Orem said. "I'm not meek enough for the one and not strong enough for the other. Why shouldn't I learn to do what servants do? Someone had to be the first servant—who taught *him*?"

"There, that's the first thing you have to lose—that insolent manner."

"Let's go," said Flea. "He just wants to talk."

The old man heard him, and shouted angrily. "Go away,

then! If you don't want what I have to offer, go away! You'll get no second chance from me!"

"What are you offering?" asked Orem.

"A job and a pass. Does that mean anything to you?"

So they stayed and listened. He beckoned them within his gate, and soon they stood before the old man, who grinned toothily up at them. His teeth were all bronze. It turned him into a statue, at least at the mouth. It was like a miracle watching him speak.

"Stand, yes, stand, that's what a servant does when his lord speaks. Stand and look at me respectfully, and don't glance away, no, and listen to every word in case I ask you a question. You can't ever be caught not hearing what I say. And stand with your foot back so, with a bow always ready, and an answer quick to your lips. You call your own master 'honored sir,' and his son is 'new master' and his second son and all his daughters are 'blest one' and his third son and later are 'hopeless sir,' said always gravely with the right respect and a touch of irony so they'll know you are their friend, though their father is not. And if the man is master of another house, he is 'esteemed sir' unless he and your master are not on good terms, at which time he becomes 'most high and noble eminence,' which is said utterly without irony lest he take its phallic meaning, and his wife you call 'esteemed lady' if she is a friend, but if your lord despises her she is 'most fecund mother of a noble lineage,' and if your lady despises her she is 'envy of nations' and if both despise her you say nothing to her but bow low and touch your brow to the ground, which will be unbearable insult to her but she dare not answer. Have you understood that? Can you do it now?"

"It's all shit, if you ask me," Flea said.

"But you, young fellow, tall and thin as the last smoke from a censer, you have another idea."

Orem smiled. "We had it just as hard at the House of God. If you speak to God with sins heavy in your heart, but there is other company and you want no questions, address God as Holy One Who Dwelleth in Heaven. If you're willing to confess your sins and your repentance, then you address Him as Holy Father Who Loveth the Weak. If you're praying for a company of your betters, the name of God is Master of the Brethren, but if you're praying for a company of common folk or if the company is mixed, you call Him Creator of All, First and Foremost, and if the King is present you—''

"Enough, enough!" cried the old man. "So you trained for a priest, did you?"

"Enough to know I'd never be a priest."

"And never a servant in a great house, either. It's not anyone wishing you ill. Not at all. We wish you well. But a servant's work is to be invisible, to have all done silently; a servant's work is to have no sign that work is done at all. A servant steps his steps like a dancer. An art, that's what it is. An art, and we're born to it and raised to it, and there's no hope for someone stumbling into it. What if the master has had too much wine, and yet asks for more?"

Orem smiled a little and shrugged. How could he know?

"Do you water his wine? Never. Do you refuse him, or give him half a glass? Never. No, you add the strongest gin you can find, so that the next glass puts him out, and then you gracefully stand beside him and bid his guests good-bye in his name, one by one, and they all touch his hand as they leave, so that in the morning you tell him, 'You shook hands with everyone as they left.' No one thinks ill of him because it was done gracefully, and though he knows the truth of what you did he doesn't mind because that's the way it's done. We are what keeps all going smoothly in Inwit. Who do you think serves in the palace? We, the fifty families. We are the only servants of Inwit and have been from the beginning. Back when God was still telling his name to strangers, we were passing the bread and bearing the meat. Does the House of Grell need a boy for stairs? I have a nephew. Does the House of Bran need a woman for children? My wife does children and teaches them dancing, too. My family is the Family Dyer, and we have a man or woman placed in every great house, and with responsibility, too. Nothing happens on Queen's Road but what we know of it.''

My feet hurt, thought Orem. What is your offer?

"Do you think these lords rule anything? Nonsense. *We* do. It's one of us who's major-domo, lording the house. Who is his steward caring for his lands, if not one of us? Oh, the master makes his decisions, but who gives him all the information he uses to decide? We are the masters of Inwit, we are the ebb and flow of everything. We give them allowances and they think that they are the ones who pay *us*! They even think they *hire* us!''

''But the offer you spoke of, what could you need *us* for?''

The old man leaned forward and smiled. ''Well, you see, while we're off tending to *their* estate, what of our own houses? We have lovely houses here, you know, the finest in Inwit, saving our masters' own. Who serves in the house of the servant? That's what we want you for.''

The servant of a servant. That's my pass. That's my entry into Inwit. Orem did not feel triumphant at getting work. Instead he kept trying to think if he had ever heard a song about a servant.

''How much?'' Flea asked.

''Two coppers a week,'' said the old man. ''Two coppers a week, and an afternoon off, another on holy days if you worship God, and room and two meals besides.''

''Two coppers,'' said Flea, awed.

''Here's the best. You'll wed here, you'll bed here, you'll sire here and your *sons*, your *daughters*, they'll do what you cannot. *They'll* wear the livery, *they'll* learn the words and times, *they'll* stand at the elbow of great men and be part of our family, the family Dyer, and do us proud forever. You'll be the sires of members of the fifty families, though you'll never belong to us yourselves.''

Orem knew then that he must turn it down. He did not understand why, not for a moment. It was work, it was a way to stay inside Inwit, but it was unbearable. His sons and daughters servants, and their sons and daughters, forever and ever, all his children bowing and vanishing, cooking and vanishing, cleaning and vanishing. ''No,'' Orem said. ''Thank you, sir, but no.''

Flea grabbed at his shirt, pulled so hard that the fabric cut at his neck. ''God's name, Scant, this is it! You don't bargain with passes and two a week!''

''The young one's crude but correct,'' the old man said. ''I won't bargain. I know I'm being generous.''

''I'm not bargaining,'' Orem said.

''Then what?'' asked the old man.

''Turning you down.''

''Then you're a fool,'' he said contemptuously.

''Yes. No doubt of it.''

"What about me?" Flea asked the old man. "Will you take me without him?"

The old man smiled thinly. "At one a week. This one can read. The two a week was for his sake, because you came together."

"One or two a week, fine with me."

"Stay, then, Flea," Orem said. "Thank you for everything. God's gifts with you." He nodded and stepped from the porch. His father had been a mere farmer, too poor to give a portion to his seventh son, but he had been a freeman, and his son was also free, and he would not bring children into the world less free than he was.

He was out of the alley, striding on into the darkening, deepening fog when he heard footsteps behind him. He knew the runner. "Flea," he said.

"You chewer," said Flea.

"That's as may be."

"Two meals a day and coppers besides. Why not, in the name of my mother's blood?"

"I came to Inwit for a name and a place and a poem."

"I thought you came for work."

"Why work? To keep yourself alive. But then, why live? Not for *that*. Don't blame me. You could have stayed."

"You chewer. I thought you knew what you were doing. A poem! My father's piss!" And Flea spat on the ground for emphasis.

"Then go back."

"I will."

"All right then."

"Tomorrow."

They walked on in silence, and stood together at the door of the Spade and Grave. The fog was deep, the night was on them, all but a faint glow above the roofs; the lanterns were lit pathetically, as if they had a chance to cast a light in air so wet. "What sort of poem?" Flea asked softly.

"A true one."

"Such a poem for you, Scanthips?"

"Why not?"

"Heroes do great things."

"I mean to do them."

"My mother's eyes."

"And there's no hope for a servant of a servant."

"So what now, Scant? Tomorrow you got no pass."

"Then I'll go out. And come back in."

"When your cheek is healed! Months from now!"

"I'll come back in another way."

Flea shook his head. "I don't know that end of the city. I don't know them as comes in that way."

"Good night, Flea," Orem said. "I'm a fool for sure. Go back to that old man and live well."

"Truest words I ever heard, God help you." And Flea stepped back away into the fog.

BARGAINS

Orem slept well that night, to his own surprise, and the next day he went downstairs and cheerfully told the innmaster to chew himself, though he still didn't know quite what that meant. Then he went to another inn and ate a copper's worth of breakfast, which made his stomach ache but tasted no worse for that. It was his gesture of defiance after nearly fasting for three days for his coppers' sake.

And as he left the inn, bellyheavy and content, he brushed past a small boy who was loitering at the door, not noticing who it was until he was a couple of steps into the street. Then he turned and said, "Flea!"

Flea looked annoyed. "You could have saved some of that food for me."

They fell into step, heading north toward Piss Road.

"I thought you'd have breakfast with that old man," said Orem. "I thought you'd given up on me."

"I should have," Flea said. "But I'm so damn dumb I believed what you said last night. If you can have a poem, Scant, why not me? I'll be twice your weight when I'm grown. My father hefted an axe for the King, my mother told me. Told me other things, other times, but who knows? Maybe."

"Maybe."

"Bring me along when you go to earn your song. Promise me."

"By my hope of a name and a poem, I promise," Orem said solemnly.

Flea answered nothing. Just silently touched Orem's hand

for a moment. And when his touch went, there were three coins in Orem's hand.

"No," Orem said.

"They aren't mine. You might as well have them."

"I can't take your coppers."

"Because I cut purse for them? I'll lie and say I found them if you like."

"You owe me nothing."

"You're going to put me in your poem. So let me help you get it started." And with that Flea ran off into the crowds of Piss Road.

Orem watched him out of sight, and still watched when Flea was utterly lost to him. He was in debt to a thief inside Inwit and to a liar of a carpenter outside. They were the closest thing to honorable men that he had found.

The line at the gate was as great as the line had been coming in, but that was because it was morning; this time the queue moved quickly on. Name, give over the pass, show the livid scar on the cheek, then through the door in the gate. For a moment he almost turned back, almost ran to the servants' alley and took a place with an old man, forgetting his childish dreaming. But then the line moved and they pushed him through, and he was glad.

There was Braisy, the weasely man, leaning against a wall watching the discouraged paupers leaving the gate's mouth. Orem walked boldly to the man.

"Five coppers," Orem said.

"A cheerful greeting. Five was all you had three days ago. What do you have now?"

"Five."

Braisy looked at him, eyebrow raised. "Resourceful little chewer, aren't you."

"Five. I want to go in the other way. If there's work there."

"I promise nothing. Hell, I don't even promise all the way in. I know the first portals, and the names of them as has names. More than you know, that's all. And it's five coppers to there."

"Then let's go."

"Eager little bastard, aren't you." Braisy licked his lips. "I tell you, maybe you're better to wait out here till your cheek's healed."

"What, trying to raise the price on me?"

Braisy studied him a moment, then smiled broadly. If he had had more teeth, Orem would have thought his smile menacing. "Well enough, then. Five coppers. Now."

"One now, one at the first door, the rest when I'm as far as you can take me, if I think it's far enough."

"Two now, three at the door."

"One now, two at the door, two at the end."

"Done. But show them all."

Orem stepped back and showed the coins from far enough that they could not be snatched away.

"Learned caution, have you?"

"One now." And he tossed the coin. Braisy caught it deftly, weighed it on a finger, and slipped it inside his shirt, under his arm. Must have a pouch there, Orem thought. I need a pouch, too. For safety. There are thieves who know how to snatch from a man's wrap.

That was why Orem broke the law to come through West Gate instead of choosing safety as a servant's servant. Tell me, Palicrovol, do you imagine that your son could choose otherwise?

15

The Hole

How Orem Scanthips was first recognized as he came into Inwit through the Hole.

A Shadow Does Not Know Him

Braisy led him on a twisting journey through Beggarstown that led at last to a tavern far from the twin towers of the Hole. It was not a bright-painted tavern like the Spade and Grave, but a dingy place, decayed outside and filthy and corrupt within. Braisy flashed a coin, and the innmaster nodded. The coin spun through the air. Before the innmaster caught it, Orem noticed that it was silver. Not copper at all. It was then that he became afraid. If Braisy's first bribe was so much greater than the whole fee Orem was paying him, it surely meant that someone else was paying Braisy for Orem's passage.

"I need to piss," Orem said.

"Not now," Braisy answered. He would not get out so easily. With a tight and painful grip on his arm Braisy hurried him up the stairs and into an open door.

Only a faint light came in through the cracks of a boarded up window. Someone else was in the room. It was too dark to see more than a looming shadow against the crack of light from the window. Heavy breathing from the shadow, and the stench of a foul mouth.

"Name." It was a whisper, and still Orem could not guess man or woman, old or young, kind or cruel.

"Orem."

"Name."

"They call me Scanthips."

"Name."

"Of Banningside. Orem Scanthips of Banningside."

More breathing. The shadow still did not believe him.

"Name of God it's true," said Orem.

A sigh like the softest whine of a keener. "I can tell neither truth nor lie."

"Stick him, then?" asked Braisy.

Orem braced himself to run—he'd not die of a blade in a place like this. But Braisy was strong, stronger than such a small man looked to be. And then the shadow's dry hand, crisp and light as paper, stroked his bare arm. "Safe, safe," came the whisper. "Safe, safe." And then a tiny prick on his arm, something edged like a razor or a sharp rock scraping off the blood that surely formed, and the shadow moved away.

"Sweet sweet Sister sister sister," came the hissing from a corner of the room. "Nothing, nothing."

"What then?" asked Braisy. His voice sounded like shouting, the room was so still.

"Pass or stay, stay or pass, all one, what can I tell?"

Hesitation.

"I need to piss."

Braisy's hand squeezed tighter on his arm. "Not now, not now, I'm thinking. What are you, boy?"

I'm scared of dying, that's what I am. You've taken my blood, name of God! Let me go. "Orem ap Avonap," he said. "Try that name."

The shadow returned quickly. "The son of Avonap? But that's a lie, a lie, a lie, there's no goldenwheat seed inside of you."

"Swear to God."

"There's word," said the shadow, "of a learned doctor."

"Would this boy be useful to him?"

"Who can say? Take the low way, low to Segrivaun, and ask for the glass of public death."

"Shit," muttered Braisy.

"Or nothing."

"And I say shit. But yes. Yes, the low way, damn you."

"And damn you," came the whisper.

Braisy dragged him now to a far corner of the room, where a deeper black waited in the black of the wall. Braisy stopped there and shoved him in. For a sickening moment he thought he was falling into a pit. Then his foot hit a step. Bad angle. He lurched, he stumbled down three more steps, and when he caught himself his foot was on fire with pain and he was frightened.

"Careful, boy," said Braisy.

"I can't see."

A door closed softly above them. Only then did Braisy try to strike a light. Click; spark. Click; spark. Click; light. A little flame in a wad of dry wool. With his bare hands Braisy gently and slowly moved the burning wool to a small lamp. It took. The stairway went down steeply, and didn't bend. The treads were only inches, the risers a foot at least, and it led far deeper into the darkness than ever the house could be. The low way.

And if I *do* escape, what then? Must remember my way back. Up the stairs, out this door however it opens, past the whispering shadow, left in the hall, down the stairs, and out. He made it a thread in his mind, a thread of words that became numbers and numbers that became words. Little mnemonics formed. Stone Road Bone Road. The stairs ended in a dirt tunnel that could not go straight for fifteen feet, with turns here and holes overhead and holes down and streams of filthy water crossing the path.

The dirt walls turned to brick, with gaps every few inches, narrow spaces a quarter of a brick wide. Out of some of them came a thin trickle of fluid. Was it raining above ground? Why did they build this place? Fly dog, sky dog, ice water, under water. The thread of the remembered path grew longer, and Orem wondered if he could hold it all in his mind. And all along the walls, the little slits.

The corridor tipped left and down, and the floor was slick hard mud with a thin skiff of water running over it. Orem's foot skidded. He braced himself against the wall. His longest finger slipped into a gap in the bricks. The water flowed down his arm.

"Name of God," Braisy said. "Get your hand out."

Orem retrieved his finger from the slit.

"Look at your arm."

It was wet. Braisy held the lamp over it, studied where the water had flowed. "Should be black. Should be black, boy. It's where they put the ashes of the dead. They fill up the slits with the ashes of the dead, and if you get the water on you, then you—but you don't turn black, do you? What are you, boy?"

They came to a stairway down. The water cascaded over the steps. They descended, a step at a time. Water began dripping from the arched bricks overhead. Now and then the lamp hissed when a drop struck it. Braisy seemed to wince with each drip that hit him.

"Quiet here," Braisy said softly. "The guards have tunnels through here, to listen for people like us, trying for the Hole. And if you think to call for help, remember this—everyone who's taken in the paths of the Hole always says they were forced, always claims they were lost in the Tombs. The guard cuts them up anyway, in little pieces, boy. Cuts them up in little pieces. Think of it before you shout for help."

The stairs stopped, and now it was rock overhead, not masonry. Here and there were posts to shore up the roof of the tunnel. The water ran sluggishly; where would it drain to, after all, at the bottom of the world?

"What are you going to do with me?" Orem whispered.

"Shut up," Braisy answered.

More twists and turns, and Orem felt the floor of the tunnel begin to incline. They were climbing now, and the water grew shallower and began to run against their path, downward, and finally they were on an upward climbing corkscrew through the rock. When the path had crossed itself three times, the stone walls and steps made way for wood.

"Slowly," whispered Braisy. "No squeaks, no creaks."

A step at a time, placing their feet at the edges of the stairs, they crept upward. Suddenly he cracked his head against a ceiling. There was a roof over them, smooth planks from side to side of the wooden stair, and the stair ran right up into it and stopped.

"That's right, knock," Braisy whispered. "Why not call out a greeting? We'll not pass you for bright, will we?" Braisy clambered awkwardly up beside him and reached with his finger until he found a hole in one of the planks. He waggled his finger around, then held the lamp up against the hole. The flame flattened, then leapt up. For more than a minute he held the lamp there, and then the board flew upward, and the one beside it, and the one beside that, until there was a way to climb out. The boards were subtly hinged and silent.

"Trying to burn us out?" asked an immense fat woman.

Her voice was soft but still had an edge to it. "Want to start a flame? Should we roast a rat over the hole? Braisy, you're a rutting hog, that's what you are, come up, come in."

Segrivaun

The woman gave them each a hand and pulled them into a room that was lit, to Orem's surprise, by daylight. Wasn't it night? Hadn't he been hours in the dark? Or could it be the next morning already? No, he wasn't *that* tired. There was no open window; just a few cracks in the wooden wall, with a roll of heavy black cloth tied above it, ready to be let down at night to hold candlelight inside. Orem wondered if this woman lived all her life here. Perhaps. It paid: Braisy handed her two silvers.

"Ah," said the fat woman. Her breasts hung well below her waist, as if she were smuggling grain sacks under her blouse. Her belly wagged to and fro when she walked. Her face, too, was draped with flesh; even her brow hung loosely over her eyes, and she actually lifted her forehead with her hand so she could look up and see Orem's face.

"What is he? Why this way? Surely not for the King, this one!"

"A shadow said to take him to you, Segrivaun, and you'd lead us to the glass of public death."

Segrivaun looked away, let her brows fall down over her eyes again. "For *him*?"

"Said he was wanting."

"Oh, yes, wanting. They brought what he wanted here just an hour ago, cloven hoof and two men binding. Only four horns, but enough, enough, a little one but enough. I want nothing of him. Go on, through here."

She led the way into a cavernous passageway. Forced to bend in the low tunnel, following right behind the woman, Orem couldn't hide from the stench of her; she was foul. But the way was not long. They came to a room with a round hole in the ceiling and two heavy ropes coming down. One rope was taut and tied to a stout iron ring bolted to the floor; the other was also taut but hung free through a hole near the ring, going down deeper into the house.

The fat woman positioned them opposite her and bade them stand away from the ropes, while she fairly enveloped the fastened one in her belly and breasts, holding to the free rope with both hands. She grunted and pulled down on the free rope. The floor rose under them.

Not the whole floor, but a circle of it, and it wobbled madly. They rose past one floor, past another, and finally stopped at the third. Segrivaun lifted them a few inches clear of the floor, then began rocking back and forth. It was a terrifying motion, and Orem couldn't balance fast enough to keep from falling. But when he fell, the platform fell also, and enough to the side of the hole that it stayed as Segrivaun stepped to the caught edge and held it there with her weight.

Braisy quickly took the lamp a few steps away, to where some heavy boards lay on the floor. He took one up, spanned the hole in the floor with it, it, and shoved it under the edge of the circle of wood. Segrivaun stepped off, and now apparently the need for whispering was through.

"Get up," Braisy said impatiently.

Orem stood, stepping back quickly from the circle and the hole. Fire searing, lecher leering, number finger, Stone Road, Bone Road. The thread was complete. Orem knew that now was his chance, if he swung into the hole and dropped to the floor below, then climbed down the free rope to the bottom, then retraced all his steps—

Segrivaun's huge hand closed on his arm. Orem tried to pull away.

"There's some tried it," Segrivaun said. "They're all dead, though. All got lost in the catacombs."

I won't.

"But Braisy's paid three silvers already, he doesn't want a dead one, does he, doesn't want a lost one. Come on."

Segrivaun opened a door, and they stepped into a tiny chamber. Braisy closed the door after them and set the lamp on a high shelf. He took a deep breath. "Strip," he said.

And meant it, for he began taking off all his clothes himself. Orem unbelted his shirt and pulled it over his head, uneasy at not knowing what was going to happen. Segrivaun, too, was undressing; modestly she turned her back to them and pulled acres of cloth over her head. Her buttocks, Orem saw, were as loose as her breasts, and nearly reached the floor.

"Take off your wrap, too," Braisy said. "And sandals."

Orem untied the sandals from his calves, let them drop to the ground. Braisy kicked them into a corner. Then, when Orem was too slow with his winder wrap, he yanked on it, pulled it free. The last of Orem's money dropped to the floor, rolled. Braisy had all three coins before they were still. "The last of what you owe me."

"Never miss a minim, do you?" the fat woman chuckled. She crossed her arms across her chest in a mockery of modesty; the huge black nipples of her dugs hung far below, where her hands could not possibly reach them. "They're ready in there, ready for sure."

Orem reached down and picked up his clothes, bundled them under his arm. Braisy reached out and knocked them down, then opened the door.

It was bright inside. A round room, with stone walls and no windows. A stairway came up one wall, curving. Candles hung all along the walls, and there was a small fire in a clay pot, which stank with some heavy, sweet smell that burned Orem's nose. The stones of the wall were so huge that Orem knew immediately that this was one of the towers of the Hole. One of the towers, and surely the towers were held by the guards; surely he was betrayed.

Then he saw the four-horned hart in the middle of the floor and he had no thought for walls and soldiers.

THE HART IN THE TOWER

The hart was alive, its eyes staring in terror. It lay on its back, a helpless and unnatural pose, its four legs tied and stretched off in the four directions, pegged to the floor. At the joint of the hind leg and the belly a cut had been made, and the hart's blood was pumping out in sluggish flows into a low copper pan held by an old man. An old man who was naked but for a deerskin over his shoulders: a doeskin, for the head was hornless where it rested on his grey and tousled hair.

"Hartkiller!" Orem cried softly. And in the moment that his name for the crime hung in the stony, silent air, the hart died. Its head went slack, its tongue lolled.

It was a deep voice that rumbled out from under the doe's skin. "A boy," he said. "And from High Waterswatch, where they keep the memory of the Hart. What have you brought me?''

''His name is—''

But Braisy was silenced by the wave of a hand. The old man's long-fingered hand seemed to have too many knuckles, too many joints. A single finger rose straight into the air, but from the back of the hand, so that the angle grew painful just to watch: all the other fingers straight down, and this single finger pointing upward.

And they waited. The hand did not waver.

The fat woman lumbered forward. The old man dipped a finger of his other hand into the copper pan and touched the bright bloody tip of his finger to her tongue. Braisy also tasted, and Orem, too, found the finger reaching for his tongue, and licked the cooling blood. It was sweet, it was sweet, and it burned all the way into his throat.

Braisy and Segrivaun stared at him with wide and frightened eyes. What was wrong? Orem grew afraid and looked behind him, but there was nothing there. It was he who frightened them. What change had the hart's blood wrought in him, that they should look at him with such horror?

''What is the price?'' asked Segrivaun in a high voice. ''Oh, God, a pilgrim's trap!''

Braisy giggled nervously. ''You didn't tell me, boy. Cheater, cheater, God hates all liars.''

Orem did not understand. What was this talk of God and pilgrims, with a hart bled to death on the floor, with the taste of hart's blood in all their mouths?

Something hot touched his leg. Orem looked down. It was the wizard's hand, still split wide like a keener's jaws, fastened to him.

''Not a pilgrim, are you?'' said the deep voice. It sounded kind. ''Not a pilgrim, and yet still we see you, we all see all, when all should have vanished at the taste of hart's blood.''

Vanished. They were supposed to disappear. And blamed the failure of it on him.

''Forgive me, Gallowglass,'' Segrivaun began.

''Forgive you? Forgive you a dozen silvers' worth, that's how I forgive you. What woe you've brought me. What trouble is here in this miserable boy. A dozen silvers, Segrivaun. You little know who guided your footsteps through the low way, Braisteneft. You little know who drew you up the spider's line, Segrivaun.''

Gallowglass stood. He was tall for an old man. He faced Orem with gaze level. "And so early, and so young. What haste."

Orem did not know what the old man meant. He only knew that Gallowglass's eyes were filled with tears, and yet his face looked acquisitive.

"How long will they let you stay, do you think?" he said softly, as if to himself. "Long enough, perhaps. Too long, perhaps. But worth this, yes. *If* you can learn—if *I* can teach—"

Abruptly Gallowglass's hand flew through the air, paused directly in front of Orem's face, and that single upraised finger lowered swiftly and sat upon Orem's eyeball. Rested on the open eye, yet Orem did not blink. He just stared at the pinkish black of the old man's finger, vaguely aware that it was hot. Suddenly the finger came into impossibly clear focus. Every whorl and twist was visible, and in them he could see, as if a hundred yards below, dizzyingly far down into the finger, thousands of people milling about, screaming, reaching upward to him out of the maze of whorls, pleading with him to release them.

"I can't," he whispered.

"Oh, but you can," said the wizard. And now his voice was not deep and old. It was adolescent, it was young. It was Orem's own voice, speaking to him out of the wizard's mouth. "You can. It is all I can do with hart's blood to contain you, even that long. What have you stolen from me just by being in the room?"

"Nothing," Orem said. What could he have stolen, naked as he was? The wizard took his finger from Orem's eye. Now the eye stung bitterly, and Orem clapped his hand there and rubbed as the tears flowed to soothe the parched glass of his vision. "Don't you know, Segrivaun, that a pilgrim would stay visible only himself? Yet you are also visible, and Braisteneft, and I, and the hart. No pilgrim. But something that is mine, surely mine. A full purse of silver, Braisteneft. Ten of silver for you, Lady Segrivaun. Enough? Enough?"

"Oh, enough, Gallowglass!" cried Braisy.

"Enough that there is no memory that such a boy was brought?"

"Already forgot."

"Enough that there is no memory of a hart whose blood failed when it was hot?"

"Already, my lord, forgot," said Segrivaun.

Gallowglass laughed. "You're both a hundred times forsworn a day. No, we swear by the Hart, yes? By the Hart." So they all, even Orem, knelt around the groin of the hart, each plunging a finger into the soft bloody slit of a wound, and all, even Orem, swore. It was a terrible oath, and Orem knew that his thread was cut in that moment. He remembered all his incantation, but there was no returning that way now.

A bag of silver changed hands. Orem knew what was happening. He had been sold. He was owned. He had left Inwit passless because he would not be a servant to a servant. Now he would be—something—to this Gallowglass. And not free.

And yet he did not mind.

The others left, and Gallowglass gave Orem his clothing. They dressed together, Orem in his dirty traveling clothes, Gallowglass in a deep green robe.

"What's happening to me?" Orem asked.

"You've been employed."

"For how long?"

"For life, I think, however long that is. But don't despair. You'll have the freedom of the city, and the best forged passes that money can buy, since with you I can't use spells to blind the guards. And all you have to do, my boy, is serve me."

"I only wanted to enter the city."

Gallowglass tossed him his belt. "And you have. Or will in a moment."

"What makes you think I *want* to work for you?"

Gallowglass only smiled kindly and patted the circled pattern on the front of his robe. It looked at first like the seven circles of a God's man. But it was eight circles. Two twos of twos. It was a fearsome thing to spell. For up it said, My blood. And down it said, Dry water. And spun down to the two and the two and the two and the two, it said, No hope.

"You're not afraid, are you, boy?"

"Yes."

"Tell me, how much magic have you seen in your life?"

"Some."

"But how much of it has actually worked in your sight?"

None. It was why he longed so for it. Magic was something that the others had spoken of, that all had seen from his infancy up, but never in his life had he seen the moment of change. For when he was there it never went right, no matter how hard they tried.

"That's right, boy. None of it. Never in your life. Your mother, did she do magic?"

He nodded.

"But sent you out of the house when she did, yes? When she wove, when she cooked, sent you out of the house."

He threatened to undam a flood of bitterness. "Yes," said Orem.

"They always sent you away. Why, boy? Why? When they said the spell of strength on you, it didn't work, did it? Never grew muscled, never grew strong. No village sergeant would have you, would he? For where you are, boy, wherever you are there's a hole in the fabric of the world. You're a Sink, lad. A Sink."

He had no notion what such a thing might be. Good or evil? If he means to punish me for it, I'll not take it without argument. "I'm Orem Scanthips."

"What do you think magic is, Scanthips?"

"Power. Bought with blood."

"Bought. Yes, that's the best you'd be able to know, I suppose. But it isn't buying. Not the way the merchants do, with their money. They separate earning from acquiring, with money in between, so the price can go up and down and lose its tie with the labor. So you can be cheated. But the prices in blood do not change."

"Earning, then."

"Not earning either, lad. For you can't *do* more and *get* more. It's there, in you, just there. In every living thing, according to the blood. The blood of life is a web, a net that we draw with us, catching the life of the world in it as we go. All the living blood draws in power, and holds it, so that when one like me, who knows the uses of that power, when I draw the hot blood I can shape, I can build, I can create and kill. But not your blood, Orem Scanthips. Oh, you catch the life as it passes, yes, the power flows into you like anyone else. Better than others, for your web is great, it trails with you, settles out around you, draws life and power from everyone, draws them to you. But do you fill with power? Is there greater strength in you?''

''No?''

''You rob the magic right from the blood, but then it drains from you, drains back into the earth, waiting for the trees and grass to suck it up, waiting for it to melt into the air, to be eaten by the cattle, to settle into the blood of other men again. You can't use it. It just drains through you and it's gone.''

''How much?''

''You drained the blood of a whole hart in an instant, Scanthips. That's power, lad. There's no limit to you. Sisters, Sisters, no limit to you except for the shape of your nets, Lord Fisher, the placement of your web, Master Spider. I will teach you.''

''Teach me?''

''How to place your web. How to swallow power where and when you wish. You will rob for me, undo the magic wherever I tell you. Who can resist me then? Who will compete with Gallowglass? Challenge me, all of you, and my Sink, my Scanthips, he will worm to the heart of your power and drink you dry.''

''Why you?''

''Because you came to me. It was no accident. Power comes to you, and you come to power. I am the greatest of the learned doctors of Wizard Street. You came to *me* for power. Oh, it's a risk I'm taking, a sacrifice I'm making. How quickly will you learn? Until you do, there's no magic in my house. You're a danger to me. If you get too dangerous, of course, I'll kill you. So learn quickly, lad. Learn quickly.''

''I will.''

''All my life I've read the stories of Sinks, but never thought I'd live to see one. Follow me, lad.''

The road out was as difficult as the road in, but now Orem did not bother trying to memorize the path. He had come to the Inwit that he had dreamed of, the Inwit of old magic from the time before God.

At last they stood in a darkened house, and saw the silhouette of the two towers far away. ''West Gate,'' said Gallowglass. ''Beauty closed it only a year after Palicrovol left the city. But West Gate wasn't its true name even then. Before Palicrovol, it was the main gate of the city. Hind's Trace, that was its name, and the ancient city wasn't Inwit, but Hart's Hope. Hart's Hope, for long before the seven circles were carved on God's Gate they lit the hundred-pointed candlestick in the halls of the great houses. And they didn't go to Great Temple then. The pilgrims came to Shrine Street, to the little broken tree that will not die. Even Palicrovol, who thinks he's a Godsman, *he* even knows the truth. Do you think that in three hundred years he has forgotten that he forsook the Hart?''

Then the wizard sent him out into the street while he magically hid the entrance to the passageway. Sent him with a warning: You have no pass, don't try to escape. But Orem did not want to escape. As he stood in the dusky street he was joyful. Hart's Hope. Hind's Trace. The broken tree that would not die. Shrine Street. The city that was before God came. It was the city Orem had come to find.

16

The Taste of Power

How Orem learned the death that gnawed at the heart of the world.

IN THE WIZARD'S HOUSE

Like all the wizards of Inwit in that day, Gallowglass lived on Wizard Street. His house looked common enough and modest from the outside. Its only advertisement was a horseshoe on a nail, for it had once been a blacksmith shop. The hinges were in such disarray that doors seemed more to lean than close, and a shutter flapped clumsily in the breeze that sighed up the street. There was dust on the porch that seemed to have been undisturbed for years. Yet the wizard seemed to see nothing amiss as he climbed the step, took hold of a door, and eased it out of the way.

"In in in," he whispered. Orem went in, ducking to avoid a heavily laden spider web whose surly mistress seemed resentful at being disturbed. It was dark inside, and darker yet when the wizard stepped within and pulled the door closed behind him.

"Lamp lamp," he said, searching in the darkness.

"What *is* this place?"

"The heavenly hearth, the kindly fire, the keeper of the heart, the place of rest and comfort. In a word, my domicile."

Gallowglass found a match. He struck once, twice; it wouldn't light. Matches had spells on them, everyone knew that, and now Orem understood why his mother sent him out of the house whenever she had to relight the kitchen fire. Gallowglass put down the matches. "We must teach you quickly, mustn't we."

He lit a flame the unmagical way. "Flint and steel, stone and ore, yes, yes, here." Gallowglass was much less deft at it than Braisy. At last there came a spark and a small fire, not on wool, but on a piece of paper. Burning paper was something Orem had never seen done before. Paper was far too precious in the House of God in Banningside. Yet it made a light, and Orem looked around the place while Gallowglass lit the lamp.

It was a cramped and crowded room, with things stacked in a hopeless jumble on shelves that sagged along the walls. There were piles on the floor, too, and on the steps of the steep and narrow stair that led to a room above. There were three large barrels against the northern wall, unmarked, yet damp and mossy. And everything was inches thick in dust.

"Is this the best place you could find?" asked Orem.

Gallowglass looked at him in annoyance. "It doesn't look like this usually. But *you're* here, and so I'll have to forego the normal furnishings for a while." As he spoke the lamp went out again. "Damn, boy, will you get upstairs so I can do this properly?"

Orem stumbled to the stairs in the darkness and clambered up into the cobwebs. Then he listened to Gallowglass wandering around below. A fire soon crackled in the hearth, though there had been no hearth in the room downstairs. And he could hear Gallowglass wander from room to room, opening and closing the doors, though there had been but the one room there before. With magic the place was a palace. With a Sink there, it was a foul place. The wizard had never bothered with housekeeping in reality, when he lived in magic all the time.

Then he heard Gallowglass speaking. "I couldn't help it," Gallowglass said plaintively. Then was there a whisper of an answer? No one had come in with them. Orem waited and tried to listen, and finally, after what seemed hours, he grew impatient.

"Gallowglass!"

"Don't come down the stairs or I'll break your brains!"

"I'm not! I haven't moved!"

"Good! It's the only thing keeping you alive!"

"I'm hungry! It's dark up here!"

Downstairs a barrel lid was tamped into place with a mallet. Soon Orem heard the wizard's footsteps on the stairs. At first the stairs were carpeted, but then, abruptly, the footsteps changed to the smack of leather on bare wood.

"May the bones of your ancestors turn to fungus." The voice was soft, but clear because the old wizard's head was now sticking up into the room. He lifted the lamp to illuminate the tiny upstairs room.

"Oh, dismal," said the wizard.

Orem silently agreed. Cluttered, filthy, and reeking of decay, it was not half so nice a place as the rooms at the Spade and Grave.

"Here," said Gallowglass. He handed him a dish of very dry bread.

"This is all I get to eat?"

"It was roast dove when I conjured it downstairs, how can I help what it turns into in your presence."

"I can't help it either," Orem said. "But I can't live on that."

"Then learn quickly," the wizard said. "I was ready for the danger of having you. But the inconvenience!" Gallowglass rummaged through the debris and pulled from it a shabby cot with a tear in the middle of the canvas. "Best I can do," he said. "But there it is. Until you learn."

"*My* bed?" Orem asked.

"Until you learn, you damnable nuisance! Don't complain when it's your flatulent fault!"

"Then teach me!" Orem retorted.

"I can't *teach* you, not just like *that*." Gallowglass snapped his fingers in Orem's face. "I can only suggest, respond, inform—you have to *learn*. It's inside you, once you learn to recognize and control it. How can I *teach* you, I've never been a Sink."

"Whatever you mean to do, begin it now," Orem said.

"Imperious little bastard, aren't you."

"Just hungry."

The wizard made him lie upon the floor with a bundle of cloth under his head. And then strange, soft commands: Reach out with your fingers, close your eyes, and tell me the color of the air just over your head. Hear if you can the sound of my beard growing. Yes, listen, reach your fingers; try to taste the taste of your sweat in the insides of your eyes.

Orem understood none of it. "I can't," he muttered.

The wizard paid him no attention, just went on. You are asleep as you lie there, listening to me, asleep as long as you think you are awake, awake only when you discover your sleep. Feel how the air gets hotter, feel it at the back of your neck, look at the sun shining, look at it through the soft place behind your knees, yes, you have secret eyes there, look how white it is there.

There was something compelling in the rhythm of the old man's speech, the cadences of it, at times sounding like prayer, at times like song, at times like the bark of an angry dog. Orem's senses became confused. He ceased seeing through his eyes, and yet was still aware of vision, or something akin to it. A grey around him, like the fog of the day before. He could hear the rush of time. He no longer felt inside him where his fingers were, but rather tasted them, and his tongue burned in his mouth, then went cold, then wilted and shrank until he lost track of what was mouth, what was tongue, and even what was Orem.

Orem tried to speak and his knee flexed, and yet he felt it as a burst of light within his chest. Orem tried to move his hand and a high hum came from his throat, but he perceived it as a great weight crushing his testicles and he wept from the pain of it.

Then something, some command he gave without knowing, caused all the grey fog around him to flex. A quick contraction. He did not know what it was he did, but there! there it was again, yes, and again. Like spasms, but he learned to flex the grey again, again, drew it in, pulled it to him, sustained the pressure. It slipped, it lapsed, he grew tired and felt the weariness as a deep green in his thighs, but this he knew was what was wanted of him. Hold this, draw it in, hold it and hold it and hold it

and now he could open his eyes and see, not an old man holding a feeble lamp in a dingy upstairs room, but a young man, blond and beautiful, the man that Orem's father had wished him to be, tall and strong, and it was not a lamp in his hands but a tiny star shining. The room was not filthy and small, either; he was lying in a bed in a room dark with heavily engraved mahogany and brown brocade tapestries, and the young and beautiful man was looking at him with diamonds at the pupils of his eyes.

"This is my home, Orem, when you let it be," said the starholder, said the jewel-eyed lover.

And then it was all too strong for him, and Orem felt something break inside him, and the grey erupted from him and his senses flew madly about the room, about the inside of his head. He writhed on his miserable cot, until at last he fell like a spider gently back into himself, exhausted, surrounded again by the filth. The old man nodded. "Not bad for a first lesson. You'll get better at it as time goes on. If you live through it."

He did get better and stronger, until within weeks he was able to hold the fog just within his skin all his waking hours, much to the wizard's relief. They could take meals together now. And in two months it was such a reflex that he controlled his power even in his sleep. Except now and then, when it slipped away from him, and he awoke again on the cot instead of his soft bed. He told Gallowglass of the lapses. The wizard shrugged and flashed his diamond eyes. "You were probably a bedwetter, too."

THE WIZARD'S WOMEN

"My pickle barrels seem to have caught your eye," said Gallowglass as they read books in his library one night.

"You must be—very fond of pickles," said Orem tentatively.

Gallowglass smiled his bright and beautiful smile. Then he pried open a lid with the crow that lay on the leftmost keg. "What I love best in all the world," said the wizard. "And not held by magic, no, not at all. That's why it wasn't undone when you came in so clumsily and wrecked the place. It's just what it seems to be." The lid came off with a sloshing of water. Orem stood to see. It was not hoarmelon floating in the water, nor onions, nor even a single cabbage as, for a moment, it seemed. For the wizard reached down with his hand, seized a loose handful of hair, and pulled up the shriveled head of a woman.

Head, neck, and naked shoulders. The eyelids hung slack, the mouth drooped open, the skin was wrinkled like a hundred-year-old raisin, and white. Bleached white as a dart's egg, white as the eye of a blindfish from the caves of Watermount.

"My love, my life, my paramour, my wife. Best beloved of all women: The dust of the pouch at my belt, the dust of her blood, here—a shake of it, not much, just a shake, and look, look.'' The blackish dust settled from Gallowglass's fingers, and Orem saw the body shudder under Gallowglass's hand. The eyes trembled and slackly opened.

''Nn,'' said the corpse.

''My lady,'' said Gallowglass.

''Nnnn.''

''I have a prentice now, who wants to see you.''

''Nnnn.''

''He's a smart lad, in his way. Has no manners, eats like a pig and smells worse, and there's no help for it but bathing, since he shuns spells like grease sheds rainwater. But ah, he has a compassionate heart. Do you think he'd be touched at your tale, my love?''

The voice was still a moan, but now Orem realized that the sluggish tongue was articulating; there were words. ''Let me sleep,'' she might have said. Or ''Dead so deep.'' Hard to hear it. And Gallowglass only nodded.

''Come so far, such a long and weary way, yes my love? And yet though the journey is long, still you know I love you. That must be a comfort to you in your death, as it is a comfort to me to have your company.''

''Nnnn,'' said the pickled head. A spurt of bile came from the mouth, and then all went slack again. Gently the wizard lowered the head again. When he turned to Orem, his eyes were emeralds, green as the growth on the barrels.

''Did I tell you that I'm the greatest of the wizards of Inwit? It's true, but small honor, small honor. Do you think Queen Beauty would let me stay, if I were strong? A strong wizard doesn't have to let his wife and daughters die of some ridiculous disease. Doesn't have to watch them waste away to nothing. A strong wizard isn't so fainthearted that he lets them die with their blood. Sleeve wouldn't have done it, you know. Sleeve would have seen their deaths, and calmly drawn their blood alive, with the power hot in it. But like a witch I waited, and took it cool, took it dead, found blood. Powdered here, with only enough power in it to bring them back now and then for conversation.'' The tears flowed down his cheeks. ''I grow maudlin, but I will not hide my heart from my disciple. Oh, Scanthips, my lad, my boy, my wife was the most beautiful of the ladies of power, saving only Beauty herself, my wife was lovely, and her loveliness was not diminished even when divided between my daughters. Look at them!''

Gallowglass unlidded the other barrels, and lifted up his daughters, and Orem looked, though he had no wish to see.

"Look at the curve of the breast—sagging now, but you can imagine it!''

Orem could not, but he murmured his assent. To him the daughter was as utterly old as the mother, for what years had not done, brine did.

"Golden hair, and her sister dark, like day and night walking through the city. I touched them with no spell to make them beautiful—it was in them, it *was* them. And ah, the men who pled with me to give them up. But I was saving them for a better lover than any man.'' Again the bright tears flowed from the emerald eyes. "I was saving them for Death, who crept in and seduced them as I helplessly looked on. Shriveled them, wasted them under my eyes. But I have enough power to waken them. I can draw them back. You saw it!''

"Yes,'' Orem said.

"Oh, by the Sisters, by the Hart, by that damnable God who broke our power and penned us in, if only I knew what the masters knew! I slay the hart in the tower, so my competitors will see the corpse and worry that perhaps I have more power than they—but I know nothing to do with that blood except foolish tricks of invisibility, and that can be done with sheep! I draw the hart's blood, and what does it accomplish? It proves to me again my weakness.'' He closed the barrels, tamped down the lids again. "My life is here, shriveling in brine. But with your gifts I will be the strongest in Hart's Hope, the greatest of them all. And yet.'' He wandered off to the stairway, intoning to himself. "Strongest of them all, and yet still too weak, still too weak, I couldn't save them.''

That night Orem did not sleep long. He awoke disturbed, and on the cot, not in the mahogany room. In his dream the pickled head of the wizard's wife had called to him, and so he went to her, because he could not deny her.

There was a faint light in the library. It came from the green luminescent slime on the barrels. He sat on a pile of rubbish in the cluttered, unmagical room. He watched.

It was the barrel that held the wizard's wife that shuddered

first; then the others, as if the bodies inside were having silent
convulsions, rocking the kegs, sloshing the water. Then a lid
popped up loudly; another split in half; the third was sucked
down into the barrel, and the water seeped and flowed over
the top of it as it was drawn down.

In the dream there had been no danger, but Orem was
afraid. Things that were dead ought to keep still, everyone
knew that. But when the dead call, only a fool refuses them.
And so he stayed and watched as a hand reached up from
one, from two, from all of the barrels, long-fingered hands,
with green light dripping slow as caterpillars down to the
wrists, into the water.

"Don't hurt me," Orem whispered.

Abruptly the hands all thrust out toward him. He gasped,
reached out with his power of negation to try to stop them;
but this was not magic, not the blood-bought magic that a
Sink could swallow up. The hands were undisturbed by his
strongest effort. They reached over the barrels' lip, and a
single finger of each began to write in the slime. Orem could
read the dark lines in the green shining, each woman writing
her word, each trembling as if an uncontainable power controlled them.

"Sister," wrote the wife.

"God," wrote the dark daughter.

"Horn," wrote the light daughter.

Then faster, as the hands grew more sure.

Sister	God	Horn
Slut	Slave	Stone
You	You	You
Must	Must	Must
See	Serve	Save

Then the hands shook violently, flew up in the air and
splashed down again, then reached out, but kept getting
sucked back in, as if they were struggling to write more,
or even to leave the barrels entirely, and something fought
as hard to keep them. The will to write was stronger: the
fingers traced in barely readable letters words that meant only
together.

Let   Me   Die

It was over; the hands splashed back into the water; the lids came quickly into place; the broken one seemed to heal as it closed. The slime began to dim, the last letters of the last words faded into a uniform blackness. Orem fled upstairs.

> Sister slut you must see.
> God slave you must serve.
> Horn stone you must save.
> Let me die.

He understood nothing, and lay halfway between sleep and wakefulness all night, trying to understand, trying not to think at all. If the last message was the wizard's women speaking for themselves, then whose message was the first part? Or was it meaningful at all? Who could lift the hands of the dead even when the power of a Sink had stolen all the magic?

Only in the first light of morning did he think to do that most obvious, most instinctive thing: he summed the words up, he summed them down, conceiving them both as columns and as rows. The upward sum of rows was *Palicrovol*. The downward sum of rows was *Beauty*. And either way the columns were added, they said, *Give all, get nothing*.

PRANKS

All through the winter and spring Orem learned to use his new senses. He had no language to describe even to himself what he felt, so he adapted what language he had. When he described it to me, it was all a tale of tongues and tasting, pinpricks and bludgeons, though through it all he usually lay still as death on his cot.

In late spring Gallowglass agreed that he was ready to start earning his keep. So he began to reach outward, finding his way along Wizard Street. He found the magics of the other wizards as if they were tiny fires, hot or cooling, depending on their power. And he tasted them or pinched them or some other inadequate word for what he did, and all the blood-purchased power was gone.

From the first the experiment was a success.

"Orem! My Scanthips! You should have heard the woe! All up and down Wizard Street! Two buildings held up by magic collapsed. One old wizard who only kept his horn with spells is so humiliated he won't go back to Whore Street for years. And never knowing when a spell will work or not. The rats and sheep that have spilt their blood in vain these weeks—ah, if only you could hear the cutters complain. In the taverns where we go, I listen, I complain along with them. They think sometimes it must be the God's men found some terrible incantation. And sometimes they think it's the Queen, putting them in their place, though it's been a long time since she worried much about our paltry powers. Some think the Sweet Sisters, and it's time for women to take the place of power in the world. None of them suspects, none of them dreams that here in my miserable filthy blacksmith shop of a mansion I have found and trained a Sink!''

"It worked, then?" Orem asked.

"Somewhat. There was an assassination over in the Great Exchange, a dearly paid-for murder—was it you that snuffed that out?''

"I don't know. There was a far one. I can't tell what they are.''

"It was poison. You killed the power of it, but the taste remained. Luckily the assassin killed himself before letting on who hired him—quite dependable fellow, a rare thing these days—but there was a wizard who stared death in the face, you may be sure, for a few anxious moments.''

"Who was it?''

"Me. This isn't going to work well if you don't learn to differentiate between my magics and theirs.''

And so they talked through everything that Orem had done, and Gallowglass showed him all his spells and powers, and Orem gradually learned to distinguish one wizard's flame from another by taste or texture or color.

That was why he came to know Queen Beauty first by her magic.

How Orem First Engaged the Queen in Battle

It was late in autumn, and Orem ranged far and wide, following all his senses where they led him. He knew by then which points of light were men, and which were women; he had already learned the difference between the whiteness of a man

who is awake and the bright silver of a soul asleep. He had
learned also that the things done in a place lingered there even
when the men were gone, so that he could taste a long and
passionate love affair and tell when the coupling was only
bought, could smell the difference between a house with love
in it and a house with hate, could feel in the ground what sort
of man had passed through a certain door. There were the
fires of wizards, whose works he recognized now easily; there
were the pools of bitter water where the Godsmen made
islands in the surrounding sweetness. Orem could follow the
life of the world as if it were a map spread before him. He
vanquished the other wizards so easily that it wasn't sport
anymore. It was boredom in the cold of an autumn afternoon that
led him to search for King Palicrovol. It was a game, to see if
he could match, in his small way, the Queen's Searching
Eye.

He began by finding the river and following it up its
course, searching for each little dot of mind that was some
farmer coming down. He searched a long time before he
came to the first town. Only then did he realize how wide a
land Burland was. He had lived too long in Inwit, had come
to feel, as so many of its citizens felt, that Inwit was fully
half the world, and everything else outside was small and
near. Instead it was far, and if he kept searching up the river
in this lazy way he'd be a week getting to Banningside.

So he rose into the air, to see if he could perceive as a bird
did, from high above. As he ascended, the sea of sweetness
in which he had always moved suddenly ceased, and instead
of the dark seeing and faint smelling he had been able to do,
he felt as though he could sense all things forever. Except that
wherever he dipped downward, there was the sweetness again
like the fog of the city, slowing him and obscuring wherever
he looked.

He tried to think what it could be, wondered if there were
some layer in the air, or if where the clouds began, his magic
vision improved. But the sweetness hung too low, never
rising much above the height of the tallest buildings—and
suddenly Orem understood. The sweet sea of fog was not
natural at all. It was Queen Beauty's Searching Eye. It was
her magic, pervading everything. Of course she did not bother
to maintain it much above the level where a man was likely to
climb. It was men she meant to spy on.

Does she see me? Or does a Sink devour the magic of Queen Beauty? Daringly he dipped down into the sweet fog and, instead of moving through it, he tasted it the way he tasted the fires of the wizards. It had no center to it, no potent place to snuff out, but he found that he could easily erase wide patches of it like clearing chalk from a slate, with no effort at all, and what he cleared stayed cleared.

At first he was alarmed at what he had done. Surely Queen Beauty would notice the gap in her vision, would come searching for him. But as he lay on his bed, feeling a little sick with fear, he realized that if he could block her Searching Eye miles from Inwit, he could block it here as well. And so he did, clearing her vision out of Wizard Street, away from the edges of the bitter island of the Great Temple, and from other places, too, so that she could not pinpoint one gap as the source of her enemy.

Enemy? Am I Queen Beauty's enemy?

He remembered Palicrovol, looking up at him with golden eyes at the House of God in Banningside. Had he, or perhaps some god, called to Orem then so he would do this very work, blinding Queen Beauty? He had never heard of a wizard daring to challenge her Searching Eye; he had never heard of a wizard who even understood how she did it. For the first time it occurred to Orem that his power as a Sink might have been given him, not to play pranks on the other wizards of Inwit, but to challenge Beauty herself. His father had found him soldiering in the dirt, childish games—but could he not now serve King Palicrovol as no other could serve him? Could he not, in fact, block Queen Beauty's power to make cowards of his men, and let his army come against an undefended city?

Now Orem searched for Palicrovol earnestly, ranging above Queen Beauty's cloud until he found a place where her sweet magic brightened and dazzled. It was here where she assailed the wizards of the King, topped their defenses, sieved through them, battered and broke them, playfully as a cat tearing at a thin paper held taut. And there was the King, a single wakeful point of lonely light within a sea of priestly bitterness, within the circle of elegant but impotent walls erected by the King's wizards. Palicrovol, the good King, still punished for a centuries-old sin, who had never passed his own suffering on to his people. I can give you ease, at least for a single hour of a single night, said Orem silently.

But before he acted, he remembered the Queen. She was the unspoken breath at the back of every speaker who fell silent, every lover who looked over his shoulder, every thinker who hummed to take a dangerous thought from his mind. He remembered that she was the helpless child raped on the back of the hart. Who was he to judge that her vengeance should be interrupted, that it was time to break her power?

You know what Orem decided, Palicrovol. You remember the night. Suddenly a wizard came in, his face white with terror, to say that the Queen had destroyed all their spells; then another came to say that the Queen's power, too, was gone. You did not dare believe that magic was so perfectly undone, until the itching at your groin let up for a few hours, your long-stopped bowels flowed normally, painlessly for a few hours, and you were able to sleep dreamlessly for the first night in three hundred years. Then you believed.

But why did Orem decide to do battle with the Queen? He did not suspect he was your son. You had done him no kindness. The Queen had done him no especial harm. It was simply this: If Orem had been alive when you ravished Asineth upon the hart's back, and he had had the power to stop you, he would have done it. He was one who instinctively fought against the strong, to help the helpless. It was his way, born into him. He hadn't the heart for necessary cruelty, the way you had. And so he challenged Queen Beauty, in part because he was brave and she was his only interesting adversary, but mostly out of pity for his weak and beaten King. Do not discount that when you judge him. There was a time when you were helpless, and he helped you.

That night Orem attacked incessantly, for hours, not just swallowing up all the magic anywhere near you, but spreading himself over as broad an area as he could, clearing away the Queen's sight, in hopes of disorienting her, distracting her, buying even more time for you. He had no hope of challenging her at the Castle, for his power was negation—he could do nothing to harm her person. But he could undo her work, and so he unwove her nets of seeing as long as he had strength to do it that night.

At last he slept, exhausted, and after several hours of

searching, Queen Beauty found you again, Palicrovol, and your suffering began anew, and sharper than before, and many of your wizards died. Orem was young, and he did not know how angry she would be, or that you would bear the brunt of her quick revenge. He assumed she would know what he was, and that she would search for him. But even so, it told you things. You knew then that if Beauty was angry, it meant there was a force in the world that could thwart her, if only for a time. You did not know if one of the gods had broken free of her, or if Sleeve had managed to free himself and work some magic, but you knew that it was a good omen, and that you should try again to bring your armies to the gates of Inwit. Admit it, Palicrovol: It was Orem who summoned you to your final battle with the Queen.

And as for the Queen, I remember that night in the palace, too. She wakened everyone with a flurry of insistent commands. The guards were alerted to stand the walls, and Urubugala was put through excruciating torture until he confessed that he knew nothing. Craven only smiled at the news— she knew he had no power that could do this. And Weasel Sootmouth told the Queen the bitter truth, as was her wont:

"You are getting old, and the power you bought is fading."

So it was that as you began to assemble your armies again, so Beauty began to look for a suitable father for her twelve-month child. Once she had found you again, and made sure that none of the gods and none of your powerful friends had broken free, she compelled the Sweet Sisters to weave a dream for her on their long unused loom. Show me the face of the consort who will father my powerful child, she demanded. And the Sweet Sisters—they knew the face to send her in her dream.

THE WOUNDING OF THE HART

He would have slept late in the morning, but Gallowglass awoke him just after dawn. "What have you done?" demanded the wizard.

"Done?" asked Orem.

"Last night the house shivered, and I awoke this morning to hear the cries of a hundred thousand birds. I looked out the window and the sky was filled with them, wheeling and turning, and then suddenly they dispersed, they flew far, but all of them dipped and turned over this house. Was it real or a vision? Did you call them?"

"I don't know how to call."

"No, it was a vision, I know it was. No magic, I'd *know* magic, I'm not likely to mistake *that*. Don't you feel how the floor is trembling?"

Yes, there was a low, low hum that shook him in his bed. He was afraid now, remembering his foolish bravery of the night before. He dared not leave Gallowglass ignorant of what he had done, since only Gallowglass would know what he must do now. So he told him of last night's battle for Palicrovol against the Queen.

"Oh, Orem," whispered Gallowglass, "no sooner do you have a grasp than you try to overreach! Touch nothing of the Queen's!"

"Is it she who shakes the house?"

"No! No, not Queen Beauty. There's no way she could know where you are. It's bad enough she knows that you exist."

"Will she know I'm a Sink?"

"She'll know that suddenly somewhere in Burland there's a wizard who can undo her doing. It will worry her. She'll search, she'll ask, and then she'll learn that here on Wizard Street also there are spells undone, and then she'll begin to wonder what's abroad in the world."

Up and down he walked, clapping his fist into an open hand. "It's a fool who tries to pit his power against the Queen! The Queen could crush us in a moment. She lets us wizards be because we do no harm. We can cure warts and other blemishes. We can do love words and vengeances on enemies, and pranks and little spies. We can even keep a hart's blood hot on the city wall and go invisible in the daylight when we have the need. But we do not darken skies or move the hearts of masses in the city. We do not question the Sweet Sisters and we do not shiver the earth. The river's course is beyond our reach, and the wind must not be spoken to, and we may not poison the milk within the breast or dry the semen in a man's loins."

Orem made no answer, for directly behind Gallowglass, stamping intermittently upon the floor, was a hart with a

hundred-pointed head, his great neck high upraised to bear
that impossible weight. Gallowglass heard the beast almost as
soon as Orem saw him, and he turned and knelt, and said,
"O Hart, why have you come?"

The Hart regarded him and did not stir to answer.

"Are you real or vision?" Gallowglass cried.

The wizard was afraid, but Orem was not. This was the
beast that he had seen before, in the bushes at Banning's
shore, watching his mother as she bathed. He looked into the
glistening eyes and knew he should not be afraid. The Hart
had not come angrily. Orem drew the covers from himself
and walked forward toward the great stag.

"Don't do anything to frighten him," Gallowglass said.

"He hasn't come for you," Orem said. "He forgives you
for the harts you've bled upon the wall." Now Orem could
see that the chest was throbbing with deep, silent breaths, and
the hart was wet with sweat, matting his fur.

Where have you been tonight? And running so hard?

Orem knelt and reached for the hart's hoof. The stag lifted
the leg, and willingly gave it to the boy; but it was not there,
Orem felt nothing, he was holding no weight at all. And yet
his hand could not close, and a great dark warmth spread
upward through his arm. The Hart, while insubstantial in
Inwit, dwelt in flesh within the city of Hart's Hope.

"Why have you come to me?" Orem asked, his voice as
reverent as a priest at prayer.

"Silence," Gallowglass softly pleaded.

Orem looked upward, and the Hart slowly bowed its head.
The weight of the horns was too much for any neck to bear,
but the neck bore. The Hart set its hind legs and braced
backward, and the head sank until the horns danced directly
in front of Orem's face, until one single horntip rested still as
a mountain right where he could not look at anything else.
And he looked, and looked again, and looked deeper, and
saw:

That the stars of a tiny heaven danced around the horn.
That he was falling down into the stars, then past them, and
the tip of the horn loomed great as a moon, great as all the
world. Then it *was* the world, and Orem could not breathe as
he raced down and down until suddenly all held still and he
hung gasping in the air over the city of Inwit.

The city teemed with life below him; boats docked and undocked at the wharves; the guard marched here and there like ants upon the city walls. But it was not the life of the city that gave it the look of constant motion. For even as Orem watched the city was unbuilding itself, as if time had come undone and it was a century, two centuries in the past. Roads changed their path; buildings grew new and flashed as brief skeletons of frames and then were replaced by older, smaller buildings. There were more and more farms within the city walls, and the settlements outside shrank and nearly disappeared. Suddenly the Great Temple was gone, and the Little Temple changed so there were not seven circles over every column, and then the Little Temple, too, was gone, and the city bent a different way. King's Street twisted sharp to the west, and the great gate of the city was Hind's Trace, West Gate, the Hole.

Then this, too, passed; the walls of the city unraveled, revealing smaller walls, and those too unwound themselves and there were no walls at all, and no castle, either, except the tiny Old Castle at the eastmost point of the King's Town Hill. This lingered, this was steady for a time. And then the castle, too, was gone, nothing but forest there, and nothing left of Inwit but a few hundred houses built in circles around the single shrine. And the houses grew fewer and fewer, and the shrine diminished, bit by bit, and Orem fell again until he saw as if he hovered only a few yards above the ground. There was no village. Only forest, and one clearing with a hut in the middle, and where the Shrine would be there was only a farmer plowing in the field.

This farmer did not plow as Orem's father plowed. The farmer himself drew the soil-cutting knife, and his wife guided it, and it made only a weak and shallow furrow in the ground. It was painful work, and Orem could see why the plot was small—there was no hope of plowing more land than that.

Suddenly there was a movement at the edge of the clearing. To Orem's relief, time was flowing forward again, and at a normal pace. A stag bounded onto the furrows, its hooves plunging deep into the loosened soil. It was frightened. Behind it came four huntsmen with bows and pikes, and dogs that barked madly at the deer. The hart ran to the farmer, who shed the harness of the plow and took the hart's head between his hands for a moment, then let it go. The hart did not move. Nor did it show fear of the farmer, and perhaps this was why the hunters stopped, to see such a marvel.

The farmer raised his hand, and the stag took a step away from him, toward the forest on the far side of the clearing. As it did, the hunters also moved, the dogs bounding forward a single leap. The farmer lowered his hand and the movements stopped, and all waited for him again.

The farmer turned to the plow. He picked it up, heavy as it was, and laid it upside down in front of the hunters' dogs. He knelt, trembling, before the plow. Then, behind him, his wife bent and took his head in her hands, helped him lay his throat against the blade of the plow. For a moment they waited, poised. It was not the wife, for her hands drew back at the last moment, too merciful to do the thing. It was the farmer himself who drove his neck sharply into the plow. Blood spurted, and Orem winced with the agony of it. Now the wife finished what the husband had begun; she drove the farmer's head down and down, until the blood spouted and the blade was almost all the way through the neck.

Then the hunters lowered their bows, and did not notice as the hart made its escape into the trees. They watched instead how their dogs came up and licked the blood leaping from the blade of the plow. The dogs went mad in the aftermath of lapping the blood; they bounded high as if they were dancing, and ran from the clearing joyfully, heading back where they had come from. The hunters knelt, marveling, and the wife dipped her finger in the blood and drew the sign of the hart upon their faces. The hunters also left rejoicing.

It was dark, and the moon rose, and the man's body still lay broken over the plow when the hart returned to the clearing. This time the hart came with a dozen harts and a dozen hinds, and then seven times seven of them, and one by one they came and licked the hair of the dead farmer. When they were through, they came to the farmer's wife, and the hart whose life the farmer had saved stretched out its neck to her. She reached out and took a small sapling tree that grew beside her hovel, and broke it as if it were brittle, though the leaves on it were lush and green. Then with the sharp and jagged end of the tree she cut the hart's belly from breast to groin. The bowels of the hart lurched downward. The bleeding hart staggered to the man and lay beside him, and their blood mingled on the plow.

Then, as Orem watched, the plow became a raft, and the head of the man and the head of the stag lolled over the edge, drifting in bright water. The raft flowed against the stream. Or did the water flow from the wounded bodies of the two broken animals? Along the banks of the river a million people knelt and drank, each a sip, and left singing.

At last the raft came to rest against a shore. Like wineskins the two bodies seemed empty, and no more water flowed from them.

Orem looked up and saw, standing beside the corpses on the bank, the living hart and the living man, whole again, both naked in moonlight.

And the farmer's face was Orem's face, and the hart was the deer that stood before him in the room, its horn lowered to offer a naked brown point.

Orem breathed to calm the violent beating of his heart. How much of it was true, and if true, what did it mean?

As if in answer came the face of a woman. It was the most beautiful face Orem had ever seen, a kind and loving face, a face that cried out like a tragic virgin starved for a man's life within her. Orem did not know her, but recognized her at once. Only one living human could have such a face, for that face cried out for a single name: Beauty. It was the Queen, and she called to him, and a tear of joy stood out in one eye as she saw him and reached for him and took him into her embrace.

Then the vision was gone, abruptly, and Orem and Gallowglass were alone in the attic room.

"Did you see?" asked Orem.

"I saw you kneel before the Hart, and it offered its horn to you, and suddenly blood came from a deep wound in your throat, and I thought you were dead."

Wound. Orem reached up his hand and yes, all across his own throat was the low welt of a cruel but long-healed wound. "I never had an injury here."

"What was it that you saw?"

"I saw how Hart's Hope came to be the name of this place. And what the Shrine of the Broken Tree is for. And I saw the face of Beauty."

There was no ambiguity when that name was said. Beauty wore only one face in Burland, though few there were who had seen it for themselves. Every man held his image of Queen Beauty in his mind, to fear and adore when he was most alone. Every woman knew her, and every woman knew the ways that Beauty mocked their insufficiency.

"Has she found me?" Orem asked.

"No," Gallowglass answered. Abruptly he turned and staggered from the room. It took a moment for Orem to know that he was grieving. The boy arose, pulled on his wrap and shirt and belted his clothing as he followed the wizard down the stairs. When he reached the hall, the wizard already had the lid pried up, and now he pried the next, the next, and then lifted up the women's corpses that floated in the brine, lifted them high and draped them limply over the barrel's edges, face upward and outward, hanging upside down and dripping slime in pools upon the carpet. "You betrayed me!" the wizard cried. "You're oathbreakers! You're thieves!" And he seized the golden daughter's shriveled head and held it so close that he spat into the staring eyes. "What are you to me, you bloated, filthy flesh! You cheated me of your power, cheated me of your lives within my house, and now the Hart has stepped within my home, and where were you? Where were you when the life flowed from the throat of my terrible boy? A sip and you would have lived, you would have lived, you would have lived!"

And the wizard stood, letting the head dangle again, bobbing back and forth a little. To the shelf, to the bag of powdered blood. Orem could not bear to see the women called forth again from the half-death that Gallowglass forced upon them. And so he sent himself out, suddenly, the way a cutpurse flashes forth his knife, and in a moment the blood was empty of its desiccated power. He knew as he did it that he was granting the desire of the dead women and breaking Gallowglass's heart. The wizard cast the pinch of blood, and now instead of quickening the women, it fell like corruption, and their faces blackened, and their hair fell to the floor in gobbets, and their flesh peeled back and slipped to the soggy carpet with tiny slaps, and one by one the heads loosened and dropped, only to dissolve quickly into unrecognizable masses of putrefaction.

Only when the bones had come apart and lay in careless
heaps on the carpet, only when the bottom halves of the
three women had slid back into the water and out of sight,
only then did Gallowglass turn to Orem, and his face was
terrible. His eyes shone with ruby light, his teeth were
bared like a badger's teeth, and Orem saw murder in the
man's hands.

He darted leftward, for the door, and shoved it open. A
hand had hold of the nape of his shirt to draw him back,
but Orem shrugged him away, letting the shirt tear as he
threw himself through the door. He ran out into the bitter
cold of the street, his shirt hanging off his shoulders, held
to his body only by his belt. He ran out into the bitter cold
of the street, under the steady drip of the melting icicles,
to race across the face of the frozen street with cold sunlight
on his back.

THE SHRINE OF THE BROKEN TREE

He ran without purpose, more afraid of what he had done
than of Gallowglass himself. By the time he was on Thieves
Street, though, a plan was forming in his mind. He would
find Flea again, and ask his help in hiding. The Queen would
be looking for him among the wizards, and Gallowglass
would never find him, for he could not use magic.

What he hadn't counted on, of course, was the enemy that
always waited for the unwary in Inwit. A troop of guards
were patrolling in the Cheaps. One look at the tattered shirt
and the frightened face and they knew that Orem was theirs.
They did not need to know his crime to know that he was
guilty. They cried out for him to stop, demanded that he show
his pass.

He had no pass with him; nor did he dare to tell them his
pass was with Gallowglass, for they would take him to Gallowglass's house to verify it, and Gallowglass could have
whatever vengeance he wanted then. So Orem turned and ran
back, ran deep into the Cheaps, dodging this way and that
among the narrow, twisting streets.

He was faster than the guards, but they were many and he
was one. Wherever he ran they were waiting, and at last they
funneled him back until he leaned upon the unkempt Shrine

of the Broken Tree. He could see that up and down Shrine Street the guards were coming. There was no avenue of escape. And so he leaned on the low wall around the shrine, and looked down on the stump, and saw that the jagged upsticking point was just as the farmer's wife had left it in the vision. The dream was true, then. It was good to know that something was true. But what, name of heaven, did it mean?

17

Cages

How the other animals kept Orem Scanthips alive until he
was recognized.

THE STEER PIT AND THE ZOO

Citizens of Inwit whose papers are in order go to Faces Hall
to plead before the Judges. Priests are tried at the Temple.
Licenses are fined and levied at the Guild Hall. But the
passless go to the Gaols, for they have no right to be in Inwit.
Their very existence is a crime.

They carried Orem with other offenders in a cart up Queen's
Road and into the vast canyon between the walls of the
Castle. The horses strained to draw the cart up the steep
slope, and the walls shut out the noise, so that all the prisoners could hear in their misery was the cracking of whips
and the straining of animals. At High Gate the prisoners
were addressed by an officer.

He told them their rights: None.

He told them their choices: Loss of an ear on the first
offense, slavery or castration on the second, interesting and
exemplary death on the third.

And to underscore the point, they were led past the Steer
Pit on their way to the Gaols. The authorities made sure that
whenever new prisoners arrived some poor criminal who
chose a eunuch's freedom was hanging there in manacles, his
hips braced in the clamp, naked and waiting for the binding
wire and cutter's shears. The men of justice in King's Town
preferred their prisoners to choose slavery, so they made
castration look as ghastly as possible. Because of that, the
machinery of justice paid for itself in sales of slaves to the
black traders who carried their captives west across the sea.

Once he had been given a good look at the Steer Pit, they
put Orem in one of the cages. The cages had no floors, no

furniture, only crossed bars below and above and on four sides. There was no shelter from the wind, and no possibility of finding a comfortable position. The cells were too short to stand in, and yet sitting meant buttocks pressed against the cold round iron of the cage. Your feet could not be tucked under you because the bars hurt them, and if you lay down, what could you do with your head? Orem tried every position while the nearby prisoners silently watched him. At last he propped himself in a corner, which of all positions was least uncomfortable for a time.

There were two tiers of cages above him, and nothing below but the ground, yet even that was too far to reach if he put his arm through the cage and reached down. He was hanging in the air and helpless and miserable.

"How long do they keep you here?" Orem asked the man in the cage next to him. The man only kept looking at him, saying nothing. "I said, how long do they—" but then he caught a glimmer in the man's eye that stopped him. It was not that the man had not heard, only that speech was not interesting to him. He got up and came toward the corner where Orem leaned. There was no hint of what he meant to do, but Orem was sure he would rather see it from the other side of the cage. The man, clay-faced and silent, pulled aside his wrap and began to piss toward Orem. It struck the floor bars and spattered. Orem retreated to the farthest corner, and for a moment thought himself safe, until he felt the hot-and-cold of his other neighbor's piss against his back, running down into his wrap. He spun to escape, tripped on the bars, and fell. His foot slipped into the gap and his hip wrenched as his body weight forced him to fall over, the leg still tangled in the bars. He was in pain, and still they pissed on him from both sides, and the man above him spat and spat. In his fury Orem wanted to shout at them, to curse them; now more than ever he wished for some power to destroy an enemy instead of the passive, useless power of a Sink.

At last the pissing stopped. The spitter above him walked away and sat down in a corner. Only the wind remained, freezing and drying the urine on his skin and in his hair; the wind and the stench. Orem was soon too uncomfortable to be angry. The piss was like the cold, to be shrugged at and borne. He could do nothing about it now. He carefully extricated his leg from the cage and rubbed his hip where it ached. Favoring that foot, he found another corner and sat in it, warily eyeing the other men. They no longer watched him.

In a few minutes the guards came for the man above Orem. They wheeled the light wooden stairway along the cages and stopped it in front of Orem. The man above did not get up from his corner. Just waited. The guards came and stood at the door. They did not come in, they did not speak. Just waited. The man inside, the guards outside, and Orem could not be sure they were even watching each other. They waited a long time. Then the breeze blew more briskly for a moment. It chilled Orem. Apparently it also whispered something to the prisoner above, for now he got up and made his precarious way to the door of the cell and watched impassively as the guards pulled the door away and slid it off to the side. They manacled his arms just above the elbow and drew the chain tight behind his back, so that his arms were straining at the socket. The man gave no sign of pain, just followed docilely.

The afternoon sun brought a sort of warmth, and Orem shivered at it, relished it. He hoped whatever trial he got would come before nightfall, before the bad cold came.

The sky was reddening with sunset and clouds when another man was brought to the cell above him. Orem watched impassively as his neighbors also began to piss on him. Most of it also fell on Orem, and could not be dodged, and with the evening breeze rising, it was even colder. But this time Orem did not cower. He did not move from his place. He only closed his eyes and tightly shut his lips, and waited until it was over. The man shouted and shouted and tried to run from place to place. There was no shelter. But because he shouted they kept attacking him. Spittle when the piss ran dry, and the man in the third tier began making as if to defecate through the cage. Finally Orem could bear it no longer. The new man's shouting and cursing did nothing but keep the rain of filth going far longer, and Orem was annoyed. He walked under where the man stood screaming at his tormentors. The man didn't see him—he was watching the silent, expressionless men who spat as often as they could work up the spittle. Orem reached his hands through the bars and fiercely pushed the heels of the man's feet. With a scream of terror the man fell straight down, only barely stopping himself before his crotch bridged the bars. Orem caught and held his feet.

"Let go of me!" he cried.

But Orem silently gripped the feet and waited. With the man held still, concentrating only on holding his crotch above the waiting bar while Orem pulled him downward, the spitters found their target enough to satisfy them. With the new man weeping in frustration, they finally quit, and then Orem let go of his legs. With difficulty the man raised himself and extricated his legs from the cage floor. Then he staggered off to a corner and whimpered quietly.

The Gaols seemed nearly full; indeed, it was as if they did not remove one prisoner until another was nearly there to take his place, as if the Gaols required the fulness of misery.

Orem could not sleep; dared not sleep, in such cold. His hands and feet became numb. He got up and walked around the perimeter of his cage, holding the bars so he wouldn't fall again in the darkness, refusing to nurse his sore hip lest that leg become too cold. Toward morning the moon arose, giving little light, just enough to mock the cold. And soon after moonrise the clouds from the west came across the sky. The new man above had stopped whimpering. Orem wondered if he slept or was dead or had simply discovered the uselessness of crying. Orem circled the cage again and again. Once a man's hand covered his on the bar. For a moment Orem feared some sharp and sudden pain, but the hand quickly lifted and Orem realized that his neighbor also was pacing.

At dawn the snow began. It stung Orem when it touched him, falling thick and fast on him. He only walked faster, around and around the cage, until in the scant light he saw that the other men were scooping up the snow from the bars with their fingers and eating it. Of course; he had gone all day without water, and who knew how long these other men had been here without food or drink? Orem also scooped the snow and sucked his finger. The water was cold on his tongue, but so clear of flavor once the first bit of pisstaste was gone that it pierced his throat to the base of his skull.

Walk on, walk on, stay as warm as you can. In the snow the guards came and took the man next to Orem, and the man behind him. Always the guards stood at the door until the prisoner stopped circling and came to them. The snow fell thicker. The man next to him stopped and shat into his hands, then rubbed the warm dung on his belly and shivered in relief.

They soon brought two new prisoners to take the old ones' places. And this time Orem joined in with the others in pissing on them and spitting. Both were brighter than the new man above. Once the shock was over, they did as Orem had done—endured. Then they quickly fell into the pattern of the Gaols, eating the slight snow that stayed for a few moments on the floor bars, circling to stay warm, sitting for a few moments when walking was impossible. When one man sat too long and began to doze, the others silently began to spit at his face, to wake him. Not a word. No voices. We have no voices here, but still we are men: we try to keep each other alive.

The man above him, however, lay still and lay still and lay still and at last the snow built up on his cold body. When it was plain that he was dead, Orem reached up through the cage roof and scooped the snow from part of the man's body and filled his mouth. It froze his teeth, but melted into a full swallow of water. When he had drunk his fill, Orem held out a handful of snow to the man in the next cage, who silently took it and filled his mouth and walked on. To each of his neighbors Orem gave a handful of the snow from the corpse above, and when they were done they took the handfuls and passed them on. The snow built up under the cages. A foot by noon, and by midafternoon clear up to the bottom of the cage. Now there was no more need to scrape snow from the dead man—there was plenty within reach of all on the bottom row. Orem saw that his skin was bluing. How long before fingers were frozen and lost? How long before the poisoning set in? How long before he simply grew too weary? Since yesterday morning he had gone without sleep, and now it was near dark again.

They came and took away the corpse at nightfall, and in the night the guards also took the last of the men who had pissed on Orem when he first came. Around the cage, around the cage, around the cage, stay warm, stay warm, and Orem sang and chanted to himself, even prayed, however futile that might be for one who had forsaken God, prayed and wondered if the vision of the Hart had been only a prophecy of his death.

In the darkness the snow stopped, the clouds slid out of the sky, and the real cold came. Now I will die, thought Orem.

For a while he stopped, sat in a corner, and trembled violently as the cold wind slapped him again and again with ever colder hands. It was only the spittle striking his face and shoulders that kept him from the gathering dream of sleep. He shivered one last, vast quake and then bounded forward, caught the bars of the cage roof and clung with all his strength, regardless of the numbness of his hands. I will live, he decided as he pulled himself up and slowly lowered himself. May the guards' children die by fire in front of them. Grimly he swung his feet up and caught them in the bars of the roof. May the guards' wives be raped by a hundred lepers. With small moans of pain he forced himself to rise, sink, rise, sink.

When dawn at last came, Orem was still staggering around and around his cage. There were many who lay still in their cages. Black lumps in the sunlight, casting inert shadows on the snow under the rows. A spiderweb with bundles safely stored in place for later devouring. Perhaps half still struggled in the web.

As if deliberately to torture him they took two new men before they finally came for Orem. How he hated them for going inside before him. But he said nothing, deliberately showed no sign of his anger, just circled, just hung from the roof and pulled himself up and let himself down with hands as stiff as paws.

Yet when they came, Orem did not run for the cage door, did not hurry. The very change in the routine of survival was too hard; it took effort, it took thought to quit moving in the set pattern. Then at last he went to the door and waited. The manacles were cold iron, but felt warm enough on his arms as they clamped them in place. They caught a little skin in the hinge, but Orem was too numb to feel the pain as the flesh tore away and some blood trickled down his arm and froze.

THE COAL HOUSE

The trial was held in the Coal House. The walls were grey and grimy from the black dust, and in the suffocating air the guards' faces streaked grey with their sweat. The heat of the place was almost more than Orem could bear, and the relief of it made his legs shake so that the guards had to hold him up. The dark morning room was lit only by small high windows and a few torches on the walls. It didn't matter; it was only the floor that Orem watched as it wheeled and spun.

The guards let him fall in the middle of the room. Orem lay gratefully on the unbarred floor and listened as a magistrate's voice intoned, "Crime?"

"Passless and unclaimed."

"Sex and age?"

"Male and younghorned."

"Prisoner, what do you have to say?"

It took Orem a moment to realize that speech was expected of him, and a moment more to remember how it was done. Don't cut me, he wanted to say. I killed the Wizard's women and deserve anything you do to me, he almost said.

"I'm a farmboy from the north, and I lost my pass," he said at last.

A guard pulled him up to his knees and turned his head to show his cheek to the magistrates. "Months healed if it's a day," said the guard.

"How did you stay out of the way of the guards all this time?" asked a magistrate.

Orem looked at them for the first time, now that the guard was holding him up enough to see. There were three magistrates on a high dais with a wire screen between them and him. They wore masks, terrible white and green masks like putrefaction, and looked at him as relentlessly as God, for the masks did not blink. "I was careful," Orem said.

"We caught him out in the open, shirt torn and near naked in the snow," said the guard. "Careful ones don't do that."

"Bring him nearer," said one of the magistrates. Since none of the heads moved, there was no way of knowing which one had spoken. As the guard pulled him staggering forward, another magisterial voice said, "The Hole, no doubt, and a false pass. Who gave you your pass, boy? Or do you want your testicles crushed and served to you in a pudding?"

It was not that Orem was courageous then—courage was beyond him after two nights in the open cage. He did not tell all he knew of the passage through the Hole because at that moment one of the magistrates let out a small cry and said, "Look at his face."

One of them motioned to the guards, who pulled Orem through a small door in the cage and brought him directly before the magistrates' table. They let him lean on the desk as the masked faces looked steadily at him. Orem was now close enough to see the whites of the eyes inside the masks, to see the lips and teeth and tongues of the speakers.

"How did you come by that scar across your throat?" asked a magistrate.

He had forgotten the mark the dream left on him. How could he answer? Only the truth would come to mind, only the truth would bend to fit: "I'm a farmer's son. I cut it as a child on the edge of a plow."

They fell silent, regarding him. Then the middle one nodded, and the others also nodded. "The Queen's dream, all right," said one.

"And come to us from the cages," said another.

"What's your name, boy?"

Orem thought for a moment, remembered. "Orem."

"Orem what?"

He couldn't remember. Hadn't he been called Scanthips? Or Banningside? Or ap Avonap? Which?

"He's in no case to make answers."

"Made one that's good enough."

"Well, what now? She said no harm to him, and look."

"How much will he remember?"

"Too much."

"How could we have known? This one was arrested before she ever told us."

The middle one made a decision of sorts. "Don't call off the search. Keep it going, and take him somewhere to sleep. Only when he's in better shape than this. Then we stop the search."

"Fool. She knows *now*."

"And damned little good to her until we restore him. Blankets and broth and a fire in his room. Hurry up about it! And bring in the next one, quick, quick!"

Orem found himself borne off again, but this time in more courteous hands, and when they came to a small hot room with a fire in it, they unshackled his arms and laid him on a feather cushion in a corner and covered him. He slept before they left the room, and barely woke for the broth they brought him, and again for the pisspot. Finally he awoke of his own accord and crawled from the blanket because he was sweating and the blanket stuck to him prickly with wool. Where the shackle had torn his skin he felt the stinging of the wound; his joints all ached, and he shuddered several times, then vomited the broth onto the bricks of the hearth.

He felt better then, and crawled off to a corner and leaned his head against the walls and watched the fire through half-closed eyes. The scene with the magistrates stayed with him as clearly as a dream not fully wakened from. *She* had set the guards to looking for him. *She* could see even now. *She* had seen his face in a dream. She could only be Queen Beauty, and now Orem understood that he would have to pay a price for having challenged her attack on Palicrovol only a few nights ago. Yet after what he had already been through, he did not bother to be afraid. What could she do to him now to hurt him further? He still had not fully returned to his body; the sensations of it still were not wholly his own again. Let her torture, let her kill, it was all one to him, all one.

Servants came with a tub, stripped his wrap from him and plunged him into the warm water. Some carried out his clothes; others mopped and scrubbed the floor while his back was harshly scrubbed and his hair was sudsed and wrung clean like the mop. The dried urine and crusted spittle of the cages came off into the water; they bore the tub away and came with another and washed him all over again, then toweled him before the fire, cut his hair and combed it, and dressed him in a simple shirt with an elaborately figured chain belt that glowed yellow as gold. Yellow as gold, thought Orem, but even then it did not occur to him that it might *be* gold. He would not have been able to tell real from sham anyway.

The magistrates looked at him one more time, to be sure. Orem did not care what they decided. It was enough to have felt the smooth cloth on his clean and aching skin, to have felt the heat of the fire, to have touched the warm brick with every finger and found that each one tingled alive, to test his feet and have them respond, living and warm.

Apparently he was the man they were looking for. "Yes. Yes, that will do. The best we can do." They brusquely apologized to him. "A terrible mistake, Orem, my boy. Just a mistake, could happen to anyone, you won't complain of this, will you?''

Complain? What did he have to complain of? Only keep me warm, he said, only keep me warm and clean and dry and I have no complaint at all. He fell asleep again before the magistrates left.

18

The Dance of Descent

How Orem Scanthips met Queen Beauty face to face, and loved her.

THE TORTURED TREES

They brought him to the palace in a twelve-wheeled carriage drawn by eleven horses, but he didn't think to count. Though he was still not fully strong again after his ordeal in the Gaols, he was dazzled by the wonders of the Palace, and gazed out the window at the mosaic-covered walls, the gilt minarets, the turquoise roofs, the bright-painted sculptures that grew in profusion beside the whitestone drive. The history they depicted was lost on Orem, but he recognized the perfection of these works of human hands.

But when he saw the sculptured garden in the circle of the palace drive, he was disturbed. Others had seen the trees and bushes growing to form elephants and giant roses and had admired them. The cleverness of the lovers grown in leaves; the heroic sculpture of the Battle of Greyling Mountain—Orem did not think they were clever or noble. He had enough of his mother in him to hate the violence done to the trees; he had enough of his father to be profoundly disturbed to see this verdure in the cold of early winter.

Then came the hands of the servants, so many hands silently touching him, lifting him weak and flexible from the carriage. "Don't the leaves fall here?" he asked.

"For a week, whenever the Queen chooses," said an oldish man. "Autumn pleases her from time to time, if only to have spring again the following day."

It was then that Orem understood the power of the Queen. He marveled that he had ever dared to challenge her. What-

ever punishment she meted out to him, he knew now that
there was no hope of resistance. He had been a shark trying to
gnaw away at the shore, sharp-toothed and dangerous, yet
unworthy of his adversary.

THE VIRGIN DANCER

They took him through rooms larger than the town of
Banningside, whose ceilings looked as distant as the sky. All
the walls were layered seven times in tapestries and metal-
work and stone. There was no marble that was not living with
the figures of men and animals engaged variously in killing
and in coitus. There was no iron that was not silvered, no
silver that was not inlaid with gold. The furniture was made
of heavy woods, yet all was delicately carved so that there
were thousands of tiny windows in the wood and it looked as
if the weight of it was borne by dark and insubstantial lace.
And through it all no one spoke to him, so that only gradually
did he come to realize that it was not for vengeance that the
Queen wanted him.

After all, in the villages and farms it was done only sym-
bolically, for they were poor. It was the Dance of Descent, of
course, the last thing Orem could have expected. And it was
done for real. He realized now that the carriage that bore him
to the palace had twelve wheels, that one of the six teams of
horses that drew it was incomplete. As he entered the Palace
he was surrounded by ten armored men, their shields marked
with nine black stones. The red-shirted barber cut his hair in
eight passes of the shears, and now seven naked women with
blood on their thighs immersed him six times in hot water and
five times in cold, so that he was given the sacrament of the
Sweet Sisters the only time in his life a man may receive it.

The only time in his life that a man may receive it, and at
that he finally thought to count; counted the women and still
could not believe. Not for this, they could not have brought
him to the palace for this. Yet when the women left, four
doors opened and through each came a young boy, naked,
without manhair. He could not doubt, though he did not
understand. He himself had been one of the Four Virgin Boys
at three of his brothers' Dances of Descent. On the farm the
Three Oils had been pig fat, sheep fat, and chicken fat, and

they had jostled and joked as they anointed and scraped. There was no joking now. The four young boys who knelt around him as he lay naked on the stone floor were sober and worked strenuously.

The oils did not reek of animals; they were delicate yet strong of scent, and the boys rubbed them firmly into his skin, each oil in turn, scraping his body between the oils. They did not even speak to ask him to turn himself over; instead, their thin childish arms reached out and their small hands gripped him firmly, and he was turned abruptly without any volition of his own, and yet without any discomfort, either. The odor of the oils went into his head, and he felt a slight aching between his eyes. Yet it was a delicious pain, and the scraping of his body was a pleasure he was not prepared for. It left him weak and relaxed and trembling, and he reached gratefully for the first of the Two Cups when they brought it in.

No rough clay cups here. The Cup of the Left Hand was a crystal bowl set in a lacy gold cradle that rested on the top of a thin spiral stem. The liquid in it was green and seemed to be alive with light, a smooth light that did not flicker with the dancing of the lamps on the walls. As he reached for the cup with his left hand, Orem was filled again with fear. This was the stuff of poems, but he was not ready, had not been warned. *I am like Glasin Grocer, chosen by chance for adventures that only the Sweet Sisters could have predicted. I am not ready,* he cried out inside himself; but still his hand reached out, and though he trembled he spilled no drop of the green. In the villages it had been a tea of mints; here it was a wine, and when it touched his tongue the flavor went through him like ice, bringing winter to every part of his body, so that he felt it sharply in his fingers, and his buttocks clenched involuntarily. Still he drank it all, though when he was through, his body shook violently and his teeth chattered. Steam rose from the empty crystal cup.

The Cup of the Right Hand was made of stone, plain unpolished stone with no figuring or sculpture on it, except that it was cut to make the proper bent curve required even on the farm. The soul of the woman he had drunk, and now he reached down with his right hand to pick up the soul of the man. The stone was not as heavy as he had expected, and he nearly spilled, but the thick white fluid was heavy and slow as mud, and did not slosh easily over the edge.

This time when he sipped the drink was hot, and did not penetrate as quickly as the cold. On the farm it had been cream, and perhaps it was cream here, too; but it was sweet, painfully sweet and hot enough to burn his tongue. Yet he drank the thick stuff down, and set the cup aside slowly, relishing the heat as it fought the cold within him and won. He knew that his skin was flushing, that his face was red. He gasped his breaths and knelt on all fours, his head hanging down nearly to the floor as his body absorbed the heat of the soul of the man.

Then the servants bore away the Two Cups, and others led him to a golden chair covered with a thick velvet cloth, where he sat waiting for the One Red Ring. Not made of painted wood, the ring they brought; it was carved whole from a ruby, a thing whose value was so beyond Orem's understanding that not until long after did he realize that the price of that ring would have bought a thousand farms like his father's farm, with enough left over to buy ten thousand slaves to work them.

Which finger? How did his brothers ever decide? All his future could hinge on this one choice.

He raised his left hand, the hand of passion, without much thinking of the meaning of it, only because that was the hand that wanted to rise. The servant picked up the ring between forefinger and thumb and waited for Orem to choose. And he chose; the one finger no man would ever choose. He chose the last finger, the small finger, the finger of weakness and surrender. He flushed with shame at his choice, but knew that he could make no other. Why? he asked himself.

But he did not know the why of anything today. It was too quick, too strange, too inexorable. He had thought to earn a poem. Instead, he had just completed the Dance of Descent, and somewhere nearby was the woman he was to marry. Marry, now, at sixteen years of age; and with all that had passed in the Dance of Descent, Orem had little doubt who his wife would be, though it was a thought so outrageous that he would never have dared to name her name aloud.

To his surprise, he was not asked to arise from the chair. Instead, with the ruby ring on his leftmost finger, he sat in the chair as porters passed rods through rings on its sides and lifted him up, bore him from the room. There was no door at that end, but the wall itself parted in a great crack from floor to ceiling, and then slid aside, and he was carried into the presence of the Queen.

Beauty's Gentle Wedding to Her Husband's Son

Behind him the doors slid shut again, and the only light in the room was the moonlight that came through great windows and was reflected off a thousand mirrors on the walls. In the mottled silver light, he saw her standing alone and naked in the middle of the floor, her bare feet white and smooth as the cold marble they seemed carved from. Do you doubt that I can describe her? Her hair was long and full, and reached below her waist; the hair of her head was the only hair on her body, and she could have been a child except for the small, perfect breasts that, in their slow and tiny rise and fall, were the only proof that she was alive.

Her face he recognized. It was the perfect, pleading, loving, inevitable face of the woman in his dream. She was the virgin, begging for his gentlest love. She was Queen Beauty, and she was now his wife.

He stood from his chair, keenly aware of his own thin, unproportioned body, tanned and weathered from the waist; yet soon he had scant thought for shame at what little he had to offer the only perfect woman in the world. For she raised her hand, and it was her right hand, and the golden ring she wore was on the impossible finger, the finger he could not have hoped for; the small finger of her right hand, her rightmost finger, and as he walked to her, his hand upraised, the rings on their fingers rested the same distance from the fingertip.

If he had chosen to surrender all his passion, she had chosen to surrender all her will.

"Are you a virgin?" she whispered, her voice soft and urgent.

He nodded.

It was not enough. Impatiently she asked again. "My boy, my husband, my Little King, has your seed ever spilled inside another woman's womb?"

And Orem spoke, though where he found his voice he wasn't sure. "Never."

She leaned forward and kissed him. It was a cold kiss, yet it lingered and Orem did not want it ever to end. As she kissed him, her breasts leaned in to touch his chest, and then they met hip to hip, and her left hand was behind his back and she clung to him. He did not think of the unfaced sisters or the whore he had been unfit to use; he had neither need nor wish to worry about what his body could and could not do. The kiss ended. "I will never love you," she whispered. "You will never have my heart." But the tones of her voice rang with love, and Orem trembled at the power she had without using any magic at all.

Should he answer? He could not. For he had worn the ring on the hand of passion, and that was a vow to love forever and completely. Yet in his heart he knew, without knowing why, that he would never love her, either. His heart was surrendered, but not to her; her will was surrendered, but not to him.

"We will have a child," she said softly, leading him to the place where the floor gave way to a vast sea of a bed.

"It will be a boy," she said as they knelt together and her hands softly touched him.

"I will give him all of myself," she said, "and that is why there will be none of me for you."

They lay together all the night, and the twelve-month child was conceived. Orem knew the moment that it happened, for the Queen cried out in joy, and for a moment her eyes were too bright to look upon. I am in and of you, Orem said silently.

Two times you had her body also, Palicrovol. Once she did not want you, and once you did not want her. But did you ever look into her face and say I am in and of you? You gave her no Dance of Descent, King of Burland. Do you begrudge her this: that once in her life she had a man who loved her with his whole heart, if only for that moment?

And if it tortures you to know that another man was with her in her life, console yourself with this: he only knew her but the once, though for weeks afterward, Orem had only to think on some moment of that night with Beauty and his body would be roused, would violently spend itself, all in a few seconds from the memory of it. When Beauty possesses a man, Palicrovol, is he to be held responsible for what his body does?

Yet I will not pretend that she forced him the way she forced you. Orem knew as no other man could know that none of it was magic. She had worked no spell on him that night. She could not have, for a twelve-month child cannot be magically conceived. What Orem felt for her was genuine, and not just for love of her perfect flesh. I know Orem truly, and I know that when he loved his bride it was not a Queen he loved, but rather the girl Asineth as she might have been if she had not been destroyed in her childhood.

Is that why you hate him so, Palicrovol? Because he knows the woman that she might have been?

19

The Queen's Companions

How Orem came to be called the Little King and met those who would most kindly, most cruelly use him.

THE LOVE OF BEAUTY

Who can blame Orem Scanthips for awaking in wonder, surprised at joy? For the first time in his life the truth was better than the dream, and more improbable. For that first hour he thought he had found name and place and poem, all in one, and that all were happy. Sunlight danced from a thousand mirrors. And more:

I believe that if Beauty had been kind to him, he would have loved her, and so we and the gods would have been undone.

Yet if Beauty had been able to be kind, it would not have taken her death to release us all from bondage.

So we go in circles. And here is the cruelest circle of all, Palicrovol: I believe that, by the end of her life, Beauty loved Orem Scanthips as much in her way as the Flower Princess loved her King. Though Orem was born when Beauty had already passed three centuries of life in power, still the girl Asineth had found her lover—a dreamer, a good man, a kind man who cared less for his plan than for the people in it. That is how he was unlike you, Palicrovol, and that is why she loved him.

Poor Beauty. May I not pity her, of all people? She loved him, but she had only learned one way to show her love— through cruelty and abuse. After all, whom did she love most in all the world? Those who had dwelt at her right and left hand for fifteen score years: Weasel Sootmouth, Urubugala, and Craven. That was what she knew of love. No wonder Orem never recognized her love when she gave it to him.

Even now, if he knew that she had loved him, it would break his heart.

But he did not know, and does not know, because this is how she served him from the first day of their life as husband and wife:

THE NAMING OF THE LITTLE KING

In the morning they dressed him in brocades and velvet, clothes so heavy that at first they bowed him and made him look a bit ridiculous. He did not know how to wear the robes of a King—that is not born in a man, as you know. Then they led him through the palace, whispering to him the names of the rooms so he could ask for them again, though he did not yet know what to do with the Chamber of Stars or the Hall of Asps, the Porch of Keening or the Room of the Dancing Bulls.

At the foot of a stair he saw an old man who seemed out of place, for instead of livery he wore only an old soiled wrap, and was covered with wood-colored stains. The old man's back was twisted, as if he had been wrung by great hands. He bent over the stair, pouring a clear fluid onto the wood and rubbing, rubbing it into the grain. Orem only paused to avoid stepping in his work. The man looked up at him. His eyebrows were heavy as moustaches, but they were the only hair on his face. The skin of his face was transparent, and the veins and arteries pulsed blue and red just under the surface. Eyes deep as amber, thick as cream, and with no pupil in them at all, none at all.

"Are you blind?" Orem asked softly. Surely he could not see without an aperture for vision; yet didn't the eyes look up at him?

"To light I am blind," whispered the old man, not taking his gaze from Orem's face.

Where had he seen such eyes? "Who are you?" Orem asked.

"I am God," said the old man. He smiled, and his mouth had neither tongue nor teeth nor anything at all—just blackness behind the lips. Then he bent again to his work, and the servants gently insisted Orem up the stairs.

Who but the Little King would have spoken to an aged,

naked servant oiling the wooden stairs? This is sure: only one who carried with him an invisible hole in Queen Beauty's Searching Eye could have heard the answer that Orem heard. He did not understand; he did not forget, either, despite all he learned of Queen Beauty before the hour was up.

Who but Queen Beauty could be noticed in the Moon Chamber, with its great discs of silver lit by a thousand candles? She used it as her private court. The servants led Orem to the edge of that huge circle of glass called now the Round Table and called then Beauty's Moon. He faced the Queen, who sat on her ivory throne.

When the servants had left, the Queen arose and stepped forward, offering him her hand. Orem took it and started to bow to her, unsure of protocol, thinking only of the night before and marveling that this woman now was his wife. But the Queen stopped him, and did not let him bow. Instead she bowed her head to him. The gasp from behind him was the first he noticed that someone else was in the room.

"Beauty has taken a wife," intoned a high-pitched voice with an edge of madness, "to last her all his life. Has she taken him to bed with poison in his head?"

The Queen lifted her head and faced the others in the room; Orem also turned. In the middle of the table sat a black man, a small man, nearly naked, with a headdress of cow's horns on his head and an immense false phallus hanging from his belt. He had not been there when Orem entered. It was he who had recited the rhyme, and now he spoke again.

> What a pretty little king,
> With a pretty little thing,
> But will the bee still sing
> When he finds he has no sting?

"Shut up," the Queen said beautifully. The dwarf turned a somersault and landed, laughing, at Beauty's feet.

"Ah, beat me, beat me, Beauty!" cried the black man, and then he wept piteously. In a moment he started tasting the tears, then retreated to a corner of the room, dabbing at his eyes with the stuffed phallus that dangled longer than his legs.

"As you see," said the Queen, "I have taken a husband. He is a common criminal from the filthiest part of the city. He is as attractive to me as a leprous hog. But he was given to me in a dream from the Sweet Sisters, and it amused me to follow their advice."

Orem could not sort out the difference between her sweet, musical voice and the harsh words she was saying. He smiled stupidly, vaguely aware that he was being abused, but unable to be angry at the song from Queen Beauty's lips.

"As you see, he is also quite stupid. He once had a name, but in this court he will be called Little King. Also, despite the fact that he has the sexual prowess of a dung beetle, we conceived a child last night."

Orem was not surprised that Queen Beauty already knew. Other women might have to wait until the moon didn't rise for them, but not *her*. With Beauty such things were not left to chance.

"You will speak of my child to the others, my Gossips. Spread it as a rumor through all the world. Dear Palicrovol will know what it means, even if the rest do not, and he will come to knock at my gates. I miss the man. I want to see him weep again."

Each in turn the Queen's Companions came to her, and she received them gravely.

The old soldier's step was slow and unsteady; he lurched under the weight of the armor. His voice was hollow and soft, full of air. He spoke to Orem first.

"Little King, I see you wear your ring wisely. Look at it often and follow its advice." Then he turned to the Queen and looked in her eyes. Orem was surprised by the force of his gaze—when the old man looked at him his eyes had been gentle and soft, but now they were full of fire. Hatred? This man had power despite his weak body and the large armor that made a joke of it. "Beauty, dear Beauty," said the old soldier, "I give your child a blessing. May your son have my strength."

Orem looked at the Queen in alarm. Surely she would be angry that the old man had cursed her unborn child so. Orem knew well the power of wishes on the unborn—many a dullwit and cripple had been the result of an ill-thought jest. But the Queen only nodded and smiled as if the old man had given her a great gift.

And then the woman. Her walk was canted a bit, so that one step was long, the next short. Her hands were gnarled and twisted, and when she touched Orem's cheek it felt as though her fingers were scaled like fish. She smiled, and Orem realized that the dirt on her lip was a scraggly moustache; her hair was also thin and wispy, and she was bald in a few patches, which had not been granted even the mercy of a wig. "Little King," she said in a voice that grated like the cry of a rutting hen, "be lonely, love no one, and live long." Then she, too, turned to the Queen. "I also give your child a blessing. May your son have my beauty."

Again the Queen accepted the cruel curse as if it were a gift.

The short man waddled up to take his turn, grinning idiotically. He stopped in front of Orem and pulled down his loincloth to reveal that he had only one testicle in his scrotum, and a penis so small it could hardly be seen. "I'm half what I should be," said the fool, "but twice the man you are." Then he giggled, pulled his loincloth back in place, and darted forward to part Orem's robe and lift his shirt and peer under it. Orem tried to back away, but the dwarf was quick and saw what he wanted to see. "Little King!" he crowed as he emerged from Orem's clothing. "Little King!" Then, suddenly, he was somber. "The Queen sees all, except that which she sees not that she sees not. Remember it, Little King!"

In the moment before the black dwarf turned away, he winked, and Orem found himself inexplicably sure that this fool knew something that Orem needed very much to learn.

"Beauty, dear Beauty," sang the little black man to the Queen,

> I bless your little unborn child
> On whom all gods but four have smiled:
> Though all his life the lad hear lies,
> He'll be as wise as I am wise.

Then, laughing uproariously, the fool somersaulted backward and sprawled under the table.

Orem was horrified at the bitter gifts they had given the Queen's child—his child, for that matter, though he was far from having much parental feeling for a creature he could not even imagine yet. All Orem knew was that a great discourtesy had been done, and he fumblingly tried to put it right. He knew no blessings for the unborn except the common one used in Banningside and the farm country, the blessing Halfpriest Dobbick had invariably used. Orem turned to the Queen and said, "Queen Beauty, I'd like to bless the child."

She half-smiled at him; he thought it was assent, not amusement. He blurted out his gift in words that in themselves had little meaning to him, only that they were a proper blessing: "May the child live to serve God."

Orem had meant it as a kindness; the Queen took it as a curse. She slapped his face with such force that he fell to the floor. His cheek was cut open by her ring. What had he said? From his place on the floor he watched as she looked imperiously at the others and said, in a voice dripping with hate, "My Little King's gift has no more power than his pud." Then she turned to her boy-husband. "Command and bless as you like, my Little King; you will only be obeyed by those who laugh at you." Then the Queen turned and started toward the door. She stopped at the threshold. "Urubugala," she said firmly. The black fool suddenly scrambled from under the table, and Orem knew it was his name.

"Come here," the Queen said. Urubugala kept crawling, whining about his sad lot in life. He passed close to Orem, who instinctively retreated from the strange man. Suddenly the fool's black hand snaked out and grabbed Orem viciously by the arm and pulled him close. Orem lost his balance, and in the struggle to get up he found the fool's lips against his ear. "I know you, Orem," came the almost soundless whisper. "I have waited long for you."

Orem was kneeling, the fool standing in front of him—they were almost the same height, then—and the fool kissed him firmly on the mouth and put his hands on Orem's head and shouted, "I name you with your true name, boy! You are Hart's Hope!"

A shudder went through Orem, violent as if the floor itself had shaken. Orem ap Avonap, Scanthips, Banningside, Little King—of all the names he was given, only Hart's Hope was given him with the Passage of Names. His priestword would have been given him that way, had he taken oaths.

And perhaps the floor *had* shaken, for the fool was writhing on the ground, screaming in agony, clutching his head. Is it a show, part of his game of idiocy, or is the pain real?

"His name is Little King, and he will have no other," said the Queen from the door.

She left. Urubugala immediately stopped screaming. He lay panting on the floor a moment, then arose and walked out of the room, following the Queen.

Orem also stood. His cheek hurt, and so did his elbow where he had hit the floor. He was confused; he understood nothing. He turned to the others, the ugly woman and the weak old soldier. They regarded him with pitying eyes. He did not really understand their pity, either.

"What do I do now?" he asked.

They glanced at each other. "You're the Little King," said the soldier. "You can do what you like."

"King." Orem didn't know what to make of it. "I saw Palicrovol once."

"Did you," said the woman. She did not sound interested.

"He covers his eyes with golden hemispheres, so the Queen can't use his eyes to see."

The woman chuckled. "Then he does it in vain, doesn't he? For the Queen sees everything."

Except where I go and take away her sight, Orem thought but did not say.

"She sees everything, like an orchestra of visions in the back of her mind. She watches always." The woman laughed. "She sees us now. And she is laughing, I'm sure."

It made Orem afraid, then. How much *did* she see? She had given him no sign she knew of his tampering with her powers. Yet if she knew nothing of his gift, why had she chosen him? Not love, that much was plain now, and he knew enough to be ashamed in front of these companions of the Queen, ashamed of being so weak and helpless and pathetic. His very shame overcame fear. If she was going to discover his power or somehow limit it, let her do it now. He let his net slip from him, just enough to fill the room, to clear the room of that sickening sweet overlay of Beauty's Searching Eye. When Beauty could not see, he spoke: "What is the boar allowed to do once the sow is serviced?"

Their eyes widened, and for a moment they said nothing, waiting, he supposed, for Queen Beauty to strike him down. Either she had heard and did not care or, as Orem hoped, she had not heard. Had not heard, and so he might have some small pathetic power here, enough that he need not be ashamed.

"I asked," he said again, "what I am free to do."

"Apparently," said the woman, "whatever you want."

The grave rumble of the old man's voice added: "You command everyone. You're the husband of the Queen. Little King is who you are, and they must obey."

It was a heady thought, and Orem distrusted it. "Tell me your names, then."

"I beg your pardon," said the ugly woman. "We spoke in error. You command everyone but Urubugala and us."

"And why not you?"

"Because we do not laugh at you."

The implication was obvious. "Then all others will laugh."

They glanced at each other again, and the woman whispered, "It is Beauty's will. And what can stop Beauty from being obeyed?"

It was not an empty question, not entirely. She was asking him if indeed he knew something that they did not know. But he dared not answer, dared not explain to them just what he was, even if he had known for sure himself. What can stop Beauty from being obeyed? Beauty sees all—except that which she sees not that she sees not. Does she not see me? And does she not see that she sees me not? Riddles, riddles. I cannot answer them because I do not know.

"The less you command," said the soldier, "the less they will laugh."

"Don't tell him that, Craven," said the ugly woman. "Little King, command all you like. Your life will be easier if they all laugh. Keep them laughing. The Queen, too, will laugh."

"If the Queen laughs, then will I command *her*, too?"

Again the moment of startlement at his impudence; again nothing happened. And this time the ugly woman smiled and the old soldier wheezed. "Who can say?" whispered the soldier.

"Craven. Is that your name?"

The soldier immediately soured. "It is the name the Queen gave to me."

"And you," Orem said to the old woman. "What may I call you?"

"I am called Weasel, surnamed Sootmouth. It is the name the Queen gave me."

"I had a name before she named me," said Orem. "Did you?"

"If I did," said Weasel, "I don't remember it."

"But you must. My name is really—"

But she put a rough and scaly hand to his mouth. "You can't say it. And if you could, it would cost you dearly. Don't try to remember."

And then he made plain to them that he was not the slim-hipped boy he seemed to be. He reached out with his subtle inward tongue and tasted them gently, where their sparks so brightly glowed. In the momentary tasting he could feel how they were bound so cold and grey, their lights smothered under a thousand spells. He did not undo all the spells, only the small spell of forgetfulness there, a common, an easy thing to do; hadn't he done it for Gallowglass?

No sooner done than regretted, however. For they looked at him with widened eyes, eyes that did not see him: they were turned inward, to see what had been lost so long from memory and now had been returned. And they wept. The old soldier Craven with his cold grey tears silently streaking his cheeks, remembering his strength; ugly Weasel Sootmouth with her face contorted more than ever, hideous with grief, remembering her husband.

Then they winced in pain and looked toward the door, and there was the Queen.

Queen Beauty, but now not haughty and imperious: now raging, with her eyes dancing as if aflame. They *were* afire, Orem saw, for flames licked outward, throwing light that danced in the silver discs and dazzled on the table. "How have you remembered what I took from you?" Her voice shook the room.

Weasel and Craven said nothing.

The Queen shouted and the discs banged on the wall. Weasel and Craven fell to the floor. Frightened as he was, Orem thought to wonder if he should pretend to be affected by whatever magic she was using. Before he could act, however, Urubugala took matters out of Orem's hands. He rolled out in front of the Queen and unfolded himself to lie supine before her, his face almost at her feet.

"You can't make Urubugala forget," he said. "What Urubugala once was, Urubugala always is."

All was still. The Queen looked down at the dwarf and smiled beautifully. It was the smile of impending cruelty; we all knew it well by then, except Orem.

"Are you?" she asked. "And what did you hope to accomplish? You couldn't stop me before; do you think some petty little spells of unmaking would terrify me?" She took hold of his hair and pulled him up as if he were no heavier than a dog. "Urubugala, my little fool, don't you know that your little unmakings caused all this? Oh, yes, Urubugala, your little try at resisting me, at helping the old cock escape me—I realized then that it was nearly time, nearly time to renew myself, Urubugala, and so the Little King is here, I called upon the Sisters for a dream and they obliged me, and sent me Little King and the infant in my womb. Do you think you can stop me?"

"No," said Urubugala, grinning.

"Or did you merely hope that I would let you die?"

"Your gracious self has long permitted me to live in your infinite mercy."

Her smile broadened, and the flames leapt from her eyes and ignited Urubugala's clothing. The dwarf screamed. As if his scream were the power of flight he rose into the air, high above the table, and there burned and burned, screaming. Orem was nauseated, stabbed with guilt. The dwarf had taken blame for all his acts, all his acts, and now was dying for it.

But not dying, after all. For as suddenly as the flames began, they stopped, and the dwarf was lowered, panting and whimpering, to the table. Queen Beauty walked near to him, reached out and took him by the ears, pulled him until she bent directly over his face, looked directly into his eyes.

"Did you block me at the cod's camp? Let me in, Urubugala, or I'll set you burning forever."

"In in in," he whispered. "All you like, see it all—" and he gasped a great rush of air and convulsed on the table. His head rose up, eyes locked on Beauty's eyes, until their faces touched, upside down to each other, mistress and slave, mother and child, Urubugala's head suspended by nothing but the force of Beauty's gaze.

She was finished. Urubugala's head dropped with a loud

crack on the table. "The truth, the truth, name of the Sisters it's the truth. I was so sure it was you."

"Oh well," whispered the dwarf.

"Do you think I'm not a match for it, whatever it is? I won't be threatened by a petty wizard who has learned your unmaking spells, Urubugala."

"Oh well."

"Don't try me, Urubugala. I won't let you have even such a victory as that." And then she touched his forehead and he suddenly relaxed. Slept. Orem saw that his skin was unmarked by the flames. The Queen addressed Craven and Weasel. "And yet, why should I remake the mercies he removed? It pleases me that you should again remember all, think of all. Will you hate me? Hate me all you like. You will watch as I am made again, and hate me as you watch, and still you will do nothing, you can do nothing, don't you see? Urubugala may give you back your memories, but I think you'll wish for the old forgetfulness again. Don't bother asking me. Ask *him*." She pointed at the sleeping dwarf. "See what *he* can do."

The Queen was gone. Craven and Weasel watched her go, then turned and stared at Orem. He opened his mouth to speak, but Weasel put her hand to her mouth and shook her head. What then? They only waited, watched him. Until he realized that they were waiting for *him* to make it safe for them to speak. So again he timidly let out his net and cleared the room.

Urubugala instantly sat up in the middle of the table. "Never again," he said to Orem. "Touch whatever you like, do whatever you like, but not to us. We three, the Queen's Companions, we are her ornaments and she'll not have us altered."

Plainly Urubugala knew what he was, and as plainly believed that the Queen did not overhear them. What could Orem do but trust him? "I'm sorry," he said.

Weasel said softly, "You couldn't know."

"Why am I here?" Orem asked.

Perhaps Weasel would have told him; she made as if to speak. But Urubugala raised his hand. "It's not for us to guess what the gods are doing. You're guided by wiser eyes than ours and we'll tell you nothing more. Only this: Seek not, and you will find; ask not, and it will be given you; do not knock, and the doors will open for you.''

Then Urubugala rolled from the table and dropped to the ground at Orem's feet. Orem looked down and met his upward turning gaze.

''Even Beauty does not know why *you* are here.''

And the black man waddled out the door, his phallus dragging between his legs; no longer funny, not to Orem, for he had seen him endure agony and speak again as if it were nothing.

The dwarf had preserved him, and borne his punishment, and kept him free. Craven and Weasel had kept their silence for his sake. If this was not friendship, Orem did not understand the word. They had his loyalty forever. Yet in truth they did not want it. They were loyal to you, Palicrovol, not to Orem, and he never understood that until the end; too late for him, and only just in time for you.

20

The Uses of Power

How did Orem use the name of King while he sat upon your throne, Palicrovol? You judged a King of Burland once before, when you were young. As Count Traffing you watched King Nasilee and thought him weak and wicked, deserving only death. What were his crimes? He was vengeful and cruel, rapacious and tyrannical. There are some who say it was his taxes that annoyed you, his weakness that tempted you, his daughter you desired, child though she was. You were ambitious, say these envious ones. But you have proved by your acts that you truly despise vengefulness and unjust punishment. So now let us judge the Little King, not by rumor, but by what he did with the power that was his to use freely. By that measure I think he was a fit son of Palicrovol.

THE LITTLE KING AT COURT

For a week, Queen Beauty presented him as her husband to all of the hundreds of visitors and thousands of courtiers in the Palace. She never spoke of him without some crude and clever jest, some taunt that set the courtiers tittering behind their oh-so-delicate hands. His thinness, his youth, his supposed stupidity, his genuine innocence, all were cause of much mirth.

Yet Orem was wise, he heeded the advice of the Queen's Companions and bore it patiently and also laughed, and soon enough, though all despised him, all were used to him and content with his role. He had his name at last, and his place: Little King, and butt of jokes.

After the first week the Queen no longer came along to taunt him. Others in a case like his might have hidden, might have stayed away from the balls and suppers. But Orem did not stay away. He came, learning to be ever more regal in his bearing. This excited much laughter among the fops, who thought he was trying to rival them. They never noticed that he was in fact what they only pretended to be. He came and openly sustained the role the Queen had forced on him. Part of Orem's role was to be a bumpkin and a boor. He learned it early and played it well.

Six weeks after his wedding he presided at a petty banquet for the resident courtiers. At his right hand sat Weasel Sootmouth; at his left sat Craven; there is order in these things. The banquet guests were perfectly willing to bait him, of course. No sooner was the first course well placed upon the table than a woman cried out, "My lord Little King, will you judge for us? My husband, there with his hand on Belfeva's thigh—he has treated me most unfaithfully." She then laid before them the shocking story—shocking, that is, to Orem—of her husband's infidelity with barnyard animals. She told it with practiced wit; only Orem of all the listeners didn't know the pleasant conventions of witty and ribald complaint. His face flushed, and his surprise at hearing such a tale at all gave way to anger at the husband's behavior; after all, there sat the husband, laughing with all the rest. Laughing! These people had no sense of right and wrong, it seemed.

Then Weasel Sootmouth leaned to him and whispered with her scaly twisted lips close to his ears, "Don't take it seriously, Little King. It's a lie, for entertainment."

At first that did little to soothe Orem's anger. After all, a lie was a lie, whether for entertainment or not. But now the laughter took on a different meaning, and he began to listen not so much to her husband's supposed sins as to the wit of her accusations. She *was* clever. It was the turn of phrase that provoked the laughter, that and the supposed clumsiness of the husband. At last she finished, and imploringly looked at him and said, "So tell me, my lord Little King, command me—should I take him back into my bed or cut off a good six inches when next he comes to me?"

"That would be too hard a punishment, Lady," Orem answered. "How can you take six from three and hope to have anything left over?"

It was more than the courtiers had hoped for. The crude accents of the country, yes; the high, thin voice of an adolescent; the innocent, guileless face, were all that could be wished. And then to have him match her bawdry—the evening promised excellence. Excellence. The Queen had chosen her bumpkin consort well.

The much-abused husband cried, "I implore you, my lord Little King! Don't make me give up *all* my liaisons! The chickens give little satisfaction and egg production has fallen off considerably. The cows I can part with. But the sow is my heart, my life, my love!"

"How can I judge from here?" Orem asked. "I have to look you in the eye. Let someone else sit here at the end of the table. Nothing against you, you understand," he told Craven and Weasel. He could sense Weasel's concern for him, that she wanted to be near enough to guide him. With the laughter and conversation loud enough to cover his words, he bent to her and said, "Now I know they laugh at clever foulness."

Then he picked up his own plate and silver, held his napkin in his mouth, and marched down to the middle of the table, displacing a particularly colorful dandy to set himself between two of the more outlandish ladies of the court. The husband and wife were both across from him, but several seats away to either hand. He peered at both of them, then laughed. "Lady, I must commend you both for your humility. You, for admitting that your rival was a sow, and he for admitting that no lovelier female would be his paramour. With such humility, I find you suited for each other. You must remain together—such candor deserves nothing less than its equal." The others at table laughed as much at his boyishness and country speech as at his wit—but no more. He would make his way and bear what he had to do.

But the unusually lovely woman across the table from him only smiled, and in her eyes was a hint of correction, even of pity. "Shouldn't you be at the head of the table?" she asked.

"Wherever I am is the head of the table," Orem answered. If *you* had said it, Palicrovol, it would have been a rebuke, and the hearers would have trembled. But in his voice and with his forthright manner, the words were ludicrous; and even if they had not been, so strong was the predisposition to laughter that they would have been amused anyway.

There was one man who was not amused, however, or at least gave no sign of it. A youngish man himself, and something of a favorite with the ladies because he was so dark and somber and strong. The sort of man one always assumes has the parts of a stallion, for which one will forgive him the manners of a hedgehog. His name was Timias. He was of that class of men who, like a flower, bloom once, with thorns, and soon fade, taking some minor post that allows them to haunt the scenes of their conquests. Yet he had a knack for truth that was part of his charm and a hint that he might end up with a more romantic and therefore brief career than others of his sort. One might suppose, uncharitably, that he was envious of the boy who had slept with the Queen. But Orem saw something else in him. Another of Orem's unsung gifts, that: to see in someone what no one else could see.

Timias was sitting on the diagonal from the Little King. The laughter died down and the ladies near him began to bask in the attention the Little King was paying them—after all, silly or not, he was the only king in Inwit. Orem made some silly comments about how much more beautiful the ladies would be without their paint—after all, said he, the country girls did well without it.

"What do they do, then, to be attractive?" asked a lady.

"They wash," said Orem. "And without paint, they aren't as slippery as you ladies—when a man takes hold, they never slip out of his grasp!" How they laughed. It was too good a show to let it lag. He called for water and made a great show of washing the face of a lady—but not the one near him, for he could see that she was in fact quite ugly and her paint was a miracle of salvage. Instead Orem washed the face of the lady across from him, who profited from the cleaning, for she had fine features. And she had criticized him, however tacitly, which gave a little pleasure to his unpainting of her. Who noticed Orem's tact and kindness in the one case, or his petty pleasure in the other? They only laughed, for it was amusing to watch him flout centuries-old traditions and week-old fashions. What a clown. What a rustic. What a boor. Delightful.

It was then that Timias acted—reached out and took the Little King by the wrist before he could follow the laughter of the crowd into washing the false birthmark off the lady's bosom. "You may be an ass," said Timias coldly, "but you needn't leap into the proof with such assurance."

All were quiet then, except for murmurs of surprise. Timias wasn't laughing. Timias was spoiling all the fun. Peace, Timias. Let be, Timias. But Orem looked at him, wearing the half-witted smile that in his home country would have been regarded as a sign of frank good will.

"What, man, is she your wife?" asked Orem.

Oh, they laughed at that. But Timias only grew colder and darker. "So your cock has filled a Queen, boy? Bloody lot of good may it do you."

It was the sort of remark that was not said, above all not in the Palace, for surely the Queen would hear.

"It's done me some," Orem said quietly. And then he remembered he needed to be amusing. "Shall we have a duel for the lady's honor?"

There were some titters at that. If it hadn't been for Timias's seriousness, there would have been more.

"The lady's honor is above the need of defense," said Timias. It was the courteous way to back down. Insult was one thing, but the thought of dueling the Little King was too dangerous. The Queen would surely not permit it. The chance of Timias losing would be too slight. But Orem would not let him drop the matter gracefully. The Little King was there to be laughed at, wasn't he? So let there be fuel for many a guffaw.

"How can you leave the lady championless, when I say her breast is in need of washing?" He turned to the lady. "What's your name, after all? Belfeva! Such a noble breast, Belfeva, and yet so friendless in this company!" He had learned the diction of the court quickly—it was just another game with words, like the puzzles and riddles he had created in the House of God. What a riotous clown, thought most who were there. How artfully he acts, thought those few who watched wisely. "I accept your challenge even if you don't offer it. And the weapon, what weapon will do, except for—yes, take your bread, sir! And your goblet! Wine-soaked bread at twenty paces."

It was hilarious, of course, just the thought of it. But more: it was impossible for Timias to bear. It's the flaw of the serious and cold—they cannot bear to be made ridiculous. "I'll do no such thing," said Timias.

"Then you'll come to my rooms tomorrow noon," said the Little King. "We have things to talk about, my friend."

"I have nothing to talk about with you." But the assurance in his manner had weakened. Alone of the courtiers, Timias now realized that Orem was cleverer than he appeared, and could turn things his own way more easily than anyone but the victim would know.

"Then bring this lady, with her breast but *without* her birthmark, and you may help me judge which is more beautiful—your companion, sir, or mine."

"No one is more beautiful than Queen Beauty."

"Ah, but Queen Beauty is not my companion. She keeps me as a pet, you know, and doesn't like to hear me bark too often or too near at hand. My companion tomorrow will be—" and he cast his gaze up to the head of the table "—will be the lady Weasel Sootmouth."

All eyes turned to the formidably ugly woman. She understood something of what Orem was doing, and so she leaned back her head and laughed. All could laugh, then. Once again the inept Little King had provided startlement enough for a week's gossip. Once again the banquet was a success.

Orem was not so stupid as he seemed to the courtiers, nor so clever as he seemed to Timias. He had no conscious plan in mind. He only knew that Timias did not laugh at him, and that attracted him; he was afraid, and lonely, and tired of the constant show he had to perform. Timias's very distaste for him made Orem want to like him.

THE FRIENDS OF THE LITTLE KING

They came as commanded to Orem's room: Timias, the woman Belfeva, and Weasel. It was a strange meeting, at first. Almost nothing was said while the servants spread a "little" meal. Orem was already used to the plenty, and wise enough not to partake too heavily. He watched Timias and Belfeva as they awkwardly ate, repeatedly asking them the same question: "Is it good?"

"Oh, very good, very good," they said. It was clear that the strain was making Belfeva more and more afraid, but the truth in Timias led him to be angry, not frightened, and at last he said, "My lord Little King, why did you bring us here? If you want me to apologize, I will. I spoke improperly last night. However you want to shame yourself is fine with me."

Orem showed no sign of noticing that it was an ungracious apology. "You're generous, but I care very little about last night."

"Then why are we here?"

"I want company. For an expedition."

"Expedition?" asked Belfeva brightly. Timias glowered.

"Am I a prisoner in the Palace?" asked Orem. "I want to go abroad. As far as the garden. Or should I be more daring? King's Town is new to me. You know it well, since you have nothing better to do than explore."

"I have better things to do." Timias stood.

"We had a name for men like you in High Waterswatch," Orem said, and the geniality was gone from his voice. "We called them cold cocks. Lots of strut, but you could leave them alone with the hens for a year and never an egg would drop."

Timias flushed, but bore it silently.

Orem walked nearer. "You're twice my strength and probably twice any other virtue I might have, Timias. Why don't you laugh at me?"

Timias looked away. "I have an idea of what a King should be."

"So do I," said Orem. "But the man who fits that idea is off in the country somewhere, wearing golden balls on his eyes and never sleeping without priests and wizards on guard against the onslaughts of the Queen. Why should I pretend to be what he is? While the true King is alive, I can only be a buffoon."

And there it was—the key to Orem's real power in Inwit. The Queen had made him the butt of ridicule, perhaps expecting him to strive for dignity and so become more and more ridiculous. But Orem had a tool she did not know he had. As long as he spun his web to capture the Queen's magic in a room, he could say whatever treason he might like and not be overheard. No one would dare *repeat* his treasons, so the Queen would never hear of them—and in the meantime, the message to his hearers was unmistakable: the Little King may say what would be death for anyone else to say, and nothing happens to him. Let the laughers laugh. Among the very people least likely to be amused by him he was seen quite differently. The Queen does not punish the Little King for treason: therefore the Little King has power.

He did not show this power to many; but then there were so few who did not laugh at him.

"Come with me, Timias, and these ladies, too."

They went with him; many times they went with him, and showed him many things, and he showed them very little, but what they saw was enough, enough: I will show *you*, Palicrovol, and perhaps you will understand why Timias has stayed with Orem Scanthips even now, when he is no longer Little King.

They toured the gardens, and annoyed the gardeners with their conversation; visited the artists' workshops where old works were furbished, new ones manufactured; made the poets at Pools Park read their rhymes to them; admired and rode the horses at Queen's Stables; even toured the armory, for after all, the Little King was titular commander of the troops.

THE UNDOING OF JUSTICE

But always Orem had in mind another visit. It seemed to come like a whim one morning when they gathered as usual in his rooms to plan the day's discoveries. "Why not the Coal House, to watch them try the criminals?"

Not even Belfeva failed to recall that the Little King had been plucked from that court to wive the Queen; but why not go there, after all? If the Little King wished to remember how low he had been in order to appreciate better where he was now, who were they to try to dissuade him? So they left the Palace—the back way, as usual, through Kitchen Street, and made their way afoot to the Coal House, where the masked judges spent their days deciding which unfortunates would be dismembered and which be merely killed.

Weasel Sootmouth, knowing what havoc the Little King's arrival unannounced might cause, instructed a servant to go ahead and warn the judges of their coming. Of course they all pretended to be surprised; of course the pretense was unconvincing. Orem had seen the place from the wrong point of view to be fooled by any show they might put on for him now. And yet he was not vindictive. He refrained from reminding them how they had met before. Indeed, he stayed aloof, showing little interest in the Coal House court itself. That was not what he had come for. It was the Gaols he meant to see.

Their guide demurred. "Common criminals," he said. "Why see them?"

Quickly enough the silence reminded him that the Little King had been just such a common criminal. The guards led them out. They tried to steer the Little King away from the Steer Pit, but he knew his way. They came to an awkward moment: the cutter was getting his tools ready to do the job. A new victim was ready, so the one in the clamps had to be cut and sent on his way.

"Of all the reliefs on the palace walls, I think this is most lifelike," said Orem.

"What will they do?" asked Belfeva. Not that it had been kept a secret from her; the great houses simply never bothered to discuss the cruelty that kept the city safe for them.

"They'll make a steer of him," Orem said. He did not realize that she would have no notion of the difference between steers and bulls.

It was Weasel who explained to her. Belfeva turned away, aghast.

In the pit the cutter waited, wondering what his spectators expected him to do. Orem could not relieve his anxiety. He himself didn't know. The victim himself had chosen—better castration than slavery. Unless Orem meant to change the law itself, what could he do but go along with the man's decision? And changing the law was beyond his reach. He could make no lasting changes, only little meddlings that would not re-shape the working of Inwit, that would go unnoticed by the Queen.

At last Orem turned away, having said nothing. The cutter wasted no time after that—they were only a little way from the Steer Pit when they heard the piteous cries of the cut man.

The Gaols were as they had been, except that now it was spring. The prisoners did not freeze now. Instead they lived in the stench and flies of their own excrement on the ground below. The upmost prisoners, as always, had it better, for the flies were not so thick where they were. It was plain that many of the prisoners were ill.

"This one's new," Orem said quietly as they walked past the cages. "And this one's been here days. He'll die before trial." They did not ask him how he knew. He knew. He showed no feelings to his companions, but they could taste his quiet, knew that this place had broken something in him, and created something else, something that had made him not the rustic that even the Queen believed he was. Weasel took his hand. He let her, but gave no sign it mattered, and soon she let go of him again. She did not mind; it was enough to see something that the Queen did not see. There was hope in that.

Up and down the rows, up and down, as if each prisoner were not identical to all the others. At last Belfeva grew sick and lagged behind, and Timias rebuked the Little King. "Haven't we seen enough of this!" he demanded. "Why did you bring us here?"

Orem had no answer for him. Hadn't he asked the same question of Flea after the death at the snake fight? *I brought you here because there were two free hours. I brought you here to understand Queen's Town as it truly is, and not as it seems to you to be. I brought you here because in the criss-cross shadow of the cages, strangers saved my life. "They spat on me to wake me in the snow."*

At that moment a prisoner on the second level cried out and ran to the bars of the cage, shouting.

"Orem! Lad, remember me, remember me! The favor, lad!"

Immediately the guards were thick between Orem and the shouter's cage. "Quiet up there!" shouted one, and several archers readied their bows for quick restoration of quiet.

Orem knew the man before he could decide whether he wanted to know him or not. "Braisy," he said.

It was enough to stop the archers. The commander of the guards came to the Little King to explain. "He's a common swindler, and not only that, he passes people back and forth illegally into the city. We were finally able to catch him within the walls, passless. Death for sure, for this one, my lord Little King."

Have you ever, Palicrovol, heard the inconvenient plea of one to whom you are in debt? And have you known that a moment's inaction would release you from his demands? But not his debt, no, there is only one release for debt. Orem stripped the place of Beauty's Searching Eye. "Free him," Orem said softly.

The guard went red. "My lord Little King, I can't."

"I confess to you, sir," Orem said, "that I took part in this man's crimes, and I insist that it is your duty to punish me exactly as you punish him. Open a cage for me at once."

"But you are the—the Little—"

"Free him," Orem said again.

Timias stepped in, spoke softly to the commander of the guards. "You heard him say the words. If she minded, would he have been permitted to say it? If she minded, would you be permitted to do it? But I assure you that if you *don't* do it, then it will be minded."

So Timias became the Little King's conspirator in a hundred little undoings of the harsh justice of the laws of Inwit. Orem's reason for working against the laws is plain: he himself had been a victim of those laws. Timias, however, had all his life been sustained by those laws. He maintained his wealth only because the guards kept the poor of Inwit too terrified to take it from him. Why, then, did Timias help undo what made him safe? Because Timias was no sycophant, as you have called him. Timias was that rare thing—a man who can genuinely grieve for suffering he has never felt.

This was the beginning of the small set of doings, the small Acts of the Little King of Burland. It is not a large chronicle: I will tell it all to you here in only a few hundred breaths. Yet at the end he had no reason, I think, to be ashamed.

The commander brought Braisy from the cage. Such an obsequious creature, so eager to lick the feet of the Little King. But Orem did not spurn him, and in fact spoke a few words kindly to him, and told the guards to give the man a pass.

"Name of God," said the commander. "How can I do it when he has no work?"

"In the pass name him servant of Gallowglass, a man of private means who is without servants at the moment. If he quits Gallowglass, he quits his pass."

Braisy's eyes went wide, but he swallowed and nodded. "Good enough for me, that's right, that's fair, that's a true favor it is."

The guards did it, and the ripple this made in the city was small enough that Beauty did not even notice it. But it was a ripple all the same, and changed forever the city you would return to, Palicrovol.

Perhaps the taste of power was heady as brandywine; but I think that Orem wasn't drunken on so small a draught. I think Orem went on to other exercise of power because he resented having done a mercy for a man that he despised, when there were others who deserved better of him who were not helped.

He began then to use the guard for his own small purposes. Find for me these two—they were my friends:

A boy called Flea, Flea Buzz, perhaps ten or so, lives in Swamptown. But put no fear in him, treat him kindly, find out where he is and tell me.

A man named Rainer Carpenter lives in Beggarstown in hope of finding work some day on a pauper's pass. Find out where he is and tell me.

A grocer from High Waterswatch comes once a year, not long from now; Glasin Grocer, who was once the Corthy Price. Find out where he is and tell me.

And they told him. Orem sat in the Coal House, where the spies of the city are controlled; Orem sat there with Timias, Belfeva, and Weasel, and heard: Flea Buzz was caught a month ago, no pass and robbing a poor pisser in Little Market. Lost both ears and now lives pimping in Beggarstown.

Tell no one who ordered it, but give Flea Buzz his pass, a full and free pass tied to no man, and give him an unlimited draw upon the Great Exchange; arrange it for me out of what the Queen lets me spend. I care very little how difficult it will be. It's either that or give him back his ears—if you can't do the second, you will do the first. And so they did it, and more: they watched over the boy, the guards who had been his terror, watched him quietly, protected him from harm; for wasn't this lad beloved of the Little King, who plainly had the blessing of the Queen?

As for Rainer Carpenter, the answer came more slowly, for he had never lost an ear and so did not figure on the perpetual records of the Gaols. At last the spies·reported. Known to be a violent, drunken man, he was killed a year ago, days after being turned away when he tried too early to enter the city on a pauper's pass.

"Has it been a year?" Orem said quietly.

"Well over a year," said the spy, making sure again on his written report.

"And so too late before I even left the city." Orem looked at the coal-blackened wall. "Had he a family?"

"In a village in the west. He was driven out when the drought made paupers of all the farmers there; came here in hope of sending money back to them. The family is barely scratching a living as free laborers now that the rains have come again."

"Give them twenty cattle and land enough for them, and money enough for safety without arousing the envy of all their neighbors. Tell them it was earned by Rainer Carpenter before he died trying to save a lad from thieves. It isn't even a lie."

Glasin Grocer they found last of all. Prospering in his village far to the north of Banningside, loved and respected by all who did not envy and respect or fear and respect him. Orem thought of vengeance, but it was not his way. Glasin had cheated him, but all the same he had a chance to sell Orem into hopeless slavery, and did not do it. Was it Glasin's fault that those who had done better for Orem had suffered more? The Sisters did not weave justice into the cloth—that would be one thread too many. So Orem told them to grant Glasin a permanent stall in Great Market, in the best place, where the square debouched into Market Street at Low Court. Never had authority taken interest in a mere grocer until now: it was enough to make Glasin chiefmost grocer and something of a legend; it added many strophes to Glasin's song.

What matter if the guards and spies thought Orem odd? It was as if he thought his life were an artifact, and he the carpenter determined that all legs shall stand flat. Saw here, plane there, even things up, set things right until all is firm and steady again.

He had forgotten that he was not an artisan at all, but rather a farmer, whose only skill was to know the calendar and watch the sky, plow when the ground is ripe, bind when the corn is dry, and save a bit of the crop to seed the field next year.

WHY DID YOU CHOOSE ME?

It became their life together. It became the way they passed their time. Belfeva and Timias spent their hours doing what no one in the Great Houses had ever thought to do: noticing the lives of the weak and helpless. They could not undo all the suffering of the city, but they could find the single acts of infamy that might be halted, to make the whole of the city that much less unfair. Then Timias and Belfeva would bring their tales to the Little King, and he would make his plan, blind the Queen, and work his small mercies. It did not go unnoticed in the city. The word quietly spread that the common people had a friend in King's Town, and among the hopeless and afraid, there grew a little hope, a little courage.

One day, when they were alone, Timias asked the Little King, "Why did you choose me?"

"Choose you?" answered Orem.

"To help you in this work we're doing." At Orem's puzzled expression, Timias laughed and explained. "Haven't you noticed that we're doing a work?"

"But—I only do this because I have you with me," Orem answered, and that was true.

But even truer was his answer when Belfeva asked him the same question. "Why me?"

"I think because whatever hand moved me to where I am, moved you to be near me."

But truest of all was the answer he gave to Weasel Sootmouth, when she asked him bitterly one day, "Why do you keep Timias and Belfeva with you? Don't you know it makes them ridiculous in the court, to be known as flatterers to that buffoon called Little King? And don't tell me the gods have brought you together, because you and I both know the gods are bound."

Orem thought for a while, and then said, "When I was a scholar in the House of God, I used to play at words and numbers, and my teachers thought that I had written truth. I laughed at them for finding truth in my play. Now I think—there's a shape to the way the world runs. Within that shape are many names that a soul can wear. I've fallen upon a name that brings me here, and whoever is named Timias and Belfeva must be with me, because that's the way of the world. All of it's a puzzle, but it's still the truth."

I think you see now that Orem Scanthips will bear his death if death is what you require of him. It is we who love you both who cannot bear it if the man who has most reason to be grateful to him is the man who takes young Orem's life.

21

Orem's Future

How Orem learned that he must die for Beauty's sake, and
what he planned for himself in the face of death.

A Chance Conversation

One evening Orem stood on a portico that hung emptily over
a roof garden. He often came there to look down on the little
forest there. Despite hours of trying, he had not yet found a
way to reach the garden itself through the maze of the Palace.
He thought sometimes that this is how the world must look to
God, close enough almost to touch, and yet so infinitesimally
small that he dared not touch it lest it break.

Out beyond the Palace Park, with its perpetual spring, a
snowstorm was covering the city, the first of that year. It had
been eleven months now since the snowstorm in the cages,
when he stared death in the face. He thought back and
remembered that he had not been afraid. He had fought death,
but with stubbornness, not fear. Not passion, either. His life
was so placid in the Palace that he now believed that he was
by nature a man of peace. Seventeen years old, and already
comfortable in the contemplative life.

Of course it was not true. He was pent-up, frustrated, but
these feelings left him languid and morose, so that the more
he needed action the less he felt like doing anything. That
was why he came to the portico and looked down over the
garden and wished he could dwell in that small place; that
was why he looked out over the city and wondered what Flea
was doing tonight in the snow.

Then voices came from below.

"Look. Snow again." It was Craven.

"Already? The time has been so short." Weasel.

"Eleven months. Rather long, I thought." Urubugala.

Do they know that I am here? thought Orem. He almost

gave them an island in the Queen's Searching Eye, so they could converse in privacy; then it occurred to him that there might be things he could learn by listening unnoticed himself. For a moment, accidentally, he could eavesdrop the way the Queen did all the time.

"How we all look forward to the joyous day," said Craven. "The birth of a little offspring."

"Beauty's rebirth and replenishment. Power for another few centuries or so. Does the Little King yet know his part in it?"

"I think not," said Weasel. "No, he does not."

"Should we tell him?" asked Craven.

Weasel answered quickly. "I think we must."

"No," said Urubugala.

"It's always better to know the truth."

"Can he stop it?" asked Urubugala. "If he tried to stop it, all would be destroyed. For the Queen to renew herself, all her power must be placed in the living blood. He will play this part better if he knows nothing."

"More merciful that way," wheezed Craven.

"Yes," said Weasel. "But will he thank you for his mercy?"

"I care nothing for his thanks," said Urubugala. "The cost of power is never paid by the one who wields it."

And then silence. He did not even hear them leave.

Orem knew nothing of the books of magic. From his time with Gallowglass, however, he knew this much: that the price of power was blood, and whatever gave the blood must die. Beauty was coming to the time of her renewal. And they would not tell Orem of his role in it because all her power must be placed in the living blood. In that moment he reached the obvious conclusion. The blood of a hart was more potent than the blood of a rat; the blood of a man more potent than the blood of a hart; and the blood of a husband more potent than the blood of a stranger.

What blood does Beauty shed for her near infinite power? The blood of her bedded husband, the Little King.

Suddenly his almost empty life in the Palace made sense. He was the fatted calf. Beauty had bedded him and conceived his child because otherwise he would not be her true husband and so would not have power enough for her. Probably she awaited only the birth of their child, and he would die.

He leaned on the railing now because he could not stand. He was still in the cages after all. He had not been saved when Beauty sent for him. He had simply been set within her plan. For an hour he watched the snow and mourned himself.

As he mourned, he forsaw many versions of his death. Would she ridicule him then, in his last moments? Or thank him for his sacrifice? More powerful than the mere blood of a husband would be the blood of a husband shed willingly. What if Beauty asked me to give my blood freely? Does it occur to her that a man might gladly die for her? He imagined himself going to her and offering his life—but he knew that she would laugh at him. She thought him ludicrous even now; he could not make a grand gesture with her watching, for it would seem ludicrous even to him.

He also thought of escape. But after thought, he scorned that, too. Had he come out of Banningside to Inwit, come from Wizard Street to the Palace, just so he could escape at the very moment that was plainly meant to be the meaning of his life? He had wanted a name and a song and a place, hadn't he?

And after an hour spent thinking such thoughts, he decided he could bear having his life end this way. He was reconciled to being a pawn in Beauty's game.

Then, suddenly, he remembered lying down in his cage because he was too weary to keep walking in the snow. He felt the other men's spit on his shoulders and face. Even when you have no hope, you do not die of sleep when you can die struggling.

Why was I brought here? Why was *I* brought here? Beauty does not know that I am a Sink. It was the Sisters who showed her my face in a dream. Perhaps I was meant to overhear this conversation tonight so that I would remember that Queen Beauty is my enemy. Though I still dream of her, though I stammer and feel the fool when I am with her, perhaps I am meant to use my power to weaken her.

If I am to die, let it not be as a willing sacrifice. Let me die knowing that while she can take my life from me, I have also taken something from her. Perhaps I have time enough in the days before the child is born to help Palicrovol. A year I've been here, and in that time I have done nothing at all with the power I have except have a few secret but trivial conversations. I may be weak, but I am the only person who can thwart the Queen at all. And if she discovers me, so much the better. Let her kill me in rage, so that much of my blood is spilled and wasted. It will be my turn to laugh at her.

It was a very satisfying story that he told himself, and it led him to do everything that he ought to do. No one but Orem himself would be hurt when he discovered that he was never meant to die at all.

THE WAR OF BEAUTY AND THE SINK

That night, Orem resumed the war that had begun with a single skirmish almost a year before. He found King Palicrovol nearer than a year ago, but not by much. The greatest change was in the number of men who were with him—he was gathering his armies in earnest now, and Orem could not even guess their number. The circle of wizards was still with the camp, and inside that the circle of priests, and inside that King Palicrovol, assailed by the sweet and terrible magic of the Queen.

Calmly and thoroughly Orem undid all her magic around the King. This time he was more discriminating—he left the magic of Palicrovol's wizards alone. The Queen did not respond quickly, and Orem used her sluggishness to cut great swathes in the cloying sea of her Searching Eye. Carefully he widened the area where she was blind, and soon it became clear that she could not even find King Palicrovol. Orem opened his eyes and looked at the candle by his bed. He had only worked an hour, and she was groping and incapable.

Back when he was pranking with his power, that would have been enough. Now, however, he knew that he had only begun. It was not enough to blind her around Palicrovol. He stretched himself to the utmost and blinded her view of whole cities, of whole counties, while she concentrated on finding Palicrovol again. Within the city of Inwit he devastated her power entirely. From wall to wall of her city, and for a mile or more outside, he undid all her spells of binding. Only King's Town itself did he leave alone, not because he could not undo her power there, but because it was better to let her think that her opponent could not pierce those defenses.

This time two more hours had passed, and Orem returned to Palicrovol one more time. The Queen still had not found him. But to make sure, he undid her so far around him that she would not find him in a day or more, if she kept searching at the same rate. Let Palicrovol have a whole day of rest. And tomorrow, I'll let him have another, if I can.

You remember that night and that morning, Palicrovol. It came almost a year after the first respite, when you first learned that another power stirred in the world. All night you waited for Beauty's vengeful counterthrust, but it did not come. In the morning your wizards tried to pretend that they had wrought your salvation, but you knew that they had not. The priests pretended that they had said some new and efficacious prayer, but you laughed at them. You knew there was no explaining what had come, only that whatever this power was, it was kind to you. There was balance in the world once more, the wheel had turned, and you began your yearlong march toward Inwit, toward the city too long denied to you. This time, you believed, you would overcome.

BATHERS IN THE POOL

Although he stayed awake hours later than usual, Orem awoke before dawn. He recognized the faint light outside his window. It was the Hour of the Outmost Circle, the time that he was wont to waken in the House of God. Not only was he awake, but he also felt refreshed and vigorous for the first time in months. He stood up from the bed and walked briskly back and forth in the room, surprised at how good it felt to move quickly again. He was a soldier; he was at war; he was alive.

Orem stood at the window and searched to see how much of last night's undoing Beauty had been able to repair. He was pleased to see how little, really, she had done. Palicrovol was still undiscovered. Perhaps more important, though, even Inwit itself was not restored to the level of control she had had before. Each member of her Guard had been bound to her with a spell of loyalty to her and friendship for his fellow guards. Many of the guards in the city had been brought back, but not all. They didn't instantly fall to quarreling among themselves or betraying her, of course. What mattered was that in a single night he could undo more than she could redo in the hours when she slept.

He was too exhilarated this morning to stay indoors. Though the sky was only faintly light, he dressed and wound his way through the rooms of the Palace, heading for the nearest door to the Park. It was woods he needed, the wild woods that no gardener tended, where it was a summer morning today despite the heavy snow blanketing the city outside the Castle walls.

There was a hurry about the servants that he passed, and urgency, sometimes even fear. That was a sure sign that Queen Beauty was feeling out of sorts. The servants always scurried then. Silently Orem apologized to them for making their day a bit more difficult than usual today. Queen Beauty, his poor wife, had perhaps had little sleep.

As quickly as possible he lost himself in the woods, wandering as he pleased until he found himself at the high west wall of the Castle. He walked north along the wall until it curved in sharply at Corner Castle, where the Lesser Donjon waited, the prison of the great, more dangerous in its gentle way than the Gaols. He could hear from within it, faintly, a distant cry; perhaps, he thought, it's only a sound from the city beyond the wall. It was not. Orem pressed his ear against the stone of the tower and the sound came clear. It was the scream of a man in agony; it was the scream of the worst terror a man can know. Not the fear of death, but the fear that death would delay its coming.

Orem could not conceive of the torture that would arouse such a cry from a human throat. The stone he leaned against was cold, and he shivered. The sun was now half-hid behind the western wall, and already the air was getting cooler. He left the tower and the suffering man inside it. He wondered if his own throat could ever make a sound like that. If it did, he would not know it: when such a sound is made, its maker is past hearing.

He walked back a different way, through the woods again, but this time brutally, thrusting the brambles out of the way and letting them whip back savagely in his face. He let his shirt tear, let his face bleed; pain was a delicious language, one that he knew how to understand. Then he came suddenly to the Queen's Pool.

It was water from the Water House, the pure spring that flowed in an endless stream as if God himself were pumping, right in the heart of the Castle. The Baths of the Water House

were public and the water good; but most of the water went
somewhere else, went in aqueducts to the Temples, to the
great houses and embassies lining King's Road and the even
more exclusive Diggings Avenue, went in bronze pipes to
Pools Park, where the artists dwelt outside the Palace, and
came here, to the Queen's Pool, where few ever bathed and
the water was as pure as a baby's tears. Orem stayed back in
the trees, just looking at the water rippling in the breeze,
transparent, green, and deep because the sun had not yet risen
far enough to shine from the surface.

While he watched, two visitors came to the pool. The first
to come was an old man in a loincloth, and Orem knew him:
the mad servant who called himself God and had no pupils in
his eyes. He came and stood across the pool from Orem,
looking down into the water. Orem did not move. They
seemed to wait forever, both of them statues in the gathering
night.

Then came the second visitor, and she saw neither Orem
nor the old man. Weasel Sootmouth, as hideous in dawn as in
bright daylight; she seemed not to see the servant any more
than she saw Orem. She stood beside the water, and then
undressed to bathe. It was ungracious of him to watch poor
Weasel's bent and shapeless body. She would surely be ashamed
for a man to see that her breasts hung like empty feedbags,
that her legs and knees were gawky and overboned. Yet he
could not leave as she descended the steps into the pool,
partly because he had the strong feeling that although she
gave no sign of seeing him, she knew the old man was there,
and had come here to meet him.

She swam slowly, barely rippling the water, never splash-
ing at all. She is misnamed, thought Orem: Not weasel but
otter is her animal self. Then she dove under the surface.

Now the servant who called himself God moved, throwing
wide his arms. Green flashed his eyes, a light so bright that
Orem looked away. And when he turned to watch again, the
old servant was naked, pissing savage green into the water,
his eyes bright green and staring into the wood. Still Weasel
had not come up. The green spread shining across the water
until the pool was all suffused with that living light. Still
Weasel stayed beneath. Then the old man bowed and bent
and knelt beside the pool, and dipped his head into the water
up to the neck. Only then did Weasel rise, only her head

above the surface, as if those faces could not live on the same side of the water. She seemed not to notice the vividness of the pool.

The tableau broke; the old servant pulled his head from the water, and Weasel turned to him, reached out and touched him. Perhaps they spoke: Orem could not hear. She kissed his brow and the servant—wept? Sobbed or cried out or spoke a single word, Orem could not tell. Then the servant arose, taking his loincloth, and walked haltingly into the well-trimmed path that would take him to the Palace. Weasel swam a few minutes more until the water gradually grew dull and ordinary. But Weasel did not become dull. Orem looked at her and realized that it was not an accident the Queen kept her close at hand. Those nearest the Queen were those most tortured; the quiet ugly woman who had come with him on so many jaunts with Belfeva and Timias was more than she seemed, surely, or the Queen would not torment her.

He cast his net for her, and counted the layers of spells, the depth of the spells the Queen had laid to pen her in, and yes, as he suspected, she was bound and tortured. Who are you, Weasel? Prisoner here as much as I, and perhaps as hopeless. I who will die, am I luckier than you? For I will soon be free of her, and you will not, bound forever in the company of a Queen who grieves you as she can; and she can so exquisitely give grief.

It was then that Orem first loved Weasel Sootmouth. Not for her flesh—Orem had known the body of the Queen. Not out of pity—he knew her too well to see her from the distance that pity requires. He loved her because he admired her. For bearing without complaint the burden that the Queen put on her. For still being gentle and loving when she had ample reason to be bitter. And because when she swam in the pool and kissed the servant who called himself God, she was, oddly enough, beautiful. Does that surprise you, Palicrovol? That of all people, your son could look at Weasel Sootmouth and see beauty?

THE QUEEN DISCOVERS HER HUSBAND

Orem returned to the Palace well before the hour when he usually awoke, and now he was weary from too little sleep and the unaccustomed exercise. He planned to rest awhile, but a servant met him at the door.

"Queen Beauty has been looking for you."

"Oh," said Orem.

"She wants you to come to her at once."

For a terrible moment he thought that his war with her was already over, that she had found him out and meant to kill him now. He did not feel as brave as he had felt yesterday on the portico. Then he realized that if it were death she intended, she would not have entrusted her message to this quiet servant. So he followed the servant to a place in the maze that he had not known existed; Beauty's apartments were well-masked, both with magic and with the illusions of clever artisans. Having gone to her once with a guide, however, the illusions were spoiled for Orem and he could find his way again easily. As for the spells, they never worked on him at all.

Queen Beauty lay in her bed looking out the window when he arrived. The servant left him alone with her. The door closed, and she turned to him.

"My Little King," she said.

Her beauty was undiminished, but her weariness could not be hidden. After all, it was a living beauty that she had, and her face was not unexpressive. She was tired, she was worried, she was grim, and her belly was heavy with the child that she had carried for eleven months. Only then did it occur to him that the pregnancy might be sapping her strength, and that was why she could not respond well to his attacks on her in the night.

"I fear I've ignored you far too long," she said.

"I've made friends."

"I know," she said. "Weasel tells me that you're pleasant company."

He could not hide the fact that it pleased him to know that Weasel Sootmouth had said such a thing—he was young enough to make more of that than was really in it. "Does she think so?"

"It's your child in my belly, you know. I'm weary with the waiting, and the child weighs me down. You should cheer me up."

"How can I?"

"Tell me things. Tell me about your country home. Tell me about childhood on the farm. They say your rustic stories are amusing."

It was a grotesque hour he spent then, telling tales of High Waterswatch to the woman who meant to kill him. It galled him to tell of his father and mother to her—but what other stories could he tell? She laughed a little when he told her of his early attempts at soldiering, and how the sergeant regarded him as unfit. She seemed interested in everything, even tales of how a farmer knows when the grain is near to harvest, and whether a cow is full of twins, and the signs of a storm.

"Look outside, and tell me if a storm is coming."

He looked. "No storm today or tomorrow," he said.

"But there'll be a storm all the same. Hart's blood, but I wish that it would come."

He turned and looked at her, wondering if she wished for the storm or the baby growing in her. Her hands were folded across the gravid mound beneath the blankets of her bed, but she was gazing neither at the window nor at her belly. When the child came, his life would quickly end, he knew. But surely he would live to see his child. Surely his future would not forbid him that.

At last, near noon, she wearied of him.

"Go now," she whispered. "I need to sleep."

He started for the door with triumph singing in his heart. She needed to sleep indeed. That was his doing, and it would be a long time before she slept well, if he had his way.

But she stopped him at the door. "Come to me again," she said. "Tomorrow, at the same time."

"Yes, my lady," Orem answered.

"I've used you badly, haven't I?" she said.

"No," he lied.

"The gods are restless," she said. "They don't bide well under discipline. Do you?"

Orem did not understand. "Am I under discipline?"

"I only noticed it today. You look like *him*."

"Who?"

"Him," she said. "Him." Then she turned her face away from him to sleep, and he left.

Orem did not understand it, and I did not tell him, but *you* know, don't you, Palicrovol? She began to love him then. And part of why she loved him was because he looked like you. Does it make you laugh? Three hundred years of torturing you, and her hate for you had twisted into love. Not that she meant to free you. Never that. But still it ought to flatter you. You're the sort of enemy your enemy must love.

This is the way the paths of our lives entwine and cross and go apart: If she had sent for him the day before, even then he might have loved her. But she did not send for him until she was afraid; she was not afraid until he undid her work; he did not undo her work until he was past loving her. If only we could stand outside our lives and look at what we do, we might repair so many injuries before they're done.

22

The Birth of Youth

The tale of the birth of Orem's son, Beauty's son, the bastard grandchild of King Palicrovol, in all the world no child more beautiful and bright.

THE BURNING RING

Orem's war with the Queen made him almost frenetic during the days, as if he had to work off some of the power he stole from her. As she neared the time of delivery, he harried her more and more, so that she spent her days exhausted after battling futilely all night. Orem, however, spent his days in ever more active games. Timias and Belfeva were surprised, but gladly joined him, even when he indulged in madness like racing horses with the cavalry on the parade ground or competing with Timias to see which of them could throw a javelin the farthest. Timias was not the sort to let Orem win, and so Orem, untrained in any of the manly arts, invariably lost. But he kept at it furiously, and gradually improved.

When Beauty went into labor for the birth of Orem's son, he was climbing up a wall of the Palace, racing to the top with Timias. This was one competition where agility and endurance counted for more than brute strength and long practice, and Orem was holding his own. He was nearly to the top, in fact, when he noticed a sharp pain like a candle flame on his leftmost finger. He looked, and saw that his ruby ring was glowing hot. He could not take it off, not without falling a hundred feet or so. Instead he endured it, climbed the rest of the way to the top, and only then tried to pry it off his finger. He could not.

Weasel and Belfeva were there, watching. "Help me," Orem said.

"You can't take it off," Weasel said. "The ruby ring will burn till the child is born. It isn't really burning you. Any-

219

way, you should be glad—it's proof that the child is not only yours, but also a son.''

"The child is being born," Orem said. Then this was the last day of his life, he was sure. He walked to the lip of the roof, reached down, and helped Timias to the top.

"You won," Timias said, surprised. "I didn't think you had it in you."

"I kept looking down," Orem said. "The thought of death makes me quick."

Suddenly Weasel cried out in pain.

"What is it!" they demanded, but she would not tell.

"Orem," she said, "you must go to your wife."

"At a birthing? The father?"

"At this birthing, with that mother, yes." She winced again.

"What's wrong? What's happening to you?"

"Help me to my room, Belfeva," Weasel said. "And you, Little King, go to your wife, I say."

"But she hasn't sent for me," Orem said. In truth, he wanted to spend the last day of his life with anyone but Beauty.

"Do you forget which finger bears her ring? She'll obey you if you command her to let you stay."

"No one commands Queen Beauty."

"*You* do," Weasel said. "But beware how you command her, for she'll obey you with cruel perfection if you ask unwisely."

"I don't want to go," he said angrily.

She winced again, and staggered against Belfeva. "Not for *her*. Your son. Your son has begun his voyage down the river to the sea. She'll have no other help but you. No one but the father can help at the birth of a twelve-month child."

Orem wanted to stay, wanted to know why Weasel was in such pain. But he knew that Weasel was wise, that Weasel did not lie; if she said he must go to Beauty, then he would go.

PARTURITION

The Queen was not in her normal sleeping room. Nor were there any servants there, to give direction. He did not know where she might have gone for her lying in. He had only one way of finding out: He spun his web through the Palace, and found her all aflame with silver sweetness, rough to his hearing, silent to his touch.

Through the corridors he went toward the place where he knew she was, but always the corridors turned, always the doors opened only the wrong way. He only understood when he stepped from a corridor and into a room, then changed his mind and stepped back again—and found that the corridor had changed direction. The short end now was on the left, the long end with the rising stairs now on the right. Queen Beauty was where he thought she was, but the magic of the Palace turned all paths away. So he let his power flow loose as a robe around him, lapping against the walls, breaking down the spells, revealing the doors where they ought to be. This was not the magic of illusion that he invariably saw through. It was true bending, and he feared that by finding her, he would confess to her what he really was.

He found her worried servants gathered at a door.

"Is she inside?" he asked.

"And alone," answered a servant. "She forbids us to come in."

"She won't forbid *me*," said Orem, and he knocked.

"Go away," came the husky, painful voice from inside.

"I'm coming in." And he did.

Beauty lay alone in the middle of a long and narrow bed. She was naked, her legs spread wide, her knees up. Some sheets had been tied to the five posts of the bed. Two were tied to her feet, and she strained against them; two she held in her hands, and pulled hard. The last lay on her pillow, and as a wave of pain swept over her, she turned her head and seized it in her teeth and bit and moaned, tossing her head, worrying the cloth like a dog with a rag. She dripped with sweat. The high-pitched moan that arose from her throat was not a human sound. Blood was trickling from the passage where the baby's head had crowned. The head was large and bloody and purple, and it would not come. Beauty looked at him through eyes wide as a deer's with fear and pain. The eyes followed him as he walked around the foot of the bed and stopped near her face as she chewed on the cloth. Even in such a state, she was beautiful, the most womanly of women.

"Beauty," he said.

And then the pain passed, and she shuddered and let the cloth slip back to the pillow.

"Beauty," he said again. "Haven't you any magic to end the pain?"

She laughed mirthlessly. "Little fool, Little King, there *is* no magic that has power over childbirth. The pain must be felt or the child will die."

Then the pain came again, and she whimpered and writhed as muscles rippled over her belly. The child's head made no forward progress. Beauty looked at him with pleading in her eyes. What did she want of him? To end the pain, but he could not do it.

"Tell me what to do, and I'll do it," he said.

"Do?" She cried aloud. "Do? Teach *me* what to do, husband!"

The child would die—he knew that much. A child who did not quickly come once it had crowned would die. Not my son, he silently said.

"Can someone bear the pain for you?"

Did she nod? Yes; and whispered: "Not against the other's will."

"Then cast the pain on me," he said, "so the child will live."

"A man!" she said contemptuously. "This pain?"

"Look at the ring on your finger and obey me. Give the pain away."

No sooner did he say the words than her convulsive movements stopped. Her heavy breathing fell to normal, her pressure on the sheets eased. He waited for the pain to come to him—but it did not. He had no time to question it, for suddenly the flesh opened impossibly wide, the bones of Queen Beauty's pelvis separated widely, and the child slipped out easily upon the sheets. It was impossible that Beauty could go through such a thing so peacefully, yet instantly the bones came together again, and Beauty reached down and picked the child up. There was no afterbirth; the baby had no trailing cord.

"Untie my feet," Queen Beauty whispered. She licked the mucus from the baby's face. The child cried, and Beauty cuddled him, held him to her breast, guided his mouth to the nipple, then sighed and comfortably crossed her legs. Orem noticed with amazement that her belly was not slack at all, but perfect in form, as if she had never carried a child at all; indeed, she had again the unutterably beautiful body he had loved, and he could not help desiring her again, for all he feared and hated her.

"Command me again, my Little King," she said. "It gave me pleasure to obey."

"But the pain didn't come to me," he said.

"You didn't command me to give it to *you*." She smiled triumphantly.

He thought back on his words and could not remember. Somehow she had tricked him, but he was not clever enough to know how. "Let me hold the child."

"Is that also a command?"

"Only if—if it will cause no harm to him."

Beauty laughed again and held the infant out. Orem looked down at him, reached to him, took the child in his arms. He had seen newborns before, nieces and nephews, and had helped to care for foundlings at the House of God. But this child was heavier, and held his body differently. Orem looked into the infant's face, and the child gazed back at him wide-eyed, and smiled.

Smiled. Minutes after birth, and the baby smiled.

"A twelve-month child," Queen Beauty said.

Orem remembered his father, Avonap, remembered his strong arms that could toss him into the air so he flew like a bird, and catch him as surely as the treelimb caught the starling. My arms are strong enough for a child this small. And suddenly he was Avonap in his heart, and he longed for the child. The child Orem had loved his father more than life; that is the sort of child who, when a man, also loves his children with a devotion that cannot be broken. You would not know, Palicrovol, but there are such men, and they are not weaker than you; you are merely poorer than they.

At once Orem knew that he must have this child, if only for a time. "You will let me see him whenever I want," he said.

"A command?"

"Yes," he said.

She laughed. "Then I'll obey."

"And you'll do nothing to bar him from knowing me, and loving me, and I him."

"You are too daring, Little King," she said. This time she didn't laugh.

"I command it."

"You don't know what you're doing."

"As long as I live I command you to let me know and love him, and him me!" She could not begrudge him that—he did not dare to ask for more, did not dare to ask to be allowed to live a moment longer than she already had in mind.

"Little King, you don't know what you ask."

"Will you do it?"

"Don't come to me and blame me, Little King. Love the child if you want, and let him love you, it's nothing to me, all one to me." She turned her face to the wall.

"A child must know his father if he's to be happy."

"I have no doubt of it. Only this, Little King: He'll eat no food but what he draws from my breast. And he'll never have a name."

That was wrong; it could not be. To have no name is to have no self, Orem knew that. "I command you to give him a name."

"You command easily now, don't you? Like a child, not guessing at the price of things. See how well your old commands have worked, before you try any others."

"Name him."

"Youth," she answered, smiling and amused.

"That's not a name."

"Nor is Beauty. But it's more name than he could earn in all his life."

"Youth, then. And I'll be free with him."

"Oh, you're a delicious fool. I've kept the three most marvelous fools in all the world with me for all these years, but you, the best of all, the Sisters saved you for the last. You will have all the time you want with the boy, all the time you can possibly use is yours. May it bring you joy."

The boy reached up and clutched at Orem's nose and laughed.

"Did you hear? Already he laughed!" And Orem couldn't help but laugh in turn.

"That's the way it is with a twelve-month child," Queen Beauty said.

"Every day I'll come to see him. He'll come to know my face, and be glad to see me; I'll have time enough for that."

Orem did not see it; but I believe that every word he said was pain to Beauty, made plain to Beauty how much he already loved the child, and how little love he had for her. It could not have surprised her, but it could hurt no less for all that.

"Give me the boy," she said. "He needs to eat."

"Youth," said Orem to the child, who smiled. He handed the infant to Beauty, and this time the child needed no guidance to the nipple. Beauty looked up at Orem with eyes strangely timid, like a doe's. She looked innocent and sweet, but Orem was not deceived. "Beauty," he said, "how did you escape the pain of this, when you didn't give it to me?"

"Does it matter?"

"Tell me. I command it."

Studying his face, she said, "You commanded me to give the pain away; you didn't say to whom."

That was true, he realized. The second time, when she obeyed him, he had not said she had to give it to him. "But who else would willingly take it?"

"The woman who of all women could not bear to see this body torn asunder. The woman whose face this really is."

Orem stared at her stupidly. Who else's face was it, if not Beauty's? Orem had never known that Beauty wore a borrowed shape. But knowing that, it was not hard to know who it was who truly owned that face.

"Weasel," Orem whispered. "You gave the pain to her."

"We always *shared* my pains anyway," Beauty said. "It seemed only fair. She had had the use of this body during her perfect childhood—we agreed that it was fair she suffer some of the pain of its adulthood." Beauty smiled lovingly at Orem. "And pleasure, too. I made sure she felt half the pleasure of our wedding night, Little King. I wanted her to remember what it felt like to be unfaithful to her beloved husband."

"Her husband?" Orem had not known that Weasel had a husband.

"What a fool," Beauty said. "Her husband, the King! Palicrovol meant to make her Queen in my place. Why else do you think I've kept her here? Weasel is Enziquelvinisensee Evelvenin, the Flower Princess. She wanted my place, so I've taken hers. Inside her perfect body. Well, her perfect body just went through a birthing that could have killed it. But thanks to you, her *perfect* body didn't have to bear the pain, or heal from the injury. Too bad for the imperfect flesh she actually dwells in, though. *That* may well die."

Orem had not realized until then Beauty's perfect malice. "It's you deserves her face," he whispered.

"Are you my judge?" she asked him coldly. "Is that why you've come to me, to tell me what I have deserved?"

He thought back to Dobbick in the House of God, who taught him that King Palicrovol brought his own suffering upon himself. "But she did nothing to you," Orem said.

"She took my place," said Beauty. "For whatever reason, I care not: she took my place in this Palace, and she pays for it."

(That argument should be familiar to you, Palicrovol. He took my place in the Palace, you said, and so he must pay. Do you then admit that Beauty was just when she punished the bride you brought from Onologasenweev?)

"I see now," Beauty said. "I see now." And her face became dark.

"What do you see?" asked Orem, afraid that she saw what he really was.

"I see that she has taken my place again."

"Yes! She's bearing the pain of the birth of your child."

"Once again she has my husband's love."

Orem looked at her in disbelief. "For a year you've despised me. How can you be jealous of a thing you threw away!" And then he lied quite cruelly to her, thinking he was telling her the truth. "I never loved you."

She cried out against his words. "You worshipped me!"

"Name of God, woman! I hate you more than any living soul, if you *are* alive, if you *have* a soul. You're three hundred years old and you have no more love in you than a mantis for her mate, and you never—you never—"

"I never what?"

"You never took me to your bed again."

"If you wanted me, boy, why didn't you come to me and ask?"

"You would have laughed at me."

"Yes," she said. "I laugh at all the weak things of the world. And when you leave me now, and go to Weasel Sootmouth, and comfort her, I will lie here laughing."

"Laugh at me all you like." He turned to go.

"But I won't be laughing at you."

He stopped at the door. "Who then?"

"At me."

He turned back to look at her. "*You* aren't one of the weak things of the world."

She smiled viciously. "Not for long, anyway. Not once I've finished what I began with you."

Orem was sure she was hinting at his death.

"Sing to me, Little King. Sing to me a song from the House of God. Surely they taught you songs in the House of God."

He sang the first thing that came into his mind. It was Halfpriest Dobbick's favorite passage in the Second Song.

> God surely sees your sins, my love,
> The blackness of your heart, my love.
> He weighs them with your suffering.
> Which is the lesser part, my love?

"Again," she said.

And when he had sung it twice, she made him sing it again, and again, and again, as she rocked back and forth, suckling their son. Despite his hatred for her, Orem had never seen a thing that pleased him so much: his baby drawing from his wife's breast, as the grain drew life from the soil. He loved his son instinctively, the way Avonap loved his sons and his fields. He regretted every word he had said that might cause her to kill him sooner, and deprive him of an hour he might have had with Youth.

At last she did not murmur "Again" when he finished the song. "Forgive me," he whispered to her. But she was asleep, and did not hear him.

So he left her, and went to find Weasel, who had born Beauty's pain at his command.

The Healing of Weasel Sootmouth

"You can't come in," said the servants standing guard at Weasel's door.

Orem pushed past them. Weasel lay delirious on the bed, crying out and weeping, calling now on Beauty, now on Palicrovol, and now and then on Orem, too. He thought that meant she loved him as she loved Palicrovol, though in fact she was crying out to save him, not for him to save her.

He questioned the doctors gathered at her bed. "We can find no cause for the pain," they said.

"Treat her," Orem said, "as if she had just given birth to a twelve-month child. Treat her as if the birthing broke her loins apart and tore her flesh."

The doctors looked at him amazed. Only Belfeva, who stood nearby, understood that the Little King might know the problem better than any of them. She strode to the bed, tore the blanket back, and now they saw that Weasel lay in a pool of blood that still flowed from a ghastly rent in her private flesh. And more astounding: there lay the afterbirth that hadn't come with the child named Youth. "Name of God," said a doctor, and they set to work.

Orem watched when he could bear it, sat by Weasel and held her hand when he could not. She knew nothing of his presence, only cried out with pain and delirium. At last the doctors finished all that they could do.

"She's lost so much blood, what can we do?" said one.

"How could this have come to be?" asked another.

Orem only shook his head. He could not explain to them that it was his doing.

The doctors left, but Orem stayed, holding her hand. Once she called out, "Little King."

"I'm here, Enziquelvinisensee," he answered. Hearing her own name seemed to soothe her. She slept. He said all the prayers he could remember from the House of God. He knew they were meaningless here in Beauty's house, but he said them anyway, because he was afraid of what he had done to her.

He must have dozed off, for he awoke suddenly to find that Craven and Urubugala waited with him beside the bed. Out of habit he extended his web to include them, freeing them to speak unheard by Beauty.

"How is she?" Craven wheezed.

"She bore the pain of the birth," Orem said.

Craven nodded.

"The Queen has been harvested," said Urubugala. "But what was the crop, little farmer?"

"A boy, named Youth."

"She'll live," said Urubugala. "Does that comfort you? Beauty won't let Weasel die."

"Her name isn't Weasel," Orem said. "Did you know? The Queen told me. She's really Enziquelvinisensee Evelvenin. The Flower Princess."

Craven and Urubugala looked at each other, and Urubugala laughed. "Did you think to surprise us, Little King? We've been with Weasel from the start."

Only then did Orem realize that they, too, were disguised characters from the same ancient tale. "Zymas," Orem said.

Craven smiled faintly. "I haven't been myself lately," he apologized.

"And you," Orem said to Urubugala. "Sleeve."

The dwarf only answered with one of his rhymes. "Who is the magical leper who cleans us with his tongue? He puts our names in picture frames and paints them out with dung!"

"You are the King's companions," Orem said. "In all the old stories—"

"The stories are very old," said Craven. "We are the Queen's Companions now." He gestured at Weasel's sleeping body. "Send for us if she awakes."

Weasel Wakes

They brought a chair for him because he would not leave her. All night he waited. And in the morning he opened his eyes to find that Weasel was awake beside him, her ugly face hidden by darkness except for the skewed eyes watching him.

"You're awake," he said.

"And you," she answered.

"I was afraid for you."

She searched his face. "You called me—I dreamed you called me by another name."

"Enziquelvinisensee Evelvenin."

"She told you?"

"After I commanded her—commanded her to give the pain away."

"Ah." The eyes closed, then opened again. "I forgive you, Little King. You didn't know what you were doing." She startled him by smiling. "Just think of it—I'm still a virgin, and yet my body has conceived and given birth." She laughed a little, then groaned in lingering pain.

"I will think of you," Orem said, "as the mother of my child."

"Don't," she said.

"It was your body that bore him."

"I would not have born a twelve-month child."

"He's beautiful. Queen Beauty has promised me that I can have him as often as I like. I didn't know how much I longed to have a son until I saw him. He already smiled at me."

"Don't love him," Weasel said. "Don't let him smile at you."

"It was your body that bore him. Queen Beauty said that you also felt it—when he was planted in her."

Weasel nodded, but turned away her face.

"I'm not ashamed," said Orem. "Weasel, I love you. Before she told me that this wasn't your flesh I loved you. Let me pretend that I'll live to see my son become a man. Let me pretend that you are my—"

"No," she said. "You have a wife."

"Have I?" he asked angrily.

"And I have a husband."

Orem fell silent then. Only after she pitied him and touched his hand did he speak again. "I was wrong," he said. "Forgive me."

"I always forgive you," she said. "Even before you ask. Little King, I will not deny my husband for you. Nor will I ever love your child. But I'll stay with you and be your friend to the end of this mad course you've chosen. Is that enough?"

"What makes you think I chose my course?" But he agreed, and let her sleep again.

Those were the very words they said, and neither one suspected that Orem had misguessed his future. From then until you came to the city gates they never spoke of it again; though they were together every day, Weasel never guessed that Orem thought that Beauty planned his death. Weasel would have told him the truth if she had known that he did not know.

I have heard it said that you were told that the Flower Princess betrayed you with Orem Scanthips, the Little King.

Of course you do not believe any such lie. But she did love him as if he were her own son. And remember this, Palicrovol: if you had been faithful to the Flower Princess, Orem Scanthips never could have been conceived. Remember that when you pass judgment on what we did when you were exiled from Hart's Hope.

23

The Freeing of the Gods

How Orem spoke to God, and learned the way to the Rising of the Dead.

FATHER OREM

We of the Palace were all too used to the ways of wealth, to nurses, governors, and tutors for a child. In all of Queen's Town was there anyone who knew what it meant to be a father? Fatherhood to us was an act of passion, soon forgot; but not to Orem ap Avonap. Never guessing that the blond and happy farmer was no blood of his, Orem had taken a part of that simple man into himself and saved it for this time. At any time in the Palace he might run by, Youth on his shoulders or, as time went by, toddling along behind. Their laughter could be heard almost everywhere. And anyone who wanted to be sure of seeing them had only to go out into the gardens, and soon they would appear, to roll together in the grass or pluck blades or play hide-and-go-find.

Did Beauty ever watch them together? I think she did, for it was in that time that she inexplicably told me of the three lessons she learned as daughter of the King. I think she envied Youth the love of a loving father. I think it embittered her, and made it easier for her to hate the Little King and his son when she needed to.

Every few hours Orem would bring the child back to Beauty to be nursed. Beauty watched Youth all the time; Orem drew his power inside himself when he was with the boy, so that Beauty would never be hindered from watching to be sure her son ate no food except what he drew from her. Orem silently gave her the child, and Beauty as silently surrendered him when he was satisfied.

Whenever Orem gave the child to Beauty, he believed that he would never see the boy again; whenever he took the child back, he regarded it gratefully, as an act of mercy, that he would be allowed to live another little while. And because he felt death to be so imminent, he wasted none of the time he had with Youth. In those days, if you wished to be with Orem you had no choice but to keep company with him when he was with Youth.

For in the evenings, when Youth slept his twelve hours, Orem retired to his chamber and spent the night battling with Beauty. Now that her child was born, she had more strength for the war, and it was a constant fight to keep her away from Palicrovol. Sometimes he even thought: I am hastening my own death by frightening the Queen. She will kill me and renew herself all the sooner. I should stop fighting her, and she might let me live.

But he knew that Beauty would not spare him, and as he watched Palicrovol's army grow, he began to hope that the King might come and save him. That's what he told Youth once: the King might save him.

Youth himself was another miracle. Like his father and grandfather, Youth was black of hair and white of skin; like his mother, he was beautiful of face. Being a twelve-month child, his life was quick, his growth all sudden. He could sit within a week or so, and stand himself within a month; before it was summer outside Palace Park the child could walk, could run his short-legged run along the paths, hiding and finding, calling for Papa or for Weel. If he had a name for Beauty he never said it in their hearing; at times Orem wondered if she spoke to the child at all, or merely fed him in silence. His teeth came in, but still she nursed him; Orem taught him to know the letters that he scratched in the dirt and name them in two orders, and still Queen Beauty nursed the child.

Orem also had some quiet hours with Youth, but they were not silent. They would lie together in the grass of the park and tell each other stories. No one was allowed to come near, for as if with one will, they fell silent at the approach of an audience. Beauty could listen, if she liked, with her arcane abilities, though usually she slept during the day when she wasn't suckling the child. But the only person permitted to attend them in the flesh was Weasel Sootmouth. Orem had told her of his game, hoping that she would pretend to be the true mother; she never said that she was playing, but her presence

let him have his imaginary family if he liked. Youth, too,
accepted her, as if he knew her heart.

They told each other stories. Orem told Youth all the stories
of his growing up. How he lived with his father; how his mother
never loved him; the tales of the House of God, and how he
was saved from the fire; Glasin Grocer, Rainer Carpenter, Flea
Buzz and the snakes; all the tales except those that would have
told Beauty, listening, that Orem was the Sink, her enemy.
Weasel listened to all his stories and remembered them.

And Youth, too, told stories. In his high, impossible infant's voice, lisping on *S*s, turning *J* into *GZ*, he spun his
tales with a serious face, and sometimes so grieved himself
that he cried, and sometimes so delighted himself that he
cried. There was wisdom in his stories, and they have not all
been forgotten.

YOUTH'S STORY OF THE SUCKLING CALF

Once there was a calf that was hungry. It wanted to suckle,
but his mother told him, "Go away, you make me tired." So
he went to his father, but the bull said, "Go away, I've got
no teat." So the calf drank from the pool in the woods and
grew horns on its head that got so heavy that it couldn't hold
its head up and it died.

YOUTH'S STORY OF THE DEAD FLOWER

Once there was a flower that got brown. God took the brown
flower and put it in his window and it wouldn't get alive
again. The old stag wore it on its antlers and it wouldn't get
alive again. The two sisters braided it into both their hair and
it wouldn't get alive again. But Papa kissed the flower and it
got alive again and turned into me.

YOUTH'S STORY OF THE SNOWSTORM

Once there was a snowstorm but it always fell on the city. Far
away under the snowstorm there were hundreds and hundreds
of people who weren't servants or soldiers or Papa or Weel or
anybody at all. The snow always fell on them, and covered

them up until they went away. The little boy told the snowstorm, come and fall on me. And the snowstorm did come and fall on him, and the little boy went away, just like the people who weren't anybody.

YOUTH'S STORY OF THE KING

The King is little but the King is good. The King never gives you anything to eat and people laugh at him when he isn't there but the King knows all the paths in the woods and someday he will find the old stag that lives in the woods and he'll let me ride on him.

YOUTH'S STORY OF THE RIVER

This was a very big river and it goes from one end of the world to the other and back again. The grocers ride on it and the farmers ride on it and a million million flowers ride on it but God never rides on the river. The river goes by a little little house where a little man and an ugly lady live but they haven't got a little boy. Then the papa planted a seed in the ground and he planted hundreds of seeds and all the seeds came up gold except one, and it was brown. "This seed is brown like the dirt," said Papa, but he liked it anyway and so he ate it and it grew inside him and made him so full that he never had to eat again.

OREM CRIES FOR HIS SON'S TALE

I do not know which of Youth's tales it was, but as he lay on his back listening, Orem cried. He cried silently, but Weasel and Youth both saw the tears well up in his eyes. One tear hovered at the corner of his eye, as if it were timid to fall and yet knew it must.

Orem noticed that Youth had stopped his story. "Go on," he said.

But Youth did not go on—instead he reached out to his father's eye and touched the tear. He gazed at it a moment on his hand, then put the hand into his mouth and tasted it, looking up at Orem with his marvelous quick eyes.

Orem looked worried for a moment; then he relaxed. "Beauty's asleep," he said. "I wouldn't want her to accuse me of feeding him." Weasel only laughed. By such small things do kingdoms rise and fall.

It was a golden summer in the Palace, the first good summer in three centuries. But then the snow began to fall again outside Palace Park. In the west King Palicrovol suddenly turned his army eastward, to Inwit. In the Palace Orem began to hope seriously that his life would be spared. But Urubugala rolled on the floor in the Moon Chamber and said,

> Twelve months blossom on the tree,
> Twelve months more and ripe you'll be.

The Low Way Out of the Palace

Orem was leaving the Queen's room, having brought Youth back to her for his evening meal. Over the Palace the clouds moved quickly, roiling with the storm that would bury Inwit if it could. Outside Queen Beauty's door, Belfeva met him, her voice and manner full of haste.

"Timias found someone in your room today," she said. "A boy. He says he knows you, but he was stealing all the same. Timias has him there."

So they hurried to Orem's chambers. Timias was leaning against a wall, holding onto the hair of an adolescent boy, who sat furious on a stool. Two years and puberty can change a child: Orem did not recognize him for a moment. Besides, the mutilation of his ears was all that could be seen at first—with the hair pulled up and away, the savage scars were ghastly. Only when he spoke did Orem know him.

"Orem, get this chewer's hands out of my hair, name of God!"

"Flea!" Orem cried.

"You know him?" Timias asked.

"Yes, I know him, I owe him my life a couple of times."

"And don't forget the three coppers you owe me," Flea said sourly.

"Flea! How are you?"

"Going bald. If I were six inches taller I'd teach this son of a puke to keep his claws in his own nest."

"How did you come?" Orem asked. "It can't have been easy to get in here."

"I came the low way."

Timias would have none of that. "The postern gate has more guards than a two-copper whore has lice."

"I wouldn't know about two-copper whores," Flea answered. "I said the low way, not the back way. Under the Palace."

Timias frowned. "There's no such way."

"Then I burrowed through the rock."

"Why do you think the aqueducts go *over* the walls? They built this place so there were no passages underground."

Flea pointedly turned his back on Timias. "Some people are so right they never learn a thing. I came to take you."

"Take me where?"

"Where you're needed. They say the time is short. You have to come."

"Come where?"

"I don't know the name of the place," Flea said. "And I'm not so sure I'd find the way too quickly on my own. I have a guide."

Flea looked toward the porch. Standing at the balustrade was a shadow Orem recognized. "God," Orem said.

"Mad as a drunk pig, isn't he?" said Flea. "He must tell everyone that's who he is. Mad or not, though, he knows his way through the catacombs."

Orem strode through the outer door and touched the half-naked servant on the shoulder. "What do you want with me?"

The old man turned around, and his eyes were dark; in the light from the room Orem could see that there was no white at all—iris only, staring through his face to see what lay behind.

"Time," the old man said. "You delay too long."

"Delay what? What have you come for?"

"You blinded her, yet still you do not act."

Orem wanted to ask for explanations, but Flea tugged at his arm. "He's just the guide," Flea said. "The others want you—they found me, brought me down, and sent me here to get you because they figured that you'd come if *I* asked. You can trust me, Orem—it's not a trick or a trap. They say it's too important for delay."

"I'll come then."

"Wait!" Timias stopped him. "You're not following this little thief down into God knows what pit—you don't believe him, do you?"

"Before you were my friend, he was," Orem said, "and with less reason."

When he saw that Orem meant to go, Timias insisted that they stop at his room for him to get a sword. The old man seemed to sneer at him for it, but what of that? Orem didn't mind knowing that Timias was with him, and armed.

The old man led them a twisted route, all through the Palace itself, sometimes up, sometimes down, into places Orem had never seen, and finally into places that seemed to have been abandoned years before, dust thick on the floor, furniture nested with rats. They left the candled rooms behind, and carried lamps to light the way, all except the old man, though he led them into the darkness. At first Flea was full of talk, but later on that stilled.

Through one door, and now the stairs were wooden, and so ancient that they walked only on the outmost parts of the treads, for fear the lumber of the middle would give way beneath them. And when the stairs ended, the floor was stone, the walls rock, the ceiling moist and dripping here and there, and shored with timbers. It reminded Orem of his trip into the catacombs with Braisy. But the catacombs had been outside the city walls, on the west side, and they were in the east here, and within the mount of Queen's Town. And still down.

The manmade tunnel widened and became a cave; narrowed again into a natural crevice in the rock, through which they made their way with difficulty, forced to bend their bodies at odd angles. Always the old man was waiting for them, not too patiently, on the other side.

"I'd like to know how that old man makes it through some of those places," Timias whispered.

"He says he's God," Orem answered.

"Look at his eyes. Have you seen his eyes?"

They traversed a ledgeless slope over a pit so deep the stones they dropped never made a sound at all. They shimmied down a chimney in the rock, scraping their knees and covering each over with the dust of passage.

"How were you so clean in my room?" Orem asked.

"I took a bath," Flea answered. "What else did I have to

do while I was waiting? I was only borrowing some clothes when your friend came in. What are you looking at?"

Orem was looking at three barrels against a wall that was only faintly lit by Flea's lamp. Orem walked closer, knowing what he would see. But the tops were off, and the barrels were empty. He breathed again in relief.

"What's written on them?" Timias asked.

Orem lowered his light. He had seen the words before, of course, and remembered well how they were written.

Sister	*God*	*Horn*
Slut	*Slave*	*Stone*
You	*You*	*You*
Must	*Must*	*Must*
See	*Serve*	*Save*

He remembered another message that once had been written on these barrels: *Let me die.* He had obeyed that command; the rest of the message waited. Now he knew he had to understand if he was to do what must be done.

"You know this writing?" Timias asked. "You know what it means?"

"Not what it means. But it was written to me. Two years ago."

God slave you must serve. Orem looked at the old man. "You are what you say you are, I think."

The eyes blazed.

"I will serve you if I can."

"At the Rising of the Dead," God whispered. Then he turned his back on them, ducked down into a low passage, and disappeared. They followed him closer to the sound of rushing water.

"What is God doing as a slave in Beauty's house?" Timias asked quietly.

Orem had no answer. And then they emerged into a vast chamber, the Rising of the Dead, where all the answers would be given.

THE RISING OF THE DEAD

There was no need of lamps here, for above them were holes that let in daylight—dim, but bright enough to see by, if they didn't look up at them and dazzle their eyes.

"The cisterns," Flea whispered.

And sure enough, there were the voices of the cisterns, rising and falling, crying out in terrible mourning. There was a river rushing along the bottom of the cave, so wide that Orem could not see across, a vast but shallow flow. And the stench was so vile that as they approached they could not breathe. The sound came from the water's edge.

"The sewers of the city," whispered God. "They all flow here."

They did not come nearer the water. The old man led them off along a ledge that paralleled the flood.

"Are we going downstream?" Timias asked.

"Yes," Orem said.

"But we're climbing, aren't we?"

Unmistakably they were. And yet they got no higher above the water. It had to be an illusion. Still, the farther they went, the steeper became their path along the ledge, while the water seemed to rise with them. It was definitely flowing uphill.

The old man clambered up the last and steepest portion of the narrow path, almost straight up and down; soon they were all gathered on a much wider ledge. It was plainly level. Just as plainly the river had no such notion: it hurtled upward, soared in an impossible cascade. The spray of it covered them—and the drops drifted downward, as they should. Orem noticed that here the water did not smell; no odor at all, and he walked near the flood and wet his hand, and tasted the water. It was pure. It was as pure as—

"The springs in the Water House." Timias looked at him in awe. He turned and shouted to Flea. "This is the source of the springs in the Water House!"

"Come and see what cleans it!" Flea called back. They followed his shout to the lip of the ledge and looked down. "With the light behind it, you can see now," Flea said. At first Orem did not know what it was that he was looking at;

then his vision adjusted, and he realized that both banks of
the river were writhing, twisting, heaving.

"Keeners," said Flea. "The place is full of keeners."

Like the rush and retreat of the waves the serpents heaved
themselves into the water, flowed back out. Millions of them,
as far as the light from the cistern mouths would let them see.
"They're eating it," Flea said. "What else could it be?"

"It rises," Timias said. "What could make it rise?"

"It rises," said a woman's voice behind them, "because it
wants to rise."

Orem whirled. He knew that voice—at once dreaded and
longed for the sight of the speaker. She looked at him with a
single eye, a twisted face, a body that was perfect as the limb
of an upreaching tree. "Follow me," she said. He followed.

Her sister sat on a rock behind the rush of the water. It was
bright here, though none of the sunlight could have touched
the place; the light had no source and cast no shadow, merely
was, merely illuminated this pocket in the rock so all that was
there could be seen. The mist-faced woman moaned.

"My sister greets you."

"And I her," Orem said.

"She says that all things come together in the end."

"Is this the end?"

"Nearly."

"Why am I here?"

"To free the gods, Orem son of Palicrovol."

Orem shuddered. "My father's name is Avonap."

"Do you think the Sweet Sisters make mistakes in such
things? We know all motherhoods and fatherhoods, Orem.
Avonap is your mother's husband, but Palicrovol sired you."

In a moment the whole dream of his own conception
flashed through his mind from the crossing of the river until
Palicrovol left the cave of leaves.

"Queen Beauty took the forbidden power, which never a
man can take, and never another woman would. She bound
us, Orem, bound us as you see us now."

Orem looked at them, looked at God. "How are you
bound?"

The old man turned his head. Orem followed his gaze. On
the floor of the cave lay the skeleton of a great hart. The
bones were so dry they should have been scattered, but
instead they were all connected, as if the animal still lived.

The skull hung in the air, suspended by the great antlers; the hundred horns were embedded in the solid stone of the cavern wall.

"See how the worlds are captive," said the Sister who could speak. "Oh, Orem, we are feeble now, and what we do is slow. We can still send visions here and there, still do little works, but it's a labor hard to bear. We made you, Orem. Shantih and I awoke your mother, named her Bloom, taught her to come to the riverbank; the Hart brought Palicrovol; God gave you Avonap and Dobbick to make you who you are. We bent your life to bring you here, watched and shaped where we could. You must not disappoint us now."

"What do you want me to do?"

But Orem knew the answer. God slave you must serve. Sister slut you must see. Hart stone you must save. But how?

"I have no power. How can I unbind what I can't see?"

"Have you looked?"

And so he looked, cast his nets. Yet there was no spark for the Hart, for the Sisters, or for God. He searched, but all the magic he could find was the simple spell that Timias had upon his sword.

"What am I to see?" he asked.

"We cannot tell you," said the speaking Sister. "We are bound."

Shantih moaned.

"My sister says that you must restore us as we were before black Asineth undid all."

But I don't know what you were *like* before—I was only born some eighteen years ago, and all these things were done before I was conceived, before my mother or her mother or her mother were alive. "I can't!"

"Be at peace," whispered God. "Only think of what you know of us; we will wait a while longer, after all this time."

Orem sat on the stone floor, reached out and touched the cold bone of the Hart's corpse. He heard Flea gasp behind him; a keener whined and unentwined itself from the Hart's ribs. It slithered off another way; it was not seeking Orem's death today.

He started with God, for he had studied Him for years in Banningside. What was God supposed to be? Kind, the father of all, perfector of the Seven Circles, raising all who would into the inmost round with him, to join in his unbodied labor, to gather all disorganized intelligence and teach it form, and—

Unbodied.

He looked at the old man, who placidly regarded him with eyes of amber, lid to lid.

"What are you doing with a body?" Orem asked.

God smiled.

Orem arose, and reached for Timias's sword. "What do you plan to do with it?" Timias asked. "Let me do it. You're not much of a fighter."

"I don't mean to fight," Orem answered. Timias reluctantly surrendered the weapon. It was too heavy for Orem's hand, and he dreaded what he must do with it, but with all his strength he plunged it into the heart of God. Blood gouted forth, but Orem watched only the eyes, watched as the amber brightened, yellowed, whitened, dazzled like the source of sunlight. Suddenly the light leapt out, for a moment filled the cavern, and was gone.

Timias bent over the old man's corpse, put his finger into the empty socket that had held an eye. "Gone," he said.

Orem laid down the sword and covered his hands with the old man's hot blood. Then he strode to the Sisters, who also smiled at him. He wiped the blood all over the face of the faceless one, and on the blind side of the one-eyed Sister. The blood steamed and sizzled on their skin. And then he took each by the hair at the back of the neck and pressed their faces together as they had been faced at birth, one looking only into her sister, the other gazing with one eye out. The heads trembled under his hands, and then were still. He loosed his grip, and the women rose. Their clothing was gone; their arms and legs so enwrapped each other that no clothing was needed for their modesty. Their hair was all one, their flesh unseamed across the expanse of their two heads. "Ah," sang the half-mouth. "Nnn," sang the other into her sister's cheek, so that both tones were a single song coming from the same mouth. Together they rose from the ground.

"Don't leave!" Orem cried.

"Free the Hart," mumbled their mouth, "and then stop Beauty. She's doing nothing that she hasn't done before. Avenge your nameless sister and your nameless son."

And they rose upward in the cavern, spinning round and round each other, joined blindly again at the face, spinning up and around and madly through the cavern like a shuttlecock, and they were gone.

"I've seen the Sisters with my eyes and I'm alive," said Timias.

Orem had three sisters and they all had names, and nothing had ever been done to them that called for vengeance. And his nameless son—what had happened to him that needed to be avenged? Orem did not understand, and so he turned himself to try to rouse the Hart.

He knew how the Hart should be—alive, and clothed in flesh and fur. But how was he to accomplish *that*, when he had no power in himself, no magic he could exercise?

"Will the old man's blood work on the Hart?" asked Flea.

"I don't know," said Orem. Now the blood was cold, and he knew as he anointed the Hart's horns and head that it meant nothing, such blood meant nothing.

Yet the sight of blood on the horns reminded him of the vision he had seen in the hart's horn in Gallowglass's house. Reminded him of the farmer who stretched his throat to the blade of the plow and spilled his blood for the Hart's sake. And he reached up and touched the scar on his throat and knew what he must do.

Timias had not seen the vision, but he knew the scar on Orem's throat. He guessed what the Little King was thinking when he touched the scar. "No!" he cried, and lunged. Orem was quick, but Timias reached the sword first and snatched it out of reach.

"Name of God, Timias, I must," said Orem.

"Have you gone mad?"

Flea did not understand at all, only knew that Orem wanted the sword and this half-chewed bastard wouldn't give it to him. It was a simple matter to knock down Timias with a blow to the balls; Flea retrieved the sword while Timias writhed, and tossed it hilt first to his friend.

He would have taken it back as quickly, if he could have, but before Flea could do more than cry out as Timias had done, Orem drew the sword hard and sharp across his throat. The blood filled his mouth and flowed down his chest, and the pain was more than he had known that he could bear. He gagged; the blood ran into his lungs; but it must not be in vain. He struggled toward the Hart's head, tried to raise himself so the blood would fall upon the horns. He hadn't the strength now, but his arms were taken by hands on either side. Timias and Flea lifted him up, and the horns were drenched with his blood.

Under him he felt the heat of the stag's body; felt it rise, felt the vast back and shoulders with their rippling muscles and the stink of strength lift him up. He saw the antlers pull away from the stone that bound them, saw the tips aglow like stars, like suns, like little jeweled worlds. And then he spun around, lost among the hundred horns, turning and turning.

He flew, he rose up with the water into the ceiling of the cisterns, to the place where it strained itself upward into the rock to emerge in the Water House. He was trapped in the water and he could not breathe. He had not had time to take a proper breath, and so he must rise, he must rise and breathe—

But no, above him he knew was fire. He must go down into the water, and then he would live. So down he sank, waiting to find the bottom. But he did not find it. Instead he despaired and breathed in deep gasps of water. But it was not water. It was pure air. He opened his eyes.

He was lying on the back of the Hart, but he was not weak now with the loss of blood. He reached his hands, took hold of the antlers, and lifted his head free from the nest of thorns. Then he swung himself down from the Hart's back.

"Orem," breathed Flea.

"My lord Little King," said Timias.

Orem touched his throat. The wound was gone; the scar was gone; his neck was whole and new, as it had been before he ever had the vision of the Hart.

"I've worn the true crown," he said. He still could feel the horns surround his head, though they weren't there.

"You're alive."

They stood and watched the Hart as it stamped its hoof. The head lowered; only then did they realize that it meant to charge them.

"Name of God, doesn't it know we saved its life?" cried Timias.

There was no time for an answer. They scrambled for the downward path and scurried and tumbled along the narrow ledge along the riverside. They looked back only at the entrance to the hewn passage. The Hart was clearly visible, pacing back and forth along the platform of rock, tossing its head.

"How will it get out of here?" asked Flea.

"He knows the way," said Orem, though he didn't know why he was so sure of that.

Orem let Flea lead them, since he had come this way twice. Like Orem, though, the others were thinking more of the future than of getting out of this path under the Palace. "What do they expect us to do now?" Timias asked.

"Not *us*," said Orem, "but I'm glad you're willing to share the burden."

"Did they mean that you're really Palicrovol's son?" asked Flea.

Orem nodded. "They showed me—how it came to be."

"She's doing nothing that she hasn't done before," said Timias. "*Who's* doing it?"

"Beauty," said Orem. "She means to renew herself. By killing me and using my blood."

"Well, at least you've had practice now," said Flea.

"But she's never killed a husband before," Timias said.

It was only then that Orem put together everything that he had learned. She has done nothing that she hasn't done before. More potent than a stranger's blood is the blood of a husband. He had got there before and stopped. But what is more potent than the blood of a husband? To a woman, the blood of her child. And a child who has taken no nourishment except from the mother's breast. Avenge your nameless son. Orem had a nameless sister, years before. Palicrovol's daughter, and Beauty had killed her for the power in her. Orem guessed it all at once, and believed it, too, and damned himself for a fool for thinking all this time that *he* was the one who was doomed. Youth! he cried out silently. Youth, my son, my son.

"Leave me!" he shouted to his friends. "Get away from me!"

They hesitated only a moment, but the agony of his face told them to obey. When they were gone, Orem leapt out of himself, and with his savage inward teeth he gnawed at all the magic he could find, exempted nothing, ravaged through the Palace where Queen Beauty was the strongest and undid her work wherever he could find it. Blinded her, loosed her bindings; he cared little now whether it was Craven that he freed or Weasel. He found the power and unmade it, and he could not, would not, be stopped.

And at last the only power was in Beauty herself; all the

other magic of the Palace was engulfed and gone. But this was where he meant to come all along. To the smiling face that held his son and meant to kill him. Layer upon layer he unwrapped her; she tried to flee but he followed. She attacked, she moved, she feinted, she tried to disappear but he was there, unmaking her at every step. He had never felt so large, and she was small as he chased her here and there in the labyrinth of sparks and smells and seas of taste and hearing. I will save my son.

And then nothing.

Nothing at all. He could not find her. He was back inside his body and could not escape. All he could taste or touch was in himself. He opened his eyes. Beauty stood above him, looking down. She held Youth in her arms. "Papa," said the boy, reaching for him.

"Youth," Orem whispered.

Beauty smiled. Orem understood. Hadn't Gallowglass warned him? He had gone too far; he had told her who he was; he was bound. She could not destroy his gift, but she could turn him in upon himself, where he could do her no more harm.

"Always you," she said to him. "I should have known the Sisters would betray me. Did you join them again? No matter. In another week I'll separate them. And you, Little King, you'll be here to watch my work. You know at last how it's done, I think. Only *you* were stupid enough to take so long to guess the price."

"Do you want to hear a story, Papa?" asked the child.

He would have killed her with his hands, except the guards had him, and carried him away from the son who was his life, away from the frozen smile of his wife.

24

The Lesser Donjon

How the Little King decided to help with the death of his son.

TORTURE

You were outside the city when they carried him to prison, Palicrovol. Your armies were gathering at Back Gate, where the towers were fewest, as if the towers meant anything. As they brought Orem up the Long Walk to Corner Castle he could see your banners. He had protected you so long that you had begun to hope, hadn't you; and even now he had cost the Queen so much that she could not attack your wizards or your priests, could only bind Craven, Weasel, and Urubugala again, then hold the loyalty and courage of her guards and hope that you'd delay just seven days.

And you delayed. Because you did not believe that it was not a trap. You waited, outnumbering Beauty's troops—a hundred of yours for every one of hers. You could have piled corpses of your fallen men to scale the walls and still had enough to sack the town and take the Castle. She could not have stopped you then, for she hadn't the strength. You could have come to her, and all the power she had could have barely turned a sword. How would you have killed her then, Palicrovol? Fire? Rope? Drowning? Any would have served— or what, had you a plan to use them all? If you had acted then, King Palicrovol, your grandson would still be alive, for as Beauty said, until the year was up he was not ripe.

But you delayed, and gathered your armies, and waited, and waited, while others took the only path, the impossible path, the hopeless path to bring her down before she was unassailable again. You could have stopped her, Palicrovol, but once again it was your son who saved you. Think of that, too, before you slay him for daring to sit upon your throne.

They kept him in the Little Donjon, and the keepers there

perfunctorily tortured him, because that was what prisoners were sent there for. He wondered as they pulled his arms from his sockets if this was what had made the man scream; it did not make Orem scream. Was it the suffocation? Needles in the soles of his feet? The binding of the testicles? The broken glass forced into his mouth that cut his tongue and filled his mouth with blood that he dared not swallow—was that what broke the other man? It did not break Orem.

For he did not dwell inside himself now. He dwelt in the body of a year-old child whose mind was five times that age, whose heart was bright, whose life was all rejoicing; Orem lived in Youth, and only watched his own agony from a distance, almost unconcerned. He had once drawn a sword through his own throat, he remembered. But the pain of that had been erased. All the pain was gone, was locked away somewhere and he could not remember where. Only the child's kiss on his lips, only the small arms around his neck. I never knew how a father loved a child until now. How did my father find the strength to ride away from the House of God and leave me? And when the pain was worst, Orem dwelt again with his father, and was four again, and saw the world from his father's shoulders, gripping the golden hair of his father's head as the world bounced up and down.

It was his comfort then, that Avonap had been his father. What if Orem had learned fatherhood from you, Palicrovol? He would have thought then that fathers do not love their sons. He would think that a father is a King, and decrees a man's death because he usurped his place. And then, when he is told that the usurper was his son, the King doubles the reward for his capture, for now he knows his son is guilty of incest as well as treason. How long would Orem have lived in Corner Castle, Palicrovol, if he had learned fatherhood from you? Not long enough to save your life, I think.

URUBUGALA

On the sixth day Urubugala came to the Lesser Donjon. It had all been a mistake, he said. Orem was not supposed to be tortured; the Queen sent her apologies.

Orem lay on his soft bed—for excepting the tortures it was a comfortable prison—and listened to Urubugala, comprehending little, caring less. Why did this small black man keep talking? "Go away," Orem whispered.

"Listen to me," said Urubugala. "Of course she ordered it. But today it stops because tomorrow is the day she means to kill your son."

Orem turned his face away.

"She can't hear us—you saw to that, she has no Searching Eye now. There's a way, only one way that we can stop her, but with your help it can work."

"There's no way," said Orem. "She's bound me. I can't get my power outside myself."

"I know she bound you," Urubugala said. "I taught her how."

"You taught her!"

"She came to me in terror as you savaged her and tore it all from her and she forced me to tell her how to bind you."

"She forced you not at all," Orem said. "I had freed you first, before I ever set myself against her."

Urubugala shrugged. "Then she didn't force me. If I hadn't taught her how to bind you, then she would have had to kill you to save herself. So you owe your life to me."

"I don't want my life," said Orem. "My son is going to die."

"Yes. Tomorrow," said Urubugala, brutally. "Your son has no hope, he never had hope, and Beauty warned you not to love him. We all warned you not to love him, but you did, for Hart knows what reason. How can we undo that? You chose it yourself, Little King. But there's still a way that when Queen Beauty kills your son she'll destroy herself as well. Listen, Little King. You know who I really am; can you doubt that I know what's possible and what is not? The Queen will do the rites that put her power into the child. All that she is she'll take out of herself and put in him. And in the moment that the Passage is complete, she'll cut him and drink the living blood, and through the blood receive back all herself, a hundred thousandfold increased."

In vain Orem cried out and buried himself in the bed, to shut the vision from his mind.

"Little King, if you do the rites along with her, but secretly, so she cannot see, then at the moment of completion, when all her power goes into the child, yours will also go. Yours will also go, Little King, Little Sink, and all the power will seep away into the earth, and when she drinks, there will be nothing, for her power, her life itself will die with the child.''

Orem heard, though he did not want to hear; he thought though he did not want to think. ''No,'' he whispered.

''Damn you, boy! Why not!''

''If Youth is dead, what is the rest of it to me?''

''Doesn't it matter to you that you're the only one in the world with the power to stop her? That the gods themselves are at your mercy? Why do you think they brought you here? Why do you think that you're alive at all?''

Orem rolled over, looked at the dwarf eye to eye, inches away at the edge of the bed. ''I don't know why I'm alive,'' he softly said. ''Once I thought I was myself, just myself, free to make what I liked of my life. But now I know from my conception on I've never been myself, but just a tool. As Beauty brought forth a daughter and a son to use for tools, so God and the Hart and the Sisters brought me forth. How are they different? If my son is not to be saved from the Queen, I at least can save myself from the gods.''

He looked into Urubugala's eyes, waiting for the argument. But it did not come. The dwarf's eyes filmed over with tears. ''You dreamed of freedom, did you?'' he whispered. ''So have I, for three hundred years. But you're not the only one who'll pay a price for Beauty's end. Beauty's power has sustained the four of us for centuries. Weasel, Craven, Palicrovol himself, and me. When her power goes, what sustains us then?''

Orem had thought that Weasel would simply become Enziquelvinisensee Evelvenin again. As she had been on her wedding night. It had not occurred to him that the intervening years would also be restored.

''And yet,'' said Urubugala, ''we'll gladly pay that price.''

''If I do what you say, it'll still depend on Beauty killing him.''

''Yes.''

''Then won't we be consenting to his death?''

''What is the price of freeing all the world? One small child. What is the price of enslaving all the world? That same child. Either way dead.''

Orem covered his face with his hands and wept.

Weasel

That night Weasel Sootmouth came to him. He did not speak,
for there was no need to speak. She took the clothing from
him and anointed him with balm, and gently rubbed his
swollen shoulders, and changed the bandages on his feet. For
an hour she labored over him. And then she covered him
again, and sat beside him. He reached his hand for her, and
she took it.

"Weasel," said Orem, "how can I give less than you?"

Weasel said nothing to that. What could she say? She only
leaned and kissed him on the hand, which set him weeping
again, for he was weak and ill and could not bear such
tenderness. He talked then, talked until he could talk no
longer, told her all that had happened below the ground and
all above, told her of the gods, of the tortures, above all of
his son, how he loved his son.

And when all was said, and Orem drifted off to sleep, still
he held her hand. She pulled it back, but he clung to her
weakly and said, "I love you."

And she said to him, because he was so young, so innocent, and so in pain, "I also. Love you." She said it because
it was true.

She left the Lesser Donjon and went to Urubugala, where
he waited with Craven in the Palace. "He'll do it," she told
them.

"If all goes well, he'll hate me forever," Urubugala said.

"Why is that?" asked Weasel.

"I lied to him," he said.

"What did you tell him?" Weasel demanded.

"I won't tell you, Enziquelvinisensee Evelvenin, or you
would tell him the truth, and then I think he would fail us."

"Why can't you believe, Urubugala, that some of mankind
will act better if they know the truth than if they do not?"

"Experience is my only teacher," Urubugala answered.
"Men are better when they know nothing."

"Then what of you, Sleeve, who know everything?"

Urubugala shrugged. "I'm just the Queen's little black
dwarf."

25

The Victory of the Hundred Horns

How Youth and Beauty died, and were borne away on the crest of the Hundred Horns.

The Readying of the Twelve-Month Child

They wakened Orem in darkness; he dressed by candlelight and walked the Long Walk with guards assisting him because he could not easily support himself. It was cold; Orem had so diminished Beauty's power that the springtime of Palace Park was broken. The winter of the world outside had come at last. The flowers all were dead, the trees that turn were turning madly red and gold; the fountains were ice, and the wind was bitter here for the first time in centuries.

The Queen was holding Youth in her arms, out in the square before the Palace. The child saw Orem and called for him. Orem did not speak, but stood silent where the guards made him stop. He tried to shut the child's voice from his mind, but could not. We who listened also thought we could not bear it, but then we did.

"Papa," cried the boy. "Where have you been? Let me tell you a story!"

Weasel, Urubugala, and Craven waited on the opposite side of the square from Orem. Only Urubugala did not hold still. He danced and pranced and rolled, cavorted here and there; only once did he come near Orem, and then only to whisper, "All she does, you do!" Then he was gone again, playing the fool at another place, pretending to be bound by spells that could not utterly bind him.

The first light appeared in the sky of the east. They were in the shadow of the Palace, but Beauty was in a hurry. She knew what was truly necessary to the rite and what was not; direct sunlight was not, and she began the Passage.

She took all the clothing from her son and laid him on the

silver table. Youth cried out, for the metal was cold; but there he stayed, cry or not, while Beauty removed her clothing, too. Orem looked at Urubugala—was this a part of it? Need he undress as well? Beauty had learned almost all of what she knew from Sleeve's books. Urubugala shook his head.

Youth cried out and pleaded with his mother to let him down, it's cold, it's cold. Orem knew he could not escape; Beauty had bound him, and his nets and webs stayed furled within him. We watched, and Orem kept himself as calm as if his son's cries were the calls of a bird, distant and meaningless.

Kept himself calm and did all that Beauty did, making every hand sign, muttering every word along with her. After a while Youth stopped crying and began to play, catching at his mother's fingers as she made the signs. If he broke a pattern she repeated it, and so did Orem. It was long, but he made no mistakes; Weasel, Craven, and Urubugala all watched to be sure of it.

As the light grew brighter, just before the sun crested the Palace, Queen Beauty smiled and took a pin from a servant, then drew the pin along her arm, drawing blood. She dipped a finger in the blood and anointed the child's eyelids with it.

What do I do? asked Orem's questioning eyes. The answer came from Craven, who suddenly began to sing a ribald, bawling song from his common soldiering days with Palicrovol's rebel army. The solemnity was broken; guards lunged to silence him; in the confusion Urubugala was near Orem and took hold of his hand. Orem was ready—he had already cut his wrist as deep as he could with his fingernail. The blood beaded on the shallow wound. Urubugala caught some on his fingers and was gone. As he rolled before the altar he jumped up, leaned out and spat in Beauty's face. She shouted at him; guards bound him as they had gagged Craven; but as he spat he had touched his bloody fingers to the child's eyes.

The disturbance quelled, Beauty went on, but she kept glancing up at the sky to see how bright it was. In the distance could be heard the sounds of gathering battle—shouts from many thousand throats. Palicrovol at last had started his attack. Too late, by now. Even if the city were undefended he could not get through the walls and barriers in time.

More words; more signs; then sunrise, full light dazzling off the towers of Corner Castle. Beauty bowed her head. All was done, except the killing and the drinking.

But Beauty did not reach and take the waiting knife. She looked to Orem and smiled at him. "My husband, Little King, who loves me loyally and with his whole heart, how easily do you think that I am fooled? Do you think I haven't seen your moving hands, your mumbling lips? Do you think I didn't see your hand cut, your blood put on our child's eyes? What a fool you fools supposed me to be. For even Sleeve is not infallible, I think, and less so when his brains are addled and put in far too small a head. The Passage may only be made between parent and child *if* the child has swallowed the fluid of your body which he took of his own power. All these months the boy has suckled at my breast; what did he suck from yours, Little King?"

Orem despaired.

The Queen said the final words of the Passage.

Youth cried out in sudden, terrible pain. All the powers, all the hatreds, all the knowledge of his mother passed into him. He screamed, and there were words he never knew in his weeping, curses in his infant voice that sounded all the more terrible because the voice should have been innocent. Even Youth, great-hearted as he wàs, couldn't bear the burden Beauty placed on him. But his cries would soon be stilled; Beauty reached for the knife.

Orem watched, unable to look away, despite the fact that Urubugala was waving his hands in supplication: See me, see me! At last Orem looked, not toward Urubugala, but toward Weasel, who also had loved the child. She motioned with her head toward Urubugala, and Orem at last saw him. He looked confused—what could you possibly want of me now? Urubugala mouthed the final words of the Passage; Orem shook his head. What good would it do?

But Weasel knew. "Papa," she cried, "why are you crying at my story?"

Orem stared at her; Beauty also paused, the knife poised in her hand. And Orem remembered Youth reaching out to him, taking the tear from the corner of his eye, and tasting it. The Passage would be complete after all, if Orem only said the words.

Beauty looked suspiciously from Weasel to the Little King. What was the trick? Were they trying to fool her into staying the knife while the sunlight was still split upon the crest of the Palace? She could not delay now. This was the day, the moment, and so Queen Beauty ignored their attempt, as she thought, to distract her. She turned back to Youth and raised the knife.

In that moment Orem muttered the final words of the rite, completing it. "Come water, come water. Come mother, come daughter. Come father, come son. Come blood and be done. The Hart makes us one, the Hind for the slaughter." In that moment all the power Beauty had bound in him left him, went into his son. In that moment all Queen Beauty's magicking was swallowed by the unbound Sink who lay on the silver altar under the knife. In that moment the knife came down, cut through the child's throat. Blood spurted, ending the child's terrible shouts in a gurgle of foam.

Did Beauty know the power was gone from the blood before she drank? Who can know. She lifted Youth and held him over the basin that a servant held. In seconds it filled enough to satisfy her. She laid down the still-living child, whose hands still struggled, whose eyes still started out of his small head in agony; she picked up the blood and drank.

It was too late. The child died. The blood was worthless. All her magic was undone. All her sustaining, all her power; she had put it on the child so it would come to her again, and stronger. Lost now. She changed as they watched her; she lost her stolen face, she withered and decayed before their eyes, then toppled forward over the corpse of Youth.

THE LAST UNDOING

Her death undid it all. The loyalty of the guards was gone; they made no effort to stop Orem as he ran forward and kissed the warm corpse of his child, weeping. They watched the Little King, some of them. Others looked at Urubugala, who had become pink of eye, stark white of skin, and tall, as all the stories said of Sleeve. Or at Craven, who suddenly filled his armor, a strong man with the fire of war in his eyes. But soon all eyes had turned to Weasel. For there before them all was Beauty again.

Beauty's face, Beauty's body. She had tricked them after all; she had survived; she was alive and would avenge herself.

They fell back from her, all but Zymas and Sleeve.

"Fools," Zymas said. "Queen Beauty is dead. This is the

true and rightful wife of King Palicrovol, Enziquelvinisensee Evelvenin. You have nothing at all to fear from her.''

It was then that Orem lifted his bloody, weeping face from the altar and realized that the Queen's Companions had not died. We saw the knowledge come upon him; saw him remember that Sleeve had told him all of them would pay the price. A lie. To trick him to do his part.

''No, it wasn't a lie,'' Sleeve said gently. ''It all depended on whether I could work a spell with the blood of your hand. I was able to replace her spells enough to keep us to the age we were when she first bound us—I wasn't sure that I could do it.''

But Orem said nothing, only looked back and forth from Zymas to Sleeve, Sleeve to Zymas.

Enziquelvinisensee Evelvenin, pitying him, ran forward to ask for his forgiveness for the lie that she had unwittingly conspired in. But he saw her face and screamed at her, flew at her to attack that face that had no right to be alive. Possibly he thought that it was Beauty—he was that distraught. They pulled him away from her, drew him back; immediately the struggle ceased, and he only hung his head and wept.

It was then that the Hart came from Palace Park and walked easily to the altar. He put his horns under the bodies and lifted. It was a curious thing: the bodies rose and yet remained, as if the Hart had found the truth of the mother and her son and raised them up, while leaving the empty bags of flesh behind. Raised them up and carried them away exultantly; they rode high among the hundred bright points of the Hart's horns.

Orem watched them out of sight into the woods. Then he shook himself like a wet dog, and made as if to walk away. The guards restrained him until Zymas called out, ''Let him go. We have to hurry and give the city back to the King, before another life is lost!'' It was enough for the guards. They followed Zymas at a run, armor and all, to the Palace gate, rushing to get to Corner Castle and raise the flags of peace; to take down and defile Queen Beauty's ermine banner.

Enziquelvinisensee watched Orem Scanthips, no longer Little King, as he walked away from the place where he lost all his loves and all his trust. Almost she called out to him. Almost she ran to him and pled for his forgiveness. But that would have been misleading. He might have thought she loved him. Might have forgotten that she belonged to Palicrovol. Might have tried to bridge the centuries. But Palicrovol, your wife was not such a fool as that. Love works no miracles; it could not have happened. She watched Orem out of sight, and then went off to look for the returning King, to give herself to him whom she had loved perfectly through all the centuries. She was still a virgin, after all; there was a wedding to complete. They would begin again what had been inconveniently postponed. But she did not rejoice in her heart. She grieved to know that Orem Scanthips hated her; grieved most of all that he had reason.

26

The Rage of the King

How the King treats his enemies.

REJOICING

You commanded the soldiers to lay down their arms when you saw the change of the flags. Beauty would either have the strength to destroy you, or she would die. You knew she would resort to no trickery. Your men laid down their arms and the city was yours. The people poured into the streets to cheer for you, though in fact they had not longed for you when you delayed your return. You wore your Antler Crown through the streets.

Zymas you embraced; Sleeve you greeted with a bow; Enziquelvinisensee Evelvenin you only gazed upon, and said, "Yes. I know you."

FORGIVENESS

All of Beauty's soldiers, all the courtiers who had flattered her, all the merchants who had profited from her rule, all the servants who had cared for her, all the magistrates who had administered her laws—you forgave all these.

HONOR

You found her body upon the altar, and the baby under her. You had them carried to the riverbank. You had the bodies burned, and their ashes cast upon the river. It was this water where you had a million flowers strewn to greet the Flower Princess. It was this water that you swam, though it was swift and cold, to get a son upon a farmer's wife.

VENGEANCE

Now with your troops you wait at the base of a mountain redoubt, not even properly a castle. Within the place you know that Orem Scanthips waits, and with him, you imagine, there waits an army, or a wizard of some terrible power. I will tell you who waits inside:

A boy with no ears, who can pick a pocket or handle a keener and live; he may bruise a soldier or two before you slay him.

A man of breeding, a courtier, the best of those who waited on Queen Beauty. He will wound five, and deeply, before he dies.

A woman of high station who serves the Little King, because Orem Scanthips taught her to value mercy above justice, virtue above rank.

A young, young man of eighteen years, dark of hair and pale of skin, with the blood of a King in his veins and the weight of the world in his heart. He flees from you only because his friends command it. He cares nothing for you. He grieves only for the ashes that you cast upon the stream.

God is not with him. The Sweet Sisters are not with him. The Hart is not with him. He finished the task they raised him up to do; they have no further need of him.

BLESSING

I write this with my own hand. I write this in your own tent. I will give it to you in the evening; when you return to the tent it will be waiting for you. If you have read it you know it is the truth.

Did you think that only wizards and witches had powers? I have pricked my finger and blotted the living blood upon this page. I have written two blessings here, which no eyes but yours are fit to read. If you are the sort of man who will abide strictly by your oath and slay the usurper called Orem Scanthips, called the Little King, then you will see only the blessing that will give you the strength to finish your work quickly, and slay him on the morrow. But if you are the man who is merciful, even at cost to himself, then you will see only the blessing that will heal your heart and reconcile you to your son. I will love you whichever man you are, and in truth I do not know which end Orem himself would wish for, if the choice were his.

Now you know what man you are, Palicrovol. Now you know your name. That is the ending of this story. Did you think this was the tale of Orem Scanthips? His tale was finished when Youth died. In Orem's short life he has already earned his name: Hart's Hope. But you: come to me now, my husband, and tell me which blessing of those I gave you, you were able to receive.

SF AND FANTASY FROM
ORSON SCOTT CARD

☐	53355-0	ENDER'S GAME	$3.95
☐	53356-9		Canada $4.95
☐	50086-5	THE FOLK OF THE FRINGE	$4.95
☐			Canada $5.95
☐	51183-2	FUTURE ON FIRE	$4.95
☐			Canada $5.95
☐	51190-5	FUTURE ON ICE	$4.99
☐			Canada $5.99
☐	53351-8	HART'S HOPE	$3.95
☐	53352-6		Canada $4.95
☐	50212-4	PRENTICE ALVIN	$4.95
☐	50213-2		Canada $5.95
☐	53359-3	RED PROPHET	$3.95
☐	53360-7		Canada $4.95
☐	53353-4	SEVENTH SON	$3.95
☐	53354-2		Canada $4.95
☐	53255-4	SONGMASTER	$3.95
☐	53256-2		Canada $4.95
☐	51350-9	SPEAKER FOR THE DEAD	$4.95
☐			Canada $5.95
☐	50927-7	THE WORTHING SAGA	$4.95
☐			Canada $5.95
☐	53357-7	WYRMS	$3.95
☐	53358-5		Canada $4.95

Buy them at your local bookstore or use this handy coupon:
Clip and mail this page with your order.

Publishers Book and Audio Mailing Service
P.O. Box 120159, Staten Island, NY 10312-0004

Please send me the book(s) I have checked above. I am enclosing $_____
(Please add $1.50 for the first book, and $.50 for each additional book to cover
postage and handling. Send check or money order only—no CODs.)

Name_____

Address_____

City _____ State / Zip _____

Please allow six weeks for delivery. Prices subject to change without notice.